THE FRAME-UP

On the television, the news reporter continued talking: "Those close to Special Agent Deering's investigation say that he believed the death threats were, and we quote, 'very credible.' One source inside the ATF said that Deering was in the final stages of developing a case against an individual known to have been stalking the candidates and believed to be very dangerous."

The picture on the screen showed some of the candidates pressing flesh. The unsaid implication was that anyone getting this close to the public would make a good target for any would-be assassin.

"There is speculation that Deering might have been shot by the very subject of his investigation. As a precaution, the Secret Service has extended additional protection to all of the major presidential candidates."

The screen changed again, this time to another story, but Claire didn't turn her head to me right away. She was clearly perplexed by the report.

"What's going on?" she asked.

"Offhand, I'd say you'd better get yourself some safety netting."

"Why?"

"Because you're being set up for a fall."

Other *Leisure* books by Alan Russell:

MULTIPLE WOUNDS

POLITICAL SUICIDE

ALAN RUSSELL

LEISURE BOOKS NEW YORK CITY

To the 1926 boys,
Mike Richter and Mark Russell.
It was a very good year!

A LEISURE BOOK®

June 2006

Published by

Dorchester Publishing Co., Inc.
200 Madison Avenue
New York, NY 10016

ISBN 0-8439-5612-7

Printed in the United States of America.

Visit us on the web at www.dorchesterpub.com.

ACKNOWLEDGMENTS

Whenever you write a book, you travel a slippery trail, and I'm thankful to the many helping hands that kept me from stumbling too badly. Kelley Ragland was there to direct me along the right path, and Ben Sevier helped me over the finish line. Cynthia Manson did her usual wonderful job guiding me over potholes. Chris Amberger was my guide through unfamiliar terrain, offering up his keen editorial eye. I am indebted to Chuck Hawks, who shared some of his firearms expertise with me and allowed me to write accurately, if not shoot straight. Russ Wilkinson of Chesapeake Bay Fly Fishing Company very kindly answered my questions, and I hope he doesn't mind that I took a little literary license with the geography of Maryland's mid-shore. Jim Tenuto educated me about life in a military academy, and former highway patrolman Jerry Rudy helped me with some technical questions. Many years ago, Bill Orilio of Grantham, Orilio & Associates introduced me to the world of mystery shopping, and regaled me with many stories. I also mined those fields with System Check in Encinitas, California, gaining yet more experience. Thank you one and all!

POLITICAL SUICIDE

PROLOGUE

By agreement the ten of us met in barracks that night. During lunchtime the Mad Cow had played the role of the righteous and wrathful god to a good part of the cadet body. The Mad Cow was one of those table commandants who seemed to think it his duty to portray a Cecil B. DeMille Jehovah when confroning plebes. His dressing-down had managed to divide our ranks, and it was clear that some of the members of our table were pissed off at Bohannon. To defuse the situation before all the recriminating and finger-pointing even started, I announced, "I've got it covered."

Nine faces suddenly looked relieved. No one wanted to take on any extra burden. We were all stretched too thin as it was. The fourth-class system is designed to overburden plebes. Plebes are referred to as the fourth class, as in fourth-class citizens. Two months into our West Point experience, we all felt as if we were four months behind. Those who have lived through the United States Military Academy swear that there is a method to the madness of the fourth-class system. Like all cadets before us, we were overwhelmed with information and pushed to our limits. The system was supposed to get us ready for the chaos of war, even if most of the time its purpose seemed more designed to introduce us to the ways of petty tyrants.

Just to make sure I was absolutely aware of the consequences of my volunteering, Eastman said, "If you can't recite the first two hundred words perfectly, the Mad Cow said our whole squad would be doing fatigue tour."

"I said I've got it covered."

At West Point, when a cadet refers to a "cow," he's talking about a junior, a second-class man. In the nineteenth century the only free time West Point cadets received was the summer between their sophomore and junior years. Their return was referred to as the time when "the cows came home." Tradition is big at West Point. Over a hundred years later, long after that summer tradition ended, juniors were still called cows. Bobby MacDonald was now a firstie, known as a senior to those outside the Academy, but his nickname from his junior year had stuck. MacDonald was a spit-and-polish honor Nazi who believed it was his mission to bedevil plebes. He didn't think much of the "kinder and gentler" army, and was the toughest table commandant at the Academy. The Mad Cow enjoyed his license to make our lives miserable.

Eastman still wasn't satisfied: "He said it had to be a cold max."

A "cold max" is cadet-speak for "without an error." All I had to do was miss a word or two and all of us would suffer.

"I'm aware of that."

During lunch, the Mad Cow had called upon our squad to demonstrate Plebe Knowledge. It's a game upperclassmen love to play. Before arriving at West Point we were expected to memorize a booklet entitled *Bugle Notes*, what we call the Cadet Bible. For some, memorizing thousands upon thousands of words on a variety of subjects proved an overwhelming task. And it wasn't just a matter of committing things to memory. When called upon, there was no time to dwell on the subject, or collect your wits. Upon the order of an upperclassman, you had to immediately demonstrate your mastery of the subject by offering verbatim quotes.

Naturally, Lou Bohannon had fucked up. Bo was my roommate. He was as nice a guy as you would ever want to meet; perhaps too nice for the United States Military Academy. Bo seemed to have a knack for drawing the attention and ire of upperclassmen. It was almost as if Bo had a KICK ME sign on his backside. Under the Mad Cow's grilling, Bo hadn't been able to recite Scott's Fixed Opinion, a statement by Old Fuss and Feathers concluding that the West Point cadets were invaluable in the war between the United States and Mexico.

"I'm sorry, guys," said Bo. "I really do know Scott's Fixed Opinion. I just sort of choked when the Mad Cow stared me down."

The sincerity of Bo's apology made everyone shift a little. Bo was a fuck-up, but he was our fuck-up. I had heard one squad member describe Bo as "annoying and yet innocent, like a little brother." That, I suppose, was the perfect summation of our relationship. The notion played on my guilt, but that was another story. Taking on the big-brother role meant that little brother's fights became my fights.

My intervention and Bo's contriteness changed the squad's mood. Instead of culling off the weakest, we once again closed ranks.

"It's the Mad Cow's look," said Anderson.

"Yeah," said Eastman. "He hypnotizes his prey, just like a snake."

"No," said Wong. "It's his voice."

"He makes 'pass the butter' sound like DEFCON five," I said.

We all laughed. It was much more satisfying having the Mad Cow in our sights than Bo. None of us lingered, though. There was much too much that all of us needed to do, and I had a speech to memorize.

In the morning all the cadets gathered outside for breakfast formation. Our squad was assembled in our assigned spot.

It's a morning ritual, the cadets marching into Washington Hall, our footsteps timed to the beat of the drum that calls us to meals. Bo was marching at my side. He was looking guilty and contrite. "I saw the light under your bedcovers after lights out."

"Better report me for an honor code violation."

"It should have been me."

I shrugged and said nothing.

"Did you get any sleep?"

I lied, another honor code violation: "Some."

"I owe you," Bo said.

"It's part of the debt owed to the long gray line."

I was quoting from the words I would soon be delivering. West Point was that long gray line. Two presidents, General Dwight D. Eisenhower and General Ulysses S. Grant, had graduated from the school. Among its other graduates were George Patton, Robert E. Lee, and Stonewall Jackson. Just as interesting, I think, are those West Point attendees who didn't make a name in the military. Abner Doubleday, the man who invented America's national sport of baseball, was a graduate, as was Buzz Aldrin, the second man to walk on the moon. Edgar Allan Poe attended West Point until he was thrown out. He must have found it a great environment for a horror writer. The painter James McNeill Whistler opted for oils over bullets, and when Timothy Leary told the world to "Turn on, tune in, and drop out," he must have been rebelling against his days in the Academy. George Custer was also a West Point graduate. As for his questionable battle tactics, perhaps they can be attributed to the fact that Custer was never a good student, and had in fact finished last in his class.

There was no shortage of memorable figures who spent time at West Point, links in that long gray line.

We entered through the huge, oaken doors of Washington Hall. Like everything else at the United States Military Academy, history permeates the room. Along the walls are portraits of more than two centuries of past superintendents, their eyes fixed dubiously on this newest generation of soldiers. There is a huge mural showing a history of war, its trail marked not in blood but by weapons and famous warriors.

The Cadet Mess is a cavernous space. It would have to be. Every day four thousand cadets assemble for breakfast and lunch, finding their places at ten-person tables situated throughout three floors and five of the room's six wings.

Once inside the hall, we removed our jackets and draped them over our chairs. Our hats were tucked away on a shelf. Before sitting, we waited for the command of "Take seats!" from the brigade adjutant. One "gunner" works at every table, making sure we have food, dishes, and silverware. There are also coffee and water "corporals" who make sure the table commandant receives his beverages of choice. Empty glasses are not tolerated.

Previous generations of plebes were forced to eat while sitting on the forward three inches of their chairs. They were required to take very small bites of food, and had to completely swallow each mouthful before taking another bite. Like an automaton, the plebe had to return his fork to the plate and place his hands in his lap between each bite. The new army has loosened those requirements, deciding malnourishment and starvation aren't the best methods for creating future officers, but that doesn't mean dining is pleasant. Nothing about your plebe year is supposed to be pleasant. The dining experience was like a five-year-old being forced to eat at his cranky grandmother's house, with the kid having to wear stiff and starched clothing, not being allowed to squirm, talk, or laugh, and having to eat whatever was on his plate no matter how offensive it might appear. All that wouldn't have been so bad if we didn't have to face up to a cantankerous elder twice a day.

The Mad Cow let us get halfway through breakfast before beginning the torture. Like any good cat, he wanted to play with the mice before eviscerating them. As he looked around our table, heads lowered and turned.

"Wong!" he shouted.

Wong jumped to his feet. "Yes, sir."

For most of West Point's history, upperclassmen could get in your face, not even offering the separation of an eyelash. That had changed, and now there was an eighteen-inch distance they were supposed to abide by. The Mad Cow kept to the letter of the law, but those who looked on could feel the narrowness of the space, like an iffy DMZ.

"Two Wongs don't make a right," the Mad Cow said.

Nearby, a few upperclassmen laughed. "Yes, sir," said Wong.

He offered up a softball question first: "How many names on the Battle Monument, plebe?"

"Two thousand two hundred and forty names, sir."

The Mad Cow looked around the table. If he couldn't exactly get in our faces, he could get in our heads. "Bartkowski!"

Another member of our squad jumped up. "Yes, sir."

"Tell me the Soldier's Creed."

"Sir," Bartkowski said, " 'I am an American soldier. I am a member of the United States Army—a protector of the greatest nation on earth. Because I am proud of the uniform I wear, I will always act in ways creditable to the military service and the nation it is sworn to guard. I am proud of my organization. I will do all I can to make it the finest unit of the army. I will be loyal to those under whom I serve. I will do my full part to carry out orders and instructions given me or my unit. As a soldier, I realize that I am a member of a time-honored profession—that I am doing my share to keep alive the principles of freedom for which my country stands. No matter what situation I am in, I will never do anything, for pleasure, profit, or personal means, even beyond the line of duty, to restrain my army comrades from actions disgraceful to themselves and the uniform. I am proud of my country and its flag. I will try to make the people of this nation proud of the service I represent, for I am an American soldier.' Sir."

"Cadet Eastman."

Eastman was on his feet in a flash. "Yes, sir."

"Tell me, what do plebes rank?"

"Sir," said Eastman, "the superintendent's dog, the commandant's cat, the waiters in the mess hall, the Hell Cats, the generals in the air force, and all the admirals in the whole damned navy."

The time-honored response drew approval from everyone in earshot at Washington Hall. Denigrating the navy is always a crowd pleaser.

The Mad Cow nodded as a matter of dismissal. For a moment it appeared as if he was done with our table, but then he seemed to remember something.

"Yesterday a member of this table was delinquent in his Plebe Knowledge, was he not?"

No one at our table answered.

"That's right," said the Mad Cow. "Cadet Bohannon couldn't accurately quote Scott's Fixed Opinion even after others at this table tried to secretly prompt him. I took that as a group failure, and said I would come by later to announce the punishment. As I left the table, I announced, 'I shall return,' then asked Bohannon who had spoken those immortal words. I was aghast at his ignorance, and could not believe he did not know that it was General Douglas MacArthur who made that famous promise during World War Two; MacArthur, a West Point graduate whose name is synonymous with this institution; MacArthur, a former superintendent here; MacArthur, who on May 12, 1962, gave his famous farewell speech to the cadets of West Point; MacArthur, who memorized that speech, all two thousand words of it, at the age of eighty-two years. And so the punishment seemed obvious."

He looked us up and down. "Now, which one of you will

be reciting those first two hundred words of General MacArthur's farewell address?"

Like every other West Point plebe, I knew that the secret to survival was not getting noticed. In the face of upperclassmen, you did your best to be invisible. When confronted, you kowtowed, genuflected, and readily admitted that you were a miserable excuse for a human being, and the sorriest soldier that ever put on a uniform. By not presuming to be anything but a pissant, you could generally escape the wrath of your superiors.

Throughout cadet basic training, what most at the Academy call "beast barracks," I had played the shorn and submissive sheep. That was the safe way, a strategy practiced by all new cadets and plebes. As I stood up, I knew that my days of flying under the radar were past.

"Proceed, Mr. Travis."

It felt as if all the eyes in the huge mess hall were directed my way. I took a deep breath and in an unsteady voice recited MacArthur's opening remaks, which bespoke of his gratitude at being the recipient of the Thayer Award. MacArthur didn't dwell on his medallion for long, and my voice firmed up as the two of us got beyond his preamble into the meat of his message.

" 'Duty,' 'honor,' 'country'—those three hallowed words reverently dictate what you want to be, what you can be, what you will be. They are your rallying point to build courage when courage seems to fail, to regain faith when there seems to be little cause for faith, to create hope when hope becomes forlorn.

" 'Unhappily, I possess neither that eloquence of diction, that poetry of imagination, nor that brilliance of metaphor to tell you all that they mean.

" 'The unbelievers will say they are but words, but a slogan, but a flamboyant phrase. Every pedant, every demagogue, every cynic, every hypocrite, every troublemaker, and, I am sorry to say, some others of an entirely different character, will try to downgrade them even to the extent of mockery and ridicule.' "

The Mad Cow was reading the speech from a piece of paper. I had finished the required two hundred words, and a few more. He opened his mouth to announce that I had successfully memorized the required words, but I wasn't done, wasn't close to being done.

" 'But these are some of the things they build. They build your basic character. They mold you for your future roles as the custodians of the nation's defense. They make you strong enough to know when you are weak, and brave enough to face yourself when you are afraid.

" 'They teach you to be proud and unbending in honest failure, but humble and gentle in success; not to substitute words for action; not to seek the path of comfort, but to face the stress and spur of difficulty and challenge; to learn to stand up in the storm, but to have compassion on those who fail; to master yourself before you seek to master others; to have a heart that is clean, a goal that is high; to learn to laugh, yet never forget how to weep; to reach into the future, yet never neglect the past; to be serious, yet never take yourself too seriously; to be modest so that you will remember the simplicity of true greatness; the open mind of true wisdom, the meekness of true strength.' "

Our wing was beginning to fill with faces. Cadets from around Washington Hall were taking leave of their tables to witness my speech. I raised my voice so as to reach all the new ears.

" 'They give you a temperate will, a quality of imagination, a vigor of the emotions, a freshness of the deep springs of life, a temperamental predominance of courage over timidity, an appetite for adventure over love of ease.

" 'They create in your heart the sense of wonder, the unfailing hope of what is next, and the joy and inspiration of life. They teach you in this way to be an officer and a gentleman.

" 'And what sort of soldiers are those you are to lead? Are they reliable? Are they brave? Are they capable of victory?

" 'Their story is known to all of you. It is the story of the American man-at-arms. My estimate of him was formed in the battlefields many, many years ago, and has never changed. I regarded him then, as I regard him now, as one of the world's noblest figures—not only as one of the finest military characters, but also as one of the most stainless.

" 'His name and fame are the birthright of every American citizen. In his youth and strength, his love and loyalty, he gave all that mortality can give. He needs no eulogy from me, or from any other man. He has written his own history and written it in red on his enemy's breast.' "

The Mad Cow's mouth had dropped open. He was still standing, unsure of what to do. As for the rest of the hall, I knew that I had them, or MacArthur did. Everyone had stopped eating. Some utensils were held in midair. For the first time in my life I knew what it was to hold a room spellbound.

" 'But when I think of his patience under adversity, of his courage under fire, and of his modesty in victory, I am filled with an emotion of admiration I cannot put into words. He belongs to history as furnishing one of the greatest examples of successful patriotism; he belongs to prosterity as the instructor of future generations in the principles of liberty and freedom; he belongs to the present, to us, by his virtues and by his achievements.

" 'In twenty campaigns, on a hundred battlefields, around a thousand campfires, I have witnessed that enduring fortitude, that patriotic self-abnegation, and that invincible determination which have carved his statue in the hearts of his people.

" 'From one end of the world to the other, he has drained deep the chalice of courage. As I listened to those songs of the glee club, in memory's eye I could see those staggering columns of the First World War, bending under soggy packs on many a weary march, from dripping dusk to drizzling dawn, slogging ankle-deep through mire of shell-pocked roads; to form grimly for the attack, blue-lipped, covered with sludge and mud, chilled by the wind and rain, driving home to their objective, and for many, to the judgment seat of God.

" 'I do not know the dignity of their birth, but I do know the glory of their death. They died unquestioning, uncomplaining, with faith in their hearts, and on their lips the hope that we would go on to victory.

" 'Always for them: duty, honor, country. Always their blood, and sweat, and tears, as they saw the way and the light. And twenty years after, on the other side of the globe, against the filth of dirty foxholes, the stench of ghostly trenches, the slime of dripping dugouts, those boiling suns of the relentless heat, those torrential rains of devastating storms, the loneliness and utter desolation of jungle trails, the bitterness of long separation of those they loved and cherished, the deadly pestilence of tropic disease, the horror-stricken areas of war.

" 'Their resolute and determined defense, their swift and sure attack, their indomitable purpose, their complete and decisive victory—always victory, always through the bloody haze of their last reverberating shot, the vision of gaunt, ghastly men, reverently following your password of duty, honor, country.' "

The triumvirate of duty, honor, and country felled even the Mad Cow. He took a chair, and like everyone else, listened with avid attention. These were words the cadets were thirsty to hear. These were sentiments and thoughts that defined who and what we wanted to be. Like Gregory Peck, I was playing the part of MacArthur. All I needed was the corncob pipe, but then smoking was no longer allowed at West Point.

" 'The code which those words perpetuate embraces the highest moral laws and will stand the test of any ethics or philosophies ever promulgated for the uplift of mankind. Its requirements are for the things that are right, and its restraints from the things that are wrong. The soldier, above all other men, is required to practice the greatest act of religious training—sacrifice. In battle and in the face of danger and death, he discloses those divine attributes which his Maker gave when he created man in his own image. No physical courage and no brute instinct can take the place of the Divine help which alone can sustain him. However horrible the incidents of war may be, the soldier who is called upon to offer and to give his life for his country is the noblest development of mankind.

"'You now face a new world, a world of change. The thrust into outer space of the satellite spheres and missiles marks a beginning of another epoch in the long story of mankind. In the five or more billions of years the scientists tell us it has taken to form the earth, in the three or more billion years of development of the human race, there has never been a more abrupt or staggering evolution.'"

I looked around at my rapt audience, and with MacArthur's words I spoke of the future, before returning to the mission of the present.

"'And through all this welter of change and development your mission remains fixed, determined, inviolable. It is to win our wars. Everything else in your professional career is but corollary to this vital dedication. All other public purpose, all other public projects, all other public needs, great or small, will find others for their accomplishments; but you are the ones who are trained to fight.

"'Yours is the profession of arms, the will to win, the sure knowledge that in war there is no substitute for victory, that if you lose, the nation will be destroyed, that the very obsession of your public service must be duty, honor, country.

"'Others will debate the controversial issues, national and international, which divide men's minds. But serene, calm, aloof, you stand as the nation's war guardians, as its lifeguards from the raging tides of international conflict, as its gladiators in the arena of battle. For a century and a half you have defended, guarded, and protected its hallowed traditions of liberty and freedom, of right and justice.

" 'Let civilian voices argue the merits or demerits of our processes of government: whether our strength is being sapped by deficit financing indulged in too long, by federal paternalism grown too mighty, by power groups grown too arrogant, by politics grown too corrupt, by crime grown too rampant, by morals grown too low, by taxes grown too high, by extremists grown too violent; whether our personal liberties are as thorough and complete as they should be.

" 'These great national problems are not for your professional participation or military solution. Your guidepost stands out like a tenfold beacon in the night: duty, honor, country.' "

The longer I talked, the stronger my voice had grown. Now I was stentorian, and my audience was responding in kind. Our wing was packed with four thousand cadets. They were like an evangelical congregation, exhorting me to greater things. I rode the MacArthur horse home in full throat.

" 'You are the leven which binds together the entire fabric of our national system of defense. From your ranks come the great captains who hold the nation's destiny in their hands the moment the war tocsin sounds.

" 'The long, gray line has never failed us. Were you to do so, a million ghosts in olive drab, in brown khaki, in blue and gray, would rise from their white crosses, thundering those magic words: duty, honor, country.

" 'This does not mean that you are warmongers. On the contrary, the soldier above all other people prays for peace, for he must suffer and bear the deepest wounds and scars of war. But always in our ears ring the ominous words of Plato, that wisest of all philosophers: *Only the dead have seen the end of war*.

" 'The shadows are lengthening for me. The twilight is here. My days of old have vanished tone and tint. They have gone glimmering through the dreams of things that were. Their memory is one of wondrous beauty, watered by tears and coaxed and caressed by the smiles of yesterday. I listen vainly for the witching melody of faint bugles blowing reveille, of far drums beating the long roll.

" 'In my dreams I hear again the crash of guns, the rattle of musketry, the strange, mournful mutter of the battlefield. But in the evening of my memory I come back to West Point. Always there echoes and re-echoes: duty, honor, country.

" 'Today marks my final roll call with you. But I want you to know that when I cross the river, my last conscious thoughts will be of the corps, and the corps, and the corps.

" 'I bid you farewell.' "

As I finished speaking, tears were raining down from my eyes, but I wasn't alone. Just as when MacArthur had spoken, there wasn't a dry eye among all the cadets. My speech exceeded the thirty minutes allotted to breakfast, but not a single soul had departed the room. For once, the strict timetables of the Academy did not rule the student body. The cadets rose en masse and started cheering. I suspect most of the applause was for MacArthur, but knew some of it was for me. Even the Mad Cow was wildly clapping and shouting.

From that moment on, I knew my veil of anonymity was lost. I had announced myself as a force to be reckoned with, but at the same time I set myself up to be scrutinized. I did this even with the full knowledge that in the military the nail that stands out is the same nail that tends to be hammered down very hard.

CHAPTER ONE

It was five minutes until midnight and I was facing the prospect of another bar and another witching hour. I took a few deep breaths and hoped that my heavy breathing would energize me. It was time to work, time to be the human sponge.

I was staying at the Blue Crab Inn located along Maryland's Chesapeake Bay. The resort featured two restaurants and one bar. I was *shopping* the property, a euphemism for spying. My job was to offer management my impressions and suggestions. I was the anonymous guest, the fly on the wall, and sometimes the fly in the ointment.

The Jimmy Sooks Lounge overlooks the Miles River. Male blue crabs are called jimmies and the females are referred to as sooks, thus the name. I knew the lay of the land, having audited the Blue Crab Inn three times in the past year. It was a good account, meaning they were happy with my work and they paid promptly. Five years ago I started my company, the Last Resort. At the time, the company name might have been a personal confession as well. The work is mostly corporate undercover. The company stationery lists my Maryland private investigator's license number, but that's strictly for show. When pressed by strangers as to my profession, I always say, "I'm a hospitality consultant," the same answer hookers usually give.

Another deep breath. Of late, it was the only kind of heavy breathing going on in my life. It was showtime. I walked into the bar and registered my impressions with one look at the room.

Jimmy Sooks Lounge less than a third full. One bartender, one cocktail waitress on duty. ESPN on television. Muzak in background. Overall, lounge appears to be clean and kept up, though some debris under the table closest to hallway is clearly visible to anyone entering the room.

There were three seats available at the bar. In less than a second I decided on the best place to sit, a spot that afforded me a direct view of the register and the point-of-sale printer. As I made my way to the counter, I gave the impression of being just another business sort out to finish my workday with a nightcap. I was wearing my Invisible Man outfit—a blue blazer, gray slacks, and a loosened red paisley tie.

Condiment tray needs attention. Fruit flies hovering over limes and cherries. Some swizzle sticks on counter. Toothpicks and a bar napkin on floor. Liquor display in disarray. Bottles not arranged neatly, some labels not facing forward. One patron with an empty glass. Bartender One slouching against back counter talking with what appears to be a friend, a white male, approximately twenty-five, with short, curly black hair, earring.

I took a seat and casually craned my neck around for a look-see. There was a mirror stretching along the bar wall that would provide me the eyes that some people swore were in the back of my head.

Cobwebs in southeast corner of bar. Nautical memorabilia also needs attention from housekeeping. Dust on anchor and dip net displays. Cellophane wrappers and other debris visible on crab traps hanging on wall. Eleven patrons in lounge. Four at counter: Earring Man; Empty Glass, who's an older white male; and Lovey-Dovey Couple, both white, she blond hair, him brown. In the lounge are three business-men at a table, all clean-shaven, two white, one black; white male in corner; a Hispanic couple in the back booth closest to hallway; a white female in booth closest to wall.

With my peripheral vision I took in the unhurried approach of the bartender. He stood in front of me and said, "What can I get you?"

No opening pleasantries, no smile. Management needs to coach staff on proper method of approaching a guest. Bartender One is Todd, a white male, six feet tall, two hundred pounds, wearing a uniform and name tag. He has short brown hair, a mustache, and a tattoo of a bulldog on left wrist.

"Vodka and tonic. Light on the ice. And a water back, please."

"You got it."

Bartender One makes no attempt to upgrade drink order. House vodka is Smirnoff. Judging by call bottles, he could simply have asked, "Stolichnaya?" Or, "Skyy?" Or, better yet, "Do you have a preference of vodka?" Bartender One uses glass to get ice instead of using ice scoop. If glass breaks in ice it is a potential hazard. Recommend that all bartenders be required to use ice scoop. He free-pours the drink. Five-count pour. Recommend to management that bartenders use shot glass and splash for a consistent pour. Lime garnish placed in drink.

The bartender returned with the two drinks, placed the napkins down on the counter, and put the glasses atop them.

"That will be four seventy-five."

No offer to run a tab. No inquiry as to whether I'm a guest in the hotel. Lost opportunity for personalization of service. Management should encourage Bartender One to start a tab as it facilitates more drink orders.

I removed a twenty-dollar bill from my wallet. When performing an audit, you always pay cash at the bar to see if the staff is following what bean counters call cash-control procedures. One of my jobs is to bloodhound the path of the money. Since time immemorial publicans have worried about ducats safely landing in the till instead of in an employee's pocket.

Bartender One immediately retrieves tendered twenty-dollar bill. Money picked up without acknowledgment of appreciation. Management should stress that all servers thank guests upon payment.

I don't particularly care for vodka, but I always make a point of ordering a clear drink because it's easy to look through. Raising my drink, I pretended to take a long sip. What I was really doing was peering through the looking glass. As the bartender approached the register, the tingle in my neck clued me to what was going to happen a moment before it did. Maybe it was the bartender's momentary pause at the cash register, or it could have been the surreptitious tilt of his head followed by the almost imperceptible look to the right, and then to his left. I always wondered if my foreknowledge was the result of physical giveaways, or if I was sensitized to some unseen vibration. It was the kind of thing I never probed too closely for fear of losing the magic.

At 11:58 Bartender One hits the NO SALE key on the register. He puts the twenty-dollar bill into the till, acts as if he's depositing money for the drink, but actually removes twenty dollars in change. In his hand he palms a five-dollar bill.

The bartender returned with my change, muttered, "Thank you," then walked off.

No receipt offered for obvious reasons. Management might consider having bartenders dispense receipts with all drinks. Fifteen dollars and twenty-five cents in change returned to me at 11:59.

I tracked the bartender's movements. He stopped as if to tidy up some glasses on the back counter, but his subterfuge was obvious.

At 11:59:45 Bartender One slips five-dollar bill into tip jar.
There was a small sense of letdown. Part of the anticli-
max was this feeling of having witnessed too many venial
sins in my thirty-five years. There was also this sense that
the last act had already been played out, but that my job as
critic required me to watch the rest of an overly long scene.
Management and ownership would feel cheated if I didn't
stay in the bar for at least an hour. They always liked the details and comments in my reports. I was living proof of the
devil in the details.

*Though the kitchen is still open, Bartender One makes no
attempt to sell appetizers and food. Management needs to
stress that all lounge staff make this offer to patrons.*
Epitaph on my tombstone, I thought: Do you want fries
with that?

*Only one table tent with bar menu visible at counter. Man-
agement should coordinate with bartenders re table tents to
make sure an adequate number are on display.*
From the corner of my eye, I watched Empty Glass signal
for a refill. The bartender, looking almost directly at the man,
missed his gesture. Obliviousness in serving staff always reminded me of David McCord's summation of a waiter's being called to heaven: *By and by, God caught his eye.*
"I'm ready for another one," I heard the man say.

*At midnight, Bartender One manufactures drink for Empty
Glass. He dispenses five-count of Dewar's and splash of
soda. Drink rung up and placed on existing tab.*
I took another sip of my drink and heard the printout
from the point-of-sales register. In no hurry, the bartender
tore off the order from the printer, read it, and then started
to make the drink.

There were several point-of-sale terminals situated
around the lounge where the cocktail servers could punch
in orders. The system was designed to allow expediency of
serving. It was a big lounge, and the setup allowed servers
to stay on the floor instead of having to walk to the bar to

turn in orders. P.O.S. systems are designed to prevent confusion and collusion between bartender and cocktail server. The drinks are specified on the order ticket going into the bar terminal. This prevents accidental and purposeful mistakes. By eliminating the "calling" of orders, management tries to control the flow of drinks into the lounge, as well as discourage the potential teaming up of bartender and server in their own side business.

I looked up at the television, pretended interest in the news story about the hotly contested presidential primaries, and then gradually let my eyes wander through the lounge. The cocktail server was chatting with the group of three businessmen. Though they were about fifteen feet away from me, I was able to tune in to some of their conversation. I also made out the writing on the server's name tag. One girlfriend I used to take on audits said I had the eyes of an eagle and ears of a beagle. She sometimes also added that I had the soul of a frog, to which I would say that my amphibian makeover was merely awaiting the kiss of some princess to transform me to my true regal self. That same girlfriend eventually broke up with me over an argument about my business, or at least that was the final culmination of other arguments. She said that she was tired of being my shill, tired of acting out her small role. I said to her, "There are no small roles, only small actors." I remember she gave me a last pitying glance and then took her leave from my life. So much for getting in the last word.

Cocktail Server One is Mercedes, five foot two inches, one hundred and ten pounds, Hispanic female.

I picked up my drink, swiveled a little on the bar stool, raised my glass, and did my sneak-peeking and sipping.

Cocktail Server One appears friendly and interacts well with guests but needs to police her station better. Several straws and bar napkins on floor. At least half a dozen empty glasses on tables that need bussing.

My head never moved, only the eyes over my glass. It

was my alligator impression. Like the reptile, I tried to disappear save for my peering eyes atop the water. My view of the swamp suddenly got a little interesting. Two heads went on alert at the same time. The heads belonged to the two singles in the lounge, the woman in the booth and the man along the far wall. I used the bar mirror to see what had perked their interest and saw a man entering the room. The new arrival paused to study the interior of Jimmy Sooks. The man who was seated gestured almost imperceptibly with his head in the direction of the woman in the booth. The signal was immediately understood. The newcomer made eye contact with the woman and then started walking toward her. Instead of watching what was going on, the man who had signaled made a point of looking the other way, suddenly absorbed in the river view.

My neck felt like it was holding auditions for flamenco dancers. Something was going on, but I didn't know what. Through the bar mirror I studied the man as he made his way through the lounge. He presented himself as looking about forty, standing six foot two, and weighing around two hundred and twenty-five pounds. The man had short, dark hair, and behind horn-rimmed glasses were dark brown eyes. In this case, looks were deceiving. The wig was the first giveaway. It was very good, but I had several that were better. I suspected that his glasses were as unnecessary as his tinted contacts. There was padding going on inside his high-collared leather coat, and lifts in his shoes. The man was smaller, lighter, and older than he actually appeared. Because my work often requires me to change my own appearance, I can spot a toupee at a hundred yards. What wasn't obvious was why the man was altering his appearance. This was Maryland, not Hollywood.

The man's posture was erect, and there was a little swagger to his walk. Definitely a military background, I thought. He had an officer's kind of bearing, wearing his authority and power like others would a vestment. Back in my spit-shine days, my cronies and I had referred to his type as Major Dick.

I shifted in my seat, raised my water glass disguise, and took a moment to study her. *White female, dark shoulder-length hair, medium build, about thirty years of age.* That would have been my description in a report. In my own mind, though, I was adding a lot more adjectives, starting with the word *beautiful.* Though she was seated, I could see she had a long torso and would be on the tall side. Her clothes were understated, a silk blouse and cashmere sweater, but looked tailored to her frame. She had bags under her eyes and her face was pale, but instead of detracting from her looks, it added a further allure to her clear blue eyes. Judging by the twisted remains of several straws, her wait had been a nervous one. Though it was apparent she didn't know the approaching man, it was also clear that she was expecting him.

My ears were straining to hear their introductions. Beagle power. "Claire?" the Major asked, extending his hand. She reached for it and then moved further into the booth so he could take a seat next to her.

At 12:03:30 Cocktail Server One approaches booth and takes drink order from couple.

I couldn't hear the order, and the interaction was brief. Claire and her new friend were already having an intense, quiet discussion.

At 12:04 Cocktail Server One places drink order on point-of-sale terminal.

I watched the printout appear at the bar printer. Bartender One reluctantly stopped talking with Earring Man and ripped off the order slip.

At 12:05 Bartender One manufactures a Cuba Libre with a four-count pour of Bacardi Rum, a splash of lime juice, and cola dispensed from the gun. He pulls a bottle of Budweiser from the cooler and places it, along with a chilled beer glass and the Cuba Libre, on the server's station counter. Cocktail

Server One picks up order and delivers it to booth at 12:06.
Customer declines offer to run a tab and shakes off server's
offer to pour the beer into the glass. He pays with a ten-
dollar bill.

By the Major's body language, it was evident he told the
cocktail server to keep the change. I watched him grip the
neck of his beer bottle with a napkin, then tilt it and take a
conservative swallow. Some people use napkins with their
drinks because they don't like getting their hands wet.
Some people also extend their pinkies when holding a
glass and drinking. He didn't strike me as the kind of person to do either of those things. It crossed my mind that he
didn't want his fingerprints left on the bottle.

His eyes shifted from hers, and he took a moment to
sweep the room with a glance. I quickly dipped my nose
into my V&T, preventing him from catching me doing my
mirror peeping.

After a few seconds passed, I shifted in my seat and casually craned my neck. Major Dick's partner appeared to
be studiously ignoring the couple, but I could tell he was
playing my game and using the window to watch their reflection. The man's face was averted from me; he was
wearing a black overcoat with the collar up, but I had
taken notice of him earlier. He had the tight facial struc-
ture and coloring of a Willem Dafoe or Christopher
Walken, and like the actors, his blue eyes seemed to have
an unblinking quality. His eye sockets barely seemed to
contain those eyes, much like those of a pug or Boston
terrier.

I sipped from my drink and went back to my mirror viewing. The Major was holding what appeared to be pictures,
and leaned close to Claire so she could see. One of the pictures slid out of his hand and over the edge of the table to
the floor. Claire bent to retrieve the photo, putting her head
under the table to look for it.

The Major did his own leaning as well, dropping something into her drink. I was pretty sure it wasn't an Alka-Seltzer.

She resurfaced with the picture, put it back on the table, and then picked up her drink. I swallowed my shout of warning, and she swallowed her drink. It wasn't a case of my being unsure about him doctoring her drink, but more that I was still trying to figure out what was going on.

I knew the logical thing to do was call the police. Maybe these two jokers worked as a team. They could be into something ugly like date rape, which would explain Major Dick's disguise and his putting something into her drink, but that didn't explain the serious conversation taking place between them, nor the pictures they were scrutinizing. This wasn't some classified-ad date. The missing puzzle pieces kept me seated and quiet. I have always been a better observer than thinker, so that's what I did. If I was hoping for some grand revelation to emerge from my watching, it didn't happen. Her wooziness came on a lot faster than any of my insights. Five minutes after first sipping her adulterated drink, she began to react to its effects. Claire's hand went up to her forehead and wiped her now-wet brow. I watched the Major reach across and lightly touch her arm with a solicitous gesture. His false benevolence decided things for me. It was time to make that call.

Because I don't like to be disturbed while I do my spotting, I had left my flip phone in the hotel room. There was a pay phone in the lobby, though. I tossed a dollar on the counter—come tomorrow, the bartender would likely need it—but then stayed my departure. The Major was a fast worker. Through the mirror I could see him helping Claire to her feet. "A little air," I heard him say, "will do you some good."

My hesitating had put her in a bad spot. There wouldn't be time to call the cops. Arm in arm, the two of them began to make their way out of the lounge. I raised my glass, sipping and surreptitiously watching the second man, Mr. Pug

Eyes. He was clearly interested in the departing couple, but he made no move to follow them. I waited until the Major and Claire were out of Jimmy Sooks before getting up.

The Blue Crab Inn and its more than two hundred rooms are spread out over four acres. The resort sports plenty of foliage and garden areas, secluded spots with koi pools and little waterfalls. The lush landscaping is part of the property's ambiance. For those unfamiliar with the word, *ambiance* means a minimum of two hundred dollars a night.

The Major seemed to know where he was going. South of the lounge was a garden area with large, rectangular planters set in a maze-like grid. They were navigating through those planters, and her legs were looking more and more unsteady. I might have been imagining it, but it looked as if she was trying to put on the brakes.

"Claire!" I yelled. "Is that really you?"

Their three-legged race came to an abrupt halt. Though the light wasn't very good, I could still make out the baleful expression on the Major's face. Medusa probably gave off more welcoming looks. I pretended not to notice and approached the woman with open arms.

"What are you doing here?" I said, sweeping her into a hug.

The Major had to reluctantly relinquish his grip on her. It was a good thing he was looking at me and not her, because drugged or not, it was clear Claire had no idea who I was. Still, she didn't seem too anxious to leave my arms. I gave her a wink and a smile and she appeared to make the quick decision that I was all right, or at least the lesser of two evils.

"Claire isn't feeling well," the Major said. He stepped toward us, ready to reclaim his prize.

With concerned voice and expression, I said, "You're not?" Then I moved her, as I would a dance partner, just out of the Major's reach.

"Sit down," I told her, "and let me look at you." To him I announced, "I'm a doctor."

Had my mother been alive she would have been very happy to hear that. For most of her too-short adult life she was an R.N., and when my brother and I were young she never discouraged us from dissecting snails or performing so-called heart transplants on grasshoppers that we diagnosed with bad tickers. Mother made us draw the line at mammals, though I once bandaged up the family dog for what I declared to be a case of phlebitis.

"The boys will be doctors," my mother often said. It was wishful thinking on her part, of course. The longstanding Travis tradition was to produce males who became warriors. I was named after William Barret Travis, who became famous for his command at the Alamo. Lost in the fine print is the fact that he was one of the first to die there. Dying for country is also a Travis tradition. The family motto is *"Nec temere nec timide,"* which translates to, "Neither afraid nor timid." I have always been convinced the family edited out the last line of the motto, which probably reads, "And not very bright, so perfect for the army."

I steered Claire to the rear of a planter, sat her down, and then kneeled down myself. Claire looked hazy, but wasn't so out of it that she didn't realize her situation had taken a turn for the worse and I was there to help. She gave me a slight nod, showing me her willingness to play along.

Exit sign twenty feet off. Stairway leads to subterranean garage. Elevator at least thirty yards away. No one in spa. No one in sight.

The Major moved to my side, his shadow lurking over me. I tried to remember what a doctor would do, recalling the few times I had undergone physicals. I felt under Claire's neck, took her pulse, and then examined her eyes. I stopped myself before asking her to look to the right and cough.

"Track my finger with your eyes," I said. The Major didn't need to be told to do the same. His eyes were burning a hole in my head. In my mind's eye I recollected other visits to the property.

Fire alarms located at every fifteenth room. Nearest one about a dozen strides away. The only security cameras are located in the lobby.

"Are you taking any medication, Claire?"

She shook her head.

"Your pulse is very slow," I said, "and your pupils aren't as responsive as they should be."

"She had some drinks," the Major said. "You'll have to excuse us now. We have some very important business to take care of."

Staying low, I turned my head halfway toward the Major. With caducean contempt, I sniffed, "I'm afraid not. Claire clearly needs medical attention. Observe her labored breathing and sallow complexion. She could be undergoing toxic shock, or having a severe allergic reaction. Did you eat any shellfish, Claire?"

"No."

For all my pronouncements, I was observing the Major more closely than I was my patient. I caught him scanning the garden area. It appeared he was expecting company.

"I have a medical bag in my room," I told him. "If you don't mind, I would like you to go get it."

The key-cards weren't designated by room number. I was planning on sending him to a distant room that wasn't my own, but his answer made me think my doctor act might not have been as convincing as I thought.

"Why don't we wait another minute?" he said. "The night air might revive her."

He did his talking while looking over my head. I followed the direction of his gaze. He was buying time for reinforcements.

Part of my mind was still in auditing mode: *Suggest more lighting along interior gardens of hotel. Inadequate illumination poses potential hazards to guests.*

Not to mention spotters.

"Better put on my coat, Claire," I said.

As I draped my blazer over her, I removed my fountain pen from an interior pocket. It wasn't much of a weapon, but it might offer an element of surprise.

"I'm feeling nauseated," she said. "Can you pass me my handbag? I would like to get a tissue."

I reached for her bag and hefted it up. It was heavy, and felt as if she was hauling the proverbial kitchen sink. She dipped her hand inside and started rummaging around. The coat began to slide off her shoulders and I reached up and draped it over her again. I thought I saw movement behind the planter to my right, and then heard the soft shuffle of feet. The Major apparently didn't hear the footfalls, but he did perk up at a second sound. There was the unmistakable metallic click of a bullet being chambered. I wondered what the hell I had gotten myself into.

My hands were on Claire's arms and I could feel her trembling. I wasn't sure if it was from the chill in the air or the realization of our situation. The Major decided it was a good time to edge away from us. That's what people do when they are afraid of being in the line of fire. If he was thinking that way, I needed to be as well. He moved back one step, and then another. When I saw him signal with a nod of his head, I shoved Claire to the ground and made my lunge. I did it all in one motion and had the Major twisted around in a bear hug when the shots went off. A cap gun would have made more noise, but the small gun with its silencer was real enough. After a few moments, the Major stopped struggling in my arms.

The shooter was the second man from the bar, the one I thought of as Pug. Either he didn't know what had happened or he wasn't deterred by his errant marksmanship.

He continued to advance while I was forced to dance with a dead man. The shooter looked all too calm, all too sure of himself, and the gun rested too easily in his upraised arm. His unblinking eyes bore into me.

The sudden blast seemed to go off right in my ear, and it surprised me as much as it did him. I turned my head and saw that Claire had evidently found a gun along with her tissue. The gun clattered to the ground as her hands were pushed back by the recoil. It was clear she wasn't familiar with firearms, but the shooter didn't know that. He dove for cover behind a planter, and I took that opportunity to drop the Major and sprint in a zigzag direction toward the hotel rooms. The fire alarm was where I had pictured it in my mind, and I broke the protective seal and yanked on it. From my perspective, there was a long stretch of silence, though it probably didn't last for more than a second. I was sure my back was probably already in the shooter's sights. During that eternity, I thought my last will and testament was going to be a final critique.

Part of management's hotel safety and security program should have involved fire alarm testing. Because the goddamn alarms didn't work, I died.

But then the clanging started. There was nothing timid about the alarms. From seemingly every corner of the hotel there was ringing. No one was going to ignore or sleep through the noise. Almost at once, windows and doors began to open.

Across the garden, a figure fled. I ran back to see how Claire was doing. The gun she was holding looked like a cannon. She somehow fitted it back into her handbag. No wonder the damn thing had felt so heavy.

"I'll call the police," I said. My voice didn't sound like my own. It was high-pitched, and my throat was so dry I almost had to peel the words off my tongue.

She shook her head. "We have to get away from here. It's too dangerous to stay."

I considered her words but still didn't move. In my business I am used to a lot of things happening at once, but this wasn't a case of a bartender handing out free drinks, or a cook taking a side of beef out the back door. There was a dead man a few feet away from me. Just to be sure of that fact, I went and played doctor again, kneeling by the Major's side and feeling for a pulse. There wasn't one.

"We can't linger," Claire said. "They'll be coming back. This was all a trap. They want me dead."

The alarms were still going off, but now it seemed as if most of them were inside my head. Combined with my pounding heart, that made for quite a chorus. "Why?"

"It's a long story. I'll tell you once we get away from here. I would drive myself, but I don't think I am in any condition to drive. Do you have a car?"

"I had a valet park it." Part of every hotel audit is to interact with as many employees as possible. I had left several marked bills in the change drawer of my car as an honesty check.

"Let's take my car, then. We have to go now."

Her voice had taken on an unmistakable urgency. More and more people were milling about outside their rooms. No one had noticed the body yet, but soon they would.

Still, I didn't move. Once upon a time I had prepared for battle, but no one had ever shot real bullets my way. This wasn't the baptism of fire I had expected. Hell, I didn't even know what battle I had joined, or what I was fighting for or against.

"Please," Claire said.

I have always been a sucker for good manners. "We can get to the garage this way," I said.

She followed me to the stairwell and we started down the steps. Claire was leaning heavily against me, her adrenaline having run its course and her doctored drink kicking in.

Even with all that had happened, I was still in the eyes-wide-open zone. Sometimes I am convinced that my ability to observe and remember things is more curse than blessing. It is neither total recall nor eidetic memory, but it is the kind of retention that some people find freaky, which is why I never pass myself off as being some kind of savant, except maybe the idiot kind.

One of the lights is out on the southeast stairwell. Cigarette butts on garage landing. Trim in need of paint.

I thought about how I was going to write up the bar audit. It promised to be one hell of a report.

CHAPTER TWO

"There," said Claire, nodding in the direction of her wheels.

Her car, a newly minted Thunderbird with a red, glossy finish, wasn't the inconspicuous vehicle I was hoping it would be. In my line of work I always drive low-profile cars, usually a new Camry or Taurus with a generic rental look. No one ever looks twice at a common car, which allows me to return to properties on a regular basis without ever being noticed. I helped Claire into her seat, and then, with misgivings, went and took my place behind the wheel.

"What are you waiting for?" said Claire. Though her words were slurred, her impatience was clear.

"How about an idea of where we're going?"

"Just drive," she said, her urgency pronounced and contagious enough for me to start the engine and do as she suggested.

"No Beach Boy music?" I asked.

Claire didn't rise to the bait, and I didn't get to falsetto, *Until her daddy takes her T-Bird away*. It was just as well.

I tried to ignore the tightness in my chest, just as I tried to ignore all my misgivings. It was just nerves, I told myself. The last time I remembered feeling like this was when I went skydiving as a plebe at West Point. Excitement and fear had seemed to hang in equal balance, though I had never considered not jumping. Apparently I hadn't learned from experience, and was still willing to take the plunge.

No one appeared to take notice of us as we exited the garage. There were few directional options by car; it would have been easier to disappear in a boat. To get to Route 33 we'd need to drive a dozen miles on a residential road and then catch Route 322 before reaching the more traveled Route 50. Once we reached Route 50, we would at least have a choice of going north or traveling south and then east. The problem with being where we were on Maryland's Mid-Shore is that most of the towns are small, and as far as I knew, none had its own police force.

"There is probably a sheriff's office in Easton," I said. "We can tell our story there."

Claire's eyes were half-closed and her head was lolling on the leather headrest. My words woke her enough to raise her head. "No publicity," she said, her announcement sounding overly loud in the enclosed two-seater.

"Dead people with the interior decoration of bullets tend to get noticed."

"Don't say a word to anyone," she said, each syllable slower and more drawn out than the last, "until I explain things to you."

"I am not liking this," I said.

Her eyes were closed now, and she didn't respond. Judging by the way her body curled into the seat, I didn't think she was playing possum. For a moment, I strongly considered turning the car around. She could sleep off her Mickey Finn at the hotel, but to get Claire to my room, I would have to carry her. Hauling around human baggage gets you noticed, and I wasn't keen on attracting any more attention. Claire's fear was contagious, and judging from what we had already been through, it was more than justified.

Despite her entreaty, I had every intention of contacting the authorities. The sooner I handed Claire off to the police, the sooner she would be their problem. I reached in-

side my sports coat and felt around my pocket before remembering my cell phone was in my room.

Claire's purse was draped over her shoulder and I decided to extend my phone search to there. She didn't react
when I unhinged the purse from her body. The bag was
heavy, courtesy of the gun. This wasn't a nine millimeter
handgun, but closer to a cannon. It looked like the kind of
gun Clint Eastwood used to hoist around in his Dirty Harry
films. I rummaged around the pocketbook. Inside it was a
smaller purse with her money and credit cards, a small
flashlight, mints, gum, antacid tablets, assorted cosmetics,
and some panty liners.

"A gun and PMS," I said. "Watch out."

You can say those kinds of things when your female
companion is asleep or unconscious.

I continued to feel around the purse. There were some
spare bullets rattling around in her bag, but no phone. Apparently she was an old-fashioned kind of girl, the kind that
preferred to shoot first and talk later.

"Praise the Lord and pass the ammunition," I said.

In her sleep, Claire groaned. Her timing didn't seem accidental.

I decided to drive toward Easton, while at the same time
keeping my eyes open for a well-lit public phone along the
way. From experience, I knew that pay phones were becoming more and more an endangered species. Before the
advent of cell phones one favorite spotter tactic was to jot
down observations while sitting at a pay phone and pre-
tending to converse with someone on the other line. The
strategy didn't always work. One spotter told me about the
time he returned to a restaurant after a long "conversation"
on the pay phone where the staff had seemed to observe
him with more than a little interest. The spotter couldn't
help but notice that after his "call," the staff's behavior suddenly became exemplary. Only later did he learn that the

pay phone on which he was ostensibly talking had been out of order for at least six months.

"They were either on to me," he said, "or they thought I was crazy."

The road was decidedly quiet. In the first mile of driving I only encountered one other vehicle, a local driving a rusted, half-ton Chevy pickup with a faded bumper sticker that said, THERE IS NO LIFE WEST OF THE CHESAPEAKE BAY.

The bay cuts through Maryland. No other state is bisected in such a way. Residents of the Old Line State claim the division extends beyond geography to a state of mind. I stayed behind the pickup for half a mile before it turned on a side road. Its absence made me feel that much more vulnerable.

The road brought me to St. Michaels, a town where I occasionally did restaurant audits. St. Michaels was named after St. Michael the Archangel, the leader of the forces of heaven that triumphed over the minions of hell. I had heard of the town before becoming personally acquainted with it, the name surfacing during a military tactics course at West Point. At the turn of the nineteenth century St. Michaels was a thriving shipbuilding center. During the War of 1812 the Brits decided to shell the town and put it out of the business of supplying the American navy with vessels. The residents of St. Michaels learned of the impending attack and implemented a scheme to misdirect enemy fire and save their town. Because the shelling was to take place at night, the locals hung lanterns from the tops of the masts of ships and from the highest trees. The British assumed they were firing at the lights of the town and overshot their mark. Only one residence was struck during the attack, a home that survives to this day and is known as the Cannonball House.

These days the town's lights are meant to draw the wallets of tourists instead of the artillery of the enemy. At one in the morning, though, the town was mostly dark. I was feeling more than a trifle uncomfortable fleeing the scene of a crime in a bordello-red car with a comatose passenger. Even the sight of redcoats would have been welcome.

"Where's the damn British army when you need it?" I asked out loud.

I was talking to myself because I was growing increasingly nervous, and there was no one to whom I could vent. If you can voice your fear, it's usually mitigated to some degree. FDR's line of "There is nothing to fear but fear itself" popped into my head. My inner voice had a succinct answer: "Bullshit."

I wasn't sure whether I cursed aloud or not.

It only took a minute to drive by the township of St. Michaels. The T-Bird was a good touring car, gliding over the road's potholes and uneven asphalt with barely a tremor. I kept checking the rearview mirror, looking for the approach of lights. There was nothing, and more of nothing. Then I caught sight of something that didn't look quite right, even though I really couldn't make it out. There was a darkness deeper than the night that was increasingly taking up more and more space in the rearview mirror. The black hole on my mirror was growing as a shadow closed on my back bumper.

Someone was driving without lights. It was possible teenagers were out on a nocturnal joyride. Since about the time of the Model T, youths have loved playing "gotcha." The rules of the game are simple: on a dark road, turn your headlights off and drive up to an unwary motorist, then scare the hell out of that driver by suddenly turning on your high beams.

These were no kids, though, and this was no game of gotcha. This driver wanted to do more than cause heart palpitations.

I floored the accelerator and the Thunderbird's V-8 responded, clearing some space between me and my shadow, but the respite was only temporary. The pursuing vehicle abandoned the element of surprise. His lights filled the back window, and though I was pushing the T-Bird to its limits, it lost ground to the other vehicle.

The Thunderbird's big wheels hugged the road tightly and took us through another set of curves. I chanced a quick glance back and didn't like what I saw. There was a truck or large SUV right behind us with a push bumper, the kind usually seen only on highway patrol vehicles. Push bumpers are designed to play a very hard game of auto tag with uncooperative vehicles. It was clear we were about to be "it."

I shook Claire roughly. "Seat belt," I shouted.

She had been groaning for half a minute, not enjoying the rougher ride. Claire opened her glassy eyes and blinked a few times.

"Put on your seat belt," I said. "Now!"

My words penetrated her stupor. She tugged on the belt and snapped herself in, allowing about a moment's grace before the collision. I was prepared for the contact, but my head still snapped forward.

The other driver seemed all too versed in this contact sport. He played bumper tag again, and before our teeth even stopped vibrating he hit us a third time, pushing us out into a half spin. I didn't immediately fight the wheel for fear of rolling over, but instead braked and gradually straightened the car out.

As a cadet I had undergone close combat instruction with pugil sticks used to simulate bayonet assault maneuvers. When fighting another opponent with pugil sticks, the effect is often cumulative, with the combination of blows often doing you in more than one hit in particular. Your opponent's slash might change your balance just enough so that his butt stroke doesn't even have to connect very hard to drop you. The other driver knew how to use his vehicle as a weapon. He was timing and measuring his ramming speed.

The first rule of pugil stick fighting is to attack your attacker, as retreating generally puts you at a disadvantage. As much as I wanted to strike back, my options were limited. I was up against a heavier vehicle with a bigger engine as well as a push bumper.

"Brace yourself," I shouted, and then braked hard, trying my best to push the pedal to the floor mat.

The T-Bird's brakes worked admirably. There was minimal smoking and shaking, but our abrupt slowing didn't seem to bother our pursuer. Our being a sitting target suited him fine, and he plowed into us hard. My braking slowed but didn't stop his momentum. The air bags went off, but I was expecting the smothering balloon and worked around it. We were pushed forward for at least fifty feet before I disengaged the brakes and punched the accelerator. Making like a scared rabbit wouldn't help us for long. The truck with its bigger engine was faster.

"Give me your purse!" I shouted.

Claire asked no questions, just handed me the purse. I twisted it around my arm very tightly and wedged it close. Nothing was going to spill out of it, and it wasn't going to leave my person.

My head moved from side to side. It was too damn dark. I wished I knew the road better.

"We're not going to be able to outrun them," I said. "I am going to pick a spot up ahead and pull off the road. If everything works out, it's going to be a controlled crash. As soon as the car comes to a stop, I want you to run toward the water, and then head south. I'll play fox to the hounds and go in the opposite direction. Got it?"

"Run like hell away from you."

"Like all the women in my life."

We were suddenly awash in lights and I didn't have to tell her to brace. The jolt shook us like one of those test crash dummies commercials. My head was ringing, and I had to shout loud enough so I could hear over it.

"We passed a town a few miles back," I said. "Let's rendezvous there an hour or two before dawn. There are some fishing boats that leave the main dock before first light. We'll meet there."

Claire nodded to show that she understood.

"Get ready."

Another nod.

"Get set."

The headlights were closing on us again. Off to the left I sensed more than saw an opening in the brush-lined road. Without warning, without braking, I turned off the headlights, then yanked hard on the wheel and we left the asphalt behind us.

The T-Bird did a bucking bronco imitation as it left the road. Even with the seat restraints, our heads played pinball with the ceiling. I pumped the brakes, and the car gradually slowed. Even before we stopped, I was in drill instructor mode: "Move! Move! Move!"

I extricated myself from my constraints, and so did she. We were both disoriented, but I was able to point out the direction to her: "That way," I said.

She shook her head as if trying to clear her ears of water, or her head of fog, then went off in what approximated a jog. If Claire was trying for a straight line it wasn't working. The good news was that she all but passed from my sight after moving only a dozen steps away.

There was only a sliver of a moon and enough shrouding clouds to make the darkness almost complete, but I didn't have any doubts that the T-Bird, with its crimson plumage, could easily be seen from the road. The bird was now a dead duck. Any question about the car being easily seen was quickly answered when the beam of a spotlight illuminated it. I cupped my hand over my eyes and made out four figures on the higher ground above. Two other spotlights joined the first beam, and I felt like a wanted man being targeted from the searchlights of a helicopter. The lights were already getting uncomfortably close, and too late, I realized my predicament. I made a dash for the brush, but the movement of flushed prey evidently caught the attention of one of the lights. There was a reason there were only three lights targeting the area. The fourth figure had something else in his hands. I heard the sound of automatic gunfire in two distinct ways. From a distance, there was the percussion of a rifle in overdrive; up close, bullets rained all around me. I pushed deeper into the resisting foliage. Brambles tried to stay my progress. It was too early for blackberry season, but not for blackberry thorns. There was another spray of gunfire, the bullets zipping through leaves. Several nearby boulders took the brunt of the shooting, and the zinging of ricocheting bullets allowed for no safe spot.

Gasping, I tried to gather my breath, and my wits. I wiped at my wet face, and came away with a bloody hand. I was hoping it was only brambles that had drawn blood. Above me, my pursuers had gone into blackout mode, turning out their lights. I could barely make out the figures along the embankment. They seemed to be having a conference, no doubt working out their strategy. It didn't take them long to come up with a plan.

From the shoulder of the road, one of the spotlights resumed its search of the area. Several moments later, a second bouncing light came into play. Judging from the bobbing, it was clear one of the torch holders was on his way down toward me. I suspected the gang of four had divided into two teams of two, with someone to light and someone to sight.

Waving a white flag wasn't going to work here. These people were out for blood. In my time at USMA we did some night field exercises, but the reality was that I spent a lot more time poring over textbooks than I did figuring out the best way to survive hostile fire. I had learned about the ballistics of wounds, but wasn't keen on getting firsthand experience. At the moment I was just another guy with a purse.

I hugged said purse close to me, leaving the handgun inside for the time being. The gun was no match for a rifle at long distances, and shooting it would likely be my last option. Any gunfire on my part would only provide a flare for return fire.

My pulse was racing and my stomach was in knots. I was waiting for my warrior caste DNA to kick in, but it seemed remarkably reluctant to show itself. My not being in the army and serving my country on the battlefield flew in the face of umpteen generations of Travises. Call me silly, but I was beginning to think I hadn't missed out on much. Maybe Napoleon was right when he said no one over the age of thirty should be in the army.

It was hard for me to be anything other than scared, but I could feel a growing anger. These bastards were intent on murder and I had no idea why. Self-preservation ruled my thoughts, but gnawing at a small part of my psyche was curiosity. I would have to live to satisfy that.

Keeping low, I tried to stay in the shadows and brush in the hopes of steering clear of the probing lights. I was glad of a steady breeze that moved the grass and shrubbery, and potentially masked my own movements. There was a sudden burst of gunfire from above that made my heart rat-a-tat-tat as fast as the round, though the shots didn't land anywhere near. The muzzle fire showed that the shooter and the flashlight wielder were separated by a distance of about fifteen yards.

There was another spray of gunfire. The shooter didn't appear to be concerned about running out of ammunition. He was firing ahead of where I was. I didn't know if he was shooting blind, or had imagined seeing something, or perhaps he just hoped to keep me reined in. I set out again, fighting the impulse to sprint. The ground was too uneven to move at more than a half trot, and I wanted to be able to make a fast stop to avoid an approaching spotlight.

There was a fourth burst of gunfire, with the shots spraying behind me. Again, I didn't think I had been spotted. It seemed more likely that there was a prearranged pattern to the shooting. At least one of my hunters appeared versed in the tactics of search and destroy. The four of them were working as a team to cut off my escape. I was being channeled like game, the high road and low road converging.

I decided two could play the triangulation game. Each of the teams was maintaining its same spacing between the shooter and the light wielder. It also stood to reason that the high team wouldn't be putting the low team in danger with friendly fire. Judging by where the rounds were being fired and the spacing of my pursuers, I might be able to avoid the enemy.

I had no choice but to move. The beam from the second light was getting dangerously close. The light wielders had to be using million-candlepower spotlights, with the beams cutting a wide swath and doing too good a job of pushing aside the darkness. I hurried forward, stumbled over some vines, and fell. Instinctively, I rolled several times. One light, and then the second, converged on the spot where I had fallen, lingered, and then moved on their separate ways.

Pent-up air escaped slowly. It was a good thing human eyes didn't reflect light the way animal eyes did. I was getting damn tired of being in the spotlight. My plan of playing the fox had worked only too well. When you play the fox, though, you're supposed to have fox-like tactics. I wondered whether I'd live to make my rendezvous in St. Michaels.

St. Michaels, the town synonymous with misdirection; St. Michaels, the town named after the archangel who managed to beat the dark angel Light-Bearer, also known as Lucifer.

The plan came to me. Let there be light.

One of the maxims from the Cadet Bible is: "A calculated risk is a known risk for the sake of real gain. A risk for the sake of a risk is a fool's chance." I suppose I had been forced to repeat that saw enough times to upperclassmen to come to believe it.

I decided on my calculated risk and began to run like hell. My incautious sprint got me the better part of fifty yards before I was noticed and the gunfire started. Instead of diving for cover, I continued on a zigzag route. The finish line I was aiming for was a stand of trees. I cleared a rise and started downhill for the trees. That allowed me a respite from being the featured attraction in a turkey shoot. Though I didn't have a clear view of my pursuers, it was evident by the lightning-like jumping of lights that Lucifers I and II were running in my direction, intent on pinning me in their lights.

I hoped I had enough of a lead. With trembling hands I pulled off my shoes, and was glad I had opted for Rockports with laces instead of loafers. I dumped the contents of Claire's purse on the ground, stuck the gun buccaneer-style into my pants, snatched up the bullets, and jammed her wallet and a few other odds and ends into my pockets. I grabbed her small flashlight and quickly examined it. There was a metal ring on its end, and I looped my shoelaces through the ring and worked a square knot in Eagle Scout time. I turned the light on and then tossed my makeshift bolo up into the branches. The shoes and light found purchase about three-quarters of the way up the twenty-foot tree.

Thank God for a misspent youth. While growing up I had left countless pairs of worn-out sneakers hanging from telephone and electrical lines. No one could tie 'em and toss 'em like I could. I always took a certain pride in my shoe handiwork, admiring the scuffed-up footwear dangling high on various wires around the country.

Now I only had time for one backward look. The flashlight was swinging. The combination of wind, moving light, and shifting branches was producing an effect better than any I could have hoped for. It was a will-o'-the-wisp effect, light moving here, there, everywhere. I wanted the enemy to shoot high, as the British had at St. Michaels.

I ran hard in the direction of the water, hoping I could outflank the enemy. My attempt at a diversion came with a high price. The land was mostly marshy, but that didn't mean there weren't rocks aplenty. Every few steps, I found a stone the hard way. I forced myself to keep running as fast as I could, though my sides hurt and my chest burned.

The sound of gunfire, not close but not far enough away, dropped me to my knees. My roosting flashlight was drawing the volley of two automatic weapons. It proved a good time for me to fall down, though. The prospect of cornered game had made the third hunter break ranks. In the dim moonlight I saw him running toward the tree. He was holding the turned-off spotlight in the crook of his arm, while the rifle was up and ready.

I waited ten seconds, but it felt like ten minutes. The shooting was still going on, but I knew my diversion would soon play out. Where was the fourth in the group? I wondered if he was already by me. I began to second-guess my calculations. Perhaps they hadn't been holding to the line I imagined.

Behind me, the shooting stopped. They were probably holding my size twelves now, and would want the rest of the package. I couldn't wait any longer.

He showed himself an instant before I rose, approaching at what seemed to be a remarkably unhurried pace. His head was moving to the right and left in a very methodical motion, like the sweeping of a mine detector. He was playing safety, trying to make sure no one got by him.

The instructor in my military arts and tactics class was a decorated battle veteran. He stressed that the first rule of warfare was to expect the unexpected. "The only thing you know for sure," he said, "is that the shit always hits the fan, but it never hits it the same way twice. You can plan for battle, but nothing ever happens the way you think it's going to happen."

My plan had been to skirt stealthily by my pursuers. What ended up happening was closer to a reenactment of the gunfight at the OK Corral. I grabbed for the gun at about the same instant the safety raised his rifle. In our panic, both of us proved to be lousy shots. He shot his burst high, and I shot all over the place. As his arms lowered, and I knew I was about to be sliced in half, I kept desperately pulling the trigger. This was no firing range where I could study where my other shots were landing. I had no scope, no real idea of where my bullets were going. The gun's strong kick added to my confusion. Then it wasn't kicking anymore, but clicking. My bullet tank was empty.

I kept pulling the trigger. I knew how stupid that was, but my finger seemed to have a mind of its own. My dry firing continued for several seconds, or about three seconds longer than my anticipated life expectancy. That's when I heard him cursing.

As I approached, my gun was held at the ready. I thought it was a better look than having an extended index finger.

He had a two-word, four letters each, interchangeable vocabulary. He was holding what remained of his right hand aloft, staring at it in disbelief. Several of the fingers on his right hand were missing.

"Who the hell are you?" I asked.

According to his answer, he was "Shit Fuck." Or maybe he was "Fuck Shit."

He didn't resist as I patted him down. Shock had set in, and his response to it was the cursed mantra. He wasn't carrying another weapon, and didn't have a wallet or identification. The only thing on his person was an ammo pack with several spare magazines.

There wasn't time to do a proper interrogation. The others would already be hurrying toward us. I slipped away into the darkness. Behind me, I listened to the monologue continuing unabated.

CHAPTER THREE

I crept through the town of St. Michaels, scaring a few feral alley cats on my way to the waterfront. They ran like hell at what they saw. The way I was feeling, I figured the cats were a pretty good judge of character.

Near the main dock I stayed out of sight in the shadows and watched a few fishing and crabbing boats being readied for departure. Claire wasn't anywhere in sight, and I wondered at her whereabouts. I was hoping her absence could be explained by her having fallen asleep somewhere. When I last saw her, she was looking wobbly.

My impression was that she came from money. She had the look and feel of someone from a privileged background, and didn't strike me as a person who frequented shoot-outs. I wondered how she had gotten herself mixed up in something so ugly. Maybe it was better I didn't know. Her no-show was probably the best thing that could have happened, but I still felt disappointed.

My feet hurt like hell. I had tried to protect them by lining my socks with the panty liners scavenged from Claire's purse. I gingerly removed the bloody socks and winced at the condition of my feet.

"There's a public restroom nearby," came a whisper from

the darkness. "If you want, I'll get you some paper towels and bring you some water to rinse off with."

Claire emerged from behind a pillar. Either she was that good at hiding, or I was that tired. She must have been watching me for a few minutes. It was possible she was cautious by nature and had wanted to make sure I was alone. The way she was standing there, though, looking ready to run if I even coughed wrong, made me think that Claire had the same kind of misgivings about renewing our acquaintance that I did.

I wanted to scream questions at her. I wanted to rail about my night from hell. Instead I answered her offer in a conversational tone: "That would be good."

Several minutes passed before Claire came back with three soda cans filled with water, and the promised paper towels. Florence Nightingale she wasn't. She left the nursing to me. I worked the water into my feet and cleared away most of the mud and the blood.

"Do you have my gun?" Claire asked.

I continued with my ablutions. Her question rankled. Instead of offering sympathetic noises and expressing undying gratitude, she wanted to know about her goddamn gun.

"Let me respond by citing Mae West's immortal question," I said, an edge to my whisper. "She asked a gentleman caller, 'Do you have a pistol in your pants or are you just glad to see me?' Here's a hint: at the moment the only things I would be glad to see are a warm tub and a bottle of aspirin."

"I would like it back."

"I'm holding it as collateral."

"What are you talking about?"

"Who are these people, and why do they want you dead?"

She took her time before answering, and was careful in what she said. "They murdered my father because of what he knew, and now they're out to kill me as well."

"And what is it that your father knew that got him killed?"

"I'm not sure," she said, "but I've been actively trying to find out."

"Well, whatever you're doing really seems to be working."

The darkness couldn't mask Claire's flush. She was either angry or embarrassed or both. "All of this proves I was right about my father's death. The authorities are convinced he committed suicide. I knew better."

"How did he die?"

"From a single gunshot wound to the head. The weapon you're holding is the one that killed him. I suppose you can say it has sentimental value for me."

I thought it was pretty strange that she would be carrying the gun that took her father's life, but given all that had gone on during the night, I suppose it was par for the course. Though she tried to keep the iron in her voice, I detected a shudder in her shoulders and maybe the smallest of sniffs. In lieu of a hanky, I reached into my pants, pulled out the oversized gun, and handed it to her. I also gave her the wallet with her I.D. and credit cards.

"You don't happen to have my purse, do you?"

"I had to lose it. The color was all wrong for me."

She examined the gun, and her frown grew larger. "They set up Father's death at his writing desk," she said, "and made it look neat and tidy, or as neat and tidy as a head shot with a .44 magnum can possibly be."

Without a purse, Claire appeared unsure as to where to place the gun. While she considered, she passed it from hand to hand. "Careful," I said. "The safety is on, but there are some bullets in there. Three, I think. I took some spares from your purse and reloaded."

I watched her doing the math in her head, but Claire never asked the question, maybe afraid of learning what happened to the other bullets. The way she considered the situation made me suspect she was a lawyer. I could almost hear her legal wheels turning. Lawyers like to control the extent of their involvement in any potentially sticky situation. She did finally say, "Thank you for everything."

I offered up a little bow of my head.

She did some more mulling before extending her hand in formal introduction. I guess she decided that after being a party to one man's death and sharing in a car chase and almost dying together, it was all right to exchange names: "Claire Harrington," she said.

I took her hand. "Will Travis."

And then she said it, she really did: "So pleased to meet you."

Before law school, I decided, there had been charm school. "The pleasure is mine, ma'am," I said.

For the most part I have rid myself of my "military school accent." It's a common speech by-product of anyone who has spent too many years in military surroundings. Those suffering from a chronic case of militaritis find it impossible to address anyone other than family or friends without saying "sir" or "ma'am."

"I was very lucky you came along."

The sound of approaching footsteps made me reach out to her. I pressed us into the shrubbery, took the gun from her hand, and raised it in a two-handed shooter's position. The fisherman didn't notice us. He was deep into what looked like a much-needed cup of coffee.

Claire touched my extended arm with an index finger, and I lowered the gun. She didn't ask for her gun back this time, apparently happy to loan it to me for the time being.

"There were four people in the car that tried to run us down last night," I said. "You have any idea how many people are trying to kill you?"

She shook her head.

"We can't linger, then. We have to get out of here."

"Let's call a cab."

"That might be an obvious giveaway." I almost added that

the only thing more obvious would have been a bordello-red T-Bird.

"You could call the hotel. They must have some kind of shuttle."

"If I was hunting us down I would have the hotel covered, and have a watch on the road. I imagine they are in the process of tightening the noose."

"I have a friend—friends in high places." She was quick in changing the singular to a plural. "They could help us. Once I got through to them they could make some calls."

"We don't have the time. We have to disappear before it gets light."

"Any ideas?"

"One, and I'm going to regret it."

I picked the smallest and least impressive of the work boats on the dock. The boat was rusted and dirty, and as far as I could see didn't even sport a name, or maybe the grime was just covering it up. There was a crew of two aboard and it appeared as if they were just about to set out.

"Hello," I yelled. I am just not an "ahoy" kind of guy.

The men looked at me and my waving hand but didn't wave back. The older of the two resignedly made his approach to me. I suppose he was the captain, though he wasn't wearing an eye patch, didn't have a peg leg, and there was no parrot on his shoulder. He resembled a walrus without the cuddlesome quality, was thick of face and body, with a spiky, unkempt mustache.

"What do you want?" He was looking at my bare feet and shaking his head with undisguised contempt.

"I need to arrange a charter."

I think I surprised him. What he expected was for me to ask him for money. But no matter, he used an all-purpose reply: "Fuck you."

"I'll pay."

"With what?"

I opened my wallet and waved some green. I was carrying plenty of money because my intent had been to pay cash at the inn when I checked out. Some desk clerks have been known to do some creative accounting with cash payments. The money got the attention of the Walrus. In a conspiratorial manner, I tilted my head toward the dock.

"My lady friend's back there," I said. "We need to disappear quickly. We have to get back to Annapolis, and time is of the essence."

Annapolis was about twenty miles across the bay, and the closest nearby city of size.

"It's a long story," I said, "but if we don't get across the bay real soon, the shit's going to hit the fan." In sotto voce I said, "Her husband," and left the implications at that.

The Walrus looked back at the other man before returning his glance to me. "Four hundred dollars."

He had bought the desperation in my tone, and had done a good job of gauging the green in my wallet.

"I'll go three."

"Let me see it."

I counted out the money and booked our passage.

Any hope I had of not being sick vanished when the ship's engine started. It was loud, smoky, and stinky, and the deck vibrated like it was being jackhammered, or at least that's how it felt to this landlubber. The work boat had a large, open deck, typical of Chesapeake Bay work boats, so I didn't have the option of going below, or finding a place to hide out. The boat had none of the grace of a skipjack; its design was for its intended cargo, which in the fall and spring was oysters, and, in the warmer months, crabs. Passengers were never one of the boat's design considerations. I took my place along the rail of the SS *Shithole*. My body language was all but shouting for everyone to steer clear of me, so naturally Claire chose that moment to stand at my side. Since boarding, she had looked pissed and done her best to ignore me.

"Why did you have to say that back on the dock?" she asked in a whisper, making sure she couldn't be overheard.

"Say what?"

"You made it sound like we were illicit lovers."

"I had to come up with a story."

"You should have come up with a different story."

"I didn't think they would buy your losing track of time while dancing at the ball with a prince, and our carriage turning into a pumpkin at midnight."

It was already starting, though I tried desperately to stave off my roiling stomach. I don't know how my forebears ever made it across the big puddle. Boats and I don't get along. The waters were flat, the waves all but nonexistent, but my stomach didn't believe what my eyes were telling it. I'm one of those people who can get seasick just by eating fish.

"You made me sound like a trollop," she said. "Those men have been eyeing me like I'm a streetwalker."

I discovered a new way of avoiding an argument. I started throwing up, and didn't stop until we reached the other side.

The ninety minutes it took us to cross the bay felt like an eternity, and when we docked I wanted to kiss the ground. Maybe I should have, and then chewed a little sand as well. My breath was awful. While feeding the fish I had caught my reflection a few times, and knew how puffy and scratched my face was. The businessman's garb I had worn the night before now looked like clothes salvaged from the trash. There were tears in the fabric, and stains better left unexamined. I limped along without shoes.

We walked away from the water, in search of a quiet spot. To her credit, Claire didn't abandon me, but she didn't exactly walk at my side. I noticed she made a point of looking away from passersby, as if afraid she might be noticed.

Annapolis was waking up. Too many people were already jogging and bustling about. I withdrew my heavy sunglasses from my jacket pocket, what I call my "blinders." Sometimes I need to make a pointed effort of shutting down and getting out of observation mode. If I don't do that, I spend the whole time looking around and trying to take notice of everything.

Despite being Maryland's capital, much of Annapolis feels more like an English township than an American city. That makes for wonderful scenery but terrible urban traffic. The main streets are clustered with administrative and religious monuments to Colonial America's red-bricked past, while the side streets, wedged between massive state government complexes, the Severn River, and the Naval Academy, are lined with row upon row of tiny mid-nineteenth-century houses.

Claire and I made our way to St. John's College. It was a place where my bohemian look might not stand out as being so out of place. St. John's is a small campus, one that is often described as being charming. The charming part didn't interest me at the moment, but its shade and grass did. I took a spot on a secluded bench while Claire appropriated twenty dollars from me and went off to "get provisions." In her absence I decided to wash up, and found a basement bathroom in McDowell Hall. Claire and I arrived back at the bench at the same time. I looked slightly more presentable, and she returned with coffee, Coke in a can, and doughnuts.

"You need to replace your fluids," she said. "The coffee shop didn't have anything for electrolyte replacement, so I went for caffeine and sugar."

"It's just as well. I don't even know what electrolytes are."

I used the can to cool my forehead, and I started in on the coffee.

"Did you know you were going to be that seasick?" she asked.

I nodded.

"So that's what you meant about regretting the choice?"

Another nod.

"Oh." With her understanding came embarrassment and she looked at me with gentler eyes. I am not the kind of person who melts at a pretty woman's glance, but I must admit to suddenly feeling better.

Claire's look didn't quite translate to words, though. "I hope you don't think I'm not grateful for all you have done," she said. "I am. It's just that I have been preoccupied. All that's happened has been rather disconcerting."

Her speech underplayed what we had experienced. "Yes," I said. "Violent death can be so annoying sometimes."

Claire shot me a look of blue-eyed permafrost, then, with an annoyed gesture, pushed at one of her dark locks that was out of place. She had been drugged, hadn't slept, had trudged along for miles in pumps, and yet somehow she looked presentable. No, that was a lie. She looked a lot more than presentable.

"We need to call the police, Claire."

She knew that but argued anyway. Definitely a lawyer. "We didn't shoot that man."

"We were there when he was shot. The police are going to want to know all about that."

She sighed, and finally nodded, but with that concession she offered a supplicating gesture, or as supplicating as possible for someone with shapely, manicured fingers. "I need to page someone, and then wait to get a response. That might take half an hour or more, and then arranging matters will take even longer. I would appreciate it if you could give me a few hours before talking to the police."

I considered her request, and then it was my turn to sigh. "All right. A few hours."

Claire went off to find a phone. More than half an hour passed, and when she didn't return I wondered if she was gone for good. When I had all but given up on her, she reappeared. Judging by her worried expression, her call hadn't reassured her any, though Claire didn't offer specifics.

"What are your plans for the morning?" she asked.

"Avoid any ocean cruises and shoot-outs. Arrange transportation to my place, then burn my clothes and take a hot bath."

"Do you mind if I join you?"

"The bath's not that large, but that will make it that much more cozy."

"I meant in your car," she said very properly, "not your tub."

She was beautiful, and intelligent, and classy. If I could ever work that stick out of her ass, she would be perfect.

"No problem."

Claire led me to the phone. I made the call at twenty past seven and was able to catch Jenny before she left for the office. Jenny Park works for me. She is one of three employees, but as Jenny is quick to tell me, she does the work of ten. Jenny was born in Korea, and though she has lived in the States for two-thirds of her life, she still has a strong accent and occasionally leaves out articles and verbs in her sentences. What she's short in verbs she makes up for in verve. I think Jenny spends most of her spare time watching Turner Classic Movies and American Movie Classics. Her speech is all her own, and talking with her is like getting an education in American slang and expressions. Sometimes what she says is not appropriate, and I am not sure if she knows that or not.

I offered up a very truncated explanation to Jenny, and then said, "Please get here as soon as you can."

"You don't need to worry about me lollygagging," she

said. "I have too much work waiting at office. Today I am busier than a one-legged man in a butt-kicking contest."

This boss tried to use a little sarcasm. "I'm sorry to be keeping you from your contest."

The sarcasm didn't work.

Jenny said, "Last Resort does not run itself, you know. The creek is rising and I am already up to my ass in alligators."

She was definitely on a backside motif.

"Let's *end* the conversation here, Jenny."

"You are right, Will Travis," she said, "time is wasting." But then she added, "Of course, a broken clock is right twice a day, too."

Jenny hung up on me first, as was the usual course of things. Claire raised a questioning eyebrow. She had stayed in hearing range, perhaps afraid that I might reconsider my promise and call the police prematurely. "Who's Jenny?"

"She works for me."

"And what is it that you do?"

In polite company I would have answered, "I'm a hospitality consultant," an explanation that puts everyone to sleep. While that answer might have been true enough, it really isn't what I do.

"I'm a spotter."

"Spotter?" Claire had never heard of my vocation.

"I'm a paid observer."

"And what is it you observe?"

"Human nature in its many forms."

She studied me, waited for my punch line, before deciding I was being serious. "You're an expert on human nature?"

"No. I'm an expert observer."

Smiling, Claire said, "Superman with X-ray vision?"

So, she could joke. "Something like that."

"Spotter. That sounds like you mark people."

"With invisible ink."

"Tell me about your work."

"Businesses come to me and request my observations. Typically I act as an anonymous guest. I do what's referred to as 'shopping a property' and report back to owners and management as to what I see. The majority of my work is hospitality-related, mainly hotels and restaurants."

"You're like a professional critic?"

"Something like that."

Claire shook her head and didn't hide her surprise.

"What?" I asked.

"Your job isn't you."

"What job is?"

"I don't know. You seem too self-assured, too much of a take-charge sort, to be someone who spends his waking hours reporting on the deeds of chambermaids."

"The preferred term these days is *housekeepers*."

"Is that what you were doing at the hotel bar last night? Spotting?"

"That's exactly what I was doing. What were *you* doing?"

Claire didn't answer immediately. She measured her words as if each was allotted to a recipe that had to be exactly adhered to.

"I was meeting with a man who claimed to have information about my father's death."

"Did he?"

"Yes. But now, for all I know, he might even have been the one who killed him."

"When did your father die?"

"On February the eighth."

His death had occurred less than three months earlier. As if to put the date in perspective, Claire said, "It happened two days after the New Hampshire primary."

"Is that significant?"

"I believe it is."

"In what way?"

"My father was Garret Harrington."

Claire studied me to see if I recognized the name, but without any context I couldn't place it.

"Congressman Garret Harrington," she added.

I remembered the name, but only because I am good at that. Had the name Garret Harrington been attached to a third-string utility infielder I had once seen making a play, it probably would have made just as strong an impression, but I didn't bother to tell Claire that.

"South Carolina," I said, some ganglions kicking in that allowed me to match a state to the representative.

"Yes," Claire said, bestowing her biggest smile yet. She waited a moment. I think she was hoping I would come up with something else about her father, but I didn't.

"My father served four terms in Congress," she said. "For him, it was a matter of duty. He didn't look upon his office as some kind of stepping-stone, but as his civic responsibility. He wasn't a career politician, and often quoted from John Sherman, who, after serving his time in Congress, returned to his farm and announced, 'I have come home to look after my fences.' To his thinking our nation was served best when the gentlemen farmers of old went to the Capitol as reluctant representatives, and then happily returned home. That was his ideal."

I didn't say anything to step on her rose-colored portrait of her father, but it seemed to me that had he really wanted to return to his no-doubt-mythical farm, then he could have done it after his first term, not his fourth.

"Your father was a West Point grad, wasn't he?"

Claire smiled at the memory. "I think he was as proud of that as anything else in his life. He served one tour of duty in the airborne division but that was before I was born."

"When did he leave Congress?"

"Sixteen years ago."

About the same time, I thought, that I left West Point. "Did he leave willingly?"

"He didn't lose an election, if that's what you're asking. He made the decision not to pursue reelection, though the campaign would have been little more than a formality. My father was very popular with his constituents, and with his party. But to answer your question, I am not sure if he did leave willingly."

There was something akin to bitterness in her voice. I waited to hear its cause.

"Our family relocated up north when I was eight. I was an only child, so it was Mother, Father, and me. We had a very full life, and Father seemed more than content in his work. He thrived on the energy of his job. We all did. There was always some event, some festivity, some meeting. My father often took me as his date to black-tie affairs. I was a young lady hobnobbing with the movers and shakers of this planet. I talked to people like Mikhail Gorbachev and Lech Walesa, world leaders who were changing the course of history. I went to parties and met with royalty and Nobel laureates, and was always attending cultural events at the Kennedy Center, or the Smithsonian, or going to plays in Georgetown. All of that ended abruptly and unexpectedly. Father was slated to run for a fifth term when he changed his mind."

I watched her do some head-shaking. The passage of sixteen years still hadn't reconciled Claire to that decision.

"It all happened so quickly. He only told Mother and me a few hours before he made his announcement. We tried to talk him out of it, and so did the Republican Party leaders, but he wouldn't be budged. Half a year later we moved home to South Carolina. But it didn't feel like home to me. I had been away too long."

These days, there are a lot of people who think the hearth is overrated. Home must have seemed drab without the likes of Mikhail Gorbachev and Lech Walesa and Queen Elizabeth II stopping by.

"So why did your father leave office?"

"His public announcement was that he wanted to return home to the great state of South Carolina, but no one knew the real reason. My mother and I speculated, of course. Both of us noticed that he wasn't himself for several months before he made his announcement, but we attributed it to his heavy workload. Now I wonder if he was just trying to avoid us."

"Why would he do that?"

"Father was never good at masking how he felt, at least to his family. I think he didn't want us to see his unhappiness."

"Do you have any idea why he might have been unhappy?"

"That was his great secret for the longest time," she said. "Long after he left Congress, his malaise stayed with him. When he was in my presence, Father always tried to act chipper, but I could tell the darkness that touched his soul was still with him. Father spent a lot of time in his study, especially after Mother died. He remained busy, mostly with his historical research and writing, but I would often catch him looking off into space with an expression I came to know only too well. Father would tell me he was thinking, but I saw he was brooding."

"Did you ever ask him what he was thinking about?"

"Many times. Usually he would say something to the effect that he was an old man studying the cobwebs of his mind. He often offered an oblique quote from Shakespeare, saying he was a prisoner of 'having sworn too hard-a-keeping oath,' but that was the price of duty and honor."

I knew those same shackles all too well. I had built my own house on duty, honor, and country, and then my house of cards fell down.

"He never offered specifics as to what was troubling him, but several weeks before he died I overheard him speaking on the phone. Father was very upset. He referred to a man's death, and how this man had been wrongly dishonored. Not long after hearing that, my father was dead."

"Killed right after the New Hampshire primary, you said."

Claire nodded without elaboration.

"Are you suggesting that something happened around sixteen years ago that caused your father to be murdered?"

"That is what I have been trying to determine," she said. "As you can see, my bringing up the past has apparently upset someone."

"Any idea whom?"

Claire nodded. I was curious as to her suspects. Since her father's death, it appeared she had been working to narrow the field. "Go on," I said.

"I believe his death was engineered by one of the presidential candidates," she said.

I absorbed the implications of her remark. "Well, thank God," I finally said.

"For what?"

"At least the pope and the queen aren't on your list of suspects."

CHAPTER FOUR

Claire didn't much like my flippant remark, and immediately became tight-lipped. After unsuccessfully trying to get her to amplify her suspicions, I said, "Look, I'm sorry if I offended you. It's just that your suspect caught me by surprise."

"No offense taken," she said, but her tone belied that.

"Which candidate?" I asked.

"I would rather not talk about it, if you don't mind."

If you liked politics—and who doesn't enjoy name-calling, finger-pointing, grandstanding, and acrimony?—it was your banner year. With the new setup of regional primaries in March, April, May, and June, the nominations were being hotly contested by both parties. This wasn't a case of the races already being decided by March, and the public yawning until November. Pundits were predicting a dogfight down to the wire. It was quite possible that the nominees for both parties might not be decided until the conventions, an unprecedented event in modern history.

There were still four candidates vying for the Democratic nomination, though one of the contenders was all but on life support and soon expected to drop out. That left a pick-'em field of three. California Governor Scott Vickers was expected to win the Golden State's May primary bonanza, but was currently trailing South Carolina Senator Daniel Greeley in the electoral vote count. Between Greeley and that nomination was a man with a lot of money, New Jersey Governor Ronald Bates. With his sizable fortune, Bates was bankrolling a huge media blitz, and many thought that made him the candidate to beat.

The Republican campaign featured only two candidates. The vice president's heart condition had precluded him from running, but he and most of the Republican establishment had early on supported Ohio Senator Bob "Storming" Norman. Of late, though, many of those early endorsements were being qualified, as Storming Norman was having credibility problems in light of allegations that he had used his office for influence peddling. The dark horse candidate was Illinois Congressman Mark Stanton. His handsome face was being pasted on advertisements that promoted him as a shining knight, and the question being asked of the American public was, Why Not a Boy Scout? Eagle Scout Stanton and his squeaky-clean image were making him an attractive alternative to the better-known Norman. So far, the Stanton campaign seemed to be playing in Peoria.

"Whenever there's a presidential campaign," I said, "I always think of Will Rogers's line: 'The best thing about this group of candidates is that only one of them can win.' "

If I was hoping to get on Claire's good side, I didn't appear to be going about it the right way. "Making sport of politics is always an easy game," she said. "It's a shame that those who try to assume leadership roles get tarred as undesirables because they dare to stand and be counted."

I almost quoted from Henry Kissinger, "Ninety percent of the politicians give the other ten percent a bad name," but refrained. She was a congressman's daughter, and I knew she revered Daddy's memory. I bit my lip a second time, remembering Kin Hubbard's line: "We'd all like to vote for the best man, but he's never a candidate."

What I did say was, "I understand the need for politics and politicians, but elections aren't something I bring out my pom-poms for."

"You see politics as a necessary evil?"

"I suppose so. Even though I live in D.C., my political passions don't run very deep. I must have genes resistant to Potomac Fever. Funny, though, I never heard that Potomac Fever was a fatal disease."

My ploy to get her talking again was obvious, and Claire decided to relent and do just that. "Something happened that made my father leave Capitol Hill," she said. "Based on what I overheard him say, I believe one of the candidates was involved in an event in the past that caused the death and disgrace of an innocent man."

"And you think this candidate would murder to protect that secret?"

"Do you have a better explanation for those men who tried to kill us?"

"I was hoping they were just aggressive Mary Kay representatives, but the truck they were driving wasn't pink."

"Do you always resort to puerile humor when you're short an answer?"

"Generally, yes."

With great certainty, she said, "My father would never have committed suicide."

"What would your father have done?"

"I don't understand your question."

"Was your father also involved in the death and disgrace of that innocent man?"

Claire didn't like the question, but it was clear she had asked herself the same thing, with some resulting tarnish on her tin god.

"I suspect my father became entangled in something

that deeply disturbed him. You might scoff at the notions of duty, honor, and country, but those were beliefs my father held dear."

She tugged hard at my Achilles' heel. By the sound of it, Garret Harrington was a man I would have understood.

"Yes," Claire said reluctantly, "I think my father was involved in some way. That would explain why he chose to recuse himself from office. His participation in this episode, whatever it was, violated his sense of propriety."

There was an utter sadness to her pronouncement. I honored it with silence.

"There were those who referred to my father as 'Saint Garret.' The nickname was not complimentary. Some of Father's critics thought he was self-righteous. It is true that he was conservative, patriotic, and religious, and there are those who find any and all of those things suspect. I do know he had a very strong sense of right and wrong, and in this matter I believe he judged himself to be in the wrong. Because of that, he withdrew. As he saw it, I am sure my father was atoning for his sins.

"He was a proud man. It wouldn't have been easy to come forward and make a public admission of wrongdoing, even after all these years had passed, but I think he was prepared to do that. He would have been willing to suffer the loss of his reputation for the sake of his country."

"Did he make those intentions known?"

"He did to whomever he was talking to."

"And that's what got him killed?"

"Imagine if you were running for president, and you had been laying that groundwork for years. Think of those thousands of chicken dinners you attended. Imagine all the handshaking and the countless meetings. Most people have no conception of the demands involved in seeking public office. I can't think of a more exhausting marathon. To get to that position, most candidates have run one race after another, and another. Finally, you find yourself a contender in that race of a lifetime, a race that you've worked up to after many years of grueling work. What would you do if you were suddenly confronted by information you knew would end your career? With your dream so close, would you just let it slip away, or would you find a way to stay in the race? People have certainly murdered for less."

When Claire had first offered her hypothesis, I thought she was certifiable. I am not one for conspiracy theories. Ben Franklin said it best: "Three may keep a secret if two are dead." To my way of thinking, conspiracy theories never take into account human frailty. People talk and words leak. Meetings get noticed, and some trail is invariably left. Still, there was something here that I couldn't readily discount.

"Let's say you're right about the secret," I said. "How do you know that one of the candidates is behind all of this?"

"Who else could it be?"

"Maybe you should be looking at the shadow lurking behind one of the candidates. It's possible the politician doesn't even know what's happening. There are always individuals or groups that make sizable investments in the candidate and expect their pound of flesh. Some of the moneylenders would make Machiavelli look like a vestal virgin. They could be the ones doing whatever it takes to get their candidate elected."

"That's a terrifying thought. If that's true, it would be like a secret war is being waged against our country."

Her umbrage seemed genuine. Even though I was just throwing out the possibility, it raised my hackles as well. Whatever was going on seemed to be stretching the boundaries of dirty politics.

Three beeps of a horn made me turn to see Jenny impatiently waving from her car. "Our ride," I said.

I made the introductions, and Claire and Jenny were polite to one another, each offering the other about as much warmth as the December sun over Siberia. East and West didn't so much meet as ignore one another.

Though Jenny was driving her own car, I told her, "Maybe I should drive. I know the way better."

"What do you mean?" asked Jenny. "I know way just fine and dandy."

In a low, advisory tone, I said to Claire, "Put on your seat belt. If you thought last night's ride was dicey, you haven't seen anything yet."

"I hear that," said Jenny. "I am good driver."

"There's a reason you don't see any Korean NASCAR drivers," I said.

"Koreans too smart to drive race cars," she said. "Go round in circle, circle, and circle. What sense is that?"

"Just get us to my place in one piece."

Jenny pulled out into the road, but instead of looking where she was driving, her eyes were busy scrutinizing me.

"In America we have a quaint custom," I said. "We call it watching where you drive."

"What happened to your shoes? And why are your feet and face cut?"

"Rocky beach," I said, "and the darn tide carried my shoes off."

Jenny's beautiful dark eyes didn't look any too pleased with my lie. "Don't piss on my head and tell me it is raining."

"Should I ever piss on your head," I said, "I won't tell you that."

"You look like you been rode hard and put away wet."

It was John Wayne with a Korean accent. I chose not to respond to the Duke.

"What about job you supposed to be doing?" asked Jenny.

"It will have to be rescheduled. I'll call the hotel and talk to the front desk about putting my luggage in storage."

"Reschedule when? Month is all booked up."

"We're going to have to bring Lucas in to do some of the jobs."

The Last Resort is a small business. In any given week we have dozens of auditors doing restaurant audits, but I try to handle all the important accounts, which includes our hotel business. Lucas Ewing is our contingency hotel auditor, but Jenny isn't very enamored with his abilities.

By way of apology to her, I said, "All of this was unavoidable."

Jenny raised her eyes and peered back in the rearview mirror, took a pointed look at Claire, and mumbled, "That boat don't float."

"Excuse me?" said Claire.

Jenny suddenly brightened. She had this ability to put on a happy face at a moment's notice. Whenever she wanted to change the subject, she just up and glowed. Jenny offered Claire a big, fake smile that showed off her pearly, white teeth. "How long have you known Will Travis?" she asked.

I wore my blinders during the drive, but they didn't quite keep the world at bay. Several of Jenny's enthusiastic automotive maneuvers were met with the blare of horns. I was glad when Mr. Toad's Wild Ride came to an end.

My Washington, D.C., apartment is in an area known as Foggy Bottom. The neighborhood is a mix of new and old, a historic area situated between Lafayette Square and Georgetown. My place is less than a five-minute walk to the Potomac River, and I can hoof it in less than ten minutes to Dupont Circle.

Two blocks from my building are the Watergate Apartments and Hotel. If I needed to be reminded about political scandals, I only had to look across the way. President Richard Nixon's Waterloo occurred inside that edifice when the Committee to Reelect the President sent some incompetent burglars into the offices of the Democratic National Committee and they got caught with their hands in the cookie jar. More recently, Monica Lewinsky hid out in the building for months while trying to avoid the media spotlight resulting from her affair with President Bill Clinton. I think Senator Orrin Hatch described the Clinton/Lewinsky relationship best: "We have perhaps the first presidential canoodler in history." Hatch was very wrong about Clinton being that first canoodler, but he did find the right description. The scandal presented the media with difficulties in explaining the president's conduct in less-than-graphic terms. It wasn't easy saying *blow job* on national television, but you could say *canoodler* and not have to worry about what grade-school children might think.

My car door opened, courtesy of Chet the doorman. Chet is a big man, tall and broad, and has been an institution at the building for at least twenty years. He noticed the state of my feet but said nothing. There is a reason Chet remains an institution.

"You coming to work today?" asked Jenny.

"I am not sure yet."

She made a disparaging sound and then passed her eyes from Claire to me in a censorious look that spoke unfavorable volumes. I suppose it was impossible for her to drive off without leaving me with a final editorial.

"Early bird gets worm," she declared.

"Yeah, but it's the second mouse that gets the cheese."

Jenny didn't look happy as she pulled away. It is rare for me to get the last word.

Claire followed me to the elevator. "I think Jenny has more than a professional interest in your well-being."

I shook my head. "Jenny is happily married. Her husband is a D.C. bureaucrat. She plays the mother hen role, even though I'm two years older than she is."

My fifth-floor apartment has a nice view of the surrounding area. For the price I pay, it should. In the nineteenth century the area was a working-class neighborhood populated by Germans, Irish, and African-Americans. Many of the locals worked in breweries, the nearby gas works, and factories. It was the smoke from those factories, combined with the fog from the low swampland along the waterfront, that earned the area its name. As far as I'm concerned, Foggy Bottom is an improvement on its earlier nineteenth-century designation, which was Funkstown.

With some trepidation, I opened the door. Maybe I was afraid of what my living quarters said about me. At least I didn't have to worry about the apartment being clean. My job requires me to eat most of my meals out, and I am often on the road, so the place always looks tidy. It also looks just this side of uninhabited.

Claire stepped inside and looked around. I was sort of hoping she would go to the balcony and comment on the view, but that didn't happen.

"Did you just move in?" she asked.

"Not long ago," I said, stretching the truth by four and a half years. "Where do you live?"

"I used to live not far from here, but I sublet the apartment after my father died."

"What about your work?"

"I took a leave of absence."

She had an answer for everything I asked, though what she said told me little. I went to the kitchen, pulled out a bottle of aspirin, and did a little castanet shake of it to get Claire's attention. She nodded and joined me. We took our pills with water—me five, her three.

"Make yourself at home," I said, "if that's possible. There might be something edible in the refrigerator, but you take your chances."

I went to the message machine and zipped through my calls. If I was hoping to show off, it didn't work. There wasn't a personal message in the lot, dammit. I checked the time and decided to call the Blue Crab Inn to avoid getting charged for staying another night. I am the last of the big-time spenders when someone else is paying, but more mindful of costs when the stay is on my tab.

After reaching the hotel operator, I inquired as to the name and availability of the front-office manager, and was connected to an individual identified as Derek Greene.

"Mr. Greene?" I said. "This is Harold Dodd."

Claire tilted her head, reminding me of a terrier suddenly alert to the scratching of a rat.

"I don't know if we have met," I continued, "but I have been a guest at your fine property several times over the years."

"Why, yes, Mr. Dodd," the manager said, his voice familiar and friendly. Hotel managers are wonderful about faking fond memories of guests they have absolutely no recollection of.

I spoke in the manner of the well-heeled, not quite patronizing, but aware of the power of my platinum card. "At any rate, Mr. Greene, I am currently registered at the inn, but I need to check out a day early, and I want to do it over the phone if possible."

"That's no problem, Mr. Dodd."

"I was hoping it wouldn't be. The only sticky wicket is that my luggage is still in the room, and I'll need someone to gather it and put it in storage."

There was a small, but to my ear telling, hesitation, before the front-office manager said, "That can be arranged, sir."

"Are you sure that's not a problem?"

Another pause. In fine hotels, managers do their best not to disappoint guests. "We will see to it, Mr. Dodd. I am wondering, though, if you happened to have a chance to speak with the authorities during your stay here."

"Authorities?" I voiced the word in wonderment, and perhaps a little indignation. "Why would I be talking with them?"

"Are you aware of what transpired last night?"

"Last night? What are you talking about?"

"There was an *incident* at the hotel last night," he said.

I could almost hear the poor man sweating over the phone. Telling me that there had been a murder in the gardens would be *outré*.

"I am afraid I spent very little time at the inn," I said. "Business took me off property. The talks went late, and the drinks went later, and an associate talked me into staying in his guest room. I didn't even get to stay in my room last night."

"What a shame," said Mr. Greene. Experienced hoteliers are able to sympathize about as easily as they breathe.

"I am not sure how we should handle this," he continued, doing his thinking aloud. "Because of the *incident*, the authorities are interviewing all of our guests currently registered in the hotel."

Claire still hadn't given me a green light to talk to the police, and I could tell that was where he was about to direct our conversation. It was time for a diversionary tactic. "Say," I said, "since I didn't really stay in my room last night, do you think you could do something about that rate?"

He politely, but firmly, went on the defensive. "I am afraid we held that space in your name, Mr. Dodd. I am sorry you were unable to use the room, but we do require forty-eight hours' cancellation notice for our room reservations."

"I am telling you the room's untouched. Housekeeping won't even have to vacuum it."

"Again, I apologize, Mr. Dodd. I hope you can understand our position, though. We didn't know that you wouldn't be using the room, and held it accordingly."

I sighed loudly. "All right," I said. "Just put it on the credit card, then. And add ten bucks to the total and pay it out to whoever takes care of my bags. There's a laptop and a hanging bag. Make sure they get my cell phone as well. I'll pick everything up in the next two or three days."

"Very good, Mr. Dodd," he said. "Let me just confirm your address and telephone number."

Sounding just a bit disgruntled, and maybe a little pouty, I recited a Manhattan address, one that matched the address I had used when registering. I also gave him a New York City telephone number. Mr. Greene decided not to press his luck, and chose to end the conversation sooner rather than later, no doubt afraid that I would once again start whining about getting a break on the rate. In his victory at holding firm on the rate, any thought of passing me on to the authorities was forgotten.

After hanging up the phone, I saw that Claire was still in her terrier pose. "Mr. Dodd?" she asked. "Mr. Dodd of New York City?"

"Pleased to meet you."

"What was that all about?"

"It's April. That's the fourth month of the year. And the fourth letter of the alphabet is D."

"Is all that supposed to mean something?"

"It means I would be in serious trouble if I ever lost my wallet. Anyone finding it would be utterly confused. In my wallet there are six credit card slots, all filled with credit cards, and all with different names that go from A to F. Behind each of those credit cards I have picture I.D. that matches the name of the cardholder."

Claire did her math. "What happens in July?"

"The alphabet starts over, so the A name that is used in January gets used in July, just as I will be Mr. Dodd again come October."

Claire looked bewildered. "Why the subterfuge?"

"My job. There are certain accounts I return to time and again. I don't want them associating a name with the audits. Some establishments post the reports for all the employees to see. It becomes a guessing game to spot the spotter. I refuse to make it easy."

"If you go to a place very often, I am sure they recognize you."

"I'm skilled at making myself very forgettable."

I was hoping she would put up an argument and say that I was incredibly unique and memorable, but she didn't. Instead Claire asked, "What's with the New York City address? And phone number?"

"The address is a mail drop. I have one for each of my six names. And I pay for a New York City answering service. It's one more veil of anonymity."

"Isn't it illegal having all those credit cards under phony names?"

"It would be if I didn't pay my bills, but I do. All the banks and credit card companies are very happy to have me as a client. My credit rating under all the names is excellent."

Claire shook her head. "Still, having so many identities seems rather extreme."

"It probably is, but there are times my work puts me in an adversarial position. Sometimes I catch people doing bad things, wrong things. There are often consequences because of my reports. I would just as soon remain anonymous."

"But the managers certainly know who you are."

I shook my head. "Sometimes they're the worst offenders. I've caught managers inappropriately groping employees, stealing, giving away food, and extorting gratuities from staff. You name it, they've done it. I can only be effective on the job if no one is aware of what I'm doing."

"Do you sometimes forget who you are?"

I didn't tell her that was one of the attractions of the job. "They say that to be a good liar, you need a good memory."

"And you're a good liar?"

"I'm well suited to my work."

"The day after tomorrow is May Day. Who do you turn into?"

"Kirk Ellis."

"You lead a strange existence."

"Blame it on my being a Gemini."

"I overheard you say the word *authorities*. What was that about?"

"All hotel guests are being interviewed about the shooting last night."

"I suppose that's not surprising."

"The manager used the word *authorities*," I said. "He didn't just say *police*."

He also called the death an *incident*, but I didn't tell her that. Maybe they teach managers those kinds of things in hotel school.

"Do you think that's significant?"

"I don't know. It might be nothing. Or it could be that someone's decided this isn't an ordinary homicide."

There was that telltale prickle on my neck. I didn't say it aloud, but I was suddenly glad to be Mr. Dodd from New York City. The alias provided me with some breathing room.

"I'm going to take a bath," I said. "I'm going to shave. I'm going to do a Mary Magdalene on my feet; and coddle them with every healing ointment in my medicine cabinet. In the meantime, make yourself comfortable."

Claire thanked me. As I closed my bedroom door behind me, I saw her picking up the television remote control.

It took a few minutes of relaxing in the hot waters of the tub for the magic to work, but gradually I started to feel like something resembling a human. The tension that had built up in my body started to slowly dissipate. I wasn't sparing with the body lotion, and lathered up so much there was a bubble bath effect. All I was missing was a rubber ducky.

The knocking at the bathroom door startled me. "Will!" Claire yelled. "Will!"

"What?"

She opened the door an inch. "CNN is doing a report on what happened at the Blue Crab Inn. They've identified the victim. What they said in the teaser doesn't make any sense."

"I'll be right out."

"They think he was murdered! They're making him out to be a victim!"

"I'm coming."

"None of it sounds right."

Claire was still talking through the crack of the door. I hadn't thought to bring any clothes into the bathroom with me, and naturally, there wasn't a bath towel on the towel rack. I stood up, grabbed a hand towel, and dried off as best I could.

"The report's being aired now!" Claire shouted.

She ran out to the living room, and I exited the bathroom with a strategically positioned hand towel. I threw on some boxers in my bedroom, but there really wasn't a need. Claire's eyes were totally focused on the CNN report.

With a grave voice, the reporter intoned, "The shooting death of Alcohol, Tobacco, and Firearms Special Agent Lawrence Deering at an exclusive Maryland hotel is being investigated by state and governmental authorities. Deering, a former captain in the marines, was found shot to death in the courtyard of the Blue Crab Inn last evening."

The screen filled with a picture of the dead man I knew as Major Dick, but this time without a disguise. Military. I knew it.

"Special Agent Deering was division director of ATF's Washington D.C.'s field management staff. Although the ATF has released few details of Special Agent Deering's investigation, it is known that he was probing into the assassination attempt and bombing of Republican presidential candidate Congressman Mark Stanton, as well as looking into death threats directed at several other presidential candidates."

The picture of Deering changed, and not for the better. Video footage of Deering sprawled among the gardens of the Blue Crab Inn played across the television screen. It wasn't a picture that hotel management would be displaying in a brochure any time soon. The shaky quality of the footage suggested that a guest was at the camera. I could imagine the narration of the home movie in front of a gathering of friends: "And here's Jane at the pool, and there's a view of the Chesapeake, and here's our hotel, and this is the body of a man shot at our hotel."

Over the footage, the news reporter continued talking: "Those close to Special Agent Deering's investigation say that he believed the death threats were, and we quote, 'very credible.' One source inside the ATF said that Deering was in the final stages of developing a case against an individual known to have been stalking the candidates and believed to be very dangerous."

The picture on the screen showed some of the candidates pressing flesh. The unsaid implication was that anyone getting this close to the public would make a good target for any would-be assassin.

"There is speculation that Deering might have been shot by the very subject of his investigation. As a precaution, the Secret Service has extended additional protection to all of the major presidential candidates."

The screen changed again, this time to another story, but Claire didn't turn her head to me right away. She was clearly perplexed by the report.

"What's going on?" she asked.

"Offhand, I'd say you'd better get yourself some safety netting."

"Why?"

"Because you're being set up for a fall."

Claire didn't want to believe what I was saying. She shook her head, looked at me as if questioning my sanity, and opened her mouth a few times to tell me how wrong I was. The words stuck in her throat, though. Too many things had happened to her for Claire to dismiss my suspicions, though she was loath to admit that being set up as a human sacrifice could happen to someone like her. Her entire life supported that kind of thinking, but the last twelve hours had offered her a different interpretation of the world. Instead of arguing, and telling me how wrong I was, she finally swallowed hard and said, "Why?"

"I think your intended obituary was written up prior to last night. You probably weren't meant to die at the inn, but in suspicious circumstances elsewhere. By living, you have forced your enemies to revise your obit."

"Care to tell me how my death is being written up at this very minute?"

I took her question seriously, even though I don't think she meant it to be. "There is the matter of Deering's body," I said. "They need a shooter, and a reason for his being shot. I suspect they want you to play that starring role."

"And how are they going to do that?"

"You were the last person seen with Deering before he was shot. I'm sure two or three witnesses from the hotel lounge have already provided good descriptions of you. Lo and behold, I'm willing to bet investigators will match your description with that of a suspect Deering already conveniently had on his books."

"What's my motive for killing him?"

"I would guess that Deering already made you a part of his investigation. That information would have been released when your body turned up. Because of your continued existence, they're going about it another way."

"So I'm supposed to be some crazed assassin, is that it?"

"That sounds about right."

"Not to me, it doesn't. Not to people who know me."

"When you think about it, you make a good victim. They already have you for means and opportunity. Now all they have to do is cook up motive. It won't take much to make you look guilty, because you already have the smoking gun in the proximity of your hand."

She was shaking her head now. "Your conjecture borders on the absurd."

"You think so? These people are playing for keeps. From the first, killing you would only have been half their plan. Killing your reputation would have been the other half. They won't do one without the other."

Claire visibly flinched. If I was reading her right, she was more upset with the idea of losing her reputation than losing her life.

"How many people know about your theory that we have a murderer running for the highest office in this land?"

Claire hesitated before saying, "No one."

"You're lying."

Her cheeks reddened. "I can assure you that I have not been going around shouting my suspicions from the rooftops."

Her indignation aside, I noticed that she didn't offer a categorical denial, but a qualified one.

I did my imitation of an attorney examining a witness. Unfortunately, I was all too familiar with that kind of interrogation. "You disputed, and continue to dispute, the manner in which the police believe your father died."

"Yes, but I didn't tell them who I suspected might be involved in his death."

"So how do you believe you came to the attention of these people who apparently want you dead?"

"When you make inquiries, you can't help but get noticed."

"What kind of questions were you asking?"

"I looked into the past. I was particularly interested in learning if my father was acquainted with the Democratic candidates, and if so, his relationship with them."

"Why did you only target the Democratic candidates?"

"I thought it likely that some political rivalry in the past prompted all of this."

"You're presuming a lot," I said. "Isn't the old saw that Republicans are involved in financial scandals and Democrats in sexual scandals?"

"My father was loyal to his party."

"Eleventh Commandment," I said, referring to the un-written law that no Republican ever speak ill of another. "Still, the Sixth Commandment might trump it."

"I suppose that's possible. Are you associated with a po-litical party, Mr. Travis?"

"Will," I said. "I come from a long line of Republicans."

That seemed to reassure Claire until I added, "I guess my being a Democrat would piss the hell out of them."

"And they would have good reason," she said.

She was right about that, I thought. "Tell me how you went about playing Nancy Drew."

"Many people already knew that my father was working on a book. My cover story was that I was finishing up some of his historical research and wanted to put it into a con-temporary context. Perhaps I was not as discreet as I should have been."

I still wasn't buying all of her story, but Claire was reluc-tant to say more. I suspected either that she was protecting someone or she didn't trust me. I suppose I blew it by telling her I was a Democrat.

The phone rang and both of us started. I was tempted to let the machine get it, but didn't want to have to endure three more rings. I picked up the receiver and answered in a slightly breathless tone.

"Did I interrupt something?" Jenny asked.

"Yeah, I was busy trying to find out how to say, 'Mind your own business' in Korean."

"Phrase escapes me."

"Phrase escapes you in both English *and* Korean."

"Mr. Lund wants to see you this afternoon."

"Why didn't you tell him I was out of town?"

"Mr. Lund could sell drowning man a glass of water. Be-sides, Mr. Lund is big account."

"He reminds me of that enough. You don't need to be his echo."

"Mr. Lund will be here at one o'clock."

"Good—he can wait, because I don't plan to be in until half past."

"I guess that is better than a poke in the eye with a sharp stick."

"I'll take your word on that."

"Since you are coming in so late, why not do lunch audit? We need someone to do George's on the River."

I realized that I was hungry, and knew the state of my larder resembled Mother Hubbard's cupboard. "Maybe," I said.

Jenny knew that was my way of agreeing. "I have to go, Will Travis. I am as busy as a paperhanger with crabs."

Jenny had a habit of leaving me with phrases—and images—that stayed with me like the annoying refrain of a bad song. Maybe that's why her speech was punctuated with colorful expressions that offered larger-than-life images. In her mind's eye she probably remembered those phrases because of their vividness.

The gift that keeps on giving. Dammit if Jenny hadn't passed on a case of the crabs to me.

CHAPTER FIVE

At the offer of lunch, Claire said she was as hungry as a horse. I warned her that she would have to sing for her oats, but that prospect didn't deter her. Before going to lunch, though, she asked to make a call or two, and warned me that the process "might take a while."

"Are you calling your friends in high places?"

She didn't answer.

"I hope those friends have your best interests at heart," I said.

"My situation is very complicated," said Claire. "If I can avoid any untoward publicity . . ."

She didn't complete her wishful thought. I felt compelled to give her a wake-up call. "You were part of an *untoward* shooting. You left the kind of footprints that will invariably lead to you, and it's going to be up to you to show they are not bloody. This isn't something you can hope to walk away from."

"I'll make the call and then we'll talk. We can better figure out our options then."

"There are no options, Claire. This afternoon we have to go to the police."

"We will. But I don't want to act prematurely. I'm waiting for certain news that will prove Father's death wasn't a suicide. With that evidence in hand I'll be able to deal with the authorities from a position of strength. It will also give me the leverage to quash any attempts at character assassination, should they occur.

"And," she added, "the information I'm waiting for might even make it possible for us to keep our names out of the news."

Since I made my living being anonymous, I liked the sound of that.

"I imagine you know any number of good lawyers," I said.

"And why do you imagine that?"

"You are a lawyer, aren't you?"

"I am not currently practicing law."

She evaded my question as expertly as a lawyer still practicing law. "I might be wrong about your being set up," I said, "but if I'm not, it wouldn't hurt to have legal representation right from the start."

"I need to make that call before I do anything else," Claire said. "What's your number here?"

I told her. Claire said, "I'll be calling a pager and waiting to get called back. When the phone rings, I would appreciate your letting me answer it."

It was clear she wanted her privacy, or maybe she was just tired of seeing me in boxers. "There's a phone in the guest bedroom," I told her.

Almost half an hour passed from the time she closed the guest room door behind her until the phone rang. The conversation was a short one, for she came out not more than two minutes later. The call seemed to have put her in better humor. She offered a smile my way.

"Good news?"

"Some hopeful developments," she said.

Claire didn't elaborate on that, and I didn't press for details.

"Ready for lunch?"

"More than ready," she said, "but I need to ask another favor that involves a hundred dollars and ten minutes."

"That sounds like an offer I can't refuse."

Her smile was now that much larger. "I was hoping you would say that. I need to stop and get some clothes."

George's on the River is a unique restaurant that combines history and political horseplay in an upbeat atmosphere. The main motif in the restaurant is George Washington himself. He is a ubiquitous figure, with a variety of icons constructed to America's Founding Father throughout the restaurant.

Our audit timeline started when the hostess seated us at 11:51. Three minutes later our server approached the table. The staff didn't quite go the Williamsburg route with period costumes, but all the servers wore white wigs. With a courtly bow our waiter said, "Milord and milady, my name is Perry and I will be serving your victuals. Can I start you off with some grog or ale?"

Solicitation of grog and ale by Server One, but no mention of product by name.

From other audits, I knew the ownership liked staff to identify several brand names to lead the patrons into an order.

"No grog for me," I said. Claire shook her head.

"Then can I interest you in some nectar, or tisane, or tea from the Indies?"

"I'll have an iced tea," said Claire.

"Very good, madam. I will bring that to you presently."

Claire raised herself after he left. "I'll be going to ye olde ladies' room," she said.

"Check out its condition," I said. "Are there adequate supplies? Is the ventilation good? Has the trash been emptied? Are there any visible hazards? Is it, on the whole, appealing?"

"I thought it was called a restroom," she said, "not a work room."

While she was gone, I inventoried cutlery, table linens, and the condition of the carpeting, and found all well-maintained.

An audit is done with all senses. Next, I listened:

Modern background music too loud. Management might also reconsider pop selections in this establishment, as they seem too modern for setting. Light classical might be better.

Then I did some sniffing about, and my nose found nothing lingering in the air, and no offensive odors.

I pretended to drop my napkin, and did a quick scan under the table.

Staff needs to police undersides of tables. Gum residue prevalent.

To myself, I hummed the immortal question written into song, *"Oh, does the spearmint lose its flavor on the bedpost overnight? When you chew it in the morning, will it be too hard to bite?"*

I picked up the menu and studied it, but not in the way most diners did. Then I also lifted Claire's menu and quickly turned its pages.

Both menus stained and worn. Smudge marks inside detract from editorial content.

George's on the River described itself as a "well-resorted tavern," taking the words directly from George Washington's description of his Mount Vernon home. Under "Fun Facts" on the menu was the claim that George and Martha dined by themselves only twice in the last twenty years of their marriage.

The menu featured excerpts from a booklet entitled *George Washington's Rules of Civility and Decent Behaviour in Company and Conversation,* including the admonitions of "Feed not with greediness," and "Lean not on the table," and finally, "Neither find fault with what you eat." In my line of work, the last would be difficult to obey.

The menu offered a wide selection of items. For those seeking culinary adventure, there was a section titled "George's Tavern Fare." Entrees included oyster fritters, mutton chops, ploughman's pie, hoe cakes (corn cakes topped with butter and honey), and bubble and squeak (the colonial description of cabbage and mashed potatoes) with pork chops.

Many of the dish descriptions were designed to elicit groans. Cherry pie was a featured dessert and was described as, "We cannot tell a lie. This is the best cherry pie in the world"; the Potomac pot roast was "well worth tossing silver dollars for"; the Cobb salad "George would flip his wig for"; and the peanut pie was so good that, "wooden choppers and all, George would be digging into it." Apparently whoever wrote the food descriptions didn't bother to take the "George Washington Quiz" that was featured in the same menu where it was revealed that George never chopped down a cherry tree when he was a child, didn't wear a wig, never threw a silver dollar across the Potomac, and that his false teeth weren't made of wood, but consisted of cow's teeth, human teeth, and ivory, set in a lead base with springs.

At nearby tables I listened to other servers describing the specials of the day. The lunch crowd was appearing in full force, and the pace in the dining room was picking up.

Claire beat her iced tea back to the table. Earlier, she had been true to her word, completing her shopping in ten minutes and for under a hundred dollars. She had bought a black A-line skirt and a white blouse. When she returned I detected the scent of perfume, and noticed that she had somehow managed to put on a gentle application of makeup. I asked how she accomplished her transformation so quickly, and Claire told me that "sales racks and cosmetic samples are wonderful things."

Claire's iced tea was delivered by a different busboy than the one I had already mentally catalogued. I added Busboy

Two to the staff list in my head, gauging his height, weight, ethnicity, and name. You can't tell the players without a scorecard.

Our waiter followed in the wake of the iced tea. "Have you had a chance to look at the menu yet?" he asked. He was smiling, but seemed a bit eager to get matters moving.

No recitation of daily specials by Server One.

I invariably ask questions of servers to gauge their professionalism. The Q&A would also buy Claire a little time to look at the menu. "I am torn between the trout meunière and the caramelized sea scallops."

"They're both supposed to be good," Perry said. "Everything on the menu is good."

I waited to hear more. I needn't have waited. Perry's grand conclusion was, "It's just that I am not much of a seafood fan."

Server One needs to offer constructive and descriptive answers to diner inquiries. He did not display any knowledge of the menu, nor did he offer any description as to how dishes are served. No feedback from other patrons offered. He could have waxed poetic on the almondine sauce used on the trout, or mentioned how the truffle sauce complimented the scallops to perfection.

I looked over to Claire to see if she had decided. Perry decided to look that way as well, his pen held at the ready.

"At heart," she said, "I am a meat-and-potatoes kind of girl, so I'll have the shepherd's pie." Claire held her tongue from saying anything else, as I had instructed her to earlier.

I ordered the scallops, and Perry said, "Okay, great." He was already stepping away from the table when I called him back.

Server One made no inquiries regarding soup or salad, nor did he make any suggestive remarks regarding an appetizer. His upselling of menu items should be encouraged.

Management should coach him in his descriptions, such as, "We have fresh oysters in today that are outstanding. Would you care to start off with some?"

Claire added the house salad to her order, vinaigrette dressing on the side, and I asked for a cup of the New England clam chowder. For an appetizer, we agreed upon splitting an order of crab cakes.

An older couple seated at a table across from us was studying their menus. The man was holding his menu away from him as far as his arms could stretch. "I forgot my reading glasses," I heard him say to his wife.

Perry stopped by that table. "Need a few more minutes?" he asked them.

Not as much as Perry needs a pair of eyes, I thought. He should have noticed the man's difficulty and offered to provide him with a magnifying glass to see the menu more easily. The fine print is a common obstacle in restaurants, and most tablecloth restaurants stock magnifying glasses for just such situations.

I watched as Perry passed by several tables with plates that needed clearing. It didn't matter that he wasn't a busboy. The old axiom in restaurants is never to make a trip anywhere empty-handed.

Server One needs to understand that a good waiter should move quickly, but not be in a hurry.

I lifted my water glass, sipped from it, and in the same motion scanned the room in search of a manager. If our server was inexperienced, he should have been under the scrutiny of a manager. Sometimes the success or failure of a meal rests on a good manager being on the floor to smooth rough edges. The manager, I saw, hadn't moved since I'd last tracked him.

Manager still not on floor. For first ten minutes of audit, manager continuously engaged in conversation with staff at maitre d' stand.

The manager was a handsome young man wearing an expensive suit. At the moment he was laughing with one of the hostesses. Throughout our meal I would continue to observe his performance. At the moment, his eyes seemed to be directed at the hostess's chest instead of at the goings-on in the restaurant.

"The view's the other way," Claire said, nodding her head at the Potomac.

"Depends on what you're looking for."

"So how did you get started in this business?"

"I suppose I am a born critic. The business started in a strange way."

Empty water glasses all around our section. No sign of anyone attending to refills.

I raised my water glass, drained it in one long swallow, and started my mental stopwatch to see if and when it would be noticed.

"Six years ago I went out to dinner," I said, continuing my story. "The restaurant was supposed to be fine dining at its best. Judging by its prices, it should have been, but the dinner was very disappointing."

From the corner of my eye I watched a hostess in the process of seating a family of five. Two in the party were toddlers.

Hostess Two walking too fast for family to keep up. No attempt to converse with patrons. Management should stress that staff should try to personalize dining experience.

"The bill for that meal was more than a hundred dollars. I reluctantly paid it and said nothing. That's what most people do. They don't complain. They just never come back. When I got home, though, I was still bothered by the whole experience. You name it, it wasn't right. The waiter was inattentive, and our food was served cold. Even the dessert was ruined when I found this big, black hair in my créme brûlée. I decided to break my silence and write a letter to the owner. The idea was cathartic for me. I got to vent my spleen and tell the owner what a huge disappointment the meal was. My letter was quite detailed and quite long. It ended up running sixteen single-spaced typed pages."

Claire laughed. It was nice to hear her laugh and see her face soften up. With all that we'd been through, there had been little enough time to relax.

"Sixteen pages," she said. "That's not a review, that's a book. How could you possibly write a sixteen-page letter about a meal?"

"Just verbose, I guess."

Deuce in corner booth departs at 12:04. Restaurant already two-thirds full.

Restaurants need to turn over tables quickly during their busy times. I marked the time to see how long it would take the staff to notice the empty table, and then clear and set it. In restaurants, timing is everything. It starts from the moment guests arrive at the door until the moment they leave. Understanding the timing in a restaurant is important in doing a critique. In the grand dance between restaurant and patron, food is supposed to be delivered in a timely matter. When that doesn't happen, finger-pointing invariably goes on between the front of the house and the back of the house.

Perry arrived with our soup and salad on a tray. "I'll bring your appetizer out shortly," he said.

Soup and salad delivered by Server One at 12:05. No notice taken of empty water glass.

Claire's fork raised itself to strike. "I'm so hungry," she announced.

"You didn't get your vinaigrette on the side."

The omission didn't slow her fork down. "You're right," she said, digging in, "but if you think I'm going to send the salad back, you're crazy. I'm too hungry to wait."

I was just as hungry, but took a moment to scrutinize the soup, noting its color and texture. Then, it was time for the Goldilocks test. The porridge passed inspection; not too

hot, not too cold. Like a wine tester on a mission, I did a little swirling and tasting. The first spoonful was for the report, the rest was pure pleasure.

Neither one of us talked while we ate. When both of us
were finished, Claire resumed our conversation. "So what
happened to your sixteen-page restaurant review?"

"The review that changed my life," I said, "although for
better or worse, the jury's still out."

I pushed my empty cup of soup forward. "Well, much to
my surprise, I heard back from the owner of the restaurant
the same day he read my letter. Not only was he very
apologetic, he was extremely grateful for my report, saying
it documented many of his suspicions. The kicker was that
not only did he insist upon compensating me for my dinner, but he paid me one hundred dollars for the report. He
also asked me to come back the following month to do the
exact same thing. To me, that seemed too good to be true.
And that's how I landed my first account."

"Did you have a background in food or restaurant management?"

"Hardly."

"So why is it that these hotels and restaurants pay for
your observations?"

"I guess they need the impressions of an everyman."

"That's your role?"

"To some degree. You ever hear someone say that they
can't see the forest for the trees? When you work in the
same environment every day, sometimes you can't see
what an outsider notices right away."

Our waiter approached with the crab cakes. He placed
the dish down in the middle of the table, and then put a
plate in front of each of us.

"Bon appétit!" Perry said.

*At 12:09 Server One delivers crab cakes. Instead of bring-
ing the appetizer on a tray, server carried plate by hand. No
check-back initiated to assure satisfaction of soup and salad.*

When the waiter was out of earshot, Claire asked, "What's wrong?"

"What do you mean?"

"The waiter did something wrong, didn't he?"

"You tell me."

She thought about it for a moment, and then shook her head. "I didn't notice anything."

"Here's your parable for the day," I said. "This man goes into a restaurant and orders a steak. Half an hour later his waiter emerges from the kitchen carrying out his plate of steak. The man notices that the waiter has both his thumbs pressed into the steak, and gets upset. 'What are you doing?' he asks indignantly. 'You've got your fingers in my steak.' The waiter says, 'That's right, sir. You don't want it to fall on the floor again, do you?' "

The light had gone on in Claire's eyes early in the story. "Our waiter had his thumb on our plate, didn't he?"

"Bingo."

"I don't care," Claire said. "These crab cakes are to die for." She cut off a large portion with her fork, dipped it into the pesto-mayonnaise sauce, and started chewing enthusiastically.

At 12:10 Busboy One begins clearing table left by deuce. Vacated tables should be attended to in a more timely fashion.

The busboy returned with the table setups at 12:12. In his haste, he dropped one of the forks on the floor. Looking around surreptitiously, the busboy decided no one had seen. He wiped the fork with a napkin, and then put it on the table.

"You get paid to eat," Claire said. "What a life."

"I get paid to watch. There's a big difference."

I felt a tingle in my neck and looked around the restaurant, but this time I wasn't doing my scrutinizing for the ownership. I had this sensation that I was the one dropping a fork, and someone was watching me.

CHAPTER SIX

The noise was building, the many voices coming together as one. The percussion from their clapping was like the pounding of heavy surf, and the way the audience was chanting his name made it sound as if they were invoking a higher power.

They were calling out his name as if they wanted a miracle.

The Candidate lifted his right arm and motioned for them to stop, but a smile played on his face and everyone was in on the joke. Monitors all around the auditorium showed his mirth. He clearly loved the moment, and was showing them that. Though his arm signaled for them to stop, his audience knew better.

The noise level increased, and his smile broadened. The true believers reacted to his delight. Now they were raising the roof. It was like witnessing something come alive, the Candidate thought. He was seeing the birth of a nation going on in front of him, and how he loved what he saw.

All eyes were on him. They were looking for him to lead them. This was his moment; this was his time. He bathed in their adulation. It was a palpable thing. He could feel it, and hear it; he could all but touch it. It was almost time to rein them in, but not yet. For now he let their love wash over him. They were telling him what he already knew. He was meant to be at the helm of the nation. It was his destiny.

The Candidate had attended sporting events where this kind of electricity was in the air, the loyal fans exhorting their team to find a way to win. That's what they wanted of him. That is what he was going to give them. Politics had all the elements of great sport; the ebb and flow; the fighting it out. It was called "the political arena" for good reason.

The chant started in one corner. "Freedom," yelled the voices. It was picked up by another section, "FReedom." Other voices joined in, and he heard the word more clearly: "FREedom." The word was identified with his campaign, and now half the auditorium was shouting it, "FREEdom."

From his youth, he had been a leader. Following was not his way. He had always found a way to govern. There had been others who were bigger and stronger, even some who were smarter, but he had always managed to accumulate power. It had been the game, the sport, he excelled at. It was not a sport for the weak of heart, or the weak.

"If you can't stand the heat," Truman had said, "get out of the kitchen."

The Candidate loved the heat.

People like Vince Foster weren't meant for the sport. After Clinton's White House deputy counsel committed suicide, investigators found a torn-up note in his briefcase. The note said, *I was not meant for the job or the spotlight of public life in Washington. Here, ruining people is considered sport.*

Foster didn't know how to play the game, but he did. In fact, part of the attraction of politics was the blood sport. Every game needs its stakes, and politics had the highest stakes of all. In order to advance, you needed to draw blood. You needed to position yourself, and claw your way higher. You only won the game by using the bodies of your opponents as stepping-stones.

The crescendo was almost there: "FREEDom!" they screamed. "FREEDOm, FREEDOM!"

He looked out and saw every mouth opening and closing in unison. Now was the time, right now.

The Candidate dropped the smile, his face now the picture of seriousness. He had a mission; they had a mission. Those not close to the Candidate saw the transformation of their leader's visage on the monitors. Their voices dropped, and the chanting stopped.

In the suddenly silent auditorium, the Candidate looked out to his audience. He turned his head and scanned the assemblage, and everyone watching him was sure that his eyes met theirs.

"This is the land of the free!" the Candidate said.

They who had been holding their breaths let out a roar.

"This is the home of the brave!"

There was another roar from the crowd, but this time it was even louder and more sustained.

"This is America!"

Those who still had voices lifted them. The din was overwhelming. People screamed and couldn't hear their own voices. Even over the loudspeakers, the Candidate couldn't be heard, but on the monitors they read his lips.

"God bless America!"

CHAPTER SEVEN

Most days I take the Metro to my Bethesda office and use the twenty-six-minute ride to do work. With a head of steam I can sometimes write up an entire restaurant audit, but on this occasion I used the time to talk with Claire instead of inputting information into a laptop.

Both of us had managed to find our second wind. Maybe it was the espresso we had after lunch (something else for the report—Perry neglected to try and sell us after-lunch drinks or dessert, and we were forced to ask for our coffee and cheesecake), or maybe we were just feeling good about being alive.

With her guard down, Claire was a different person. She didn't entirely lose her reserve, but offered glimpses of what she was like when people weren't trying to kill her. Though blessed with beauty, Claire wasn't obsessed with keeping up appearances. She walked by mirrors and windows without stopping to appraise herself. In my experience that's a rare quality among the very attractive. Claire was a good listener, and peppered our conversation with questions. There was a part of me that realized her curiosity might have been a tactic, and that by keeping me talking she saved herself from being on the receiving end of the third degree, but even if that was her ploy I couldn't help but enjoy being the object of her attention.

"Doesn't your job make you feel like you're a spy?" Claire asked. "No, worse than a spy. What's that word? Narc!"

"I am not a narc," I said.

"Come on," she said, "it's not like Perry wasn't trying."

"There is an art to service, and he needs some guidance. Remember the acronym of TIPS—to insure proper service."

"Poor kid will probably get fired."

"My feedback will include as many positives as negatives."

"Such as?"

"His alacrity. And let's not forget his upbeat temperament." I acted like I was racking my brain to find something else good to say. "And he was prompt, though usually that was after we reminded him that he'd forgotten to bring us something."

I made a face, as if desperate to remember any other positive attribute. Claire was trying not to laugh, but she was. "Oh, yes," I said. "That white wig of his was well kept up."

"Oh yes, extremely well kept up."

"It was one of the better white wigs in the restaurant."

"The best," Claire said. "And if called upon, I will swear to that."

"I'll hold you to that if we have to go to court."

"Does that happen?" Claire asked.

"What?"

"Have you had to testify in court because of your work?"

"It happens." In fact it had happened only the week before, but I didn't tell her that.

"And how have you done?"

"I am still in business."

Claire thought about that. "Maybe his wig wasn't really that white."

"In truth, it was a bit gray."

"His shoes, though," said Claire. "Now, they were polished."

"I'll give their luster at least a paragraph."

"I want to read that report."

"I'll get you a copy. You were a good partner."

"Really?"

"Really. You were very natural. No one would ever have guessed you were shopping the restaurant. I've been with people who all but wear 'spotter' in neon."

"How so?"

"They don't know how to do their looking subtly. Their observing is about as obvious as someone working a gun turret. Most make the mistake of constantly checking their watches for the time. The biggest giveaway, though, is a self-conscious spotter. If they're working with a partner they often clam up when staff comes around, as if afraid of being found out. You weren't like that at all. Instead of being stiff and awkward, you acted very natural and didn't come off as if you were working from a script. That's how a good audit is done. You have to let the meal unfold at its own pace, but at the same time be alert to what's going on all around you."

With a little bit of Groucho eye movement, I said, "You have good eyes."

She batted them. "I'm so pleased you noticed."

The mutual flirtation was fun, and I think that surprised us both. We had met during a moment of crisis, not the best way to get to know someone. The more time I spent with Claire, the more I wanted to spend more, though I could do without any more flying bullets.

"We'll have to do another audit together," I said. "It's always better when I bring a partner along. I get double the input that way, and it makes me less conspicuous. With two people, you can also interact more with staff. I usually try and bring extroverts along. They're the ones who get noticed, while I am just the observant wallflower."

I thought about a recent example of that, and Claire saw my smile. "What's so funny?"

"Have you heard about Wolfgang Puck's new D.C. restaurant?"

She nodded.

"Three weeks ago I did an audit there. My partner for the night was a very attractive woman. Now, as it happened, Wolfgang himself was on site, and like the knowledgeable restaurateur he is, he was making rounds of the tables. From what I observed, Wolfgang appreciates a beautiful woman as much as he does a wonderful meal. Because of my partner, he took a little extra time at our table, and I used that opportunity to ask him what wine he thought we should be ordering with our meal. After determining our entrees, Wolfgang said, 'I know the perfect wine. Let me handle the selection.' And so I did just that.

"From the first sip, it was clear that Wolfgang knows his grape squeezings. The cabernet sauvignon he selected was exquisite. When the bill was presented to me, the reason for the wine's excellence became abundantly clear. Wolfgang had selected a one-hundred-dollar bottle of wine.

"Like most successful restaurateurs, Wolfgang keeps a keen eye on the bottom line, and my expense report from that audit immediately raised red flags. He called the office and demanded to talk to me personally about the shop of his D.C. restaurant. 'How could you have ordered such an expensive bottle of wine?' he asked me, but before giving me an opportunity to answer, he started in on me again. 'We have excellent wines,' he said, 'that are far less expensive. Better yet, you should have ordered a glass or two of the house wine. Do you expect me to pay for this bottle of wine? I will not!' He did some more venting, and on maybe my sixth attempt I finally got the chance to speak. 'Mr. Puck,' I said, 'you were the one who selected the wine.' I then reminded him of his visit to our table, and my asking him for his wine recommendation, and how he had insisted upon doing the choosing for us."

"This really happened?" asked Claire.

"Cross my heart."

"So what did he do?"

"At first he tried to tell me that I should have clued him in to the fact that I was shopping the restaurant. I told him that was something I could not, and would not, ever do. I said my anonymity was essential, and that he needed to know how everyone on the staff acted, including himself. 'Apparently I am very generous with other people's money,' he said. I told him after drinking the wine I was appreciative of that fact. Then he asked, 'Did you love the wine? You better have loved that wine.' I told him it was a wonderful bottle, and he seemed to get some satisfaction out of that."

"He'll remember you next time," Claire said.

"No, he won't. He even commented about that. 'I remember the woman you were with,' he said. 'She was very beautiful. But I don't really remember you.' I told him that's the way I like it."

Looking at Claire, I reconsidered my statement. Not being noticed was the way I usually like it, but not always.

"So you didn't lose his account?"

I shook my head. "He actually ended up having a good sense of humor about the whole thing. I suppose he thought that anyone asking Wolfgang Puck to play the role of sommelier deserved to pay the price. When his own boomerang returned to hit him, he enjoyed the irony enough to be able to laugh at himself."

Claire and I continued to chat on the three-block walk from the Metro to my office. We took the elevator to the fifth floor. The name on the entry door to the office is the same as that listed on the lobby reader board: TLR Enterprises. We get few visitors to our fifth-floor offices, and because of that there is no receptionist. It's a bare-bones operation, Jenny running the office and doing the scheduling and payroll, and Brenda and Brad (Jenny calls them the "killer bees," usually with an accompanying sigh) doing the word processing and answering of phones. Even our field auditors almost never visit the offices, as all reports are submitted electronically.

I opened the door for Claire, and let her proceed ahead of me. Though a partition separated us from being able to see Stevie Lund, we weren't spared his voice.

"So," he said, playing up his southern accent, "this fellow goes into a restaurant, and sets himself down at a table. This waitress, who's quite the looker, comes over and hands him a menu. Now this fellow looks at the menu for a minute or two, and then his waitress comes back. All friendly, giving him a big smile, she asks, 'Have you decided yet?' And this fellow looks her up and down and says, 'I want a quickie.' The waitress changes her tune but fast. Right hasty, she loses her smile and her friendly, and in a frostbit voice asks, 'What would you like to order?' Well, this fellow's not deterred. He smiles at her big, and repeats, 'I want a quickie.' That gal is even less pleased to hear this the second time around. She'd just as soon spit on him as talk to him, but manages to choke out the words, 'I'll give you one last chance—what do you want?' It's clear that she's mad as a wet hen, and this fellow's not sure what to do. He looks at the menu, and looks at her. Just then a helpful diner from the next table leans over and whispers to this fellow, "I think it's pronounced *quiche*."

Over Jenny's laughter, I said, "After what we've been through, I hope you haven't been telling that joke at work."

"I'd just about given up on you, Lone Ranger," said Stevie. The week before, he'd bestowed that nickname upon me.

When he saw Claire standing at my side, Stevie made a few appreciative sounds. "Then again, there are some things worth waiting for," he said.

Stevie motioned for our forbearance, and took his leave of Jenny. "Good-bye, my lovely lotus flower," he said. "Remember, when you decide to leave your ungrateful employer I got a job just waiting for you."

He joined us in the hallway, and as I offered introductions, Stevie Lund took Claire's hand and kissed it. Some think Stevie's gallant; others consider him a dirty old man. What's agreed upon is that he's a character.

After disengaging his lips, Stevie asked me, "What's the matter with that joke?"

"It could be interpreted as inappropriate, especially in a workplace."

"Well, let me ask this pretty lady if she thinks it's inappropriate."

I didn't tell him that some people considered the phrase *pretty lady* inappropriate as well. There was a good reason why the lawyer representing Stevie had tried to limit his answers to "yes" or "no" during the recent trial.

"I think Will's right," said Claire. "It's not appropriate. What kind of a man would order quiche?"

Stevie started laughing. "She's got me there, Ranger."

"Ranger?" asked Claire.

"Yes, ma'am," Stevie said. "As in 'Hi-yo, Silver, and away.'"

Stevie put his right hand around Claire's side. "You ever see the Long Ranger show on TV?" he asked. "Hell, you're probably too young. The Lone Ranger and Tonto were always showing up in the nick of time. Our boy's gotten into the habit of doing the same thing."

"I have the notes on your employee handbook in my office," I told him. No one seemed to be able to hear me.

"Does he leave behind a silver bullet?" asked Claire.

Stevie appeared delighted that she knew about the Lone Ranger. He turned to me and said, "She's right, Ranger. Silver bullets are just what you need."

"In your case, I'm thinking a silver stake might have a better use."

Stevie wasn't about to be detoured any further from his story, and turned to Claire to tell it. "I've been in the food business my whole life," he said. "I started as a dishwasher when I was fourteen, and fifty years later I own three restaurants. The way things were looking last week, I was wondering whether I'd be going back to dishwashing again.

"The long and short of it is that I fired a bartender for giving away drinks based on what old Ranger here observed and put in his report. That same bartender turned around and said the real reason I got rid of him was for being gay. When he first sued me, I looked at it as just another nuisance suit aimed to extort some of my money. On principle, I refused to settle, even though my gutless insurance company encouraged me to. Hell, they are always ready to raise a white flag and then raise my premiums. The way I figured it, my ex-bartender's contingency lawyer would do a disappearing act when he saw that I had every intention of making a dogfight out of it. I am sure he would have, too, but suddenly the state and the feds got all interested in the case. Then it was like a whole pack of dogs barking the same tune, everybody saying this is a case of *discrimination*. And it's no longer just one lawyer looking to pick my pocket, but the government. Now I wasn't afraid of taking on some shysters, 'cuz I got a whole passel of pit bull lawyers of my own. When it comes down to a case of you show me yours and I'll show you mine, I know mine is damn well going to be bigger. But once the government got involved, all bets were off. I knew it was a whole new ball game then. Ronald Reagan, God bless him, told it true when he said that the nine most terrifying words in the English language are, 'I'm from the Government and I'm here to help.'"

Stevie stopped to shake his head. He was a showman from way back. I wanted to put a quick end to his storytelling, but he had a pretty woman who appeared interested in his tale, and for him that was more than audience enough.

"Before I knew it, all these governmental agencies are investigating me, and in their learned opinions they're saying my actions might have constituted a violation of state and federal law. No one wants to hear the reason that I canned this guy was for thievery, plain and simple. Since when is it legal to keep passing free drinks to your boyfriend? People always say the government moves slowly, but not this time. Lickety-split, the state empanels this group of three judges to hear the case and judge its merits, and I'm shitting bricks. My former bartender is trying to make himself the poster child for the Civil Rights Act. Only problem is, no poster child I know of ever posed for the kind of pictures he did."

For the sake of brevity, I tried to explain. "Just a few days before he was fired, the staff learned the bartender posed for a graphic nude pictorial in a gay pornographic magazine. Those pictures were widely circulated throughout the restaurant. Though many on the staff already assumed he was gay, the bartender didn't come out of the closet until after the magazine spread."

"The whole case hinged on what the Ranger here had to say," said Stevie. "I don't think it was looking very good for the home team before their shyster called him up for cross-examination. That same bastard had already twisted me every which way on the stand."

"You didn't exactly help your case." Stevie's salty tongue and off-color jokes were legendary. It had been easy to paint him as a homophobe.

"Jesus Christ himself would have looked like an apostate once that lawyer got his hooks into him."

"To make a long story short," I said, "we ended up convincing the judges that this was not a matter of a civil rights violation, nor was there any precedent being set here."

I tapped my watch and tried to impart a certain urgency to Stevie. "Claire and I have to leave within the hour," I said, "so we had better talk about that handbook now."

"What happened?" Claire asked.

Choosing between the two of us was an easy choice for Stevie. "Why, the Lone Ranger happened."

"I was able to document how the audit was part of an on-going series of performance reviews being conducted at the property," I said, "and how the employee was not being targeted. My testimony was believed."

Stevie thought my description was a tad short on details. "The first thing their lawyer did was try to discredit Ranger. He challenged his expertise and his credentials. He went about making a big point to the judges that Ranger didn't have a background in the hospitality industry, and sure didn't have a degree in restaurant management. I guess food service isn't something stressed at West Point."

"West Point?" Claire was suddenly on the alert. She looked at me, but I didn't meet her eyes. I hadn't wanted to bring up that connection with her father. It made me feel unworthy.

"I attended," I said, "but I didn't graduate."

Stevie said, "Our side countered their innuendo, of course. We emphasized how Ranger had spent years in the field being a hospitality consultant, and further established his credentials by showing he's been a licensed private investigator for the last four years."

"You are full of surprises," said Claire.

"Anybody can be a P.I. in Maryland," I said. "It's something to put on the company letterhead that makes the Last Resort look official."

"Things got real interesting, though," said Stevie, "when that ambulance chaser tried to challenge Ranger's recollections from the night in question. Remember, five months had passed from the time of his audit. Now sometimes yesterday's hazy enough for me, but the Lone Ranger here is the proverbial elephant. He don't forget."

Once again, I tried to cut to the chase. "I was able to recollect the circumstances surrounding the free drinks I saw dispensed."

Stevie chuckled. "You recollected a hell of a lot more than that." He drew Claire a little closer to him. "Our boy here rattled off everything that occurred during his ninety-minute audit. He had times, drinks, and descriptions of who served what. I never seen anything like it. That lawyer who was supposed to be grilling him apparently hadn't, either. He tried not to look flummoxed, but he was. Guess he saw all those dollar signs floating away. Anyway, this lawyer started getting more desperate. He implied that Ranger here must have had access to the bar tape and memorized everything on it in preparation for the trial. There were all sorts of objections, of course, and then that shyster tried to get even trickier. He started asking all these really nitpicky questions, and unbelievably, Ranger kept answering them. Finally, in exasperation, this lawyer asked if the bar television set was on during the audit, and if so, what was playing. Ranger here said that for most of his time at the bar the station was tuned in to *Late Night with David Letterman*. So their lawyer, in a sarcastic voice, asks, 'I suppose you can tell us the Top Ten topic.' And then Ranger not only tells him the topic, but he's able to give him seven out of the ten answers. I wouldn't have believed it if I hadn't seen it."

Claire looked at me as if expecting a comment. I didn't offer one.

"I knew Ranger was good," said Stevie, "but not that good. You see, about a year ago there was this attempted stick-up in the lounge of my Tin Pan Alley restaurant. This guy's drawing a gun, but before he even got it all the way out, he was cold-cocked from behind.

"The next morning I'm reading all about the incident. I got me a police report and a write-up from the bar manager. Funny thing about all this paperwork is what isn't included. Apparently, with all the excitement going on, the hero vanished before they could get his name or anything else. Hell, no one could even provide a half-decent description of our Good Samaritan. I didn't think anything more about it until I was reading an account of a bar audit performed at the Tin Pan. Something about the date and times stood out in my mind. I did a little checking and found out that Ranger here just happened to be in the bar at the time of the attempted robbery, and he decided to take the law into his own hands. The funny thing, though, is that he didn't mention that."

"When someone with an obvious drug habit and a bulge underneath their jacket enters a bar just before closing time," I said, "it does draw your attention."

"No one else seemed to notice," said Stevie.

"It's my job to notice things."

"And then just disappear?" asked Stevie.

"Who was that masked man?" Claire said. She didn't say it quite the way they did on the old show. There was a speculative quality to her question, and her look.

I met her glance, and both of us smiled. The more time I spent with her, the less I wanted to wear a mask.

"Hi-yo, Silver," I said.

But I didn't say, "Away."

CHAPTER EIGHT

While Stevie and I hammered out details on the employee handbook for his three restaurants, Claire disappeared into a vacant office. Months before, during a weak moment, I had agreed to help Stevie with the project. Though this was our third go-round, it took an hour of haggling before Stevie was satisfied with the final product. His impetus for doing the handbook was to avoid future lawsuits. Most of the time Stevie kept on topic, but he did manage to slip in a few of his jokes ("Waiter, there's a dead fly in my bottle of wine." "Well, sir, you did say you wanted something with a little body in it"), and tell a few of his stories ("And so I told this hostess of mine, 'Do not underestimate your abilities. That's my job' "). Another lawsuit, I decided, was probably inevitable.

"Well, Ranger," said Stevie, finally rising to leave, "I am much obliged. You know what they say: Friends help you move, real friends help you move bodies."

Jenny popped out of her office just in time to hear those words of wisdom. She nodded, as if blessed by the scattered pearls of a wise man. I didn't doubt I would soon be hearing those words from her lips.

"I don't mind telling you, Ranger," he said, putting his

arm around Jenny's shoulders, "last week when I was in court I was nervous as a whore attending church. With that lawsuit dismissed, I feel twenty years younger."

He turned his attention to Jenny. "Walk with me to the door, dear, and by the time we reach its portals, perhaps I'll have talked you into running away with me."

"We have been round that tree before," Jenny said.

"And such a pleasant journey it is," he said.

I returned to my desk and left the two of them to their homilies. What Stevie had said was too close to my own situation: *real friends help move bodies*. There were a few other words rattling around in my head, including the phrase *leaving the scene of a crime*. The Puritan guilt of my ancestors was kicking in and insisting that I make my overdue visit to the authorities.

Claire must have picked up on my vibes. She magically reappeared, and looked quite pleased with herself. "I just got the call I was waiting for," she said. "We need to go to the Department of Justice and meet with Leslie Drabowsky, the assistant attorney general of the criminal division. She's expecting us."

"You give any thought to bringing along a lawyer?"

"We won't need a lawyer." She made her pronouncement as if the fix was already in.

"As soon as I hear anything resembling Miranda, I am not saying another word."

"The assistant attorney general will be helping us with this matter. She's on our side."

"No general has ever been on my side."

"You didn't tell me you attended West Point."

"No, ma'am, I didn't."

"That explains some things."

"If you say so."

She sensed my reticence to talk, and didn't push the envelope any further. "Are you ready to go?" Claire asked.

"Metro, cab, or get Jenny to chauffeur us?"

"Anything but the last."

Jenny turned the corner just as the words were out of Claire's mouth. She gave both of us a dirty look, then stomped off muttering a stream of Korean under her breath. I keep threatening that I'm going to take a Berlitz course in Korean some day. According to Jenny, it won't help because her office vocabulary won't be in the course curriculum.

"I'm not sure if I'll make it back this afternoon, Jenny," I shouted.

I heard another muttered reply in Korean, or perhaps a curse, to show that she'd heard. Jenny was right. In some matters, ignorance is bliss.

We waited half a minute for the elevator. The doors finally opened, revealing a man inside wearing a business suit and holding a briefcase. Claire stepped in, and I followed. She pushed the button for the lobby, but as the doors started to close I stuck a hand out and stopped the door from closing.

"I just remembered. I left my briefcase in the office."

"Are you sure you need it?"

Instead of answering, I stepped out of the elevator and continued to hold it with my hand. Claire reluctantly followed behind me. When I heard the elevator door close behind us, I took a quick look back, then said one word to Claire: "Hurry."

She didn't have time to question the command, as I was already running toward the office. We were both breathless by the time we reached the office. Behind the closed door, Claire gasped, "What?"

"The man in the elevator didn't look at us," I said.

"What are you talking about?"

"He made a point of ignoring us. His face was expressionless."

"What difference does that make?"

"You put on a poker face when you don't want to show anything. His lack of expression made him stand out."

"You're not making any sense."

I didn't have time to give her a lecture on nonverbal communication, and how my job and my nosiness made me hyper-aware of body language.

"Does this make sense then?" I asked. "The elevator was going up when it arrived on our fifth-floor landing. When we got in, he pressed the fourth-floor button. He was going up, but suddenly planned to get out on the fourth floor."

"I miss my floor all the time," Claire said.

"Maybe that's what happened. Maybe I overreacted and read the situation all wrong. But I didn't want to take a chance and find a reception committee waiting for us on the fourth floor."

She was shaking her head, but I wasn't waiting for her reasoned arguments. I double-timed it to Jenny's office, and rushed inside. She met my appearance with a scowl but dropped it after seeing my serious expression.

"I don't have time to explain. I need you to take the stairs and go to the law office below us. If anyone stops you on the way and asks where you're going, say that you need to borrow some paper for our copier. Without attracting any attention I want you to take notice of anything you see on the stairway or in the fourth-floor hallway. As soon as you get to the law office, call me up here."

Jenny read the urgency in my voice. She asked no questions, and only offered a short editorial as she set off on her mission: "That girl is trouble."

I followed her to the door, and before she exited the office I asked, "Where are Brad and Brenda?"

"Killer bees take break together," said Jenny. Under her breath she added, "Killer bees always on break," then disappeared out into the hallway.

Claire was still regarding me as if I had lost my mind. The look intensified when I started to muscle a desk toward the entry door.

"What are you doing?" she asked.

"Moving a desk by myself because you're not helping."

"You're panicking because of a preoccupied business-man on the elevator."

"Did you notice the looseness of his jacket?"

"Why would I?"

"Because if you want to conceal a weapon, you don't wear a tight jacket."

At that she began helping me with the desk. For the first time since making the purchase, I was glad for having opted for cheap pressboard over natural wood. The press-board was heavier, and might buy us time from unwanted visitors.

The phone rang just after the barrier was put in place. "Big man on stairway between fifth and fourth floor," Jenny said. "He didn't say anything as I passed, but just stood there pre-tending to tie shoe. Outside elevator on fourth floor I saw two deliverymen standing around a big box. It looked like they were bringing up refrigerator or something like that."

Or maybe a coffin. "Don't come back up here, Jenny."

"What is wrong?"

"Call Brad and Brenda on their cell phones. Tell them to extend their break. Tell them to take the rest of the day off. Got it?"

"Okay, but—"

I hung up, dialed 911, and when asked the state of my emergency, I said there was a man out in the hallway walk-ing around with a gun. I gave the address and floor num-ber, repeated it again, and then hung up.

There was only the one door into the office. With the ele-vator and stairway covered, our options were limited. Up was a dead end, and our downward escape was blocked. Maybe the cops and their sirens would happen sooner rather than later, but that wasn't something I could count on.

I ran into my office, yanked open my window, then leaned out and looked below. Because the building is only six stories high, windows can actually be opened and closed. The joke among the tenants is that it's a suicide-friendly building. My fifth-floor office had never seemed that far up until that moment. I directed my attention to the third floor. It was a warm afternoon, and I could make out two opened windows. I gauged the distance, and then did a quick inventory. No ropes. No sheets. One extension cord, though, and some heavy computer cables. I started running in and out of offices, yanking the cables out of the computer towers and throwing everything over my shoulder. Claire followed me from doorway to doorway.

"Take off your panty hose," I said.

"What?"

"Do it."

I knew that Jenny kept two boxes of spare panty hose in the supply closet, and I ran to get them. When I returned, Claire had divested herself of her panty hose. I started lining up the cables, panty hose, and extension cord. "I'll take that," I said, reaching for Claire's reluctant offering.

I did my mental calculations, and decided it should be long enough. The panty hose would help bind the unwieldy computer cables. I hoped they would support my hundred and seventy-five pounds. Claire watched as I started tying everything together.

"You can't be serious."

Second knot done: "As a heart attack."

I had experience with making one-rope bridges. Constructing those bridges and putting them to use over obstacle courses is part of West Point team building. They also had us rappel down a seventy-five-foot cliff, but with nylon lines, a metal D ring around our waists, and a girdle of nylon rope called a Swiss seat which worked as a safety net. Unfortunately, I didn't have any of those things in the office.

Claire looked out of my office window and apparently didn't like what she saw. "There's no fire esc—"

"No."

I finished with the fourth knot. Two more.

"Get your gun out," I said.

She went and retrieved it, and then asked, "What did Jenny see?"

"People who shouldn't be here."

"You already called the police. Why are you doing this?"

My hands navigated the fifth knot. "Insurance."

"I hope you're wrong."

"That's two of us."

Then we both heard something at the door, the first exploratory push. Then there was a second attempt at entry, this time more forceful. The Big Bad Wolf was starting in on his huffing and puffing.

Sixth and last knot done. I grabbed the makeshift rope and ran to my office, Claire following just behind. At the back of my desk I looped the rope around the leg closest to the window and pulled tight. Everything cinched up and seemed to hold. I jumped up, threw a quick loop under Claire's rib cage, and cinched it. She wanted to object but I didn't allow her the opportunity. I took the gun from her hand, set the safety, and then looped it through my belt inside my pants.

"We're going to play leapfrog," I said. "You'll have to bypass the fourth floor. They're gathered there. Go through the first opened window on the third floor."

I helped her up to the windowsill, and then wrapped the line around her hand so that Claire had a loop to hold on to. She was shaking, but game. We could both hear the squealing of a moving desk.

"Hurry," I said. "I'll be coming right after you."

Claire nodded, and then went over the railing. I braced a leg against the wall and started playing out the line, but not as fast as I would have liked. While I belayed, Claire kept slowing for footholds along the way and I chafed at her progress. *Move, move, move,* I wanted to shout. I continued to play out the line, feeling her progress while also hearing the encroachment of the enemy. It was all going to be too close. Then I felt some slack in the line, and stuck my head out the window to see. Claire was pulling herself through the opened window, but at a turtle's pace.

"Come on, come on," I said, watching her get one foot over the railing, then a hand on the window, then her butt up on the sill.

Though I didn't have a view of the entry door from where I was, I could hear explosive grunts and the thudding of shoulders against resisting wood. Inch by inch, the desk barricade was being breached. I looked below, chafing to act, but I had to wait for the baton to be handed to me. Claire finally disappeared from view.

I couldn't wait any longer, and straddled over the sill and started downward, going hand over hand. It had been a long time since I had rappelled. Now I barely felt qualified to say the word, let alone practice it. I didn't do much kicking off the building, though, not trusting my makeshift ladder. During the descent I focused on one grip at a time, fighting the temptation to look up to see if I was in someone's crosshairs. Amazingly, no one on the street or in the offices had taken notice of Claire's downward passage, and I didn't seem to be the object of any finger-pointing. I skirted by the fourth-floor windows and continued downward.

The computer cable rope was not something you'd want to use on Everest. The line was thin and slippery, and I found myself sliding and hard-pressed to get a decent grip. My brake-stops were the panty hose, allowing me something I could grab onto. That was an unexpected bonus. The panty hose stretched very thin, but didn't appear in imminent danger of ripping. One more use for panty hose that Help Me, Heloise could offer as a helpful tip. *When escaping from bad guys, always remember the efficacy of a panty hose ladder.*

Claire had unleashed herself, but I could feel her anchoring the bottom of the rope. I continued on my way down. It wasn't pretty. Grip, skid, and then hold on for dear life. It probably didn't take me more than ten seconds to navigate the two floors, but my heart was in my throat for most of the ride.

I wriggled and flopped through the window, and Claire helped to land me. The office we were in was very well appointed, and I remembered the space was rented by an accounting firm. I listened through the open window for any sounds of alarm coming from upstairs. Still nothing. I flexed my rope-burned hands, brushed at my coat and pants, took a deep breath, and then extended an elbow for Claire. She encircled her arm through mine and I could feel her trembling. Smart woman.

"We walk through this office like we own it," I said.

She nodded, and we started forward. The office space was much larger than mine, with a completely different layout. We followed a maze of cubicles, and several people looked up in surprise. I nodded and smiled, and they responded in kind. We wended our way toward an exit, but unlike my office, they had a receptionist. She didn't appear completely won over by my affable routine, looking a bit confused by our sudden appearance, but she didn't stop and ask us for our papers, either.

I opened the door enough to look right and left, saw that all was clear, and tugged on Claire's arm. We walked at a brisk pace, but not so fast as to be noticeable, toward the stairwell.

"We are going to have to be very quiet on the stairs," I said. "Someone might still be stationed a floor above. What I want you to do is give me a fifteen-second head start. They know what you look like, but might not know my face."

She nodded, and then we continued our navigating through the shark-filled waters. When we reached the door to the stairwell, I raised a cautionary hand. She waited, and

I soundlessly opened the door just enough for us to pass through. It wasn't one of those open stairwells, which was a good thing. Our line of sight was only up to the next landing, and there was no sign of the sentry. With a patience born of necessity, I gently closed the door behind us, and then motioned for Claire to wait.

I stayed to the side of the stairwell and tiptoed down the stairs, doing my best to make haste slowly.

At the bottom of the stairs I put on my business face, an expression that combined being overworked, underappreciated, and dreaming of a tropical island somewhere. The final layer of the look was that of wistful disappointment, the certain knowledge that the pipe dream of retiring to that island wasn't going to happen in this lifetime. It's one of my looks I have been practicing for years, most of the time unwittingly. It's the same unguarded expression on the faces of most people working jobs they don't love. Patting my shirt, I felt the gun. It was an insurance policy I preferred not to use.

I opened the door only enough for me to slide out, and hoped that the noise of its closing wouldn't carry upstairs. Without seeming to take notice of anything around me, I started toward the street. There were three people in the lobby area. Two of them were waiting for the elevator, and I remembered having seen them in the building before. I also thought I recognized the third individual from the night before. He'd been part of the group trying to kill me. Luckily, there was no mutual recognition. I continued walking, thinking desperately through the countdown in my head.

Eleven, ten . . .

Claire wouldn't be so fortunate. The guard was positioned in an alcove, with a perfect view to the elevator or door to the stairway. As soon as Claire opened the door to the stairwell, she would immediately be in his sights.

Eight . . .

With my back to where he was, I came to a sudden stop and reached into my coat pocket. I was sure the sentry was watching me. At that moment he might even be reaching inside a pocket of his own to have a gun at the ready.

Six . . .

I palmed my hand and lifted it up to my ear, counting on the fact that some cell phones are so small that they are hidden in the depths of a hand. "Hello?"

Five . . .

I turned around, offering him a view of my head that blocked his line of sight to the right hand that was now held up to my ear. With a scowl, I said, "Now? But I just came down. Can't it wait?"

He seemed to visibly relax.

Four, three . . .

"Jesus," I said, shaking my head in disgust. "All right, I'll come up." I pantomimed shoving the phone into my coat pocket, started walking toward the elevator, then seemed to awaken to the fact that the door was closing. "Hold it!" I yelled, counting on the fact that it was too late for the door to be reversed.

Two, one . . .

I slowed up in apparent disgust at having missed my upward train. The sentry was only about eight steps away, and I could feel his eyes on me. He didn't appear to be spooked, but neither did he look totally relaxed.

Two things happened at the same time: his phone started to ring and the stairwell door began to open. As he reached into his pocket and looked past me to the opening door, I charged him. There was an instant of indecision before he dropped the phone and reached inside his coat. He was pulling the gun free with his right hand, while his left arm was coming up in a defensive posture. I feinted as if I was going for his face, and then came down hard on the instep behind the ankle of his forward leg.

I heard the crack of bone, followed an instant later by the explosion of his gun. My attack had caused him to raise his shooting hand, and the shot went high. I followed through with a head butt and shove, and he fell backward, his gun sliding across the marble floor. He didn't run after it; his broken ankle prevented that. For the moment, at least, he was like a turtle upended, flailing with all fours.

The dropped phone rang for a third time. Between its first and third rings, a battle had taken place. My guess was that the call was being made from the fifth floor.

Claire stood frozen just outside the stairway door. "Run," I shouted.

She only had to be told once, and followed me in a sprint to the sidewalk. I paused long enough to look all around the front of the building. As far as I could determine, no alarm had been raised and no enemies were waiting. Behind us, the phone suddenly stopped ringing.

"This way," I said.

I walked in the direction opposite the Metro stop, assuming that's where they would head first. We kept close to the buildings, moving in and out of foot traffic. Our immediate problem was getting away. Bethesda isn't like New York City, with fleets of cabs cruising for fares. I had to arrange transport another way.

We came to a corner where a stoplight had traffic backed up, and I quickly scanned the drivers and their cars. Three I passed up immediately: a businessman in his Beemer, a thirtyish woman driving a Toyota Supra and talking into a cell phone, and a crew-cut older man in his GM Yukon.

The winner was a white woman in her mid-twenties with bottled red hair and long loop earrings driving a Ford Focus. On the back of the car was a slightly faded George

Washington University bumper sticker. Next to that was a newer bumper sticker from a local radio station that rewarded listeners sporting its call letters with cash prizes if picked out by their search patrol.

Her driver's-side window was down. "There's our ride," I said to Claire, and swooped in on the vehicle.

"What's your favorite radio station?" I asked and waited expectantly with a big smile. The station's shortened nickname, I remembered, was "the Rocking Z."

Caught off guard, the driver froze for a moment, her face registering her uncertainty of both me and my question.

Claire came up behind me and chimed in, "I am afraid we need your answer now."

The woman seemed to be reassured by the sight of Claire, and blurted out the station's call letters on her bumper sticker.

"You're a winner!" I said. "What's your name?"

"Shelley Reeves!" She was slapping the wheel and squealing with laughter.

The light changed. "Just pull over to the curb, Shelley, and collect your green."

She didn't have to be told a second time. As Claire and I made our way back to the sidewalk we could see Shelley carrying on in her car. She was acting as if she had won a million dollars. I didn't listen to the station often, but seemed to remember that those tagged by the prize patrol won five hundred dollars, an amount I didn't have.

I pulled out my wallet, withdrew three hundred dollars, and walked up to Shelley. Maybe if I just handed her the green she wouldn't notice.

"It's your lucky day, Shelley," I said, and passed her the money.

"This is so great!"

Trust is a rare commodity in the world these days. She started counting the money.

"Three hundred dollars from the Rocking Z," I told her. "It's a shame you weren't tuned in to our station. That would have earned you five hundred dollars."

"Oh." Shelley sounded disappointed, but she wasn't distracted enough to stop with her counting.

"But you are eligible for Rocking Z's million-dollar grand prize drawing."

She immediately brightened: "Really?"

"It's going to be held two weeks from now."

"Good luck!" said Claire with cheerleader enthusiasm.

"Do you have a business card for the drawing?" I asked.

"Um," said Shelley, "not really. I just started in graduate school, so I'm working this part-time job."

"That's okay," I said. I pulled out a pen and pad. "We'll need a number to reach you, though," I said, "and you'll have to spell your first and last name for me."

"Sure."

"Maybe you can do us a favor," I said. "We've been searching for a winner for the last hour, and we parked a ways from here. Could you give us a lift while we get your information?"

"My feet would really appreciate it," said Claire with a well-timed giggle.

I wasn't even aware that she knew how to giggle.

"Sure," said Shelley. "It's kind of messy, though."

"You ought to see the station's van."

We didn't give her time to reconsider, but were already piling into her car. "We're about a mile north of here," I said, "on Wisconsin Avenue."

"You did walk far," Shelley said.

"And to give away money yet."

"I thought the prize patrol drove around in a van."

"We do. Today we just decided to go the pedestrian route. We never imagined it would take us so long to spot a winner."

I didn't know enough about the station's promotion to try and fake it very well, so I changed subjects by clicking my pen. "Now about the spelling of your name," I said. "We want to get it right for that million-dollar check."

"Oh, God! That would be like the greatest thing that could ever happen." I dutifully wrote her name down, and then jotted her home number, work number, cell number, and the telephone number of her parents into my notepad. Shelley didn't want to take any chances on missing that million-dollar call.

Whenever lottery winners are asked the inevitable question of how they intend to spend their money, their invariable response is, "I am not sure." Shelley didn't have that problem. She offered a travel itinerary, the car she would buy, the house she wanted, and the city where she intended to settle. As we neared the ride's end, I felt bad for the deception. Shelley's enthusiastic daydreaming was positively beguiling. Claire played into her conversation, expressing delight at all of Shelley's plans. Claire's acting ability continued to surprise me, especially in light of what we had just endured.

We continued along Wisconsin until I told Shelley to turn on West Cedar. Two blocks from our destination, I directed her to pull over. For her sake, and ours, it was better she not know where we were going.

We thanked her for the ride, and Shelley turned around and said, "No, thank *you*. Thanks a million."

She realized what she said and started laughing. "Knock wood," Shelley said, searched around in vain, and ended up putting a knuckle to her head. She drove off with a smile, no doubt fantasizing about a big payday and not noticing there was no Rocking Z prize patrol van where she left us.

"I probably should have prepared her for the disappointment," I said. "I could have clued her in to the fact that the government would tax half of all the winnings anyway. That would have put a pin in the million-dollar balloon."

"Why spoil her fun?"

"It would have assuaged my conscience. When you go from a million to half a million it almost puts my story in the white lie category."

"Is that so?"

Both of us were acting a little too cute and casual, dancing around what had just happened. Claire spotted the rental car sign and divined my intention.

"I intend to pay you back for everything," she said, "including your time."

"I'll be billing for combat pay."

At the rental window I decided not to be Mr. Dodd. It was possible that my identity had been flagged at the Blue Crab Inn, and I didn't want to take that chance. Besides, it was the last day of April anyway. I pulled out Mr. Kirk Ellis's license and credit card, and waited while they were processed. Because I keep all my identities separate, I was relatively sure no connection could be made between them. Still, when handed the keys to a car, I was glad Mr. Ellis had passed muster.

We drove off in a Honda Civic, an unpretentious car with a built-in invisibility quality. Claire didn't question the route I was taking, though it was obvious that we weren't headed in the direction of the Department of Justice. We didn't talk, and I used the quiet time to consider all that had happened. I drove to North Bethesda, putting what I hoped was more distance between us and our attackers, and ended up in the parking lot of the cavernous White Flint Mall.

Claire took notice of our surroundings and said, "Bloomingdale's. How did you know it was my favorite store?"

"Maybe you should find a new favorite, one that sells Kevlar vests."

She looked at me without smiling, waiting for what I had to say.

"What happened earlier?"

Claire shook her head. "I don't know."

"You made some calls. Did you tell someone where you were?"

She hesitated, nodded slightly, and said, "No."

I laughed without being amused. "You're not a very good liar, Claire."

"Why do you think I'm lying?"

"You mean other than the fact that you didn't deny lying? And then there was your classic mixed message as well. While your lips were saying 'no,' your head was nodding, 'yes.'"

"You're trying to trick me."

"No. I am trying to get a straight answer out of you."

"I gave out the telephone number of your home and your office to my contact. That's all. The person I gave the numbers to would not have given those numbers to anyone else."

"Did you give my name?"

She shrugged her shoulders. "I suppose so. Yes. But that was necessary to get us the appointment with the assistant attorney general."

"So how did they find us?"

"It's possible word leaked out of the Department of Justice. But I think it's more likely that they tracked us down through your credit card number."

"There are firewalls between the real me and Harold Dodd."

"Then why did you use your Kirk Ellis's credit card for the rent-a-car?"

"I did that as a precaution."

"You were worried that all your identities might have been compromised." I wasn't the only one of us observing the other.

"Maybe I've been given good reason to be worried. Who the hell are we up against?"

"I don't know."

"Lawrence Deering worked for ATF."

"I never saw him before last night," Claire said.

I thought about that, and considered our situation. There seemed to be only one solution. "Let's go shopping," I said.

We skipped Bloomies, opting instead for a phone store where I bought a cell phone. Instead of activating a calling plan I prepaid for air time. I wanted to keep as many buffers as possible between me and my enemies.

When we returned to the car I didn't immediately hand over the phone to Claire. She wanted to call Assistant Attorney General Leslie Drabowsky and explain why we were late, but I decided that call should wait a few minutes. We needed an update on the Deering situation, and I wanted to see if the attack on my office had made the news.

The rental's pre-sets were easy listening, so I scanned for something more interesting and settled on a news-and-talk station. Usually the station was far more talk than news, but I caught one of the headline news stories with which they punctuated the show.

With dramatic intonation, the news correspondent said, "There are new developments in a murder investigation that link the assassination attempt on Republican presidential candidate Congressman Mark Stanton with the murder of ATF Special Agent Lawrence Deering."

Claire's head almost did a Linda Blair, and her eyes fixed upon the radio as if she was staring at a television set. I turned up the volume.

"Lab and ballistics reports show that the gun used in an attempt to assassinate Congressman Mark Stanton appears to be the same firearm that was used in the killing of Lawrence Deering last night in the courtyard of a Maryland inn. According to the ATF, Deering was initially brought into the case in January when a bombing occurred at Stanton headquarters. His investigation was broadened after the assassination attempt on Stanton, and when other presidential candidates received death threats."

The broadcaster paused for effect, and the timbre of his voice deepened: "Although no arrest warrants have been issued at this time, authorities say they are looking to question thirty-two-year-old Claire Harrington. Those close to the investigation say that there is evidence that links Harrington not only to the shooting of Stanton but also to the stalking of at least one other presidential candidate. There are also reports from several witnesses saying that a woman matching Harrington's description was seen talking with Deering just minutes before his shooting death. Authorities are advising the public that Harrington might be armed and dangerous."

Claire's normally pale complexion turned a sickly white that extended even to her lips. Her head swayed, and I was afraid she was going to faint, but she managed to steady herself.

"No," she whispered.

Then, instead of shouting vehement denials, Claire said, "How can I undo that kind of damage? Even a retraction won't be enough."

"Won't be enough for what?"

"I'm tainted by the scandal," she said, doing her thinking out loud. "My only chance for vindication will be to prove that my father was murdered, and that everything else occurred as a result of that. That's the only way."

"You care to tell me what the hell you're talking about?"

"It's very complicated."

I didn't like that answer. From the first she had been secretive, holding information back. I opened my mouth to tell her that, to demand some answers, but she spoke before I could.

"I'd like to hire you," Claire said.

"What do you mean?"

"I need a private investigator. I need you."

CHAPTER NINE

The so-called "Open Media Forum" was neither open nor was it really a forum. The Candidate was meeting with a handful of invited media. In the tried-and-true method of most politicians, the Candidate wasn't really answering their questions but instead giving them snippets from his stump speeches. In this way he avoided questions he didn't like, but at the same time tried to make it appear as if he wasn't sidestepping any issues. Answering in this manner allowed him the freedom of not having to measure his words or thoughts. With the cloth already cut, all he did was follow the pattern. This saved him from having to worry about being misinterpreted, and also spared him from having to think. He was an actor reciting lines while his real thoughts were often elsewhere. One of the rules of political survival is never to speak your mind anywhere near the proximity of an open microphone. In the 2000 election George Bush had leaned over to running mate Dick Cheney and said, "There's Adam Clymer, major league asshole from *The New York Times*." The open mike caught his comments, and they became a national news story.

The public could forgive profanity a lot more easily than they could honesty. The Candidate kept his answers short and simple; those made for the best sound bites. His advisers counseled him that the best strategy for victory was to accommodate short attention spans and appeal to the lowest common denominator. That's what he was doing now.

Naturally, the media did their best to ambush him, but the Candidate had learned from the mistakes of others. In the 2000 campaign Bush had been asked to name the leaders of Taiwan, Chechnya, and Pakistan, nations that were then in the national news. Bush hadn't been able to come up with the name of even one leader. The Candidate had prepared for that trap and countless others. His staff had prepped him by giving him index cards with the names of world leaders and the nations they governed, and had quizzed him tirelessly. He knew who was running every banana republic and third-world nation. Those weren't the only index cards his staff had force-fed him. He had digested so much information that he felt like a human atlas. Even his enemies conceded that he was well versed in international issues.

Of course, the media was always trying to set new traps. The Candidate acknowledged a hand, and the reporter stood up.

"I wonder if you could clarify some issues, sir. You are known to be an ardent supporter of the death penalty, and yet you call yourself 'pro-life.' Do you see any inconsistency in your positions?"

Such a transparent ambush, the Candidate thought. The reporter hadn't even tried to hide his snares.

With gravity, and emphatic hand gestures, he said, "I believe in the rights of states to deal with convicted criminals in a manner that is in keeping with the wishes of their citizenry and the laws of both the federal and state judiciary. As commander in chief, I will uphold the laws of the land whether they apply to capital punishment, abortion, or whatever other issues are before me."

The Candidate addressed another raised hand, and was asked about how he planned to build up the military without raising taxes. While he offered up another scripted answer, he let his mind drift to what was really on his mind.

Claire Harrington should have been dead by now. The plan had always been first the father, then the daughter. There really had been no other way to deal with her. The world was too small now, and news too instantaneous. It had been easier hiding problems in the past. In 1921 the Republican National Committee had sent Mrs. Carrie Phillips and her husband on a slow cruise around Asia to keep the media from asking about her long-standing affair with Harding. As it turned out, though, Mrs. Phillips was only one of the women Harding was dallying with. There was also Nan Britton, with whom Harding fathered an illegitimate child. Britton later said their girl had been conceived in Harding's senate office. When Harding became president, their relationship continued. After Harding died, Britton admitted that they had had sex in an office closet at the White House.

Of course, sexual peccadilloes paled in comparison with other scandals in the Harding administration, notably Teapot Dome. The American public hadn't known what they were getting with Warren G. Harding. He was a compromise candidate, selected by a group of powerful senators in a smoke-filled room. The senators and power-brokers had asked Harding if he had any skeletons in his closet, and he had opted not to tell them about his nervous breakdowns, time spent in a sanitarium, and sundry affairs. Money brokers always wanted those assurances. To fill the campaign coffers, the Candidate had been similarly vetted. Like Harding, he had chosen not to answer fully. He liked to think of it as an omission.

The Candidate thought about that skeleton in his closet. He was making sure it would stay there forever. He was burying the bones.

The Buck Stops Here. Those words had been written on

a placard sitting on Harry S. Truman's desk. Truman had to grow up in the job very quickly after FDR's death. As vice president he had been kept out of the inner circle. FDR hadn't even told Truman about the Manhattan Project. It wasn't until Truman became president that he learned our country had developed the atomic bomb. Having the bomb and using it were two different matters. As commander in chief, Truman had to make the tough decision to drop that bomb.

The Candidate was ready for those kinds of difficult choices. He knew that no one served as president without getting bloody hands. Every president was forced to condone one form of murder or another. Death came with the job. The president was responsible for military actions, reprisals, and war. Life-and-death decisions were part and parcel of the presidency. By acting as he had, the Candidate had already shown his mettle, had shown he was ready for that top job.

What he had done was really nothing more than on-the-job training. The nation needed a tough leader, a man who wouldn't shrink from hard decisions. In his mind, the Candidate believed he was that man. The office would validate him. For as long as he could remember, his life had been one campaign after another. It had all led to this. It was his moment, his destiny, and nothing was going to get in the way of that.

The Candidate acknowledged the raised hand of another reporter.

CHAPTER TEN

I listened to Claire's job offer with incredulity. "You need a good lawyer a lot more than you need me as a private investigator."

She shook her head. "I won't be put on the defensive any longer. If I get entangled in some kind of legal battle, that will work to their advantage. At this point, I am only a suspect."

"From the sounds of it, you are about an hour away from being a fugitive."

"Then we'd better make use of that hour."

"In the words of Tonto, 'What do you mean *we*, white man?'"

"*We* need to investigate my father's death."

"I'm not qualified."

"I've seen how observant you are. We're still alive because you notice things."

"We've been lucky and we can't count on that luck lasting much longer. You have to be smart about this. The first thing you need to do is hire the best lawyer in town."

"Even the best lawyer might not be able to prevent me from being railroaded into jail."

"There's a thing called bail."

"There is if I live long enough to get it. Who's to say that a

Jack Ruby won't be waiting for me?" She paused a moment before adding, "Besides, I won't allow myself to be taken away in handcuffs. That kind of disgrace could never be forgotten or forgiven. The very thought of that is unacceptable."

By the tone of her voice it was clear that the fear of being humiliated scared her more than anything else, something that didn't make sense to me.

"Getting killed is what should be unacceptable. Everything else is a moot point."

"Not for me."

She didn't elaborate, and I was tired of trying to divine her secret agenda. "I can't help you."

"You *won't* help me. You are a licensed private investigator. I am coming to you as a client. By establishing terms we can come to agreement on a verbal contract."

"Will that verbal contract include a Get Out of Jail Free pass? Do the phrases 'obstructing justice' and 'aiding and abetting a felon' ring any bells?"

"As of this moment, I have not been charged with a crime. Accepting me as a client now would likely be a mitigating factor in freeing you from criminal liability."

"I would hardly call that bulletproof."

"You have seen their methods, and how they will stop at nothing. Are those the people you want running our country?"

"I am one person. You need the cavalry. Bring the FBI in on this, or the Secret Service, or Homeland Security, or Justice."

"What about the ATF?" she asked. "Lawrence Deering worked for them."

Her point was well taken. It was hard knowing where to turn.

Claire pressed on: "Besides, do you think anyone in those agencies will believe my story? If you hadn't been through all this with me, would you believe my story?"

"There has to be evidence—"

She interrupted. "From the sound of it, they have manufactured the so-called evidence to point my way. What they have done is put the smoking gun in my hand."

I didn't answer right away, and Claire must have detected that I was weakening. "Edmund Burke said, 'All that is necessary for the triumph of evil is for good men to do nothing.' During his lifetime, my father often reflected upon those words. He used them as a yardstick by which he tried to measure his own actions."

It was a favorite line of my own, or at least it had been once, but I didn't tell her that.

"When you heard the news account of Deering's death, the first thing you said was that I was being set up. At the time I didn't believe you, but now I do."

Sometimes you don't want to be right. This felt like one of those times.

"I am not asking for your assistance only for myself," said Claire. "This goes beyond me. This is service to your country."

"Oh, shit," I said. She was hitting below the belt now. All that was missing from her recruitment campaign was her humming "The Battle Hymn of the Republic."

"In your heart you know I'm right."

"I think that was a failed political slogan."

"People tried to kill you."

"I decided not to take that personally."

"You went to West Point. You took an oath to defend this country against its enemies."

"I never graduated from there, and never got my commission in the army."

"Have you forgotten the notions of duty, honor, and country? That, more than anything else, is what West Point stands for. Those are the ideals my father took away from that university, ideals that served him so well."

"Are you sure about that? Maybe those ideals killed him."

"Help me to find that out, then."

I opened my mouth but I honestly didn't know what I

was going to say. For the longest time I had kept a side of me bottled up, and now a cork had been loosened and all the old yearnings were bubbling to the surface. Putting aside my dream of a military career was the most difficult thing I had ever done. Now, it almost felt as if I were being given the opportunity to serve again. It was foolishness, though. I was at a stage in my life where I knew more about analyzing food service than I did battlefield tactics.

I looked at Claire, and if my goal was to think rationally, that wasn't where I should have been staring. The more I looked at her, the more I wanted to look at her. I wanted to help, wanted to please her, wanted to be with her even when doing those things made no sense.

"To get their way," Claire said, "these people are apparently willing to do anything. Their actions are the politics of extremism, the kind of tactics you would expect from Brown Shirts, or the Red Guard, from the minions of Hitler and Pol Pot and Stalin, but it's not happening far away or in another time, but right here and now on the hallowed soil of our country."

MacArthur's words—my words recited in Washington Hall—came back to me: *Whether our strength is being sapped by deficit financing indulged in too long, by federal paternalism grown too mighty, by power groups grown too arrogant, by politics grown too corrupt, by crime grown too rampant, by morals grown too low, by taxes grown too high, by extremists grown too violent; whether our personal liberties are as thorough and complete as they should be.*

I thought of MacArthur's farewell address to the Academy: *The long gray line has never failed us. Were you to do so, a million ghosts in olive drab, in brown khaki, in blue and gray, would rise from their white crosses, thundering those magic words: duty, honor, country.*

"A million ghosts," I said.

Her brow furrowed. "Excuse me?"

"I surrender," I said.

* * *

Claire's fugitive status required us to stay on the move. We talked while I drove. Just staying mobile was not a battle plan. As of yet we had an unknown enemy whose assets and resources were also unspecified. We were trying to fight blind. Intel was the first thing we needed to gather.

"You believe something happened about sixteen years ago," I said, "that somehow incriminates one of the presidential candidates. You also believe your father was privy to whatever happened."

Claire nodded.

"On several occasions you've spoken of your father's doing research on a book. What was he writing?"

The memory brought a smile to Claire's lips. "He jokingly called it his magnum opus. He'd been working on it for years, and whenever we talked I would always ask him if it was finished yet, and he would tell me it was still a work in progress. The book was on American political scandals."

"Have you read it?"

Claire shook her head. "Occasionally he would give me a few pages to look at, but those were doled out sparingly. I was going to read it after his death, and try to see to its publication, but I got"—she had to think of the right word—"sidetracked."

"What's it titled?"

"The working title is *Political Passions*, but my father usually called it his '*Et tu, Brute*.'"

"And you, Brutus." The words of Julius Caesar directed at his friend Brutus as he was stabbing Caesar to death. Few political assassinations rivaled the intrigue of that death. It was arguably the most famous political assassination of all time.

My neck started doing its dance, with the tingling extending along my vertebrae. Garret Harrington's book suddenly sounded like a must-read to me.

"Where can we get a copy of the book?"

She hesitated before saying, "I imagine it's somewhere in his study at the family house in South Carolina."

"You don't sound very sure of yourself."

"His study"—she paused before continuing—"was a mess."

I remembered Claire's saying that her father had died at his desk. It had probably been hard for her to go through the room where he was shot.

The gun reminded me of something else that was troubling me. "According to those news reports, the gun that killed your father is the same weapon used in the Stanton assassination attempt. How do you explain that?"

Claire shook her head. "I can't."

I let the silence build and Claire finally started talking again. "I was shocked when I heard that. I don't know why my father's murderer also wanted to kill Mark Stanton."

We both thought about it. Claire must have decided confession was good for the soul. "There's a second gun," she said, her voice little more than a whisper. "I think it's an exact duplicate of the one I have."

She reflected for another moment before adding, "It looked just like my gun, looked just like the gun that killed him."

"Go on."

Claire looked embarrassed. "I found it in Father's safety deposit box in Charleston. Before he died, I was certain he didn't own a gun. That's what I kept telling the police. That's one of the reasons I was so certain he didn't kill himself. When I discovered that second gun I was devastated, because here I had been arguing the whole time that he couldn't have even owned one gun, let alone two."

"Where's the gun now?"

"It's still in his safe-deposit box. I was afraid to tell anyone else about it. The police were already digging in their heels on their suicide theory, and I didn't want to give them

what they would have certainly construed as further sub-
stantiation of that. Even after discovering that second gun I
was still convinced he was murdered."

Most people have guns because they like to think they
provide personal protection. Having a gun in a bank
wouldn't have done Garret Harrington any good.

"Do you have the key to his safety deposit box?"

"It's at the house. I returned it to Father's hiding place in
the study. Father didn't tell me what was in that safe-deposit
box, but I wish he had. It wouldn't have come as such a
shock to me. In retrospect, I can now see why he didn't set
up the safe-deposit box in a bank in town."

"Was anything else in the box?"

She shook her head.

"Do you know how long he had the safe-deposit box?"

"According to the slip I signed at the bank, he opened it
sixteen years ago. Father made me a signatory on the box
just a few months before he died."

"Let's go get a book and a gun," I said, but instead of traveling south I got on Interstate 95 going north.

"Where are you going?" Claire asked.

"We need money," I said, "and they know I'm with you. I'll
stop at some ATMs on this route. If they're tracking my banking records maybe they'll think we're headed to New York
City. I want those transactions to be our only credit card or
banking activity. We'll have to steer clear of hotels or motels."

"We can stay with my best friend, Jenny Mitchell, on
Hilton Head Island," said Claire. "She and her husband,
Paul, have a house in Port Royal."

I shook my head. "That would be an obvious place for
them to search for you."

"So if hotels and friends are out, where will we stay?"

"We'll camp somewhere tonight."

Claire gave me a questioning look. "Don't worry," I told
her. "I'll get the fixings for s'mores."

We stopped at four ATMs, and I took out the maximum

amount of money from each, before reversing our route. I exited from 95, traveling west and then south. I bought clothes and camping gear at a Maryland WalMart, and purchased a book on campgrounds of the southeast. As we drove, Claire read from its descriptions to help us decide where to stay.

"No federal or state campgrounds," I said. "Better to avoid that kind of potential scrutiny."

Claire listed some stipulations of her own. "Flush toilets on the property," she insisted.

"Off the beaten path," I said, "but not out in the middle of nowhere."

"Showers would be nice."

"Not one of those RV parks. I want a camping area primarily designated for tents, not Winnebagos."

We settled on a campground in Central Virginia that was less than a two-hour drive from Washington, D.C. I hoped that would be far enough away from our enemies. Now that the danger wasn't so imminent, I began to feel angry about being chased away from my workplace. There was a sense of violation. They had come on my turf, and forced me to leave. No, worse than that, I had fled. Overdue guilt kicked in, and I pulled out my flip phone and called Jenny.

"Can you talk?" I asked.

"Office closed today," she said. "Gas leak."

"People are there, aren't they? It's hard for you to say anything, isn't it?"

"You're right as rain."

"I am going to be away for a few days."

"Okay-dokey."

I had the impression Jenny was condoning my flight, at least within limits. "I am sorry."

"It is always something," Jenny said, "but right now I could chew nails and fart tacks."

"That's not the high-fiber diet I'd recommend. I wish I

hadn't left you holding the bag, but I'll make it up to you. I promise."

The gentleness in her voice belied her reply: "Wish in one hand, shit in other, and see which gets filled up quicker."

"You take care as well," I said, and ended our conversation.

"We'll get gas at the next exit," I told Claire. "You'll want to change into that clothing I bought you before we get to the campground. I went for mostly oversized T-shirts and sweats."

"As a rule, I don't wear T-shirts or sweat suits."

"I figured that out all on my own. I also figured out that the people looking for you are expecting a fashion plate, not someone in sweats."

With misgivings, Claire dug out the articles of clothing I had bought. Her look of consternation continued to grow as she inspected my selections.

"These are all quite horrid."

"They were out of good Republican cloth coats."

"I am beginning to believe you really are a Democrat."

Perhaps I had been a little sadistic with my choices. The shirt Claire was holding had a picture of a Hershey Bar and the caption *If They Don't Have Chocolate in Heaven, I Ain't Going*.

She shuddered for effect and made me laugh. "I was torn between that one or getting you the T-shirt which read '*Next Mood Swing, Six Minutes.*'"

Not sparing any sarcasm, she said, "I can see what a difficult choice that must have been."

"Don't feel picked on. My novelty shirts aren't any better."

She arched a disbelieving eyebrow, then reached for the bags in the backseat and started rummaging through them. Claire puzzled over my FISH EXCUSES T-shirt, which was filled with explanations: *The Water Is Too Warm; The Moon Is in the Wrong Quarter;* and *The Scale Broke Under His Weight and He Fell Back In.* She shook her head, then using the tips of her fingers as if holding something that might be carrying a communicable disease, she folded the shirt and gingerly put it back in the bag.

I said, "You haven't found my favorite one. It says, 'I Didn't Climb to the Top of the Food Chain to Be a Vegetarian.'"

"To paraphrase Lily Tomlin's observation about the individual who created Muzak, doesn't it worry you to think that the person who came up with that clever shirt is inventing something else at this very moment?"

"Hope springs eternal."

"Is there any other reason besides public humiliation for us to be wearing such outfits?"

"I thought that was a good enough reason. And you'll see very little formal wear in campgrounds."

I paid cash at a gas station, and Claire and I used the restrooms to change. For me it was a relief trading in my button-down shirt for a T-shirt, and wingtips for sneakers. Claire wasn't quite as enthusiastic about her change of clothing. She slunk back to the car, and then sank down into the passenger seat where she worked at adjusting her red, white, and blue baseball cap. There was a bald eagle on it, but the rendering was not exactly Audubon-like. The heavily muscled eagle was chomping down on a cigar and looked ready to kick some butt. Claire took notice of my observing, and by managing not to smile I probably saved my life.

"The loose clothing hides your figure," I said, "and the shadow of the cap effectively covers your face. It will be difficult for anyone to recognize you."

"Thank God for that," she said.

Our intended camping spot was along Virginia's Lake Anna. The area was near some of the Civil War's most famous battle sites, and Claire perked up as we approached Fredericksburg.

"My father was a Civil War buff," she said. "He used to take me on pilgrimages to this area. I was introduced to where all the fighting took place around Spotsylvania, and on one occasion we even rode around on horseback to better appreciate the cavalry battle at Trevilian Station. We spent many a weekend tromping around Fredericksburg and Chancellorsville and Petersburg. Father made men like Robert E. Lee, Stonewall Jackson, Jeb Stuart, Joseph Hooker, and Ambrose E, Burnside come alive by describing their exploits and strategies. I remember crying when he showed me where Stonewall Jackson was shot. Father wasn't entirely sympathetic to my tears. He told me, 'There were thirty thousand others like him who died at Chancellorsville.' I couldn't believe that so many died in one battle."

"And just two months later another fifty thousand men died at Gettysburg," I said.

I shook my head thinking about that figure. "Our country has participated in major wars that have spanned years with fewer men killed than died during the three days of fighting at Gettysburg. Two of my kin fell there, one fighting for the North, the other for the South. Family lore has it that they died in each other's arms."

"Is that true?"

"Their deaths were true enough, but as for the rest, I doubt it. Dead men tell no lies, but the living sure do."

I was no stranger to the area myself, and on impulse turned on to Route 3 and drove west toward the Chancellorsville Battlefield Visitor Center.

"I thought you wanted to have us keep a low profile," Claire said.

"It's off-season. And besides, no one would recognize you with that shirt and cap."

"I hope you're right."

I paid the park's entrance fee, and we drove over to the

visitor center. For a time we stood and looked at the Battle Painting, which reconstructed the major players and battles that had occurred back in 1863. General Joseph Hooker's trepidation, and General Robert E. Lee and General Thomas "Stonewall" Jackson's daring, had carried the day for the South, this despite the fact that the northern army had a huge numerical superiority over the rebels.

We decided to take one of the walking tours, with the signs along the way providing us a roadmap to the past. The historical perspective offered us a respite from our own situation, and also gave us a bridge that made it easier to talk to one another. We were able to forget our own problems, especially while strolling along the walking trail of the Old Mountain Road.

It was a perfect day for the walk. The woods along the path were showing their spring greenery, and the brisk air put color in our cheeks. Bird calls far exceeded human voices, and in most stretches we were alone.

"Father and I walked along here many years ago," Claire said. Her smile was wide at the memory. "He gave me a blow-by-blow account of all the fighting. He loved retelling how Lee and Jackson and Stuart outfoxed Hooker."

"It was a huge gamble."

To surprise the enemy, Jackson led his Second Corps of twenty-eight thousand soldiers on an exhausting twelve-mile march along uncharted trails. The path was narrow, in most places only allowing four men to march abreast, and wound through hills and dense woods. At the end of their march, Jackson's troops attacked the right flank of Hooker's northern army while engaging the Union's Eleventh Corps. The fighting raged through the afternoon into the evening, with the Confederates gaining a decisive victory.

Claire remembered the hero of that day. " 'There is Jackson standing like a stone wall,' " she quoted.

Jackson had earned his nickname during the Battle of Manassas when he stood strong against the Union Army, but the Old Mountain Road we were walking along didn't lead to a Jackson victory. It led to his death. He was shot by friendly fire on the evening he had led the South to their greatest battlefield triumph, was wounded in two places on his left arm and hit on his right hand by a volley from the 18th North Carolina Regiment that thought Jackson was part of a Union attack.

"When the doctors amputated Jackson's left arm," I said, "and Lee was notified of what happened, he said, 'He has lost his left arm, but I have lost my right arm.'"

Claire nodded. She had heard the story before, no doubt from her father.

We continued our unhurried walk. There were somber reminders of the past, but our trek wasn't depressing. In Claire's presence I saw the past as I had never seen it before. And the present. The world was brighter somehow, the colors more vibrant, the air more invigorating. It felt as if we had been given leave from our own battle, and the freedom was exhilarating.

"Father liked to say that Chancellorsville was a West Point versus West Point battle. Hooker and most of his generals were West Point graduates, as were Lee and Jackson."

I nodded. "In some instances," I said, "roommates from the Academy squared off against each other on the field of battle."

"Do you come from a military family?" asked Claire.

"Yes, ma'am. My father was career army, as was his father, and his father before that, and so on. My kin fought in the French and Indian War and the Revolutionary War. Sometimes I think that ours isn't a family tree as much as it is a battalion. Or a graveyard. Pater actually survived his time in the military, something exceedingly rare for a Travis."

My surname awakened Claire's memory. "The commander of the Alamo was named Travis, wasn't he?"

"My namesake and relative," I said. "Colonel William Barret Travis. When General Santa Anna and his army of four thousand rode up to the San Antonio de Valero Mission, the colonel wouldn't consider giving up the Alamo even though he and his ranks were slightly outnumbered by a ratio of about twenty to one. In inimitable Travis fashion, all hundred and eighty-eight defenders under his command died. The colonel was only twenty-six years old when he met his end."

"Are you trying to reassure me?"

"When it comes to lost causes, we know how to pick them."

"Wasn't Colonel Travis the one who drew a line in the sand with his sword?"

"So legend has it."

"I saw that in a movie," Claire said. "He said that anyone crossing that line would agree to fight to the death to defend the Alamo, and those who chose not to step forward could just saddle up and leave. And everyone crossed that line except for one man, who rode away."

"All Texans are certain it happened that way, all except the historians."

Claire didn't look happy at my putting a pin to great-great-great Uncle Will's reputation, so I decided to salvage it a little.

"Two years before he died in the Alamo, Uncle Will wrote in his diary about setting out on a journey. Apparently rivers were overrunning their banks, and the prairie was a quagmire, and after swimming and trudging for days and not getting anywhere he finally had to give up. In his diary he wrote it was 'the first time I ever turned back in my life.' That speaks of him, and most of my kin. We don't like giving up, especially if common sense dictates that we do."

"Determination is a good thing."

"Remember the fucking Alamo," I said.

Claire laughed, and in a moment of daring I stuck my hand out to her. She clasped her fingers between mine, and hand in hand we continued along the Old Mountain Road.

CHAPTER ELEVEN

Because it was midweek on the last day of April, the campground was less than half filled. We arrived at sundown and found a secluded spot that had enough brush to effectively shield us from any probing eyes.

I walked the perimeter of our campground, ostensibly gathering firewood, though my main purpose was to scout the area around us. There were no visible threats if you didn't count some panhandling chipmunks that dogged my trail for around fifty yards. Most of those staying at the campground were older couples who were enjoying an unencumbered leisure without the concerns of children or work.

While I was doing the scouting, Claire remained in camp unloading the car. Day was giving way to night when I returned. I dumped the gathered wood in our fire pit, turned on a lantern, and set up the propane camp stove.

"Spaghetti? Or canned beef stew? Or both?"

"Hot water seems to be our element," said Claire. "I'll boil the water for spaghetti."

"I'll set up, then."

I put up the tent, inflated the air mattresses, and unrolled the sleeping bags. When I surfaced from inside the tent, the spaghetti was already in the boiling water and the table was set up with place settings of paper plates and plastic forks and spoons. Anchoring the paper plates were cereal bowls filled with pears in syrup. Claire had made the table positively homey by going out and gathering some wildflowers. The empty pear cans were positioned in the middle of the table and served as flower vases.

She wasn't the only one with a surprise. I had secreted a bottle of wine in a cooler and brought it out. The glass was cold to the touch. With my Swiss Army knife I worked the cork free and then poured the wine into two Dixie cups.

"You definitely deserve a merit badge for this one," Claire said.

We clinked plastic cups, or approximated such, and took a sip.

"Cold even," said Claire. "I am very impressed."

Our glasses emptied quickly. While Claire drained the boiling water and poured in the jar of spaghetti sauce, I refilled our cups. Both of us had an appetite, and we dug into the pasta.

"I guess running for your life makes you hungry," said Claire. "It's hard to believe all that's happened since last night."

"My mother always warned me about girls like you."

"She did not," Claire said. "I am the kind of girl all moms want their boys to marry."

"Uh-huh," I said, acting as if I was very dubious.

"In high school I was a candystriper, the president of the Spirit Club, a member of the National Honor Society, did volunteer work for the elderly, and was a majorette."

I continued my doubting Thomas act. "You a majorette?"

Claire rose to the challenge—literally. She walked over to the fire pit, sorted through the branches I had dropped there, and found one she liked. After feeling along the length of the wood and smoothing over a few rough edges, she carried the stick into a clearing. Claire gave me a pointed look that announced it was comeuppance time, and then started twirling the stick in her right hand. It began rotating faster and faster, and without breaking rhythm she transferred it to her left hand. Back and forth it went, and then she started chanting a tune I was all too familiar with. She must have picked up the cadence from her father.

> *"When my granny was ninety-one*
> *She did PT just for fun.*
> *When my granny was ninety-two*
> *She could do PT better than you."*

PT was army talk for physical training. In the army, cadences are called "jodies." Drill instructors love using good cadence calls. They go hand in hand with double-timing in formation. When I finally controlled my laughter, I joined in.

> *"When my granny was ninety-three*
> *She got up before dawn to do PT.*
> *When my granny was ninety-four*
> *She ran three miles and then ran three more."*

Claire was able to cadence and twirl at the same time. There was no doubt but that she had done majorette duty. The stick never stopped twirling, and she moved it around her head, behind her back, and through her legs. I cheered her on and thought the show was all but finished when Claire decided to attempt a grand finale at the end of her cadence.

> *"Granny met St. Peter at the pearly gates*
> *She said, 'St. Peter, I hope I'm not late.'*
> *St. Peter said with a big, wide grin*
> *'Get down, Granny, and knock out ten.' "*

With just the light of the moon to guide her, Claire threw the stick high into the air. This was no conservative throw. Claire was going for all or nothing. I lost sight of the stick as it spun end over end upward. Just as I decided the stick had disappeared for good, it fell from the sky and dropped into her expectant hand.

Entirely too nonchalantly, Claire tossed the stick back into the fire pit from which it had come. I lowered myself to my knees, and then raised my arms up and down in a supplicating "we are not worthy" gesture. Claire accepted it as her due, and even offered a little curtsy in return.

I started a campfire, freshened our Dixie cups with a pour of wine, and we relaxed in front of the flames.

"Some show," I said. "I especially loved your twirling a baton to a jody call."

"Father's influence," Claire said. "Whenever we walked together, or when we did chores, he'd always call out cadence. I fell into that habit as well."

"Jodies always seemed to take some of the sting out of hikes and work," I said.

Many of the rhythmic chants are full of bravado, or just plain silly, but they have been working as marching tonic for soldiers for a lot of years. There are those who claim that "Yankee Doodle" is one of the first cadences used by an American army. I sipped a little wine, and then offered up one of those silly jodies:

> *"Me and Superman got in a fight*
> *I hit him in the head with some Kryptonite*
> *I hit him so hard I busted his brain*
> *And now I'm dating Lois Lane.*
> *Well, me and Batman, we had one too*
> *I hit him in the head with my left shoe*
> *Right in the temple with my left heel*
> *And now I'm driving the Batmobile."*

Claire was not about to be outdone. "Father served in the airborne," she said, "and a lot of his cadences reflected that." She started in with one of those:

> *"C-130 rolling down the strip*
> *Airborne daddy on a one-way trip*
> *Mission unspoken, destination unknown*
> *We don't know if we'll ever come home."*

I was familiar with that one and joined in on the chorus:

> *"Stand up, hook up, shuffle to the door*
> *Jump right out and count to four*
> *If my main don't open wide*
> *I got a reserve one by my side."*

We laughed together, both pleased that we could share some army tunes together. I tested Claire on another one.

> *"Momma, Momma, can't you see?*
> *What the army's done to me*
> *Momma, Momma, can't you see?*
> *What the army's done to me."*

I looked at Claire expectantly, and she didn't miss a beat.

> *"I used to date a beauty queen*
> *Now I hug my M-16*
> *I used to drive a Cadillac*
> *Now I hump it on my back."*

It almost felt as if we were singing camp songs. I didn't want the night to end. The more Claire revealed herself, the more beguiling she became. At the age of thirty-five I had begun to get used to the idea that I would be single for life.

In the wisdom of my years I had come to the conclusion that the concept of love was a female thing, and that it was a notion perpetuated by bad poetry. The idea of feeling so deeply for someone else had always escaped me. In the firelight, I was getting some understanding of that thing that made the world go round.

I watched Claire's face as she turned serious and offered up the cadence of "She Wore a Yellow Ribbon," singing it with more soul than I had ever heard.

> "Around her hair she wore a yellow ribbon
> She wore it in the springtime in the merry month of May
> And if you asked her why she wore it,
> She'd say she wore it for her soldier who was far, far
>   away.
>
> Far away
> Far away
> She wore it for her soldier who was far, far away.
>
> Around the block she pushed a baby carriage
> She pushed it in the springtime in the merry month of
>   May
> And if you asked her why she pushed it
> She'd say she pushed it for her soldier who was far, far
>   away.
>
> Far away
> Far away
> She pushed it for her soldier who was far, far away.
>
> Around his grave she laid the pretty flowers
> She laid them in the springtime in the merry month of
>   May
> And if you asked her why she laid them

She'd say she laid them for her soldier who was far, far
    away.

Far away
Far away
She laid them for her soldier who was far, far away."

When her last somber notes faded, we both became
more contemplative and quiet, each of us staring deep into
the fire. She had put a different twist to an old standard,
emphasizing the words instead of the rhythm.

"I guess we should be thinking about sleep," Claire said.

"It's that time."

"Is there only the one tent?" she asked. Her voice
sounded higher than usual.

"Yes. I wanted us to look like a couple. I thought it would
be less conspicuous that way."

"I suppose you're right, but I have to admit to feeling a little awkward at that arrangement."

She stopped talking, and averted her eyes from mine.
"Will," she said, "I should have told you before. I'm involved
with someone."

My stomach went hollow, but I pretended noncha-
lance at her remark. Acting overly cheery, the usual male
reaction when confronted by something hurtful, I said,
"That's no problem. I guess I was thinking more like a
bodyguard than anything else. How about I sleep in the
car tonight?"

"That's really not necessary," Claire said, but it was clear
she would be more comfortable with that arrangement.

"Yes it is. I snore."

"Well, if you don't mind . . ."

"Not at all."

I went and retrieved my sleeping bag from the tent.
There were three pillows in the tent, and rather petulantly I

took off with two of them. I was only willing to be a martyr within reason.

Claire was cleaning up while I relocated. She seemed a little embarrassed by having discommoded me, or maybe she was reconsidering her majorette display and the intimacy of our shared jody calls. I had the feeling she wouldn't be doing any twirling or singing again any time soon.

Both of us went to bed without our s'mores.

In the morning I gingerly eased out of the Civic and then walked around the campsite with a little bit of exaggerated stiffness. There was some residual awkwardness between us, but that soon passed. Claire took sympathy on my hobbling, encouraged me to sit down, and then went about boiling water again. While she was making instant coffee and oatmeal, I put batteries into a portable radio I had bought the day before and began fiddling with the dial.

"*Voilà*," said Claire, serving up the breakfast. She must have decided the oatmeal and coffee weren't enough, as she sectioned a chocolate bar and put some on each of our plates.

"Part of a balanced diet?" I asked.

"That shirt you bought got me to thinking," she said.

The radio reception proved surprisingly good, and I found something resembling a news station. The impending May primaries were getting lots of air play. There's nothing like a close horse race to get the onlookers screaming.

"We need to—"

"Shh!" Like an avenging librarian, Claire shushed me. She was listening intently to the western polling results, the area where the regional primary elections were soon to be taking place. She looked as intent as a sports fanatic trying to catch the score of his favorite team. In this case, it was hard to tell which of the candidates she was cheering for, but she did appear to be satisfied with the results.

Claire was not nearly as happy with the follow-up news story.

"Suspected murderer stalking the candidates," the newscaster said. "We have this report from Brian Jensen in the Capitol."

Another self-important voice took to the airwaves: "Yesterday afternoon an arrest warrant was issued for Claire Harrington, aged thirty-two, for the murder of ATF Special Agent Lawrence Deering.

"Deering, aged forty-eight, was killed while conducting an active investigation into the assassination attempt on Congressman Mark Stanton. Deering was also probing into death threats issued to at least one other of the presidential candidates.

"Harrington, a longtime Washington, D.C., lobbyist and daughter of former Congressman Garret Harrington of South Carolina, reportedly suffered a mental breakdown after her father committed suicide in early February. In addition to shooting Deering, Harrington is also wanted for questioning in the New Hampshire assassination attempt on Republican presidential candidate Congressman Mark Stanton. The Secret Service announced that ballistics reports link the gun used in the Deering shooting with the same gun which fired two shots at Congressman Stanton and resulted in a wound to his left arm.

"The Secret Service also confirmed that Harrington has apparently been stalking Democratic presidential candidate Senator Daniel Greeley by working as a volunteer in his campaign. Her travels reportedly took her to at least two states where she is said to have assumed a variety of disguises. Because of the threats to Greeley, the Secret Service has increased its security to all candidates.

"Harrington, believed to be armed and dangerous, was seen in Bethesda, Maryland, on Monday afternoon. Authorities have set up a toll-free number for anyone sighting her to call."

While that number was recited, and then repeated a second time, I stared at Claire. She had lost all color in her face and was shaking her head.

"This is far worse than I could have imagined," she said.

"That's two of us," I said.

"My God, this is character assassination."

"No, it's being called attempted political assassination, and stalking."

"You know I didn't kill that man."

I asked the Paul Harvey question: "What about the rest of the story?"

She got the color back in her face very quickly. Red and angry, she said, "You think I tried to shoot Mark Stanton?"

"Tell me you didn't."

"That's the last thing I would ever do."

"What were you doing in New Hampshire prior to the primary?"

"I was working on the Stanton campaign."

"Legitimately working? Did you have a paid position?"

"I was a volunteer doing whatever was needed. I very much want Mark Stanton to be our next president."

"Were you in New Hampshire the day his headquarters was bombed and when someone took some shots at him?" The events had happened simultaneously, the bomb apparently providing a diversion for the shooter.

She looked genuinely upset, and if I wasn't mistaken, even shuddered. "Yes. I thought it was awful."

"What about those charges that you were stalking Senator Greeley?"

Claire didn't meet my eyes. "You wouldn't understand."

"Try me."

With apparent reluctance, she went about doing that. "Because no one was willing to believe that my father was murdered, I was forced to conduct my own investigation. Yes, I went undercover as a political volunteer for Daniel Greeley to see what I could learn."

"So it's true you went around in disguises?"

"Out of context, I know all of this might sound a little crazy, but if I hadn't altered my appearance I certainly would have been found out. The same press pool follows the campaigns from state to state. Because of my work on the Stanton campaign, as well as my work as a lobbyist, I was already acquainted with some of the reporters covering the candidates."

"You're right," I said, "it does sound crazy and it doesn't matter what context you put it into. You're not a detective. How did you think you were going to learn anything? It's the rare politician who's honest with his own mother. Did you think Greeley was suddenly going to come clean while just happening to confess in your vicinity?"

"I was never that naïve. I knew it was unlikely that I would get to do much more than shake hands with the candidate, or be near him and cheer wildly at the rallies volunteers are encouraged to attend. But I know how stories surface during a campaign. I was listening for those, and throwing out conversational gambits that I hoped would lead back to my father. In retrospect I know all of that doesn't sound very sensible, but I hoped I could pick up some clues."

"What was it that you were looking for?"

"I wanted a window to the past."

What a Quixotic quest, I thought, and then remembered that I had signed on to find the same thing.

"Why did you suspect Daniel Greeley?" I asked.

"Like Father, Greeley is from South Carolina. My father had already served three terms in Congress when Greeley was elected. Instead of being deferential to his seniority, Greeley targeted my father and was antagonistic toward him. Some of that might have had to do with Greeley being an up-and-coming Democrat, and my father's being a well-known Republican, but the animosity between the two of them extended beyond that. My father was not the sort to castigate others, but I remember once hearing him describe Greeley as 'having the stick-to-itiveness of a hemorrhoid, with the same apparent fondness for assholes.' For Father, those were most condemning words."

"That's your evidence?"

"There were a number of turf wars going on between them in South Carolina. Before being elected to Congress, Greeley was a very vocal member of the state assembly. On several occasions he targeted my father, and his attacks seemed more personal than political. He went so far as to call Father a 'carpetbagger.' It's no wonder then that my father accused Greeley of 'skullduggery and disingenuousness.'"

"About what?"

"A land deal Greeley was involved with. The whole thing looked dirty, and smelled dirty, but nothing was ever proved."

"Anything else?"

"Greeley was always an opportunist. Father said you could count on Greeley to cast his vote for what was popular instead of what was right. He thought him dishonest."

"I can see how that would be annoying," I said. "I once heard that the definition of an honest politician is one who when he is bought, stays bought."

Claire shook a dismissive head, and then offered a more philosophical political observation. "My father always said, 'A politician thinks of the next election; a statesman thinks of the next generation.' I suppose that's why Father didn't think of himself so much as a politician as he did a statesman. Father had disdain for those who stayed in office just to get elected. He liked to quote from Adlai Stevenson, who said, 'The hardest thing about any political campaign is how to win without proving that you are unworthy of winning.'"

"Did your father know any of the other candidates?"

Claire nodded. "He was acquainted with all of them, but

some more than others. Bob Norman was serving in Congress at the same time my father was, and they served together on several committees. I've also determined he had a nodding acquaintance with Mark Stanton, Scott Vickers, and Donald Bates, but I can't find anything that would suggest any more of a relationship than that."

"So that's why you keyed on Greeley?"

Claire nodded.

"How did your meeting with Deering happen to take place?"

"He was the one who called me, though he never identified himself as ATF. By the time he contacted me I had already called hundreds of people trying to get information about what was really going on behind the scenes during Father's time in Congress. My cover story was that I was finishing up my father's book, but the whole idea was to get people talking and reminiscing. Over the phone Deering told me he had some information about a sub-rosa group of politicians that would make Iran-Contra look like child's play. He said it appeared that Father had gotten wind of what was going on, and threatened to open the curtains on the shadow government. He said he had documentation of this, and arranged for our meeting at the Blue Crab Inn."

I was watching her carefully, doing my own lie-detector reading. "When and why did you start carrying the gun?"

The question caught Claire by surprise. She broke off our eye contact and tugged a little at her hair. Before speaking, she cleared her throat. Her body was announcing the lie.

"After the police concluded that my father committed suicide they gave me the gun back, and that's when I started carrying it with me. Because I was sure my father was murdered, I was afraid someone might come after me."

"So all this time you have been carrying around the same gun that killed your father?"

"I needed it for protection."

She was sounding more emphatic about it, getting comfortable with her lie.

"If it was me," I said, "I think I would have found it hard to be carrying around the gun that killed my father. It would be just too grim a reminder."

Claire narrowed her eyes, and tried to think of a logical answer. "It sort of stayed buried the whole time in the bottom of my purse."

"That must have been like having a brick in your purse. It's a heavy, long gun. For the sake of concealment and comfort you could have bought something half its size and weight. Remember Nancy Reagan and her 'itty-bitty gun?'"

She cleared her throat again. Claire was not a good liar. "I guess I never had the time to get another gun."

"Or maybe you thought it would be poetic justice to use that gun on Greeley. Were you stalking the congressman, Claire? If you had found the evidence you were looking for, were you prepared to take that gun and shoot him?"

"No," she whispered, and then said, "I don't think so."

I waited for her to continue.

"I fantasized about pulling the gun on him," she finally said. "But I don't think I could have pulled the trigger."

"You're not sure?"

In a voice stretched to an emotional thinness, she said, "Sure enough to know it would have ruined my life. I have too many things to live for, too much I want to accomplish, too many of my own ambitions, to do that.

"Though," she whispered, "I would have wanted to. I even had a dramatic scene I sometimes played out in my mind. I imagined myself holding the gun on Greeley and saying, 'This is the gun that killed my father. And now it's going to kill you.' But my fantasy never ended with my shooting him. I saw the gun as leverage for getting his confession and learning why my father was murdered."

If it wasn't exactly the truth, it sounded close to it. I watched Claire dab at her eyes from her own tearful admission.

I wanted to offer her a hanky and a hug, but kept my distance, cautioned by my suspicions that she was keeping other secrets from me.

CHAPTER TWELVE

The Candidate picked up the ringing phone on his night-stand and listened without saying anything. The familiar officious voice of an aide said, "This is your wake-up call, sir."

He took a look at his watch. Five A.M. Three hours' sleep, the Candidate thought. That was better than most nights.

"Thank you."

"You have a six-thirty breakfast talk and prayer meeting, as well as a talk at nine o'clock. Would you like some coffee in the meantime, sir?"

"That won't be necessary."

"There's a freshly pressed suit in your closet, sir."

"Got it."

"Will you need my assistance with anything?"

"No, I'm fine."

"Mr. Smith and Mr. Jones are hoping for five minutes of your time before the first breakfast. They are waiting in the hotel lobby now."

"Smith and Jones" was a generic phrase for deep-pocket contributors or potential contributors. They were always looking for five minutes of his time. Nothing overt was ever said in the meetings, but there was the pressing of flesh along with their identifying who they represented. The unsaid was always more important than the trivialities uttered in such meetings.

"Give me fifteen minutes."

"Yes, sir."

The Candidate went to the bathroom, adjusted the flow of water in the shower, and while waiting for it to get hot ran an electric razor over his face. He shaved three times a day. No way was he going to lose this election, as Richard Nixon had in 1960, to a five o'clock shadow. He brushed his teeth quickly. They were bleached white and didn't need much work. The shower took less than a minute. There was no need to shampoo today.

While dressing, he thought about the *other* matter. He hoped that before the day was out, everything would be resolved. Garret Harrington had known just how far politicians would go to satisfy their passions. He had documented the selling of the political soul in his book, but with all his insights into political passions, Harrington still hadn't realized his own imminent peril, or that of his daughter.

The Candidate thought it a shame that Harrington's book would never be published. Saint Garret had done his research well and showed just how far the pursuit of politics could lead its practitioners astray. His book was self-serving, of course. Saint Garret's hands were as dirty as his, or at least almost as dirty, though Harrington had tried to wash them clean. The Candidate suspected that Harrington had found that the bloodstains ran very deep.

It was a shame he hadn't been able to keep a copy of Saint Garret's book for himself. He had even thought of putting the pages into some secret cache, and bringing them out on those rare occasions when he could count on absolute privacy. For a time the Candidate had owned some special pornographic pictures that he stored in a vault. Every few weeks he would bring them out and look at them. He still thought of those pictures, and wished he had them, but he'd destroyed them years before. There could be no possible taint of scandal, not now, not when he was so close. Just as he disposed of those pictures, the Candidate had also shredded Garret Harrington's book, but not before reading it several times. He could close his eyes and recall passages. In some ways, probably because of the forbidden pleasure aspect of it, the book was as exciting as those pictures had been. He found the political animal, with all its venality, sins, passions, and raw ambition, a compelling figure. Anyone reading Harrington's book could not have accused him of being anything other than bipartisan in his assessments. There was no shortage of sin or sinners on either side of the aisle, Republicans and Democrats sporting ample villains and villainy. All the stories Saint Garret unearthed further justified the Candidate's opinion that the ends justified the means and underscored the fact that his actions were really not unique. He would not be the first president with blood on his hands. It stood to reason, the Candidate thought, that there were other secret stories like his. He suspected that the known scandals were just the tip of the iceberg. Everyone harbored secrets, and politicians more than most.

Since 1970 more than thirty members of the House and Senate had been convicted of some type of criminal activity. The witches' brew included such offenses as mail fraud, racketeering, bribery, perjury, tax evasion, and sex with minors. The Candidate suspected that the surface had only been scratched. The deeper pool, and the larger crimes, were beneath that surface.

He finished with the buttoning of his shirt and then looped his red, white, and blue tie around his neck. Image was more important than reality, though the bubble of image was sometimes not immune from the pinpricks of truth.

Just a few years ago Larry Flynt sent his peers running for the hills. The *Hustler* publisher hadn't liked the holier-than-thou attitude of politicians venting on Clinton's affair with Monica Lewinsky, so in essence he put a bounty on Senate and House politicians with the express purpose of wanting to air their dirty laundry in public. When Flynt and others started turning over rocks on Capitol Hill, the chorus of "mea culpas" was loud and long. Congressman Henry Hyde admitted to a nine-year affair, and Congressman Dan Burton came clean about fathering a child out of wedlock. While Newt Gingrich was speaking of "family values," it was revealed that just like Clinton, he was also having an affair. Gingrich relinquished his position of Speaker of the House, but his successor, Bob Livingston, was only able to hold the post for a few days because his own past affairs were suddenly revealed. Flynt seemed to get particular satisfaction from ferreting out hypocrisy. Congressman Bob Barr's second ex-wife said that he not only supported her decision to have an abortion, but he paid for it as well. Even as the abortion was taking place, Barr was having an affair with a woman who ended up being his third wife. In his public life, Barr was strongly pro-life and a self-avowed supporter of family values. The conservative congressman had even received a Friend of the Family Award from the head of the Christian Coalition. Like many leaders, Barr's private life was something altogether different from his publicly expressed values.

The Candidate's phone rang again, and once more he heard the voice of his aide. "Mr. Smith and Mr. Jones are in the meeting room," he said.

"I will be outside my room in two minutes."

"Yes, sir."

There was always a Smith and Jones waiting. They wanted access to power, and were willing to pay for it. Among federal, state, and local governments, almost three trillion dollars was spent each year. The way money was divvied up caused all sorts of jockeying. Questionable expenditures were labeled "pork politics." But there was discretion and leeway that surrounded even legitimate funding, and the resulting manner in which businesses jostled each other for that money reminded him of how piglets fought for the favored teat of a sow.

Saint Garret had written about how James Buchanan had gone to his friend George Plitt for campaign contributions, and how after Buchanan became president, Plitt received lucrative naval shipbuilding contracts. He wrote about how Rutherford P. Hayes, ultimately known as Rutherfraud, made shady deals to become president.

You scratch my back, and I'll scratch yours. It was the accepted political quid pro quo.

The Candidate stepped out of his room. He wondered if he yelled "sooeeeey" whether Smith and Jones would come running.

CHAPTER THIRTEEN

After leaving our campground, we made good time traveling south, but I left the freeway not long after crossing the Palmetto State's border, choosing a roundabout way to get to the Harrington family home.

Claire inquired about the detour: "What are you doing?"

"Taking the scenic route."

Her look told me she wasn't buying my answer.

"I was hoping that by traveling along a few blue highways, we could avoid announcing ourselves."

"Do you think they'll be looking for us here?"

"It's no secret that people on the run tend to go to places familiar to them."

Several times I slowed down to look at parked cars, and Claire couldn't figure out what I was so intent on. "What are you looking for?"

"Scavenger hunt items," I said.

Finally I stopped to take a close look at an older Buick Regal that was mostly hidden in a grove of pines and resting on cinderblocks and jacks. Judging by the abundance of spider webs and dust on it, the car repairs were going very slowly. Though the license plates were dirty, the tags were still current.

"Keep the engine running," I told Claire.

I ran up to the Buick, made sure the coast was clear, and then did some quick screwdriver work and removed the plates.

"I'll need you to spit shine them," I said, handing the plates to Claire. "They have to look new."

Claire didn't ask any questions, just found some wipes and started in with the elbow grease. By putting on the South Carolina plates I hoped we would blend in that much more.

All of Garret Harrington's papers, and his hoped-for book, were in their family house in Summerville, a town about twenty-five minutes away from Charleston. As we drove, I asked Claire about the house and the surrounding area. Since her father's death, the residence had been unoccupied. Although Claire didn't have a key to his home, she told me the spare was hanging under the sill of the window to the left of the front door.

The house was situated on two acres in an area bordering what was referred to as Old Summerville. According to Claire, Summerville had recently been selected not only as one of the fifty best small towns in America, but also as one of the hundred best places to retire.

"Maybe that's why the police are so sure my father committed suicide," said Claire. "A murder might get the town delisted."

Claire still hadn't finished cleaning the license plates when I made my next scavenger hunt stop, this time pulling up to the front lawn of a house that was for sale. There was no one around, but I still went through the routine of pretending interest in the property. What I was really interested in was the FOR SALE sign. According to the sign, the house was listed by Lloyd Durkin, the Duke of Real Estate in Dorchester County. It took several hard tugs to unearth the Duke's sign; I tossed it into the trunk.

"The Duke is not going to like that," Claire said.

"I'm trusting to the Duke's noblesse oblige."

She looked me over. "You don't look like Duke."

"What about an earl?"

"No real estate agent would be wearing a *Top of the Food Chain* T-shirt."

"I plan to remedy that."

It only took a few minutes of driving to find a secluded spot. I changed license plates, and then pulled out my blue blazer, button-down shirt, and khakis. There was no crest on the blue blazer. Duke Durkin would probably not have approved, but Claire did.

"Now you look more like a real estate agent," she said.

"You really know how to turn a guy's head with your compliments."

Before leaving the open, grassy area, I picked up a good-sized rock for pounding the sign into the front lawn of the Harrington home.

Aloud, I tried to work out final details of the plan. "You said that the backyard of the house opens up into wetlands?"

She nodded.

"How far do the wetlands extend before they come to a road?"

Claire thought about that. "The nearest road is about three-quarters of a mile north."

"Is there a path through the wetlands?"

"There used to be a few old trails, but they might be grown over by now. Why?"

"Always have a contingency escape route."

"There are a lot of shrubs and brambles," Claire said, "but the way is passable unless it's been raining hard. The area is called the wetlands, but what it really is more than anything else is a flood plain. There's a creek down there that runs through the canyon, but it shouldn't be hard to ford. I'd worry more about the poison oak and mosquitoes. If calamine lotion and Off! aren't part of your contingency plan, they should be. Don't believe it when they say the Great Carolina Wren is the state bird. It's skeeters."

That wasn't the kind of bloodletting I was sweating over. "Is the phone in the house still operational?"

"It should be. I never had it turned off. The real estate office has a firm that keeps up with landscaping, cleaning, and the like."

"What's the number?" I asked.

Claire told me, and I tapped it in on my cell phone. I let it ring several times before hanging up.

We drove over to where the wetlands played out to the road, and I took a long look at the surrounding area. From the road, no houses were visible. As far as the eye could see, there was only brush and trees. I looked around for any landmarks or markers, but the terrain was all but indistinguishable.

"Where's your house?" I asked Claire.

She figured out her bearings, and then pointed. I set my mental compass to her finger, and then handed Claire my cell phone.

"What's this for?"

"We'll need to split up. I want you to stay mobile until you hear from me. I'll call you once I get inside the house, and then you will proceed to this location. Remain here until thirty minutes pass, or until I call you again. This is where we will rendezvous unless I tell you differently. Understood?"

Claire nodded.

"Let's take the roundabout route back to your father's house," I said. "If the enemy has set up position, I don't expect they'll be camped on the doorstep, or parked on the street. It's possible the house is wired, and they're waiting somewhere nearby for someone to trip it. It's also possible they picked a good spot for surveillance, so what I want you to do is drop me off a few blocks away, and then drive away and wait for my call."

"Do you want the gun?" Claire asked.

"You keep it."

We drove around Summerville's winding roads with its elegant Victorian-era houses and the picturesque look and feel of the Old South. The area was awash in trees and greenery. As innocent as everything appeared, I still wasn't feeling comfortable.

"You know the town," I said. "Have your escape route thought out just in case. If you get out of sight of your pursuer, make some left-hand turns."

"Left-hand turns?"

"The other driver is more likely to turn right."

Both of us got somber and quiet. Neither of us said anything until Claire pulled over to the curb.

"Walk to the corner," she said. "Make a left, and the house will be the fourth up on the right."

"Make sure no one's following the car when you leave," I said, and exited with sign and stone. "If you think you're being pursued, the best thing to do is drive directly to a police station."

"Be careful," said Claire, and then pulled away, following my directions not to linger. As far as I could see, she didn't even pause for a backward glance. I wouldn't have minded had she lingered for that.

I set off for the house at a very deliberate pace. As I drew nearer, I acted as if I were taking some impressions of the area. For the sake of anyone who might be watching, I started stopping at all the mailboxes along the street where the Harrington home was, and acted as if I were leaving a business card in each. Luckily, the homes were spaced far apart, and no one appeared to take notice of my impersonation of a real estate agent.

The Harrington house was a two-story colonial with

white columns. I took several steps up the pathway, and then decided to unburden myself of the sign. Using the rock, I pounded it into the ground and claimed another kingdom for the Duke. I raised my arm to toss the rock aside, but then thought better of it and crammed the rock into the confines of my coat pocket.

From the outside, the house spoke of old money. There was a wraparound porch that extended around the front, a reminder of when people didn't cocoon themselves inside their domiciles. The brick fronting wasn't veneer, but the real thing. The house was set back a long way from the street, and I became ever more aware of the distance as I walked up the pathway to the door. I couldn't help but wonder if I were in my enemy's sights and being targeted for an ambush.

The key was where it was supposed to be, and I opened the lock without any trouble. I stepped onto heartpine floors into an atrium of vaulted ceilings that was almost hotel-like. A bona fide real estate agent would have stopped and taken five minutes with a client to discuss all the extras that were immediately visible. Instead, I made a beeline for the phone in the hallway, pulled up the receiver, and called my cell number. Claire picked up on the first ring.

"Is everything okay?" I asked.

"No sign of anyone following me."

I looked at my watch. It was ten after four. "Proceed to designated location then, and wait there for the agreed-upon time."

With the stopwatch ticking, I ran by the living room and opened the door to the library where Garret Harrington had kept his office. By itself, the library was about as large as my apartment and used to house wall-to-wall books. There was no time to browse through the titles, but it was evident that many of the books were old and leather bound, though there was no shortage of newer books as well. The volumes seemed to be divided into sections, including history, philosophy, biography, politics, and fiction. One entire bookcase appeared to be devoted to Alexander Hamilton, Aaron Burr, and political feuding. The Dewey decimal system wasn't being used to tag the books, but I had been in small-town libraries with fewer volumes.

The library didn't contain only books. Some of the shelves held curios and keepsakes and memorabilia. There were also display cases stocked mostly with historical souvenirs and relics, the majority with a South Carolina emphasis, but not everything in the cases was an antique or had some particular significance. Claire's mother had collected snow globes, and there were at least a hundred of those, with no two alike. The globes were different sizes and colors; some were simple and quiet, others loud and elaborate. Most had the snow in common, but even that wasn't universal, as some contained colored glitter.

Claire had told me about the snow globes. During her reminiscing she had forgotten her troubles, at least for a few moments. "Our family was steeped in Christmas traditions," she said with a smile. "Daddy would get the tree, always a blue spruce, and we would decorate it together. After that, we brought out this elaborate crèche and set it up with its own display light. There was real straw in the manger, and the wise men were carrying actual frankincense and myrrh. On the opposite side of the living room we'd put up this winter scene of antique, colored pewter figures. It was almost out of Dickens, with men in their top hats and women with their winter finery. There were boys running with dogs, and girls hauling their dollies along in sleds. Most of the figures were skaters designed to look as if they were gliding over their pond made of cut glass. We all participated in putting together our miniature winter wonderland. Only when everything was done would Mother bring out the snow globes. She put them in strategic spots around the living room and sitting room, and when people came over, my father used to always belt out the Jerry Lee Lewis line: 'There's a whole lot of shaking going on.' And there was. Everyone would be shaking the snow globes. It never felt like Christmas until those snow globes came out."

I scanned the globes, ignoring the smaller ones in favor of those that were larger. There was a New Year's scene with revelers, Santa landing his sleigh atop a roof, and a Grandma Moses painting of a winter scene. The snow globe with the Statue of Liberty was not the largest, but there was abundant snowfall at the feet of Lady Liberty. I wondered if Garret Harrington had chosen to hide the safety deposit key in that particular globe because of the ample snow-drift, or whether there was more significance than that.

I turned the globe upside down, caused a flurry of snow, and something else. The key, now revealed, drifted downward. After unscrewing the bottom of the container, I was able to fish out the key, along with about half the water. As I worked, I kept being confronted by the tiny lettering of the statue's inscription:

Give me your tired, your poor, your huddled masses yearning to breathe free, the wretched refuse of your teeming shore. Send these, the homeless, tempest-tossed to me. I lift my lamp beside the golden door.

The wet key went into my pocket, and then I paused to listen. There was no sound, but then the room was well-cushioned from any noises because of all the books and shelves. The room offered no view to the outside; if there were windows, they were covered up by books. On another occasion I might have enjoyed the feel of the almost hermetically sealed library, but not now. It felt too much like a trap.

There was a huge rolltop desk off in the corner of the

room, and on each side of the desk were mahogany filing cabinets. I approached the desk and raised its hood. There was some discoloration to the wood's otherwise sleek finish, and I remembered Claire's telling me that her father had died at his desk. The wood must have soaked up his blood.

I quickly went through the desk and the adjoining filing cabinets. The book wasn't there, nor were there any notes. I walked through the study, looking to see if it was on a shelf somewhere. There were plenty of other books, but no sign of *Political Passions*. I returned to the desk and started going through the cubbyholes. From what I knew of Garret Harrington, he was an orderly man, though the state of his desk did not reflect that. There didn't seem to be any rhyme or reason for where things had been stuffed. It was apparent the police—or someone—had been there nosing around before me.

One of the filing cabinets was devoted to correspondence going back half a century. There was no time to make a dent in it, and I would have needed a U-Haul to remove all of it. I flipped through the tabs, and found the year that Harrington had left political office for good. The folder seemed particularly light, especially when compared to the folders holding correspondence for Harrington's other years in Congress. I thumbed through the letters, but didn't find anything of interest.

The other filing cabinet consisted mostly of financial records. According to the statements I saw, Claire was now worth several million dollars. I was surprised the media hadn't already picked up on that. Tania the revolutionary meant nothing; Patty Hearst was another matter entirely. An heiress-assassin would play much better on the tube than a run-of-the-mill assassin. I thumbed through tax records, property deeds, insurance information, check ledgers, bill statements, and various warranties before reaching the bottom of the cabinet.

I searched the desk again, but could find no manuscript, and no evidence of the book Garret Harrington had been working on for at least a dozen years. In the cubbyholes there was plenty of typewriter ribbons and Wite-Out, and next to the desk was a case that housed a manual typewriter. Garret Harrington had grown up without computers. There was no file to be retrieved, no handy diskette with the heading "Political Passions."

I went back to the filing cabinet with the correspondence and thumbed through the letters from the last two years of Garret's life. Nothing jumped out at me.

The quiet room was growing increasingly oppressive. This was the room where one man had died. I had no desire to be part of a trend.

I tried to think how a real detective would open a window to the past. Phone records, I thought. Claire had overheard him talking with somebody. It was her eavesdropping that ultimately convinced Claire that her father had been murdered.

Harrington, or his accountant, divvied up bills on an annual basis. There was a manila envelope for every calendar year. Within those envelopes were statements from credit card companies, as well as gas and electric, water, phone, sanitation, and the other dunning agencies that reach into all of our wallets. I pocketed the phone statements from the last two years.

My forehead was damp with sweat. I checked my watch and saw that fifteen minutes had passed since I had called Claire. Maybe Harrington had placed his book in one of the bedrooms. I would have to extend my search to the rest of the house.

From outside, even through the room's insulation, I could hear the cries of a jay. At first I dismissed it for a male's incessant mating piping of "Here I am," but then I reconsidered. This sounded more like a scolding than a love call.

I ran to the door of the library and stopped to listen. There were no sounds of human activity, but the jay continued his scolding. Looking right and then left, I saw there was no one in the hallway. I took a long, silent breath, almost as if preparing to jump into deep water, and hurried down the hall.

Staying out of view, I moved to the side of the front window and was able to get an angled view out to the street. There was a van parked up and across the road that hadn't been there before. It looked like a painter's van, with lettering on its side and a roof rack loaded down with ladders and the like.

It was time for that contingency plan.

I ran to the kitchen, and from behind the blinds looked out to the backyard. Beyond the tennis court the ground sloped down. There was no high ground in the immediate vicinity, so I didn't have to worry about a sniper. Closer to home, I tried to eliminate all the likely vantage points for an ambush. There was nothing obvious, and I couldn't afford to wait.

Making my way to the patio door, I inched it open and then stepped outside. There was a huge magnolia tree about forty yards away that could provide cover. From there it would be maybe another fifty yards until the property started sloping down into the wetlands.

Waiting wasn't an option. I looked around again, saw nothing, and then took off for the tree. An instant after I started my flight, a figure in paint-splattered overalls turned the corner, but he wasn't holding a paintbrush in his hand. It was the same shooter with the pug eyes who had fired at me at the Blue Crab Inn.

His gun rose in the air, and I desperately started to zigzag toward the tree. Over my steps I heard no noise, but as I neared the magnolia I saw its bark flay and shatter. I was ten yards from the tree when I dove headfirst and then rolled. It wasn't artistic, but I ended up behind the magnolia. I saw a puff of dirt rise up about eighteen inches from my foot, and then the shooting stopped.

I moved to the other side of the tree, did a quick bob and look of my head, and saw the shooter moving, crablike and low, toward me. Everything in me wanted to run, but it would have been a sucker's bet. The shooter was ready for my flight now. My back was going to be his bull's eye.

"I give up," I yelled, and chanced another quick look.

This time I heard the shot, but it sounded more like a cap because of the silenced gun. The round hit the tree.

"Shit!" I shouted. "I said I give up."

I had seen the direction he was moving, and now I heard his voice.

"Come out then," he said.

"How do I know you won't shoot?"

"Because if you don't come out with your hands held high, I'll shoot you anyway."

It was the kind of logic I couldn't argue with, but it wasn't assurance I wanted. Now I had my update on where he had moved. In my mind I locked on the target and weighed the rock in my hand. It was heavier and bigger than a baseball. I would need to take that into account.

"I'm coming out, then," I shouted. "I know where the woman is. She hired me, but I don't want anything more to do with this, so don't shoot. Okay?"

I didn't have to fake my fear. It was there in my voice, but the shooter didn't respond.

"Okay?" I shouted again. What I was really yelling was, "Marco."

"Okay."

Polo. I had two things going for me: twelve years of organized baseball, and countless acorn fights as a boy where my specialty was whipping out from behind a tree and throwing on the fly.

Heavy breath to focus, the bending of my knees to balance, the wind-up, then I was leaping to my right. My attempt to parlay hadn't impressed the shooter. His silenced pistol was already up and aimed. I threw the rock on the move, and immediately knew it was off the mark. The stone was going to land short.

Luckily, the shooter didn't know that. He raised a defensive hand as if to ward off the hurled projectile and his shots went wide.

The rock struck about ten feet in front of my assailant, but the ground barely slowed it. I suppose it must have bounced on a straight line, but I was running too hard to see that. From behind me, though, I heard a yelp of pain.

I ran as fast as I could downhill. There were trees all around that provided cover. The leafy ground gave little indication of what was beneath it, and it was a balancing act not to break an ankle or a neck.

Fifty yards, a hundred yards, and still no indication I was being shot at. That didn't mean anything. Pug had a silenced pistol. I had read somewhere that silencers inhibit the velocity of bullets. The silencer and small gun were good for stealth, but not fire power. At the Blue Crab Inn the bullets hadn't penetrated through Lawrence, which meant the gun wouldn't be effective shooting at long range.

I turned my head around and didn't see pursuit. It had been a long time since I'd taken an individual tactics and techniques course. My breath started coming in gasps. All those damn restaurant audits, all those meals with appetizers, desserts, and drinks. Sure, I did my obligatory workouts at the gym, but I wasn't in battlefield shape. I needed to get through boot camp alive so I could participate in the war.

I took an inadvertent tumble, did two forward rolls, and then got to my feet. For a few moments I saw two of everything except pursuit. It dawned on me that not being chased wasn't necessarily a good thing. If the enemy wasn't after me, they might have already figured out where I would be coming out. I was the little fish, not the bigger fish they wanted. I pushed that much harder, this time in a race against an unseen foe.

Spring runoff had pushed the creek's waters high up on the banks. I could see how a downpour would flood the bottom of the valley. The water was halfway up my calf, and it took me three steps to get through it. My shoes squished under my feet. They were the proper footwear for a realtor, but not someone in a life-or-death sprint, or what should have been a sprint. Now the way was uphill, and every step was a fight against gravity.

I had this feeling I wasn't making any headway. I was Sisyphus with a rock, struggling mightily but futilely. My feet kept slipping, the mud denying them good traction. I felt like one of those dying insects upended on its back whose legs kept moving out of instinct.

God, I'd made a mess of things. My command decisions had been pathetic. The only battle tactic I had demonstrated was fleeing for my life.

Another step, and another.

I had to pick up the pace, and tried pushing myself with a gasped-out jody call:

> *"One mile no sweat,*
> *Two miles better yet,*
> *Three miles think about it,*
> *Four miles thought about it,*
> *Five miles feeling good like I should."*

The words kept me going, and I was able to think about something other than my next breath. It was clear they knew things about Claire. They had figured she would return to her father's house, and they had set the trap. Maybe they already had her. I wasn't their target. I was only the foot soldier. They had probably welcomed my going into the house. They might have even monitored the phone call.

I kept going. I could beat them to her. She would be there. She had to be. I was too stupid to give up, and too stubborn. I snatched a look at my watch. It was four-thirty. Claire would be waiting for my call.

People have always thought I am smart because of my memorization ability, and powers of observation. They don't realize that what I do is only a skill, like juggling, or a carnie guessing weight. I was a sideshow act, not a hero.

Closer to the top, closer. I felt like a mountain climber approaching a summit. Every step was pure agony. There wasn't enough air. My brain was operating on fumes. But something kept my feet moving. The rise wasn't far now. Only a few more feet.

I reached level ground and all at once I could see more than the hill in front of me. What I didn't see was Claire's waiting car.

All my fears were realized in an instant. I sucked in air and tried to think what to do.

Flag down a car. Get the police. Neither was the right answer. I might stop the wrong car and end up dead. And involving the police would mean having to spend time answering too many questions.

I ran in an unsteady line to the street. There was no traffic to be seen, and I remembered how quiet the road had been when we scouted it out. There were no buildings in sight, and the nearest house was at least a half mile away.

The goddamn finish line had been moved on me.

I threw the blazer over my shoulder and started jogging along the street. My feet were sore from two nights before and running in mud-soaked shoes wasn't helping them. With every step I realized there wasn't a part of me that didn't hurt. I no longer looked like a real estate agent. I looked like an escapee from the asylum.

I suddenly woke from my recriminating to hear a car coming up behind me. Too late, I realized I should have been conducting myself as if I were behind enemy lines, not out for a stroll. I was acting as if I had never had military training, making the kind of novice mistakes that get you killed.

I veered off, heading back for the wetlands. That's when I heard the honking. I looked over my shoulder and then stopped running. Hands on knees, I waited, doing my looking while sucking in air. If it was a trick, it was a good one, and I was now dead.

Our rental car was being driven very quickly. As the Civic came closer I could see that Claire was driving it, and there didn't appear to be any other passengers. The car came to a shrieking halt and she threw open the passenger door.

I jumped inside and Claire punched the accelerator.

"Where the hell were you?"

"Staying alive," she said.

"What do you mean?"

"I had this feeling something was wrong," said Claire. "I kept sitting here as the minutes ticked by. The wait kept getting more and more difficult and finally I decided to move the car. I drove up the road, came to a residential area, and pulled into a driveway. Luckily, no one was home, so I was able to just sit there and wait. I kept my head low and out of sight, but positioned all the mirrors to see behind me. Five minutes went by when I heard the approach of this vehicle. I could hear the car braking as it came closer. From my mirrors I watched a large sedan slow to a crawl just in front of the driveway. I am sure it was studying every car it passed, but I have never been so scared in all my life. It felt as if I were being stalked by something terrible. I couldn't see the monster, but I knew it was there. All I could make out were those tires turning over at a snail's pace. I couldn't even breathe. I suppose the car only slowed up for a moment, but it felt like hours. Then it accelerated away. I didn't move, I couldn't move. My hands were white from gripping the gun. I can't be sure, but I think the same car went by

YES! ☐

Sign me up for the Leisure Horror Book Club and send my TWO FREE BOOKS! If I choose to stay in the club, I will pay only $8.50* each month, a savings of $5.48!

YES! ☐

Sign me up for the Leisure Thriller Book Club and send my TWO FREE BOOKS! If I choose to stay in the club, I will pay only $8.50* each month, a savings of $5.48!

NAME: _____

ADDRESS: _____

_____

TELEPHONE: _____

E-MAIL: _____

☐ **I WANT TO PAY BY CREDIT CARD.**

☐ VISA   ☐ MasterCard   ☐ DISCOVER

ACCOUNT #: _____

EXPIRATION DATE: _____

SIGNATURE: _____

Send this card along with $2.00 shipping & handling for each club you wish to join, to:

**Horror/Thriller Book Clubs
20 Academy Street
Norwalk, CT 06850-4032**

Or fax (must include credit card information!) to: 610.995.9274.
You can also sign up online at www.dorchesterpub.com.

*Plus $2.00 for shipping. Offer open to residents of the U.S. and Canada only.
Canadian residents please call 1.800.481.9191 for pricing information.
If under 18, a parent or guardian must sign. Terms, prices and conditions subject to change. Subscription subject
to acceptance. Dorchester Publishing reserves the right to reject any order or cancel any subscription.

JOIN NOW!

again a few minutes later, but this time in the opposite direction. That's when I decided to look for you."

"It's a good thing you're not a soldier," I said.

"Why is that?"

I whispered some Tennyson: " 'Someone had blunder'd. Theirs not to make reply, Theirs not to reason why, Theirs but to do and die.' "

"What are you talking about?"

"I blunder'd," I said, using the poetical pronunciation. "If you had obeyed my orders, you would probably be dead."

During the Crimean War, the Battle of Balaclava became famous for The Charge of the Light Brigade. Because of ambiguous orders, over six hundred British soldiers engaged in a cavalry assault on Russian guns. Armed only with sabers and lances, the British charged into a withering fire of cannons. Because of a poorly written command, and subsequent miscommunication, the Light Brigade was decimated. The soldiers knew the orders they had been given were all but suicidal, but all of them did their misguided duty. One fourth of that cavalry never rode out of that valley, and almost half of the survivors suffered wounds.

"Let's get the hell out of the valley of death," I said.

CHAPTER FOURTEEN

Both of us started breathing a little easier when we saw the signs to Interstate 26.

"Which way?" Claire asked.

"Charleston," I said. "We need to visit your father's bank first thing in the morning. I'm hoping your face or your name won't jar a teller's memory. Does anyone know you there?"

Claire shook her head. "It's a large bank. That might be why my father chose it. I don't think anyone there knew him, either."

"Do you have any idea where he could have gotten those two guns?"

She shook her head again. "Like I told you, finding that gun in the safe-deposit box was a shock, especially after I had kept insisting to Sheriff Vargo that Father had never owned a gun."

"Is he the one who knows your case best?"

Claire nodded. "The Summerville Police Department was the first on the scene, but because there was a death with potentially suspicious circumstances, most of the investigation was conducted by the county sheriff's office. Dorchester County only has about a hundred thousand people living in it, so the force isn't that large. Sheriff Vargo is as familiar with the case as anyone."

"I need to find a way to talk to him, then," I said.

"That should be easy," she said. "Tell him that you're a national news correspondent and that before sending a film crew to see him you need to run some questions by him first. He'll talk for sure."

"And why's that?"

"The county sheriff is an elected official, and this is an election year. The sheriff won't want to miss a photo opportunity like that."

Claire didn't voice any objections about staying in the car while I talked with the sheriff. I told her that for security reasons I wanted to call from a pay phone, but the truth of the matter is that I wanted to have the conversation with Claire out of earshot.

Experience had taught me that hotels are a good place in which you can be anonymous. I parked in a subterranean garage of a downtown Charleston hotel, and after tidying up I ventured inside the property and gave myself a self-tour. Outside of a third-floor banquet room I found a bank of pay phones. There were no meetings going on, and very little foot traffic in the hallway. Clark Kent probably could have changed into Superman and not been observed. Now I had to change into reporter Clark Kent.

I looked at my watch, saw it was almost five o'clock, and hoped the sheriff wasn't keeping banker's hours. After dialing a number Claire still remembered by heart, I tried to impress a very southern, very bored, female voice by announcing myself as Jack Petit of ABC News looking for Sheriff Vargo. I said my name as if it meant something, as if it deserved not 911 priority, but 1011.

"I'll see if he's around," she said, with languid unconcern.

Half a minute passed, and then a voice said, "This is Vargo."

I again did my self-important introduction, but the sheriff didn't seem inclined to do somersaults, either. "Thought I already talked with you boys," he said.

For a moment, I didn't understand what he was saying. "You mean my network?"

"That's right. I talked to a reporter out in front of the building. They brought a news van for a satellite feed."

"That must have been local news," I said. "I'm with national in D.C. In fact, Peter Jennings is considering coming down there tomorrow and talking with you personally. Before we make those arrangements, though, I need to do some fact-checking."

Vargo sounded a little more enthusiastic: "Shoot."

"The media is categorizing Claire Harrington as being 'mentally unstable,' Sheriff. In your dealings with her, was that your impression?"

"I can't say I knew her well enough to form an opinion. I can tell you that on several occasions when I talked with her she was very upset. At the time I thought that was understandable, though, what with her daddy dying and all."

The sheriff had a folksy way of talking, but I had a feeling the pone in his speech was there by design. More than anything, he sounded sharp, and seemed comfortable in his dual role of lawman and politician.

"You ruled her father's death a suicide, is that correct?"

"That's what the medical examiner, and the detectives investigating his death, concluded."

"But Ms. Harrington thought it was a murder?"

"That's right."

"Why was she so adamant?"

"Several things bothered her, but I think what stuck in her craw most was the 911 call."

"Tell me about it."

Over the phone, I could hear the sheriff flipping some pages. "The congressman made that call on January twenty-eight at a quarter after nine. He said there were some suspicious characters lurking around his house."

"He saw more than one suspect?"

"He said he saw one sitting in a car, and one attempting

the break-in. Officers were dispatched to the scene. They did a thorough search around the house and found nothing that would indicate an attempted home invasion. There were no footprints, and no signs of forced entry. The officers canvassed the neighborhood, ringing doorbells and asking questions. None of the neighbors saw anything. One of them walked his dog right by where Congressman Harrington said the getaway car was parked, but he didn't recall seeing any car. After doing all their checking, and talking with Harrington, the officers on the scene suspected he was making up his story."

"Were there any other factors that led them to believe that?"

"Uh-huh. The logistics weren't adding up. When questioned, the congressman was vague on all sorts of details. Even though he offered descriptions of the suspects, it turns out he couldn't have seen them from where he said he was doing his looking."

"Any guesses on why he bothered to make a phony call?"

"False calls are part of police work. Sometimes people are lonely. Sometimes old people are frightened but don't want to admit it. The elderly often need reassurance. Believe me when I say that we're used to people making up emergencies. At the time, the officers assumed it was just one of those things. Later, we decided the call was the congressman's way of preparing for his death."

"I am not following you."

"Did you know that Harrington was a very sick man?"

I did not know that. It hadn't been part of Claire's edited version of the facts.

The sheriff didn't wait for my answer, but continued talking. "He had cancer of the colon, and his prognosis wasn't good. We learned about his cancer after he died. That's when everything started making sense to us."

"Why don't you make sense of it to me."

"As we see it, Harrington wasn't comfortable going out as

a suicide. We've seen that before with old-schoolers and military types. For them, there's a bad stigma associated with suicide. They see it as a coward's way out. Because of that, Harrington decided it would be more honorable to set up his death to look like a murder. His 911 call was his way of creating bogeymen that would ultimately explain his death."

"He wanted a break-in on the record."

"An armed break-in."

"Did you do a gun residue test on his shooting hand?"

Just a touch of testiness entered the sheriff's voice: "It was inconclusive," he said, "but even the lab boys will tell you that the results from a GSR are less than reliable."

I racked my brain, trying to sound as if I knew something about forensics and crime scene investigations. "Was his death consistent with a suicide?"

"He made a lot of amateur mistakes in trying to make it not look like a suicide. That's what made it so obvious that it was."

"What obvious things are you talking about?"

"He broke a window so it would appear there was a forced entry of the house, but we determined the break came from inside the home, not outside. The signs of a struggle in the library were also clearly manufactured. There were overturned book racks and displaced furniture, but no bloodstains, hair, or trace evidence from that apparent struggle. He wanted to make it look like he fought his killer tooth and nail before dying."

"He was found dead atop his desk, is that right?"

"Uh-huh. And forensics tells a story there as well. The tattooing of the gunshot wound showed the weapon was fired at a very close range. The blood splatter also confirmed that."

"Was the gun found in his hand?"

"It was not," said the sheriff, "which is consistent with

most suicides with handguns where usually the weapon is dropped. Hell, sometimes it's even tossed, especially when you got a handgun with a kick like this one. Being military and all, Harrington would have known about guns and counted on that happening to make it look more like a murder."

"Did you do a history on the weapon?"

"If you're asking do we know where and when he bought the gun, no, we don't. The feds are looking into that now. What we do know is that it's an older model, about twenty years old, a Smith and Wesson Model 629 .44 magnum with an eight-and-three-eighths-inch barrel." He paused a moment before asking: "You know anything about guns?"

I offered up some old NRA propaganda: "Yeah, they don't kill, people kill."

The sheriff surprised me by laughing. "What you got here is one heavy gun. It weighs about three pounds empty. This kind of gun is popular with hunters."

"People use handguns to hunt?"

"They use this kind of handgun to hunt. It's big and accurate, and can be loaded to shoot bear, and I mean that literally. Some of the good old boys like nothing better than going out with a big-bore six-gun like that magnum and hunting big game. They get themselves some three-hundred-grain ammo and they're really throwing lead."

"What does all that mean?"

"That it's a gun capable of handling a big load. Plinking bottles is one thing; shooting a deer or boar at a hundred yards is something else entirely. Put some high-grain ammo in this gun and you can hit your target from a long distance off."

"What kind of ammo did you find in this gun?"

"Nothing too high up on the grain count. It wasn't special pack, but just something bought over the counter. The ammo was old. I imagine it was bought with the gun."

"You said this gun has an eight-inch barrel?"

"Eight and three-eighths inches. It's about as big a barrel as you're going to find. That same model came in other barrel sizes, though, with a four-incher and a six-incher."

I eschewed the Freudian interpretation, and instead asked, "Why would anyone want a gun barrel that long?"

"Accuracy. You see guns like that used for target shooting. It's one of those guns of choice for long-range handgun shooting events. Not all gun people like them, though, especially indoor range operators. They hate big forty-fours 'cause they're so noisy. Some shooting ranges even ban them. Other people don't like those kind of guns 'cause they kick like a horse. I hear tell they got over twenty pounds of recoil energy."

Firsthand, I knew that. Even when I'd been expecting the recoil, the gun had bucked and packed a punch. Claire Harrington hadn't been able to handle that recoil at the Blue Crab Inn. She had dropped the gun after firing it, and acted surprised by its kick, as if she had never shot it before.

"Claire Harrington is wanted for the murder of Lawrence Deering and the attempted assassination of Mark Stanton. Has the gun that killed her father been linked with those shootings?"

"The government boys are doing ballistics tests right now, comparing groove impressions, projectile samples, things like that. We do know casings and ammo for a forty-four were found at both of those sites."

"Didn't the Stanton shooting occur two weeks before Harrington's death?"

"That's about right."

"So what do they think, Claire Harrington got the gun, went target shooting on Stanton, then returned it back home in time for her father to shoot himself?"

"If you want a sensationalistic news slant, I suppose you could work the story that way. Maybe you could even get Oliver Stone to direct the segment."

"Simplify it for me, then."

"The government has evidence that shows Claire Harrington visited her father two weeks before he died. They can also prove that right after her visit Miss Harrington went to New Hampshire. They can show that shots were fired at Stanton very near the motel where she was staying. And two days after the New Hampshire shooting, Ms. Harrington was in South Carolina visiting her father again. Do you find it so hard to believe that she took the gun, used it, and then returned it again?"

"I'm easy to convince," I said. "I'm one of those rare people who can't even find fault with the findings of the Warren Commission. But if what you say is true, and Claire Harrington did borrow her father's gun to try and shoot Stanton, then I assume you found her fingerprints on the firearm when you had it in your possession."

Sheriff Vargo sighed. "Ms. Harrington's fingerprints were not on the gun, but again, that means nothing. These days anyone with a lick of sense knows you wear gloves when you're using a firearm in the commission of a crime."

"How many sets of prints were found on the gun?"

"We identified three sets, with Congressman Harrington's predominating."

"So you're saying at least two other people handled the gun?"

"I'm surprised we didn't get more than two sets of prints," said the sheriff. "It's not like the gun just magically appeared one day."

"What was the condition of the gun?"

"What do you mean by that?"

"Could you tell if it had been used a lot?"

"When our boys tested it, they said they doubted whether more than ten rounds had ever been fired."

"A gun that old, a gun which at that time was supposedly used in an assassination attempt, and then a suicide, and it's hardly ever been fired?"

"That's about the size of it."

"How did you determine this gun actually belonged to Harrington?"

"In a death like this, we don't call it a suicide without doing some serious looking. In our investigation we talked to friends and relatives of Garret Harrington. That's how we learned about his terminal cancer. That's how we learned he wasn't acting like himself the last few months of his life."

"Is it true that Claire Harrington told you that her father did not own a gun?"

The sheriff paused before answering. "She made that assertion," he said, "but became less vociferous about it as time passed. I do know that while Garret Harrington was a congressman, he was a friend of the gun lobby. That's public record. It seems to me that a man who was consistently on record for the right of citizens to bear arms would probably have one of his own."

"Why do you think she backed off on her claim that he didn't own a gun?"

"I'd only be guessing, of course, but maybe she started getting nervous about our looking closely at the gun and finding a possible link with the shooting that went on in New Hampshire."

"When did you give the gun back to Claire?"

"She reclaimed all of her father's possessions that we were holding on March the twenty-third."

"In retrospect, you probably wish you hadn't given her the gun."

"At that time, Ms. Harrington had a clean record, had not been convicted of a crime of violence, was not a known member of a subversive group, and appeared to be mentally competent. In South Carolina you don't need a permit to purchase a gun, don't need to register a firearm, and don't need a license to have one, so I had no choice but to pass on the firearm. The Second Amendment to our Constitution is taken very seriously in these parts."

"Did you ever consider that someone might have made the murder look like a suicide, up to and including the staging of those so-called amateur mistakes?"

"That was Ms. Harrington's interpretation of what occurred. So we asked her if that was the case, what was the point of someone going to all that effort? Why didn't they just murder her father and dispose of his body? She could never answer that question."

I thought about it. I couldn't, either.

"Do you have a transcript of Garret Harrington's 911 call?" I asked.

"Sure do. You want me to fax it your way?"

"That's not necessary," I said quickly. "If it's not too long, I'd appreciate your reading it to me."

The sheriff didn't comment, but I could hear him sorting through some papers. "You want me to read everything?" he asked.

"Just what Harrington said."

"All right—the dispatcher asked about the nature of his emergency, and Harrington said, 'There's an armed man trying to break in through the downstairs window. I can see him from here. He's holding a very large gun.' Then the dispatcher got his name and address, and told him she had already dispatched a squad car. That's when Harrington volunteered, 'Tell the police to watch out. There are two of them. One is waiting out in the car, and the other one is doing the break-in.' The dispatcher asked if he could get a make, model, or license plate of the car, but Harrington said, 'It's too far off to see. But I have a good view of the driver. He's an older white male, about seventy-five years old, with wavy, white hair. The one who's breaking into the house is younger. He is a white male, very clean-cut, about fifty years old, with short, black hair. It appears he's holding some kind of bag in his left arm.' The dispatcher heard him getting worked up, so she told him to remain calm and assured him that help was on the way. At that point he interrupted her and said, 'He's running back to the car. He must have been scared off. Now he's in the car. They're driving away.'"

I heard the crackling of paper. "Do you want me to keep reading?" asked the sheriff. "That's really about it. The dispatcher stayed on the line and chewed the fat with the congressman until help showed up at the door, but she did almost all the talking."

"No, that's fine. Thanks much."

"So, you say Peter Jennings might be coming out here tomorrow?"

I decided to head off any technical questions before they might be asked. When short on facts, pour on the bullshit. "That's the plan. If Peter does fly down there, make sure that neither you, nor anyone on your staff, make any Canadian jokes."

"Say what?"

"Peter's Canadian. He has this big chip on his shoulder when it comes to Canada. Do you know the capital of Canada?"

"I got no idea."

"It's Ottawa. Remember that. Before starting in on an interview, Peter always throws out that question in a casual kind of conversational way. Believe me, he's a lot more pleasant to you if you know the answer."

"Ottawa."

"It's in the southeastern tip of Ontario. If you say the words *Ottawa* and *Ontario* in the same breath, he'll be eating out of your hand."

"Much obliged."

"Likewise, Sheriff."

Claire was waiting for me in the underground parking lot of the hotel. She greeted me with a big smile and was much more cheery than I remembered her being when I left. I wasn't as enthusiastic with my own semi-grin, but she didn't notice.

"Did you get through to Sheriff Vargo?"

I nodded, started up the engine, and then turned to look at her. "Why didn't you tell me your father had colon cancer?"

"What difference would it have made?"

"People with terminal illnesses often choose their own way of going out."

"I hope you haven't bought the sheriff's interpretation that my father was at death's door. He was somewhat weakened by his cancer, but he was not daunted by it."

"You're assuming your father was murdered because of something he knew. Are you sure the attempt on your life was a result of your investigating his death?"

"I believe that has to be the case. It was only after I started making inquiries into his death that I was targeted."

"Not long after the assassination attempt on Mark Stanton, you returned to South Carolina."

"As you have learned, my father was ill. Because of that, I was a frequent visitor the last few months of his life."

Claire had answers for everything, and despite evidence to the contrary, was convinced her father was murdered.

"In your father's 911 call, he referenced that the man breaking into his house was holding a large gun."

"That's proof he saw the gun," Claire said.

I didn't know what it was proof of, but I didn't say that. Maybe the gun at the bank would offer more answers. We pulled out of the subterranean garage.

"Which way?" I asked.

Claire offered directions to the bank and I followed them. My questioning her was only interrupted, not put to an end, and both of us knew that. Surprisingly, my interrogation hadn't seemed to put a damper on her good mood.

The bank was the anchor property to a strip mall just outside of Charleston. Judging from its exterior, the bank did a high-volume business, with three drive-up stations and a fourth lane with two drive-up ATM machines.

I parked away from the bank, left Claire as a lookout, and walked over to a third ATM for those who wanted to do their banking outside their automobiles. There were two entrances into the bank, and from the outside I counted nine walk-up windows. The interior of the bank was set out in the shape of a large square. In a corner behind where the tellers were stationed was the vault and safety deposit room. While continuing to do my scouting, I pretended to make an ATM transaction, mindful of the cameras everywhere. There was a newspaper machine next to the ATM, and I dropped in some change and pulled out a copy of the *Charleston Post & Courier*.

When I returned to the car I tossed the newspaper on her lap, and Claire saw her picture on the front page.

"As if all the lies aren't bad enough," she said, "they seem to have found corroborating pictures. I look like Snow White turned anarchist. And the guilt by association doesn't help, either."

Next to Claire's photo were pictures of Squeaky Fromme and Sara Jane Moore, failed assassins of President Gerald Ford. The headline read WOMEN JOINING RANKS OF ASSASSINS.

"No one's going to associate you with Squeaky Fromme," I said. "She came out of the ranks of the Charlie Manson family. You, on the other hand, emerged out of the Daughters of the American Revolution. That makes you much more interesting. Because of you, the FBI will probably start investigating the D.A.R. as a subversive organization."

Claire wasn't amused, and tossed the newspaper into the backseat. "When I'm vindicated," she said, "I'll hold the biggest press conference of the year. When people learn all that I've gone through, everything will change at once. They'll see how I was terribly wronged because of one man's blind ambition. I'll be surrounded by some very visible supporters, and the tide will instantly turn. I will not only get my good name back, I'll get justice."

"You have your Cinderella story already scripted."

With a fierce adamancy, she said, "Yes, I do."

Maybe that vision was the only thing keeping her going. "And they lived happily ever after."

"That's the ending I have in mind."

"In that case, we'd better get our pumpkin parked before midnight strikes."

"Can we stay in a hotel tonight? I so want a shower."

"I don't think we can even chance a tent tonight," I said. "We're going to have to find a quiet place to park, a spot that won't attract the attention of police. Tell you what, though. I'll give you the choice of the front seat or back-seat."

Claire sighed. "I'm not a very good fugitive."

"I know. I was thinking of reporting you to the Social Register people."

"You make me out to be such a silver spoon sort."

"Aren't you?"

"It's true that I come from a privileged background, but it's not as if I spent my time hanging out at the country club. Ever since I was a little girl, it was made abundantly clear to me that I was expected to give back to community and country, and I'm not talking about just writing a check. Whenever I could, I pitched in and worked, and while I might have been sheltered I was still given periodic doses of reality. Every year my mother had me help out at a food line for the needy, and she also made me volunteer at a homeless shelter. At the time, I didn't like it much, but now I'm thankful for all those lessons. Last year alone I did more than two hundred hours of pro bono legal work, as well as heading up several service organization projects."

"In other words, you were a member of the Junior League."

Claire laughed. "You're a jerk," she said, "but you're right. You make me feel so predictable."

"You're anything but that."

My compliment made her smile linger.

As a girl, I was willing to bet Claire had made more Brownie points, and sold more boxes of Girl Scout cookies, than anyone in the state. As a woman, she still seemed to be trying to earn those Brownie points. I wondered at her motivation, but didn't ask.

I took my eyes off the road for a moment, looking at Claire's hair and face. She looked like a younger version of Michelle Pfeiffer with dark hair. Claire used very little makeup, but with her classical good looks she didn't need much.

"What are you looking at?" she asked.

With her blue eyes and light coloring, blond hair would look very natural. I said, "Maybe we should take a chance on finding a place with a shower after all."

CHAPTER FIFTEEN

From the platform of the train, the Candidate waved to the enthusiastic gathering. On cue, the conductor sounded the whistle and the crowd raised their voices to cheer.

Their special charter train was making its way down the California coast. They had started in Santa Barbara, and would end in San Diego. Each stop lasted fifteen minutes, time enough for him to shake hands, kiss babies, and give a short, passionate address.

"I need your vote!" he shouted. "Can I count on you next Tuesday?"

They responded to his entreaty with loud cheers, and by waving the small red, white, and blue flags provided by his campaign.

The whistle-stops were getting wide media coverage. His campaign manager said there had been news spots on every station in California. In Los Angeles and San Diego they had even patched in live feeds to their nightly news broadcasts.

People loved trains as much as they loved parades.

"Together," he said, "we can send a message to Washington, and to the world. It's time for the politicians to listen to the people."

The clapping was long and sustained now. It didn't matter that he was an entrenched Washington insider, because he always talked himself up as an outsider.

He put his fingers up to his ear, and assumed a pose of someone straining to hear something. His gesture prompted the loudest cheers yet. "You know what I hear?" he asked. "I hear the message that America is back."

The train whistle sounded, the audience cheered, and the Candidate offered a thumbs up.

"Next Tuesday, show them that America is back!" he shouted.

Slowly, ever so slowly, the train pulled out of the station. All that was missing was the locomotive effect of billowing smoke. His people had done a fine job of choreographing all of these miniature appearances. Each station was almost like a movie set. Working from the train allowed him a forum for short, sweet, and highly visible presentations. There were placards along the side of the train that announced THE WHITE HOUSE EXPRESS. One of the pundits had said there was more corn in his campaign than in the state of Iowa, but at the same time admitted the corn was working. It was. All the polling results indicated his numbers were on the rise. Arizona and Washington had swung his way. And this train idea was bringing California into his camp. Next Tuesday could put him over the top.

As they pulled out of the station, he almost felt like one of those heroes who ride out of a town after rendering justice. In deliberately regal motion, he continued waving until the crowd was out of sight, and then finally made his way inside the coach car.

Applause greeted him as he stepped inside the compartment, and the Candidate bowed and smiled. His people were in high spirits. Just being aboard the train had put everyone in a celebratory mood. It was like riding a juggernaut. Nothing could stand in their way. As the Candidate passed down the aisle, he offered up praise to everyone he encountered. He knew his staff willingly worked harder than galley slaves. They liked his message, and they liked him. He was known as being affable and friendly and approachable. No one knew how long and hard he had worked on his personality in order to appear that way. He had studied tapes of Ronald Reagan, seeking to emulate the Great Communicator, to have his folksy charm.

With the back-patting and homilies behind him, the Candidate took a seat. There was a sleeper set aside for him, but by not using it, he signaled to those in the senior staff that he was available to them. The media had labeled his three kingmakers as "the Magi," though individually they were often referred to as "the Pit Bull, the S.O.B., and the Poet." The Candidate's campaign manager was his attack dog; his strong-willed chief of staff the one who said "no" on behalf of the Candidate; and the Poet was the chief speechwriter and media consultant.

The Candidate felt good, and not only because the crowds and the polls were pumping him up. There was that other thing, that secret thing. By tomorrow, his ongoing problem would disappear. Claire Harrington would no longer be a distraction.

The Pit Bull was already making his way down the moving train to have a word with him. His campaign manager had the reputation of being a hatchet man. The Candidate was able to play the good cop, while Pit Bull was the bad cop. It was a perfect setup, with his campaign manager the lightning rod for most of the criticism.

"You're kicking ass," the Pit Bull said.

"Thanks to you," the Candidate said. "You might remember I was skeptical about these whistle-stops."

The campaign manager's expression was just shy of a smirk. "I used a little ancient history," he said. "Harry Truman's whistle-stop tour got him elected when everyone said he didn't have a chance. I just dusted off his strategy."

"Well, I encourage you to keep dusting."

He nodded. "We got plenty more rabbits to pull out of the hat down the homestretch."

The S.O.B. and Poet joined the gathering, taking their seats in the berth across from his boss. The chief of staff was smiling, as usual. Critics called it his "executioner's smile." Though outwardly affable, the S.O.B. often quoted H. R. Haldeman's assessment that the White House Chief of Staff needed to be "the president's son of a bitch." Even though they weren't in the White House yet, he was practicing for his job.

"How is your voice holding up?" the Poet asked. She was always worried about his voice because it was the instrument for reciting her words. "There are four more stops to go."

"In the words of Hubert Horatio Humphrey, 'I am as pleased as punch.'"

"Speaking of punch," said the S.O.B., "there will be about a hundred people at that dessert tonight in La Jolla. They're all popping for a thousand dollars."

It was the modern version of indulgences, the Candidate thought. People no longer tried to buy their way into heaven, but instead purchased their favors for the here and now.

"Sugar *and* spice," the Candidate said.

Laughter greeted his remark. Like a comic, the Candidate had learned how to best deliver one-liners. He knew how to pause on certain words, and what to emphasize for maximum effect.

"They tell me there's a huge backyard at the house with a sweeping view of the Pacific," the S.O.B. said. "They've set up a gazebo there, and after your talk they'll be serving champagne and cordials and brandy. I promised that you'd stay long enough to smoke a cigar and pose for pictures."

The American voters didn't like their leaders assuming too many airs. In an effort to appear as "one of the guys," the Candidate had admitted to the vice of an occasional cigar. Now everyone wanted to indulge him, and it seemed that at every intimate gathering a smoke break was written into the agenda. Both men and women adjourned and lit up with him. There was something just a little bit naughty about holding a cigar in one hand and a brandy glass in another. It harkened back to a more innocent age and image. The tobacco industry loved his tacit endorsement of smoking, and as a result their contributions to the campaign were substantially up. There were a lot of people who thought it had been too long since a cigar-smoking, red meat-eating leader had taken up residence in the White House.

"Better save your voice," said the Poet. She rose, and the other two kingmakers stood with her.

"Fifteen minutes until the next stop," said the Pit Bull.

The Candidate nodded. After the Magi took their leave, he leaned back in the seat and closed his eyes, a signal for others not to disturb him unless there was something important to discuss. There were no media in this coach car; it was reserved for staff. He listened to the undercurrents of conversation going on around him. There was something almost Darwinian about the campaign. It was survival of the fittest, and even with the tremendously long workdays his staff was doing more than surviving. They were thriving.

The Candidate thought back to his qualms about campaigning on a train. He supposed his doubts stemmed from the last "whistle-stop tour" he had taken. The Scandal Tour is a popular sightseeing service unique to the Washington, D.C., area. Those taking the tour are treated to the kind of history lessons not taught in school. The Scandal Tour's "whistle-stops" include visits to such spots as the Watergate Hotel and Apartments, the Washington Tidal Basin, (stripper Fanne Fox jumped into the Tidal Basin to try and avoid arrest after a night of drinking and fighting and carousing with House Ways and Means Committee Chairman Wilbur Mills), and even the steps of the Capitol Building (not to talk about the distinguished personages who have walked up and down them, but to point out where Congressman John Jenrette and his wife Rita had made love). The Jenrettes's fifteen minutes of fame were not well spent. John Jenrette was caught stuffing bribe money down his pants during the Abscam scandal, while Rita shed her pants and everything else for a *Playboy* pictorial.

Those taking the tour got to hear about the Capitol Hill version of "Parkinson's Disease," and how the scandal made the hands of politicians shake. When lobbyist Paula Parkinson admitted to having affairs with a dozen congressmen, and revealed she even had sex in their offices, public approval for Congress plummeted. Buying a vote was one thing, selling it for sex another. Even Parkinson grew disgusted with the behavior of the politicians. "My morals might be low," she said, "but at least I have principles." Politicians didn't want to own up to having had sex with Parkinson, nor were they willing to live with the consequences. When Parkinson became pregnant, an antiabortionist congressman gave her five thousand dollars to have an abortion.

With such associations, it was no wonder that the Candidate had needed convincing to conduct his own whistle-stop campaign.

A voice interrupted the Candidate's musing: "We're coming into the station, sir."

The Candidate opened his eyes and saw one of his officious assistants standing there waiting to attend to him.

"Thank you," the Candidate said.

He straightened his tie and the assistant held a mirror up for him to see. The Candidate repositioned a few errant hairs. Outside, even over the noise of the train, he could hear the cheering.

The Candidate started walking down the aisle. As he had

in the previous stops, he would tell his supporters the children's story of *The Little Train that Could*. That was their train, he would say, a train running on ideas. But he needed their help to get beyond the "I think I can, I think I can," to the "I knew I could, I knew I could." Everyone always loved a good children's story.

The P.A. system was already starting up. The announcer was a popular southern California radio personality. "All aboooooaaaarrrrrd!" he shouted, "on the presidential express!"

That was his signal.

To uproarious cheers, the Candidate stepped forward to the platform.

I knew I could, he thought, I knew I could.

CHAPTER SIXTEEN

"Do you think he suspected?" Claire asked.

"No."

"How do you know?"

"You want the long answer or the short answer?"

"Your choice."

"He didn't turn his body away from me, and there was no change in his eye contact. His voice remained steady, with no alteration in pitch or speech. There was no nervous movement of his hands, feet, or legs, and his usage of 'ums' and 'ahs' remained constant. His body language was consistent with conversation. I didn't detect any mixed messages."

"I should have asked for the short answer," said Claire.

"That was the short answer."

"When did you become a human lie detector?"

"I had a girlfriend who worked as a psychic who got me interested in analyzing speech and body language. I was always amazed at Rebecca's ability to do a 'cold reading.' That's the term people in the clairvoyant business use to describe a session with someone they know nothing about. I drew from Rebecca's techniques, and learned others besides."

"Was she some kind of Gypsy?"

"Rebecca could have been from Sunnybrook Farm. She was a midwestern Episcopalian who graduated from the University of Illinois with a degree in Renaissance poetry. I knew she wasn't a real psychic when she agreed to go out with me."

"So you did a cold reading on the desk clerk?"

"In essence, yes. Our transaction was rather brief. He is used to people paying cash, and used to them not wanting to give their real addresses. And I was busy giving off the vibe of a man here for one reason."

Claire laughed a little nervously. The motel was off the beaten path. I had consulted the yellow pages to find it. Most communities, even those that consider themselves respectable, have such motels. People call them "hot pillow joints," or "no-tell motels." Some are quiet, innocuous even, surviving and even thriving because of their anonymity. Others flaunt their purpose by advertising hourly rates, boasting about their videos, ceiling mirrors, waterbeds, and vibrating beds. If it quacks like a fuck, it usually is.

Our motel was the quieter kind of getaway. The driveway leading up to our room was gravel, and as we drove along the path, the car's tires seemed to crunch with reproach. The rooms were set back in the shadows of large pine trees. There was maybe a touch of the Garden of Eden to the setting, but to my mind, the area felt more sleepy than sexy. There was no neon, and no glittery lights. Energy-saver bulbs in the fixtures outside the rooms gave off just enough light to see, but at the same time allowed for privacy.

I backed up the car, positioning it for a quick escape. We brought very little inside, though I did carry our recent purchases from a drugstore. Claire's teeth were chattering as I opened the door. There was a chill in the air, but she was more nervous than cold.

At first glance, the ceiling mirrors were the only giveaway that this was anything other than a motel room. The king bed took up most of the room. There was a large television set suspended from the ceiling, and on the bed stand was a remote control.

Claire did an uneasy inspection, opening the door to the closet and then looking in the bathroom.

"At least there's soap," she announced, "but I wish they'd provided disinfectant as well."

I picked up the remote. "Better check out the latest news," I said, and clicked on the TV.

The last viewers hadn't been watching the news. They had also liked the volume up on the loud side. I changed channels, and found different humans engaged in the same activity. Claire pretended not to see or hear what was going on while I again switched channels. At last I found some people on the screen not coupling. I muted the sound just in case, and after some more channel surfing found CNN.

Rather than sit on the bed, Claire took a seat in the room's lone chair. I plopped down on the bed and melted into the mattress. The impending primaries were the big story. In five days most of the western states would be holding their primaries, and all the politicians were heavily courting the voters. Their rhetoric was now more strident and desperate than it had been before. For many, a two-year marathon was now coming down to a sprint. The coverage flipped from one campaign to another.

"If only they could bottle all that hot air," I said.

"Shush."

"Personally, I would rather be watching the adult movies."

"That doesn't surprise me," said Claire. "Now be quiet."

For fifteen minutes the political coverage continued. I had thought I would be glad when it ceased, but I wasn't. Suddenly it was my face on the television, and if that wasn't bad enough, it was my mug shot photo being displayed. The only thing missing was the caption "serial murderer."

The news correspondent said, "There has been a second suspected shooter identified in the murder of ATF Special Agent Captain Lawrence Deering.

"Will Travis, age thirty-five, has been identified as an accomplice of Claire Harrington, the woman wanted for questioning in Deering's death, as well as the assassination attempt on presidential hopeful Mark Stanton. Travis is believed to have been with Harrington when Deering was shot. Investigators say that two different guns were discharged at the shooting, and they believe that both Travis and Harrington fired upon the ATF agent.

"Travis is an accomplished marksman. He attended West Point for two years before being discharged for an honor code violation. Although the United States Military Academy has refused to provide details of his violation, it is known that Travis has a history of gambling, and was charged with felony battery in a gambling-related altercation."

The picture changed to show Claire. At least her photo wasn't a mug shot. The story went on to say that the two of us were thought to be traveling together and believed to be armed and dangerous. In numb disbelief I continued to watch the story. They were talking about me, talking about us. I was on national news, and I looked like a scumbag. This wasn't the Ralph Edwards version of *This Is Your Life*.

When the story finished, I continued to stare at the screen. That wasn't me up there, I wanted to yell. That was somebody else. But it was the version of me that I wished had never been, with the low points of my life highlighted for all to see. Leaving West Point with my tail between my legs had always been my own personal disgrace. Now, that underwear was airing in public.

I felt a hand on mine. Claire had joined me on the bed. "I am so sorry," she said. "I know I got you into all of this."

"I was never convicted. Those charges were dropped."

"It's not important."

"It *is* important. The report implied that I have a gambling problem. That's not true. When I left West Point I drifted for a time. My only skill was soldiering, so I had to find another way to make money. I used my memory. As you might already have noticed, when I have a mind to I can retain large chunks of information. That's why I turned to counting cards."

Claire continued to stroke my hand.

"Casinos don't like people like me, people who win. They like the system stacked in their favor. I didn't count just face cards. In my mind I could reconstruct every card played, and not just for a single deck. They could throw four decks at me, and I could still recall most of the cards that were played. I didn't bet extravagantly, but I never liked to leave a table without a pocketful of black chips."

Now she was using her other hand to stroke my face. I could barely feel it.

"The casinos work together. They circulate pictures of card counters and criminals, and security seems to lump the two together. Even though I never played too often in any one place, I eventually was designated as a card counter and became persona non grata at the casinos."

I shook my head and Claire's light hand didn't detach itself from my face.

"I never liked gambling," I said. "It was just something to do to earn money. For me, sitting in a chair and memorizing cards for hours on end is anything but exciting. I didn't get a thrill from beating the system, and I had no itch for gambling. It wasn't the work I wanted, wasn't close to the life I wanted, but for a time I really didn't know what else to do."

"You don't have to explain," Claire said.

I shook my head. I did have to explain. "That felony charge happened almost ten years ago. I was playing at a blackjack table when the pit boss asked me to accompany a security guard to the manager's office. I didn't protest my innocence, and I didn't raise a stink. I did as I was told, and this guard just happened to take me to the one place in the casino where there weren't any security cameras. He led me to a room where two security guards were waiting for me. The muscle was wearing gloves. They wanted to hurt me without leaving any marks. I didn't go along with that plan. I was carrying a whole lot of anger, and I used it on those two security guards. When the Judas Goat guard saw how things were going, he ran out of the room and raised an alarm.

"Naturally, all three of them colluded to say that I had instigated the fight. Charges were filed, charges that were mysteriously dropped a few days later."

Claire said, "If you want to quit this job right now, I wouldn't fault you, and I wouldn't second-guess you." In a smaller voice she added, "I hope you don't, though."

"Quit?" I shook my head. "You forget, I'm a Travis."

"Are you going to draw a line in the sand?"

"No, I am going to cross a line."

Her caresses and concern emboldened me to kiss her. Claire's surprise was only momentary. She returned my kiss, and our breathing turned to panting as our faces ground into one another and our tongues danced. I pulled her close, and our bodies rubbed together as if we were two sticks intent on making fire. Then, abruptly, Claire broke off the kiss by pulling her head back. Palms facing out, she raised her two hands up against my chest. She didn't quite push me away. It was more like she was dispatching evil spirits. I broke apart from her.

"I'm sorry," she said. "That was my fault. For a moment I

forgot myself. I told you I was involved with another man, but it's more than that. We're engaged."

"Are you sure?" Her lips hadn't seemed sure at all.

"Yes, quite sure."

"So where is this fiancé?"

"He works in D.C. Since my father died I've seen very little of him, but he's been more understanding than I deserve. He is the reason I'm so desperate to clear my name. Because he has such high morals, I imagine he would find my even being in this room unforgivable."

"It's not as if we had much in the way of a choice."

"Still, I don't know how I would explain it to him."

I pretended the stiff upper lip: "You won't have to. Consider it a closed subject."

"If we had met under different circumstances," Claire started, and then chose not to finish her thought.

I didn't want solace. I wanted her. But in my best Bogey, I said, "Of all the gin joints in all the towns in the world, she walks into mine."

"You don't want to hear me sing *La Marseillaise*."

The singing I could live with, I thought, but I could do without hearing any more about her Victor Laszlo.

Claire slid away from me, but she didn't make a quick escape of it. I wondered if she wanted me to reach out for her again, but the moment passed and then she was away from the bed. She went and retrieved one of our drugstore purchases.

"I have never changed my hair color before," she said. "The idea of doing it feels strange to me."

"Maybe you'll find a whole new you."

"Maybe that's why I'm so scared."

"I promise I won't make any blonde jokes."

"You really think dying my hair is necessary?"

"Just going to the bank is chancy. If your name jars the teller's memory, I want you to have a different look from the one on the front page of the local bugle."

"You'd better not laugh at my transformation," Claire warned.

She withdrew into the bathroom and shut the door behind her, but didn't completely close it. Through the crack I caught glimpses of her disrobing. I didn't feel right about being a voyeur, but I didn't look away either. I did most of my viewing from the mirrored ceiling, which allowed me the pretense of staring at the television. Through the mirror I saw Picasso images of Claire's flesh. She finished taking off her clothes, then reached into the shower and turned on the water. Claire finished working the handles, and then disappeared behind the shower curtain. I let out a lot of pent-up air.

From start to finish, the coloring of Claire's hair took less than half an hour. She emerged a wheat-colored blonde, and I studied her critically before nodding.

"You look good," I said, "and different."

"I think I'll kill myself before being arrested with this hair color."

I tried to match her light tone, tried to pretend I was fine and dandy playing second fiddle to her fiancé. Edward G. Robinson-like, I said, "They'll never take us alive."

"Shall I call you Clyde, and you call me Bonnie?"

"I'd prefer Sundance."

"Which would make me Butch, right?"

"If you say so."

Claire hovered around the bed, but thought better of landing there and instead took a seat in the chair. For a minute, she played nervously with her hair.

"I'm worried I won't be able to pull it off tomorrow," she said. "I'll probably do something stupid, and the next thing you know they'll set off one of those silent alarms."

"All you have to do is get in and get out," I said. "I'll be the lookout. While you're going for your safe-deposit box, I'll be posing as a customer asking about opening a new account. If something looks wrong to me I'll signal you."

"You'll be doing a cold reading of the bank employees?"

"That's right."

"Did your psychic girlfriend ever feel bad about deceiving people?"

"Who said she deceived them?"

"Her clients must have thought she had certain powers, or was connected with a higher authority."

"And how is that different from someone in sales, or advertising, or politics?"

"Those people don't claim to be something they're not."

"They tell people what they want to hear, and that's exactly what Rebecca did. Yesterday you asked me why I was so cynical about politicians. With no disrespect intended to your father, I guess it's because I have been given an education on their shell games. Rebecca taught me the tricks of their trade."

"What tricks?"

I thought about them for a moment. "Rebecca came across as super-confident, as someone very sure of herself. She had her list of stock phrases, and could deliver them without even thinking. One of her talents was delivering ceremony. She could make a dramatic moment out of a look or gesture. Even if a reading wasn't going well, Rebecca knew how to flatter people into making them feel good about themselves. But what she did best was give the impression that she knew much more than she was saying, as if she was tapped into some divine and immutable truths."

The more I spoke, the more upset Claire seemed to get. "I have never seen a politician with a crystal ball."

"Yes, you have. A crystal ball is only a prop. Politicians have plenty of those, and use them for the same purpose. Props provide atmosphere and make a statement. Why do you think politicians wrap themselves in the flag, or apple pie?"

"Don't you think they believe in those things?"

"I hope so. But they're certainly not above using them for their own purposes, either."

"From firsthand experience I can tell you that I know leaders who clothe themselves in garb other than the flag and sheep's clothing."

"You forgot to mention another one of their favorite outfits, the worst of all."

"And what is that?"

"When they parade around in their emperor's clothes and expect us to believe that they are draped in finery, when in truth there is nothing to them at all."

Her clipped response was offered in cold anger: "How lucky for us, then, that we have you to point out their nakedness."

"Why are you getting so mad?"

"Is that what your psychic training is telling you?"

"I don't know what it's telling me. Maybe it would be better if you just told me."

"Maybe it would be better if we just went to sleep. I'm exhausted."

CHAPTER SEVENTEEN

We shared the bed, each of us staying to our own side and neither of us coming close to no-man's-land. Claire dropped off to sleep quickly. She was more forgiving when asleep, and turned on her side toward me. In the darkness I watched her. Her breathing was soft and steady and I could just make out her reposed face. Apparently she was one of those people who could go to bed angry and not have it affect her sleep. I am not one of those people.

Her proximity wasn't making it any easier for me to sleep. Even though she stayed on her side of the bed, I could feel her body heat under the covers. I turned my back on her, but it was still there, touching my flesh like a furnace.

I thought about taking a cold shower, and not only because of Claire. My picture and biography as reported on national news was eating at me. I had never wanted to be anything more than a patriot, and now I was being called an enemy of the state. Now that I had a few moments to do something other than just stay alive, I could reflect about what I had gotten myself into. One thing was certain—my life would never be the same.

Still, that had been my choice. From the first, I could have walked away. For most people, that would have made sense, but not for me. I had needed something in my life, maybe not something as extreme as this, but some kind of change.

I had started and succeeded in my own business. I was good at my job, but it wasn't as if I felt wedded to the work. Maybe because I had settled in my professional life, I had also been willing to settle in my personal life. Claire kept stirring up these feelings in me. She brought on this storm inside that I couldn't pretend did not exist. I didn't think I was alone in sharing these feelings. When Claire and I had held hands, and when we kissed, she had returned my passion.

Since leaving West Point, my life had been one compromise after another. Growing up, I had wanted to be a soldier as much as most young boys want to be professional athletes. Duty, honor, country. It was a mantra I had stopped reciting, but one in which I was still a true believer. Recognizing that helped to ease my anger.

I will talk with Claire, I promised myself. Bowing out gracefully wasn't something I was going to let myself do. I could lose, but I wasn't going to compromise.

With that resolved, I felt a strange peace. It didn't even matter that I was a public enemy. I was doing what I believed was right, and that is as much as any soldier can ever hope for. That said, I didn't want to be a martyr; I wanted to beat the enemy. That enemy had me scared, but being afraid wasn't all bad. It reminded me that I was alive, and awakened me from what felt like a Rip Van Winkle slumber.

Finally I surrendered to need, and fell into an exhausted sleep.

"You do snore," Claire said.

She was already dressed and made-up, and her new blond hair was neatly brushed.

"What time is it?"

"Half past eight."

"You should have awakened me earlier."

"I didn't have the heart."

I couldn't detect any residual anger from the night before. I wondered if she had picked a fight because of our brush with intimacy. Our argument had set up barriers between us. Maybe, consciously or subconsciously, Claire wanted to avert the possibility of another encounter or to avoid any temptation altogether.

It had worked. We had spent the night not touching one another while sharing a king-sized bed in an adult motel. That was probably a first.

"It's raining outside," Claire said.

I listened to the pelting on the roof. "Good."

"Good?"

"We'll dress you up in layers and a raincoat. Everyone looks the same when they bundle up for bad weather."

I considered what needed to be done. "We'll stop and get you a large handbag as well. Don't linger when you're in the vault. Just drop the gun into your purse."

"You seem to think this second gun has some great significance, don't you?"

"Your father wouldn't have wrapped it up and put it away like that if it didn't. He wanted you to discover the gun, and the history behind it. That's why he put you on as a signatory to his safe-deposit box, and showed only you where the key was hidden. I just wish he had made the same arrangements when it came to his book."

"I've been doing some thinking about his book," said Claire. "My father was very old-fashioned, and didn't readily embrace modern technology. Not only was he computer illiterate, my father didn't even know how to type. He only knew how to hunt and peck."

I didn't see her point, and questioned her with my eyes.

"As I told you, over the years he gave me some pages of his book to read. Those pages were very clean. There was no Wite-Out on them, no misaligned or indistinct letters, not the usual blemishes you would expect to find in a typed manuscript."

Belatedly, I understood what she was getting at. "Someone typed it for him."

She nodded. "Someone who, I expect, saved the file and kept it for Father whenever he needed a printout."

"Holly's Secretarial in Ladson," I said, remembering an invoice. "She billed by the hour with no notation about what her services entailed."

Because whoever rifled through the office had left the invoice, I thought, there was a good chance that they hadn't connected her billings with the book.

"I'll call her," said Claire.

"Let's contact her after we finish with the bank," I said, "and the earlier we get there, the better. People tend to be more preoccupied at the start of a work shift."

I reached over to the bed stand and found a notepad. At the top of the pad was a silhouette of a naked woman's body along with the words TAMI'S OUTCALL MASSAGE. I wrote down a name and two telephone numbers, and ripped out the page.

As I handed the piece of paper to Claire, I said, "I'll be shaved, showered, and ready in ten minutes. Be ready to go."

She read the name on the paper aloud: "Lou Bohannon?"

"He's a captain in the Buffalo Police Department, the youngest in their history. The top is his work number, the bottom his home number."

"And why do I need his name and these numbers?"

"You don't go into an operation without preparing for the worst. In the event something happens to me, call Lou and use my name. Say that I told you to call in a favor on my behalf. He'll help you."

"Is he a good friend of yours?"

"He was," I said, "though it's been more than fifteen years since we talked."

"How is it you have these numbers?"

"He sends a Christmas card every year and I memorized them."

"How do you know him?"

I didn't answer, just closed the bathroom door behind me. Claire had her secrets, and I had mine.

We went to a drive-through and bought fast food and coffee. I parked several blocks away from our destination and while we sipped and nibbled I went over the bank plan. I kept coming up with "what if" scenarios, and "what to do in case of" situations. We pulled out our camping book and picked a spot to meet in the event we were separated; we agreed on legal strategies if caught; we went over escape routes. She was still holding on to my cell phone and I told her to keep it. The two of us decided it would be better if we went into the bank unarmed. After all, Claire would be coming out with another gun. All the planning didn't make her any more confident. Being reminded of the many things that could go wrong only made her more nervous.

"Let's get it over with," Claire finally said.

"Most battles are won or lost through planning."

"The rain's letting up," she said. "I'm going to look pretty silly walking into that bank and looking like the Morton Salt girl if it's sunny outside."

"All right," I said, "let's do it."

I drove over to the bank, and circled around the lot, looking for anything out of place in the vicinity.

No pedestrians walking around strip mall save to and from cars. Rain keeping people inside. No guard appears to be on duty. No one lingering in cars. Twenty-three cars parked within immediate vicinity of bank. Delivery truck parked in white zone in front of Italian restaurant kitty-corner to bank. Two entrances to bank, south door and west door. Equal amounts of foot traffic through both. Doesn't appear to be anyone lurking in vicinity of doorways.

I parked the car out of range of the bank's cameras, and was mindful of positioning it for quick accessibility to the street. "See you inside," I told Claire.

She gave me an intense nod, and I started walking along the rain-slicked asphalt parking lot. The plan was for Claire to set out for the bank as soon as I was inside. I would enter the building through the south door, and she through the west.

Two parking spaces open out front, and a third car leaving. Dry cleaner, Asian male five foot seven inches, one hundred forty pounds, putting out sign, WE ACCEPT COMPETITORS' COUPONS. Fogged windows of tan Chevrolet Caprice, but no sign of occupants. All windows of blue Ford Explorer cracked open. Shadow of movement inside.

The shadow revealed itself in the form of a shepherd mix. He barked at me from the backseat, then jumped to the front and continued to bark. The dog wasn't showing any teeth, but was telling me to stay clear.

I opened the south entry door to the bank, and held it for a woman who was leaving. It wasn't entirely chivalrous. I used the extra moments to scout the inside of the bank.

"Thank you," she said. After appraising the weather, she said, "It's turned into a nasty day, hasn't it?"

"It has indeed," I said, but I was already looking past her.

Staff moderately busy. Half situated behind the counter, the other half in public area. Ten staff on duty. Three tellers at open windows. Drive-up teller with headphones working window but also assisting out front. Assistant manager working behind the lines and handling business accounts. On the other side of wait area are suits at their desks. The accounts manager talking with older couple; investment officer punching in numbers; loan manager in discussion with twentyish male; employee leaning over manager's desk and going over paperwork.

Behind me I heard the dog, his bark penetrating through the glass. I looked back and saw the woman I'd held the door for pass by the car. Then I turned my attention back inside the bank. I tried to give the impression of being uncertain where to go, an explanation for my looking all around. After a few moments of scrutinizing, I appeared to find what I was searching for and made my way over to the desk where new accounts were being handled. The woman talking with the couple saw me standing there expectantly and gave me a smile.

"I'll be right with you," she said, pointing to some vacant chairs. "Why don't you have a seat."

I did as she suggested. From behind me, I heard a door opening. With my peripheral vision, I watched Claire enter the bank through its western door. No one seemed to take notice of her presence.

Claire proceeded directly to the most eastern window. There was a sign above it which said BUSINESS ACCOUNTS/SAFE DEPOSIT. The assistant manager noticed her standing there, and came out from behind her desk. The banker was a young woman, heavily made up, without a wedding ring. I thought those were all good things. Those south of thirty-five don't tend to follow the news as closely as those who are older.

"May I help you?" she asked.

"I need to get into my safe-deposit box," said Claire.

Outside, the dog barked again. Several seconds after that, the door opened and a woman holding a banking slip and some checks entered the building.

The assistant manager pushed a card forward for Claire to sign. "I'll need you to fill this out," she said, "and we also require two forms of identification."

Claire completed the card, writing her name and then penning her signature. Then she reached into her purse and produced a license and a credit card, as well as the key to the safe-deposit box.

I had imagined that if things were going to go bad, this would be the moment. There was no getting around

Claire's out-of-state license, or the name on that license being in the news. Changing Claire's hair color and style might have made her look different from the fugitive, but it also offered a different face from that on her license. The rain had helped in that regard. She was wearing a scarf over her hair.

The assistant manager scanned the identification, gave Claire the briefest look, and then picked up the card. "I'll be right back," she said.

Her walk was unhurried. There was no change in her posture, no telltale signs that something might be amiss. She opened a filing cabinet and did some thumbing through folders. Her hands didn't shake, and her fingers didn't fumble. She appeared to find what she was looking for, and compared the card to the signature on file. I only had a view of her back. Her breathing looked steady. She returned the card back into the folder, then closed the filing cabinet.

I casually turned my head as if stretching it, and took in the room. Nothing struck me as being out of the ordinary. Claire stood at the counter looking very poised, very patrician.

One of the bank's customers exited the door. She waited until she was outside before opening her umbrella. Superstitious, I thought. Judging by the dog's frenzied barking a few moments later, he didn't much like the umbrella.

The other door opened, and a middle-aged man in a business suit hurried in. As he brushed beads of water off his jacket, he looked distinctly annoyed. The rain made his clothes cling. He wasn't carrying a gun.

The older couple rose from the account manager's desk, and I was sorry their business didn't continue for another few minutes. The account manager looked my way, smiled, and said, "I'm sorry to have kept you waiting."

The nameplate on her desk said VIVIAN CARTER. Her coffee mug said WORLD'S GREATEST GRANDMOTHER. There were several pictures on her desk of a towheaded young boy. I was pretty sure I was seeing the grandson of the world's greatest grandmother.

"Just glad to be out of the rain," I said, making with the folksy patter.

"It's been coming down buckets, hasn't it?" Vivian said.

"Raining cats and dogs."

She didn't up the cliché stakes, but waited for me to state my business. Sitting on her desk were glasses. I decided I wanted them to stay right there. Vivian looked like the kind of woman who might remember faces from news reports.

"And how might I help you, Mr.—?"

"Paulsen," I said. "Jack Paulsen."

To my left and behind me, I saw the assistant manager press a button. Claire pushed on a gate, and was in. One major obstacle surmounted.

"Well," I said, "I guess I came in here because I'm not exactly happy where I'm presently doing my banking. You see, every month when I get my checking statement I feel like one of my hounds after a day in the brush. Those dogs always come out with lots of ticks, and darn if that's not the same kind of bloodletting that goes on in my account. You can't believe all the service charges for this and that."

Vivian made some sympathetic noises.

"So I just decided to come in here and see what kind of accounts you offer. I got a savings account with my bank, a checking account, and some IRA money as well."

Vivian had questions and brochures, and I pretended answers and interest while at the same time trying to monitor the goings-on of the bank. The rain had picked up, and was falling so hard on the roof it almost sounded like the playing of drums. I heard the western door open, and I tilted my head to see a mother pushing her baby in a stroller.

"We do have a checking account that offers interest," said Vivian. "Might you be interested in signing up for that?"

"What kind of interest rate does it pay?"

Almost three minutes had passed since Claire disappeared into the vault, and I was getting more and more concerned with each passing second. Still, as far as I could see, there was no unusual activity, nothing to indicate anything out of the ordinary was going on inside the bank.

Vivian was discussing having my work check directly deposited when Claire reemerged. The assistant manager was with her, and they appeared to be chatting amiably.

The heavy drumming on the ceiling let up, and the background static seemed to disappear. Even the weather now seemed to be cooperating for us.

"You've been a big help," I told Vivian. "Right now I got to run for an appointment, but all this sounds good to me."

Vivian didn't want me to leave without another brochure. I took it, and started for the door I had entered through. Claire would be exiting through the opposite door. Before stepping outside, I heard the dog start barking again, and through the door noticed a woman walking away from the bank. Though her back was to me I could see that she was talking on her cell phone.

The plan was for me to get the car, bring it around to the front, and pick up Claire.

The dog finished his barking about the same time the woman put away her phone. The dog had been consistent, warning off anyone approaching his car. I looked at the ground. There were waffle marks of small hiking boots leading not quite all the way to the door. The woman who was walking away was wearing hiking boots.

I wondered why she had stopped short of entering the bank. There were plenty of possibilities; she could have left something in the car, or been called on other business before doing her banking.

Or she could have been watching from the door and waiting for Claire to emerge from the vault.

Though the dog was now quiet, in my head his barks seemed more insistent than ever.

I changed directions, walking around the side of the

bank to the western entrance, but at the same time surreptitiously monitoring the woman in hiking boots. She was
now getting into a white Jeep Cherokee parked next to our
rental. I wondered why she hadn't parked closer to the
bank on a rainy day. I also didn't like the coincidence of
her car blocking my view to the Honda.

I caught Claire as she came out the door, and smiled as if
greeting an old friend. For a moment, her face registered
alarm. "Just relax," I told her. "Smile like this is an unexpected pleasure."

Claire managed to do that.

"It might be nothing," I said, continuing my smiling and
gesturing "but I think we'd better change plans."

"What's wrong?"

"Keep smiling," I advised her. "It's probably just nerves on
my part. Do you have the gun?"

Claire nodded enthusiastically as if I had said something
wonderful.

"Okay," I said. "I'm going to give you a nice, long hug. As
I'm doing that, slip it out of your bag and hand it off to me."

I drew Claire to me, but left her hands free to do their
work. She reached into her bag, and passed over a heavy
object covered in bubble wrap. While finishing off the hug,
I stuck the gun into my pants and hoped to hell it wasn't
loaded.

We disengaged, and I continued to offer the kind of man-
nerisms and enthusiastic speech you would to a good
friend you have run into. "Now we're going to separate," I
said, "but just for a minute. I want you to stay close to the
bank. If the bad guys are around here, they're going to be
mindful of not wanting to be caught on *Candid Camera*.
Walk over to where the drive-up window lanes are and wait
there. I'll pick you up in just a minute."

Claire's smile was failing her, and her breath sounded
strained and ragged. I patted her arm to reassure her, and
said, "It's almost over, okay?"

She nodded.

"I'm going to run over to the car," I said. "At the same time I want you to do some fast walking over to the drive-up area. Keep your eyes on me. If anything happens, I want you to run back into the bank and scream bloody murder. Okay?"

Claire gave me another nod.

I hugged her again, but this one wasn't scripted, and then I took off.

No cars moving in lot. No brake lights showing anywhere. White male, early fifties, leaving chiropractor's office. Walking gingerly as if back is bothering him. Delivery truck that wasn't in lot earlier parked in front of Italian restaurant. Impressions in asphalt of a dolly or cart leading from truck to restaurant.

I made it to the Honda, but stopped before inserting the key into the door, noticing the asphalt. It was obvious where the mystery woman's jeep had been parked, as the asphalt was almost dry. There was also a dry area near the driver's door that shouldn't have been there. Now that it had stopped raining, the asphalt was no longer awash in water. That was how I had made out the woman's waffle shoe patterns, and the wheel tracks from the cart. This time I wasn't looking at an impression so much as a lack of one.

The dry spot was out of place on the wet surface.

Maybe it was just the grading of the asphalt. It was possible the water had been funneled into another direction. I bent down a little closer. There wasn't one dry spot, but two. The areas were oblong and parallel to each other. They resembled two large loaves of French bread.

No, larger than bread loaves, I thought. More like two legs.

I matched my own legs up with the dry spots and found myself looking under the car. One look was enough. I pushed away hard, scraping my palms and tearing the seat of my pants. Then I was up and running away from the bomb.

The woman had been a lookout, advising the bomber or one of his lookouts of our movements.

"Claire!" I screamed.

She didn't hear me, her attention diverted by a tow truck with flashing lights that was parking on the street below the drive-up lanes. They had probably planned to detonate the bomb when we were driving on a deserted stretch of road. The tow truck would have been just the right touch. No one would have questioned a vehicle with flashing lights coming to the assistance of a car on fire.

The tow truck wasn't the immediate threat to Claire, though. The real danger would be coming at her from another direction.

I sprinted, unmindful of the wet asphalt and oil-slick surface. "Claire! Claire!"

She looked up and saw me. "Get into the bank! Now!"

Wheels squealing, a gray sedan with tinted glass turned hard into the parking lot and shot toward the drive-through lanes. The car came at Claire and she jumped back on a cement island. The sedan stopped well short of the drive-up window. Claire's eyes were focused on the passenger-side window. I assumed she was looking at a gun.

Someone was talking to Claire from inside the car. The good thing was that they weren't shooting yet. Instead of running up to Claire, I ran by her, stopping at the curb. The back window on the passenger side opened, and a gun leveled itself on me. There were three men in the car. One of the faces was all too familiar. It belonged to the man with the bulging eyes who had tried to shoot me first in Maryland, then the day before in Garret Harrington's backyard.

"Let's trade," I said.

From inside the bank the drive-up teller could see me standing there. Her voice, polite and curious at the same time, came out of the intercom, "Can I help you, sir?"

"Just give me a minute, please," I said.

To Pug I said, "I have what you want. Get out of your car and let her drive away and I'll give it to you."

"What is it we want?" At least this time he was asking a question before shooting at me.

I reached into my pants and pulled out the bubble-wrapped gun. "This." I pulled back some of the wrapping, making the contents unmistakable to them.

His frown intensified, and his eyes bored into me as he considered whether to shoot me or not.

"Maybe if I were an unknown, it wouldn't matter what you did to me. But you've made people curious about me."

From the intercom, the teller's voice asked, "Is there a problem, sir?"

I looked at him before answering. He offered a small shake of his head. "No, ma'am, no problem," I said.

He wanted me dead, but couldn't chance a public shooting. "The girl can walk away if you give me the package," he said.

"She drives away first, and then you get it. That's non-negotiable. And it has to happen now."

Claire said, "Will—"

"No discussion, Claire. Just drive away, and make sure you're not followed. I know they have a tow truck and a Jeep Cherokee in their fleet. It's possible there are more."

From the intercom, the teller said, "Sir, this is a drive-up banking area. You and your friends will have to leave, or otherwise I'll call the authorities."

"Yes, ma'am."

The gun was still pointed at me. I waited for the longest three seconds of my life, and then the car's engine cut out and the doors opened. When the men stepped out they weren't holding guns. Pug had the keys to the car in his hand.

"You give me the package," he said, "and she gets the keys."

"She drives away," I said. To Claire I said, "Take the keys and go."

Claire stumbled off her island, collected the keys, and hurried over to the car. Without being told, the other two men stepped between me and the car to make sure I wouldn't have any chance of driving off with Claire.

She started the engine, but didn't leave immediately. "Will!" Claire called.

"Get the hell out of here!"

Claire stifled a sob, and then hit the accelerator. The drive-through lot emptied out into the street where the sign said RIGHT TURN ONLY. Claire made a left. Smart girl.

The three men had spread out around the island, wary that I was going to run, but I knew that wasn't a race I could win. The gun was the important thing. I couldn't let them have it.

I considered tossing the gun onto the roof, but knew that would only delay their getting it. There was only one place the gun would be safe. As they started to close in on me, I turned and grabbed one of the banking tubes. I suppose they thought I intended to use it as a weapon, and they stayed clear as I swung it around.

It was a feint, my attempt to misdirect them like a magician might. The Great Travisini needed to disassemble a weapon, and fast. Cadets are timed when they disassemble their rifles, and then assemble them again. I had to detach the barrel off the gun in record time. There was only one way.

I smashed the barrel against the curb, putting all my strength in the blow. It wasn't enough. On the second attempt I heard a crack. The third time was a charm. Pug and his friends had closed in warily, unsure of what I was up to. I grabbed the pieces of the gun and forced them into the canister. They divined my intention then, and rushed at me. One of the men went airborne, tackling my right leg. I pushed with my left, much like a running back trying to bring a football over the goal line. My goal was the pneumatic chamber. I spiked the tube inside, and as I was falling, punched the "Send" button.

From the ground I looked up, expecting the tube to sail into the bank, but it wasn't holding a deposit slip or some paper checks but a heavy gun. For a moment I thought I was seeing a replay of the "four-inch flight" where the Project Mercury rocket barely got off the ground before falling to the earth again.

This time, though, gravity didn't have its way. We all watched the tube as it slowly made its way along and up the clear plastic tubing until it was hidden behind the metal casing. Even then we could hear its progress, or lack of it. But somehow it kept going, rattling and rumbling along. Then the tube dropped down the slot inside the bank.

Behind the glass barricade, I could make out the darkened face of the teller. Her mouth was open in surprise at what I had sent her way.

"Take care of my deposit," I shouted.

CHAPTER EIGHTEEN

For a moment, I wondered if I had miscalculated. Pug stared at the drive-up teller window as still and fixed as a bird dog signaling prey. He's going to do it, I thought. He's going after the gun and damn the consequences. Too late, I remembered the mother and her baby and the other innocents inside, people I had unwittingly put in harm's way.

The Jeep Cherokee, driven by the woman in hiking boots, suddenly pulled up next to us. Abruptly, he made his decision, turning away from the bank to stare at me. "Get in the car or die," he said.

Everything about the way he said it left no third option. I slid into the backseat and was immediately sandwiched in on both sides by the other men.

No one said anything as we drove off. Three sets of eyes watched my every blink. Since I was the center of attention, I decided to try and plant some seeds of doubt.

"They have all of your faces on the security tape," I said.

No one replied. The SUV swung out onto the road, and I threw some more fertilizer on the doubt seeds. "Remember, I am the big, bad fugitive who's assisting the crazed assassin. Law enforcement professionals are going to try and figure out what happened at the bank. They'll review the tapes over and over again. The gun I deposited will interest them. I imagine they'll run all sorts of tests on it."

Even though they didn't respond, there were more than a few telltale signs that they were listening. I watched the man with the gun closest of all. He was clenching and tightening his jaw, and I decided that was a good thing.

"As far as I'm concerned, there's been no crime committed. If you're smart, you should be thinking about cutting a deal. No one cares about the little fish. You know how government agencies are. They want that trophy fish."

From the front seat he gave a little nod, and the bookends grabbed my arms. Pug swung his gun and hit me on the side of my head. I suppose I was lucky it was a small gun. The blow didn't quite knock me senseless, but it rattled my brain pan enough to leave me dazed and bloodied.

We drove for what must have been at least an hour, but for most of that time my head was down, my mind out of commission. Any sudden movement made me dizzy and nauseated. I tried to think through what must have been a concussion, but my hoped-for brainstorm never occurred.

When the Jeep finally stopped I raised my head and looked around. We seemed to be in the middle of nowhere, a rural road with no buildings in sight. The rain had resumed, and was coming down hard. There would be no witnesses in this remote spot, and I wondered if this was where I was going to die.

Pug regarded me with a calculating look, and I must have blinked, for in his expression I saw a flicker of amusement. He had played my own game, and read my fears. No one said anything for a half a minute, and then a truck pulled up behind us. Everyone but me apparently expected the vehicle. At its arrival, Pug nodded again, and once more I became the center of attention for my two neighbors.

Each grabbed an arm. I tried to fight, but they held on

even after I kneed one of them in the chin. That's when Pug lent a hand again. He slammed a fist into my stomach that seemed to come out my back. For the next few minutes I did my fish-out-of-water imitation, gasping for air that didn't seem to come. While I was incapacitated, his two helpers tied up my ankles and wrists. When they finished with their rodeo roping they hoisted me into the air and carried me over to the truck. They had missed their calling in life by not working as baggage handlers for the airlines.

Pug decided to add insult to injury. "Strip him," he yelled to the men.

I was dropped to the ground, and then my buttons were popping and my clothes were ripping. It didn't take them long to make rags out of my clothes. The men seemed a little uncomfortable with their assignment. They didn't strike me as the usual criminal muscle.

"We'll meet later as planned," said Pug.

His henchmen walked over to the Jeep Cherokee and disappeared inside. I heard the vehicle drive away. Being alone with Pug didn't make me feel any better. The only thing I could think was that he didn't want to kill me with any witnesses around.

The rain pelted down on me, and I was cold and muddy, but apparently I hadn't been humiliated enough. Pug came and stood over me, hawked up some phlegm, and then spat on my face. Then he pulled me to my feet and shoved me into the cab.

Inside the truck, Pug changed from his wet shirt into a dry one. Under his shirt I noticed that encircling Pug's waist was a girdle of sorts with canisters connected by wires. He noticed me observing him.

"You like my hair shirt?" he asked. "It's always with me, but I rarely notice it anymore. Still, it's probably not a good idea for a fragmentation jacket to get too wet. Wouldn't want a wire to short out, would we?"

Pug seemed a lot less concerned about that possibility

than I would have been. If what he said was true, and my quick look at what was under his shirt seemed to confirm that, he was a human bomb.

"Was that your handiwork under our car?"

"It was fast and dirty work," Pug said, "not up to my usual standards, but it would have done the job."

I considered how I might signal a passing vehicle, but the opportunity never arose. There was no passing traffic on the country road and as we drove, the way seemed ever more remote. After about ten minutes of driving, the landscape changed, with a canopy of trees blocking out light. The road grew rougher, and the pavement became spotty until it gave out completely.

Being tied up made the off-road driving an exercise in punishment. I tried bracing for dips and jolts, but it was like preparing for a beating, with no good way of going about it. I was tossed around the back, every jolt adding to my misery. I was also worried about Pug's fragmentation jacket. How much jostling would it take to set it off?

It was hard gauging the distance, but we traveled for at least one difficult mile before Pug stopped the truck. I sat up and saw a chain blocking access to the road. He turned and looked at me, and I had the same sinking feeling as when I had been punched in the stomach.

"Don't worry," he said, "I intend to take good care of my deposit." He seemed to enjoy throwing my words back at me, as his parchment face broke into what approximated a smile.

He had a key to unlock the padlock on the chain, which told me more than I wanted to know. This wasn't some random spot, but a place familiar to him. Instead of leaving the chain up, he took it with him.

We drove for about ten minutes along a rutted path before stopping again. This time he turned off the ignition and the headlights. Though it was only around noon, the rain and clouds made it seem as if night had already arrived.

Maybe it had.

Pug sat and said nothing. I didn't break the silence, remembering the feedback from my last unsolicited conversation.

"Where is she?" he finally asked.

"I have no idea."

He let the silence build again before asking, "Where is she?"

"You saw what happened at the bank. You caught us off guard. There was no way we were expecting that ambush."

He ignored my denials. "Before we're through," he said, "you'll tell me where she is."

"I can't tell you what I don't know."

"What is it that you do know?"

I wanted him to believe I was cooperating. If he did, then maybe he would decide I was telling him the truth about not having any idea where Claire was. Offering up some details seemed the best way to go. They clearly knew things about us, and were aware of where we had been and what we had done. To appear credible, I had to stay as close to the truth as possible.

"I know that Claire believes her father was murdered. I know that people have been trying to kill her. She's sure that something happened in her father's past that set all these things in motion. Claire also thinks there's a political motivation behind all of this."

"What motivation is that?"

"She believes one of the presidential candidates is dirty, and that there's a past scandal waiting to be exposed that would derail his candidacy."

"Tell me about that scandal."

"I can't. I have no idea what it is."

"Then how do you know there is a scandal?"

"She says that whatever happened drove her father to leave politics. The way he abruptly quit never made sense to her until she overheard him talking on the phone not long before he turned up dead. She said her father implied that one of the presidential candidates participated in a criminal act in the past."

None of what I said appeared to be a revelation to Pug. "But you don't know what crime?"

I shook my head. "No," I said, "but I suspect that the gun was involved."

"Why do you think that?"

"Congressman Harrington opened that safe-deposit box in Charleston not long after leaving office sixteen years ago. He carefully wrapped that gun and put it away. Why would he store the gun in that fashion unless it was of some importance?"

"You tell me."

"I wish I could."

"You shouldn't have meddled in what you couldn't possibly understand."

"Your people tried to kill me. I understood that."

"To accomplish great things, small sacrifices are sometimes necessary."

"Excuse me for not willingly lying down and dying."

"You have been an inconvenience. That is all."

"What great things are you trying to accomplish?"

"There is a rot in this country's core. That rot has been spreading. We need a leader not afraid to cut out the cancer and make the hard decisions."

"Holy shit," I said. "She's right, isn't she? There's a murderer running for president."

"There's a great man who will be president."

My circumstances were forgotten. I had to know. "Who is he?"

Pug smiled. I had thought I was playing him, but he was the one who had the information he wanted. He had tested me to find out how far my knowledge extended. I had a few pieces of the puzzle, but by themselves they told me nothing.

I needed to keep him talking. "Great men don't sanction murder."

"You're right, they prevent murder. We call ourselves a civilized country, and yet every year more than a million innocents are murdered."

For a moment I didn't understand what he was talking about. "Do you mean abortions?" I asked.

"I mean just what I said: murder."

"You haven't seemed to shrink away from attempting murder yourself. How does that make you different from those you condemn?"

He shook his head as if unable to believe my ignorance. "If someone had murdered Hitler before he came to power, would that have been an act of murder, or the prevention of a holocaust?"

"You're talking apples and oranges."

"I'm talking about the preservation of human life. I can stop a terrible ongoing holocaust by helping a leader get elected. What are the lives of a few people when compared to millions?"

His words were passionate, but his face wasn't. I decided there was a reason for the surprised look in his eyes, and the mask-like appearance of his face. Some cosmetic surgeon had done extensive work there, with a little too much nipping and tucking. That explained the tautness of the skin over his cheekbones. It explained a few other things as well, like the bomb around his waist, and the bomb he'd wired to the car.

"You've had plenty of experience with bombs, after setting off so many in health clinics and hospitals."

"My targets have been murder mills," he said by way of correction.

"You're Sam Roper," I said. "You're the Baby Bomber."

"That's the name that the Alcoholic Tobacco Foul-ups and Federal Bureau of Incompetents came up with for me. What I am is the baby defender."

I reconsidered the quality of his plastic surgery. He no longer looked like the Sam Roper whose face had been displayed in the media in connection with at least half a dozen abortion clinic bombings. For the last year two years he hadn't been in the news, though. There had even been speculation that he might be dead, blown up by one of his own bombs.

"You've been quiet lately," I said.

"On the contrary, I've been very busy."

"Was it your bomb that went off near Stanton campaign headquarters right before the assassination attempt on him?"

"That was a very rudimentary explosive," he said smugly. "If you ask the ATF or FBI they'll tell you it didn't fit my profile."

"Were you the one who killed Garret Harrington? And did you set Claire up to look like an assassin?"

"She did a good enough job of setting herself up."

"One thing's been bothering me since this morning," I said. "How did you know to expect us at the bank?"

"Some people aren't very good about keeping secrets. If you want to prolong your existence, maybe you should follow Miss Harrington's example and talk."

I didn't want to believe that Claire had betrayed me, and yet I didn't know any other way to explain the reception committee waiting at the bank. Roper looked as if he was enjoying my discomfort.

"What do you want to know?" I asked.

"I'm shocked," he said. "Here I thought you would only give me your name, rank, and serial number."

"I don't have a rank or serial number, and I'm no hero."

"No? Then why have you risked death?"

"She promised me a million dollars if we got the goods on the killer. That's my kind of combat pay. I even had her sign a contract stipulating that payment. Yesterday I mailed it to my P.O. I wasn't counting on any of this, though."

A frown crossed his face. "You could have gotten away at the bank, but instead you came to her rescue."

"She's my Golden Goose." In an insinuating voice I added, "And the rewards haven't only been financial. Besides, I knew that once you got the gun we were dead. It was our only bartering tool."

Roper didn't seem convinced.

"Look, in the heat of the moment I acted out of instinct. It's true I've been involved in this thing, but I've never been committed and there's a big difference between the two. It's like an eggs and ham breakfast. The chicken's involved in the breakfast, but the pig is absolutely committed. I'm the green eggs type, not the ham."

"You want to be the chicken?"

"I want to be alive."

"Why should I believe you?"

"Because I'm in this for myself. You know what I do for a living? I lead the good life, eating at restaurants and staying in hotels. When I had a chance to reach for the golden ring, I did. You can't blame me for doing that. I saw it as my opportunity to get the big money. Now I just want to save my hide."

"Tell me where she is."

"Maybe she went back to our no-tell motel. That's where we spent last night."

He wanted to know the details, and I gave them to him. I also added a few, and Roper's facial mask managed to come alive. He pretended to be the protector of unborn children, but the better I got to know him the more convinced I was that he believed women were inherently evil, and that they needed someone to control their uteruses.

"Where else might she be?" he asked.

I appeared to search my mind before shaking my head.

Roper threw the truck door open, and then he dragged me out into the open by my bound ankles. He pulled me over a landscape of roots, mud, and the occasional rock.

With all the gouging and scraping, I left a trail of skin. I didn't accept the pain quietly, but instead yelped and cried and called out for him to stop. I wanted him to believe I was the coward that I had painted myself to be.

He stopped dragging me. With the cold rain pelting down on me, he said, "I want you to think a little harder."

As incentive, he directed a kick at my ribs. I didn't have to fake my cry of pain.

"Where did the two of you spend the night before last?" he asked.

He had an expectant look. I groaned to try and buy a little time. While planting the bomb in the rental there was a good chance he had seen the camping gear, but the problem with admitting we had been camping was that it might put Claire at risk. Our meeting spot was supposed to be James Island County Park outside of Charleston, and if they checked nearby campgrounds they might find her.

"We camped," I said, "right on Lake Anna in central Virginia. It was a nightmare. All she did was complain. She was groaning about her back, and the bugs, and how she was so cold. I was trying to save her life, and she was having a fit because she couldn't order room service. Nothing was good enough for her."

I looked up and saw Roper nodding. I had passed his litmus test by admitting we had camped. It also seemed that the more bad things I said about Claire, the happier he was.

"So now that you've had some time to think about it," Roper said, "where will she be staying tonight?"

"Probably in the car—"

I didn't get to finish. He kicked me again. "Think." Another kick. "Think." The third time was the charm. "Think."

I'm not sure how much acting I did. I wanted him to believe I was weak and scared and afraid of being hit. Being tied up, naked, cold, and hurt made my performance all too easy.

"Shit, stop!" I cried, and rolled around some. "Enough, already. Let me think, goddammit. Shit, I think you busted some ribs."

He raised his right boot.

"Hilton Head Island," I said. "She has good friends who live there, Jenny and Paul Winchell. They have a house in Port Royal. If she doesn't go back to our motel, she'll go there."

Roper didn't immediately bring his foot back down to the ground. He let it hover above me. It might not have been as sharp or final as a guillotine, but it was almost as intimidating, and was meant to bring out the penitent.

"No more," I begged. "I've told you everything I know."

He kicked me anyway, and cur-like, I yelped. As I shivered and trembled I told myself that what I was doing was all an act to stay alive and give myself a chance. I wanted to believe that.

"Get up," he said.

Tied as I was, it wasn't easy, but I pushed myself to my feet and managed to stay erect.

"Don't move."

I didn't have much choice. I could either continue to stand, fall on my face, or try hopping away. Roper went back to the truck, and when he returned he was holding the chain.

Pointing, he said, "Over to the tree."

I thought about lunging at him. Once he was down I could use my hands and my head. I think he sensed my desperation, and brought out his small, silenced gun and leveled it at my chest. It was an effective way of making me reconsider my plan. I hopped over to the tree he had pointed out, and as I came closer I made the decision to lean against it face-first.

From behind me, Roper wrapped the chain through my body and around the tree. When he finally finished, he padlocked the links behind me.

"You can't leave me like this," I said.

"I am afraid I must. I need to find Miss Harrington. I hope for your sake that I do, because if I don't find her I will return in a very bad mood and extract what I need to know from you. Pray that doesn't happen."

"I'm freezing. I'll die of exposure."

"I don't think so, but I'll take that chance."

"I gave you the information you wanted. You can't leave me like this."

Roper said nothing. He started walking away.

"Come back here! Where the fuck are you going?"

My screams were muted by the woods. I heard his truck door open.

"I'll pay you whatever you want, do whatever you need!"

The door shut, the engine started, and I heard him drive off. It was what I wanted, or at least what I thought I wanted. I was still alive because Roper suspected I hadn't told him all that I knew. If he found Claire, Roper wouldn't need to return, believing that the elements and my imprisonment would take care of me soon enough. If she eluded him, I had some more torture to look forward to.

I preferred a third option. Exhaling completely, I felt the chains loosen around me. While Roper tied me up I had inflated my chest with air. Now I had a little breathing room, but not much more.

I tried shifting around, but only managed to get chafed by the bark. At the best of times I'm marginally limber, and when I go to the gym I'm always amazed by women who can make pretzels of themselves during yoga classes. Naturally, I always pass up the yoga classes, choosing instead to pump iron. I twisted without success, trying different motions. Snaking and flexing didn't help, and neither did doing my version of the hokey-pokey. I strained against the tree. Apparently the chain didn't know there was supposed to be a weak link in it somewhere.

How the hell had Harry Houdini gotten himself out of situations like this? I had seen pictures of him all chained up, shackled from head to toe, yet it usually only took him moments to wiggle free. I thought about those death-defying Las Vegas acts I had seen on television where the performer was trussed up like a turkey and, with the clock ticking, was faced with some terrible fate unless he managed to get clear of the chains.

I had the same ticking clock but seemed to be meeting with considerably less success.

After ten minutes I was huffing and puffing and feeling like my bag of tricks was all but played out. I was still trying to remember anything I had ever heard about how escape artists wiggled out of their bonds. Some had picks hidden on their bodies, I recalled, and there were those who could separate their shoulders, and others who were amazingly double-jointed. Hell, the best I had ever done in a limbo contest was third place, and there had only been a handful of us competing.

The limbo, I thought. How low can you go? Maybe the tree's root system wasn't that extensive. I knew that towering sequoias, some three hundred feet tall, had roots that went down six feet or less. The rain had already worked the soil into mud, and I started rooting my feet into it. What I discovered wasn't encouraging. In a relatively small area I unearthed a dozen thick roots, each feeling like an impregnable anchor.

No getting under it, I decided.

"Help!" I screamed. "Help!"

It was a waste of breath, I knew, but I felt a little steadier for venting my panic.

Study your enemy. They had taught me that at West Point. My enemy was a tree. I looked it up and down. The tree was about fifty feet high, with a trunk diameter maybe two feet around. The bark was furrowed. It looked as if elongated "S" shapes were running up and down it. There was a sweet fragrance to the wood, especially in spots where I had scraped the bark away. The scent was familiar to me, as I had sniffed it out around Washington, D.C. Trees like this one were planted around the city, and I had heard them referred to as bee trees.

That was all I knew about my captor.

"Someone should have chained Joyce Kilmer to a tree," I said aloud. "Bet you he wouldn't have written that damn poem if they had."

I was trying to keep it together by talking to a tree. Zen question: If a man babbles in the middle of the forest and no one hears him, is there sound?

I thought I had the answer to that Zen Koan about a tree falling, and I didn't much like it. As far as I could tell, there was no sound.

Can't go under it, I decided, but what about over it?

I tried to find some kind of purchase in the mud with my tied feet. Bending as much as the chains allowed, I pushed up and off from the roots. My squirming didn't get me very far, the only tangible result being that of bark flaking off. In frustration, I shook myself at the tree.

I had to have overlooked something. As plebes we were taught to react to adversity. One colonel at the Academy always quoted from Carl von Clausewitz's classic text, *On War.* "Presence of mind is nothing but an increased capacity of dealing with the unexpected."

Think. There had to be a way. I did something between tapping and rapping my head against the tree, and was quickly reminded of the blow I had suffered earlier. Still, there was something more than pain penetrating my head. I could sense it there, even if I couldn't quite grasp it. I did a few more woodpecker-type taps with my noggin.

That was it. There was a hollow sound to the tree almost akin to that little echo you get when tapping a melon. My bee tree wasn't completely solid.

For the first time in hours, I felt a twinge of hope. Maybe I could use my own bonds to cut into the tree. I shifted back and forth, sliding the chains along the bark, but after a few minutes of Chubby Checker twisting, the result was disappointing with only the slightest groove registering.

I tried rapping my shoulder into the tree. Again, I could hear the hollow sound. I remembered what Roper had said about the rot in the country's core, and how his candidate would cut it out. I hoped that rot extended to the insides of this tree.

There was only one way to find out. I drew my face toward the bark. It was ridiculous, of course, but I was short any other recourse. I bit into the bark, did a dog-like shake of my face, and sheared some of it away. Then I took a second bite, and a third.

It wasn't quite like biting into rock, but neither was it a meal I would recommend to any creature other than a beaver.

As bark goes, I was chewing into soft wood, but that seemed a very relative thing. Marble is soft when compared to a diamond. If Roper had tied me up to a maple or hickory tree, the first bite would have stopped me. With the bee tree, I was at least able to do some nibbling.

I tried to remember my botany. Past the bark was the phloem, and then came the cambium. After that was the sapwood, and heartwood. I tried biting into the wood, but it seemed to repel my teeth, so I settled into some gnawing. The going was already getting difficult, and I had barely started my wooden entree.

At least I wouldn't need a toothpick during the meal.

I tried to be an automaton, not letting up with my combination of scraping, gnawing, chewing, and nibbling. After a while my mouth grew as numb as my tied hands and feet, but I kept pressing my lips and teeth into the wood. The rain didn't let up, and water ran down into my face. When the wood seemed particularly unyielding, I collected water in my mouth and spat at the exposed gouge, hoping to make it more pliable. I don't know if that helped, but at least it was doing something.

While my teeth worked, my mind drifted. As a boy I remembered hearing a joke about Euell Gibbons, a man famous for writing books on eating wild plants, and even more famous as a cereal pitchman. "You hear about Euell Gibbons getting sick?" the comic said. "Yeah, he started vomiting and threw up a forest."

At the Academy we had gone through survival training out in the woods. The acronym GAP-C was drilled into us— grasses, acorns, pines, and cattails. Our instructor told us that pine phloem was edible, and that its seeds and needles could be boiled into a tea, but he hadn't been nearly as enthusiastic about the edible uses of pines as he had been about eating insects to survive. When it came to obtaining protein through bugs, the man was positively rapturous. We gave him the nickname of Renfield, the tortured servant of Bela Lugosi's Dracula. Whenever he was out of hearing range we recited Renfield's famous line, "Flies, why eat flies when I can have nice, juicy spiders?"

Maybe I was thinking about Dracula, because it was my own blood I was seeing in the exposed wood. What I was doing wasn't something that regular teeth cleanings could prepare me for.

Somehow I needed to make flesh and blood stronger than wood. I kept gnawing at the tree. First my mind had bitten off more than it could chew, and now my teeth were doing the same. I thought about that oversized gun Garret Harrington had put away for safekeeping. It was odd that its mate had turned up as the weapon that killed the congressman. Claire hadn't even known her father possessed one such gun, let alone two. In the days of automatic weapons, that kind of pistol seemed anachronistic. Apparently, though, it was still popular in some circles. The sheriff said magnums like that were used in shooting contests, and even for hunting large game.

I worked my front teeth into the wood, and was able to pull away a small strip. Then I did it again. The wood was like string cheese, coming apart in threads instead of chunks. The process was painstakingly slow, and yet I could now see that I had taken a bite out of the tree—literally. It was only an apple-size bite, but it was a start.

For a few minutes I was exhilarated. I could do this thing, I thought, and was inspired to chew more vigorously. I remembered a county fair pie-eating contest. I once entered on my girlfriend's behest. The rule was that you couldn't use your hands, which meant all the contestants had to dig in face-first. The end result was that there was no way of avoiding getting pie smeared all over your face. We had all come out of the contest looking like clowns.

Somehow, I won the contest going away. No one would have guessed that outcome, as several of the participants were NFL-sized, but I guess there's something to be said for a big mouth. My reward was a certificate to a buffet restaurant, just what I didn't need.

I backed away from my chewing, took a big breath, and tried to see what progress I had made. The indentation in the tree didn't seem to have grown any, and my exultation vanished. This was no pie-eating contest. Shit. I fought back tears. Minutes before, I thought I could rip through the tree, but now the task seemed all but impossible. Still, what else could I do? I went back to termite duty, and tried to use my front teeth like a grater. Forget the pain, forget everything. There was only the scraping.

I thought about how, during the course of her celebrity interviews, Barbara Walters always asked, "What kind of a tree are you?" I was ready with my answer: I'm a fucking bee tree, Barbara.

At least Roper hadn't crucified me, hadn't nailed me to the tree. If I had been hung up on a cross, I wondered whether I would have tried to eat my way free. That struck me as being funny, as did the idea of the subsequent interrogation: "Centurion, where is your prisoner?"

I had heard of animals biting off a limb in order to get

free of a trap. Could I do the same? Freedom. It was all about freedom, but not just mine.

Take the tree. Take no prisoners. Grind it out. Under my command were twenty-eight soldiers made up of molars, incisors, bicuspids. We will not retreat. To stop is to deny duty, honor, and country. Failure is not an option.

Maybe my being captured had prompted Claire to go to the police. That's what we should have done from the start, I thought, but I had respected her wishes and not done that. Something even more than pride had kept Claire from seeking out the authorities. She was afraid of permanently staining her name. Under the circumstances, her behavior seemed silly. What was she afraid of? I should have questioned her more before agreeing to help her.

You get stupid when you fall in love.

That's what it was. That was the word I hadn't whispered, even to myself. Or maybe I needed the threat of death to allow myself the luxury of feeling that way. She had a fiancé, after all. That was something else I needed to know more about.

The shadows deepened. Afternoon was passing into night. The cold continued to get worse, and I felt its numbing hand reaching up my body. The paralysis was slow but sure, moving up my legs into my trunk. For a time I staved it off, cracking my legs and hips against the tree, but gradually all feeling from my waist down left me.

The coldness wasn't only in my limbs. I was afraid. I felt as if I wasn't making inroads into the tree, but was merely gumming it. I tried chewing louder and harder, and to my own ears I sounded like a rodent intent on his gnawing.

The darkness grew complete, and clouds covered the moon. I could not see, but knew that my face was deeper and deeper into the tree. My lesson in forestry had been up close and very personal, my chewing taking me through different variations of wood. In my mind's eye I tried to imagine the tree cut through. Every stump tells a story, the layers of rings in the wood marking the passage of time.

Those were the lifelines I needed to grind through. The tree's circles were intersecting with my own. I had the task of navigating through Dante's circles of hell.

The wood was more fibrous now. Like a dog, I worked that bone, ripping, crushing, and gnawing. I kept tearing into the tree's tissue, all the while trying not to acknowledge the state of my gums and jaw and teeth. The more I worked on the tree, the more it felt as if I was chewing on thorns.

At least I was still feeling something. Below my neck my body no longer felt like my own. I didn't want to think about lack of circulation, and what it was doing to me. There was only the tree.

My head was deep into the wood now. I craned my neck and came in at an angle. That was how Dracula worked. Again, I thought of my wilderness survival course, and the instructor we called Renfield. "Flies? Why eat flies when I can have nice, juicy spiders?" There hadn't been a class on hewing trees with your teeth. What I should have learned was how to avoid being in the position I now found myself.

General George S. Patton said it best: "No bastard ever won a war by dying for his country. You won it by making the other poor, dumb bastard die for his country."

Because of poor grades, Patton had been forced to repeat his plebe year at West Point. One of the great military leaders of the twentieth century had almost been bounced out of the Academy.

Over my own gnashing of teeth, I could hear sounds from the bee tree. It seemed to be whispering to me, voices arising out of the creaking limbs. Among that chorus I heard General Patton: "Thirty years from now when your grandson asks where you were for the Big One, you won't have to say, 'Well, I was shoveling shit in Louisiana.' "

What did I do in the war? I attacked a tree in South Carolina with my bare teeth.

I started lunging at the gouged wood like I was going for the jugular vein. The hollow sound was louder now, like a watermelon ready to split open on its own. I had given no thought as to which direction the tree would fall. Could it topple backward and crush me? I didn't know, and was beyond that kind of planning. My one and only goal was for the damned thing to drop.

Damn the torpedoes, full speed ahead.

I chopped at the tree with my front teeth as if wielding an ax. One cut, two cuts, and a third. There was a crack, but it didn't come from the tree. For a moment I was in shock, and then I cried out in pain. Ever so gingerly, I probed with my tongue and touched on a raw nerve. It felt as if half of my right front tooth had broken away.

The exposed tooth was so sensitive that even contact with air made my mouth feel as if it was on fire. I couldn't go on. The very thought of more of that kind of pain made me feel sick to my stomach. To continue would be the worst kind of self-torture. It would be like sticking my tooth in an electric socket. No one could expect me to subject myself to that.

No one and no group, not even the fucking long, gray line.

The kibitzers emerged, voices emanating from the crackling bee tree. The chorus was talking to me again. *"He chipped his tooth and he thinks he's earned his Purple Heart."*

Carefully, so as to try and not touch my tongue to the damaged tooth, I said, "You don't know how it feels. It's like I have an exposed wire in my mouth."

"Duty," said the voices.

"Isn't dying enough?" I asked.

"Honor," they replied.

"Is there a more abused notion than honor?"

"Country," said the chorus.

"Go away," I said.

But they couldn't go away. They were inside me. Ghosts I thought long exorcised asserted themselves.

I opened my mouth and let the rain fall inside it. Even the raindrops hurt like hell. I drank the runoff of sweat, tears, and blood, and tried to steel myself to a last assault. The tree would fall or I would. It was groaning, and so was I. Through the darkness, I tried to make out the damage. My eyes might have been playing tricks, but it looked like I was breaking through to where the hollow was.

Whispering "Once more unto the breach, dear friend," I brought my teeth to the wood. Though I tried using only half my mouth, I could not shield the cracked tooth from the job. With every bite I pleaded to God for the pain to stop, or for the amnesia to continue.

My nerve circuits must have overloaded, and I blacked out. When I stirred again, there was a little break in the cloud cover and I was able to get a better look at the tree. My heart gave a little jump. There was a light at the end of the tunnel, a dime-sized opening into the hollow. With my tongue, I explored the hole. Yes, I was through now. I tapped with my chin. The echo seemed to indicate that the cavity was extensive. By the sound of it, I was dealing with little more than veneer, though the tree seemed to be standing as stubbornly as ever.

"Fall, damn you!"

What was holding it up? I had chewed away the living matter, exposing the gutted corpse, but still it resisted toppling. Using my lower teeth, I kept digging into the opening, widening it. The hole gradually expanded, but not fast enough for my liking. I started hitting at the opening with my chin and head. Each blow brought about rustling and shaking and swaying. The assaults started a crackling in the tree that continued to grow louder, but the tree resisted my efforts and gravity. I tried reawakening my own dead limbs, tried putting my lower body into the mix.

The crack was sudden and sharp, an explosion and implosion right in my ear. I didn't have time to be afraid. Wooden shards splintered into my body. Chained to the tree, it felt as if I was in the middle of an avalanche. For one long, violent moment I was shaken, and then the tree toppled around me.

I offered a silent prayer of thanks, and had a little taste of why there are no atheists in foxholes. Freedom proved elusive, though. With my hands and feet tied, and my body in Sleeping Beauty mode, getting loose of my chains was slow going. I had to work up and out of my prison. Inch by inch I made my way over the split tree, finally falling into a heap. For a few minutes I didn't move, and when I raised myself it was to crawl. With the chains clinking behind me, I went in search of something with a sharp point. It was a rocky area, but most of the stones seemed only of a size to stab up at me from the mud. At last I found a boulder with an adequate enough edge. I started with the rope bonds on my wrists. The fibers were stubborn, but there was a benefit to all the rubbing. The friction brought heat back to my wrists and arms, and after working at the rope for several minutes my hands became my own again. There seemed to be no avoiding the flaying of skin, and I paid for freedom with my pound of flesh, but finally I shed my bonds.

With my hands free, I worked on untying my ankles. The knots were stubborn, and while picking at them the warmth generated from my movements faded and I found myself shivering again. Though the temperature was probably around fifty degrees, it felt as if it was freezing. With the state of my chipped tooth, my chattering teeth hurt like hell. Unable to control my trembling, I stuck a fair-sized twig in my mouth to keep my teeth from grinding.

Inclement weather has always had a great bearing on war. During the retreat of Napoleon's Grand Armée from frozen Russia in 1812, one French military surgeon succinctly noted: "The bald men died first."

Half of heat loss occurs through the head, and stemming that flow was my most immediate concern. I scouted around, looking for potential shelter, but there was nothing in the immediate vicinity that jumped out at me. The woods appeared to be second or third growth, though it didn't look as if any of the trees in the surrounding area had been chopped down for some time. The only sign of humanity I discovered was a long-abandoned black plastic garbage bag snagged in a lower branch of a tree. I took the bag and pulled it apart. On the top of my head I strung together a hat, bandana style, and around my groin I made a makeshift diaper. My relief might have been more psychological than actual, but my violent shivering tapered off.

Most of the wind seemed to be coming from the north, so I looked for a good spot at a right angle to the prevailing breeze. The nearby rise with its thick layer of leaves looked promising. I did some exploratory reaching in. The pile of leaves and branches was more than three feet high, and the dampness didn't extend more than six inches down. Beneath that point there even seemed to be a little heat, with nature's composting at work.

I had never built a debris hut, but I knew the theory. In a sleeping bag, air gets trapped by the insulation. I wanted to create that dead air space in my shelter. From the bee tree I collected branches, and then layered them atop the leaves. After gathering armfuls of leaves I covered the branches over and then repeated the same process and built a third layer.

Before settling into my shelter I went and retrieved the chain. It was about ten feet long. I hefted it in the air, getting the feel for its weight, and then practiced swinging it. There was no mistaking the chain for a bullwhip, but by using both hands I could get a good snap to it. I picked a spot just outside the clearing, marked it in my mind, and then covered the chain with leaves.

Back at the debris hut, I snaked inside the leaves and

branches. My shelter was far from perfect. At any other time I would have found the damp intolerable, the scratchy leaves insufferable, and my throbbing tooth impossible to bear. On this night, though, I fell asleep almost immediately.

It must have been hours later when I heard the approach of a vehicle. I stuck my head out of my nest and was glad to see it was still dark. By the sounds of it, the truck was straining through the muck and mire of the dirt road that was now a bog. There was no sign of the headlights, so I had enough time to get myself in place.

I backed away from my shelter, trying not to leave footprints, but offering up misdirection if I did. It was possible that Roper was bringing all of his underlings with him. If that was the case I would have little choice but to melt into the woods.

I hoped that wasn't the case.

Roper wouldn't have come back unless Claire was still free. He would be coming with a head of steam, ready to lay into a helpless captive to get answers, or maybe just to vent his anger. He had enjoyed the last torture session all too much.

The rain was steadily dropping again. It wasn't quite raining cats and dogs, but the downfall was at the kittens and puppies level. Good. The rain would hide most sounds.

Some light from the truck's headlights jumped around the clearing, and then the truck came into view. It slowly pulled up to a stop, the engine still running. Roper appeared to be by himself. I could see his face staring out the window, the wipers bringing him into focus, and then the rain blurring him. He was peering intently, and not liking what he saw. The downed bee tree was in his headlights.

You're in the right place, I wanted to call out, but I stayed hunkered down and silent. I touched my tongue on my tooth's exposed nerve and fed on the pain. At last Roper turned off the engine, but left the lights on. Before leaving the truck, Roper used his left hand to sweep the area with his flashlight. In his right hand he held a gun. After determining there was no immediate threat, Roper stepped out of the truck and locked the door behind him.

With extreme caution, he made his way over to the bee tree. Gun and light worked as if the two were connected. Wherever the light went, the gun followed. I watched as he bent down over the tree and dug something out of it. He examined his find, and then tossed it aside in fury: "Shit!"

The lower half of my front tooth, I thought. Apparently he wasn't planning to put it under a pillow as an offering to the tooth fairy.

Roper fanned the nearby area with his flashlight, and then seemed to realize that it would be impossible to find me in the darkness. Impossible, that is, unless I wanted to be discovered.

During the Civil War the Confederate troops were often ill-fed and at a provisional disadvantage to the Union army. Battle was sometimes initiated by the rebels because of the lure of their enemy's food. "There's cheese in their haversacks," the Confederate officers told their soldiers. It was a desperate exhortation, something just short of cannibalism.

My incentive was almost as visceral. The truck would get me out of here. Roper must have known that. I wondered if he was using it as cheese to lure the mouse. He retraced his steps, light and gun in synchronized dance, but then he changed the script. Roper started shooting the gun. As he turned in an arc, he clicked off the shots. The silencer and the rain and the forest muted all the sounds. I pushed my face into the ground and when the firing stopped came up silently spitting out leaves and dirt.

Roper chose speed over caution as he hurried toward his truck. He must have thought his gunfire had dispersed any possible threat. My hand felt for the chain and gripped it. When Roper reached into his pocket for his keys, I silently rose to my feet.

The rain beat down, covering up the sounds of my approach. Roper sensed something, though, and began to turn. I brought the chain down hard. The links caught him along his cheek and knocked his head back. His finger had already closed on the trigger, and several rounds were directed at the clouds. I swung the chain again, this time catching him along his right side and staggering him. It was too dark to tell if he was still holding the gun or not. I dove at him, and drove him into the truck. The fight in me was fueled by hate and madness. I used my hands, feet, and head, striking him all over. When he fell to the ground I jumped on top of him and continued the beating. When Roper realized this wasn't a fight he was going to win, he tried to snake his hand into his pants but I was expecting that. I rammed my elbow into his arm, and then pinned both his arms down with my knees. I decided the best way to keep him from trying to blow both of us up was to beat him senseless, but I didn't even need that encouragement.

Finally, I couldn't even raise my arms. Beneath me, Roper's face was cut and bloodied. He was breathing, but not moving unless you counted some involuntary twitching. I got off of him, and then felt around for his gun. There was mud in the silencer and barrel, and I wiped the muck away as best I could. Then I started shivering, suddenly abandoned by my inner fire of madness.

It was quid pro quo time. I tied his hands behind his back with his shirt, and then continued taking off the rest of his clothing and transferring every stitch to me. Roper was taller and thinner than I was, and his shoes were at least a size larger, but no fit had ever felt so perfect.

With his keys, I opened the truck door and turned off the lights. I didn't want the battery running out. There was a half-eaten box of powdered doughnuts, and unmindful of my throbbing tooth, I jammed them into my mouth and started chewing ravenously.

Roper was trying to get to his feet now, but without much success. He reminded me of a boxer who knew he had to get up, but was abandoned by his body. With his own shoe I kicked him in the face and he stopped being so eager to rise.

I wrapped him in chains, and then dragged him a few feet back. When I tied one end of the chain to the tow bar, Roper awakened to what I was doing and started flapping around in an effort to free himself. He kept shifting, and I wasn't comfortable with the possibility of him loosening wires on his fragmentation jacket. I put the gun at his head for him to stop squirming.

"You're going to tell me what I want to know," I said, "or we're going to go for a little ride."

Roper said nothing.

"Who are you working for?"

He didn't even look at me.

I went over to the truck, started it up, but left it in park. Then I walked to where he was tied and stood over him. "If you don't want to leave skin behind you from here to Charleston, you'll start talking."

"Just try it," he said. "That kind of friction will set off the bomb."

It was possible he was bullshitting me as much as I was bullshitting him. Or maybe he was trying to lure me into taking off a booby-trapped fragmentation jacket. As much as I liked the idea of exacting my pound of flesh, I had no intention of dragging him along the road. Revenge might make me feel better, but it wouldn't get the information I needed. Roper had probably always envisioned himself dying a martyr, and I wasn't going to realize his dreams for him. Even though there was a large part of me that was convinced the planet would be better off if Sam Roper no longer inhabited it, acting upon that conviction wasn't something I was prepared to do.

I went and unhitched his chain from the tow bar. My act of charity drove him to speak, but he didn't say, "Thanks."

"May God strike you dead, and may you rot in hell forever."

"You have a nice day, too."

CHAPTER NINETEEN

The Magi and the Candidate were waiting in the hotel conference room for the fourth kingmaker, a man everyone thought of as the Numbers Guy. He was their pollster, and much more, and as usual he was breathless when he rushed into the room. The Numbers Guy was loaded down with all his equipment. He never traveled without a laptop, camcorder, and overstuffed briefcase. After greeting everyone, the pollster took a heavy seat and sighed. He was short, squat, and hairy. Someone could have made a case that he was the missing link, save for his wonderfully analytical brain.

"Which way is the wind blowing?" asked the Pit Bull. The campaign manager acted as if he was never quite sure whether the Numbers Guy was the real deal, or a witch doctor. "And don't tell me up my ass."

The Numbers Guy expelled some air. "Benjamin Disraeli once said there are three kinds of lies. Lies, damn lies, and statistics."

"So what you're telling us is that you're a professional liar."

Everyone joined in with the laughter and the Numbers Guy said, "I suppose I am."

He passed some paperwork out. "Thumbnail sketches from our overnight polling."

Everyone scanned the sheets. Satisfied expressions appeared around the table.

"As you can see," said the Numbers Guy, "the approval rating is up two percent from three days ago. That's significant."

"What was your polling sample?" asked the Poet.

"A thousand people. The usual."

"Look at name recognition," said the S.O.B. "That's up five percent."

The Numbers Guy said, "You can also see a positive response to the most recent ad campaign. The message is not only getting out there, it's being received."

The Candidate continued to study the data. He was wary of any dark clouds. "The undecided percentages are still high. Almost a third."

"That's true," the Numbers Guy conceded. "But you've been making inroads into the women's vote."

"Reel them in by their panties," said the S.O.B., "and we'll win."

"Don't make those kinds of remarks in public," said the Poet, "and we might have a chance to do that."

The Numbers Guy hooked up his camcorder to the monitor, and then dimmed the room's lights. There was still enough light for everyone to continue reading from the sheets, but the lighted screen in the front of the conference room drew everyone's attention.

"As you know," he said, "we have half a dozen focus groups running. There are eleven to fifteen people in each group. Yesterday we ran your two latest speeches by them. We set everyone up in the focus groups with laptops so they could instantly respond to what you were saying. By analyzing their responses, we were able to chart positives and negatives for such things as phrasing, gestures, and message. The line graphs you're looking at further amplify this."

"Lies, damn lies, and statistics," the Candidate said.

"Look at that," said the Pit Bull, pointing out a pattern he saw in the numbers. "Everything spikes up during the Up With People routines."

The Poet took some umbrage: "That's not what we call them."

"It doesn't matter what you call them," said the Numbers Guy. "What matters is that the audience responds enthusiastically to an upbeat message. Those are the spikes you see. Most of the valleys occur during prolonged discussion of issues."

The S.O.B. said, "So your advice is to stick with the cheerleading, and stay away from any serious discussion of the issues."

It was hard to tell if the Candidate's chief of staff was being facetious or not.

"Our man has a talent for making people feel good," said the Numbers Guy. "It makes sense for him to give them what they want."

The Candidate didn't respond. He was still studying the information on the screen. "What are those three circled areas?"

"Those are the times during your talk you made prolonged eye contact with the camera."

"Valleys," said the Poet, surprised at what she saw.

The Numbers Guy nodded. "From what we could determine, the audience didn't respond well to that."

"And why is that?" asked the Candidate.

The pollster took a breath, and then answered without sugarcoating the message. "You don't come across as sincere," he said. "You play better to an audience, or an interviewer, than you do to the camera. Of course, the data is only as good as its interpreter. Nonetheless, you can see that with all the focus groups you lost ground when you looked too long at the camera. Our advice is that less is more."

"Last week you advised him to engage the camera," said the Poet.

"That's usually the best tactic," the Numbers Guy said, "but in this instance the data suggests that people prefer the long view to the up-close one. We've been testing for that and other things in these focus group studies. We're keying on the negatives, because you can be sure other people are looking for your Achilles' heel."

"Willie Horton," said the S.O.B.

"Exactly," said the Numbers Guy.

The campaign manager nodded knowingly. "It takes a lot longer to put up a building than to tear one down."

The Numbers Guy offered an explanation to the Candidate. "In 1988 George Bush was trailing Democratic nominee Michael Dukakis by double digits. Most pundits were saying Dukakis had the election in the bag. The Republicans put together a focus group in Paramus, New Jersey, and tossed every known negative about Dukakis their way. By the end of that session, the Republicans had their strategy for victory. Give the voters a diet of a prison-furlough program, and put the threatening black face of Willie Horton on television screens around the country, and *voilà*, you had white flight votes for Bush. Lee Atwater, the campaign director, was quoted as saying, 'I'll make Willie Horton Dukakis's running mate.' And he did."

"Where am I weak?" the Candidate asked.

The Numbers Guy said, "There is some question as to your ability to handle either a domestic or international crisis."

He pulled yet more paperwork out of his briefcase and placed it in front of the Candidate. "You can see right here where we asked the focus groups whether they would be confident with your leading our country in the midst of a crisis. The positive is that people perceive you as being a 'nice guy.' The negative that goes with that is they're not sure you can be the mean son of a bitch we need when the chips are down."

"I see. Any solutions?"

The Pit Bull said, "It's time to take the gloves off."

"Be firm," advised the Poet, "without being pugnacious."

"Show 'em your steel edges," said the Pit Bull.

"Within limits," said the Poet. "Don't be harsh, though. You don't want to alienate women in the process. They don't like sour grapes. Bob Dole's kiss of death in 1996 was that women perceived him as being bitter. That's a turnoff."

"Just as men are turned off by the appearance of indecision," said the S.O.B.

The campaign manager made eye contact with the speechwriter. "We've got that national news interview coming up. Maybe we should rehearse a little Bush/Rather vignette."

She considered that, and after a little reflection, nodded.

"You want to explain that shorthand?" asked the chief of staff.

The Poet said, "In 1988 George Bush needed to lose what was known as the 'wimp factor,' and used a Dan Rather interview to do that. Instead of being passive, Bush went on the offensive. When Rather emphasized his involvement in Iran-Contra, Bush told him it wasn't fair to judge his career by rehashing Iran. Then he said to Rather, 'How would you like it if I judged your career by those seven minutes when you walked off the set in New York?' That was in reference to Rather's leaving the set in a snit earlier in the year. And suddenly it was Rather who was on the defensive instead of vice versa. That interview changed public perception. People suddenly thought Bush could and would stand up to bullies."

"We'll pick out your bully," said the Pit Bull, "and set up your response."

The Candidate nodded.

The Numbers Guy turned on the lights. He pulled out some more paperwork from his seemingly bottomless briefcase. "These are the figures on those ads you wanted me to test-market."

Everyone scanned the results. "The flag burning," said the Poet. "I told you that would play best. Symbols beat issues every time."

"The numbers are also good on the attack piece on Governor Beam-me-up," said the Pit Bull. "If we pin the right nickname on the opposition, Leno and Letterman will do the rest."

"It worked on the likes of Jerry Brown and Bob Kerrey and Michael Dukakis," said the S.O.B.

"You mean Governor Moonbeam, Cosmic Bob, and Rocky the Flying Squirrel?" asked a delighted campaign manager. He was clearly relishing the prospect of throwing off the gloves and engaging in hardball politics.

They talked for ten more minutes, and the Numbers Guy further elaborated on the focus group findings. Much of what he suggested would have been applicable for the Miss America pageant, the Candidate thought. He was just in a different kind of beauty contest.

After the meeting broke up, the Candidate retired to his hotel room. It was ironic, he thought, that the voters considered him a "nice guy." And it was even funnier that his own handlers were making plans for him to appear tough. If only they knew. Oh, how he was ready to be commander in chief and make the difficult decisions. Let the other candidates engage in wars of words. He had shown he was willing to do much more than that. For the sake of his country, on behalf of the national interest, he had already sanctioned three murders. One down and two to go. Those last two deaths were overdue. Claire Harrington and her friend had used up nine lives and more.

It was just another case of a woman being a major hindrance to a candidate. Garret Harrington had cited quite a few examples in his book. A woman scorned could prove particularly nettlesome in any century. Elizabeth Ray told the country she couldn't type, though for years she had been on Congressman Wayne Hays's payroll as a secretary. Ray served as Hays's mistress, but had believed she would be moving up to a higher position as her boss's second wife. When Hays married his legislative aide instead, Ray blew the whistle on their relationship.

Sometimes it wasn't only political careers that were lost. Senator Arthur Brown learned the hard way not to trifle with a woman's affections. For years Utah's first senator had carried on with Anna Addison Bradley, the secretary of the fifth ward Republican Committee. Bradley even bore Brown a son. When Brown's wife learned of his affair, she threatened bodily harm to Bradley. Senator Brown gave a pistol to Bradley for her own protection from his wife. That threat disappeared when Brown's wife died. With Mrs. Brown out of the picture, Bradley accepted her lover's proposal of marriage but as time passed he proved remarkably unready to walk down that middle aisle. Senator Brown kept putting Bradley off, claiming the time wasn't right, and that for the sake of propriety they should wait. When Bradley was three months pregnant with Brown's second child, she discovered he was having an affair with another woman. Many considered it poetic justice that she killed Brown with the same gun he had given Bradley to protect her from his wife.

In a way, thought the Candidate, he was indebted to Garret Harrington and his stories of political passion. They put all his goals and aspirations in perspective. Harrington should have learned some lessons from his book. Instead he became a victim much like Senator Arthur Brown.

The moral of the story, thought the Candidate, is that you

don't give a chance for your skeletons to get out of the closet.

You don't give them a chance to rattle.

You shoot them dead before they even think of shooting you.

CHAPTER TWENTY

It was a little past five in the morning when I got a working signal on Roper's cell phone. As I tapped in the number I tried not to notice just how much my fingers were trembling. Never in my life had I so wanted to hear one voice, and my anxiety increased exponentially with each ring. By the fourth ring I had gone from anticipation to despair. That's when she picked up, sleepy voice and all, and for a moment I couldn't speak.

"Claire?"

She was quick to awaken. "Will? Is that you?"

"Are you all right?" We asked the same question at the same time, and then our mutual assurances echoed each other's.

"How did you—?" started Claire.

I interrupted her and said, "Just to be safe, let's wait to talk until we're face-to-face."

"Are you sure you're not hurt? You sound funny."

"I'm fine," I said, trying to navigate sounds through my damaged front tooth. "Did you get in touch with my contact?"

Claire hesitated a moment before saying, "No. I kept hoping I would hear from you."

She should have called Lou Bohannon, I thought, though I wasn't surprised that she hadn't. From the first, Claire had actively avoided involving anyone else. As public enemies went, she was positively private.

"Are you at the prearranged spot?"

Again, she didn't answer immediately. "It didn't feel safe, Will. And besides, the camping equipment was in the rental car at the bank."

"Without being specific, where are you?"

She considered her answer for a moment and then said, "It's snowing."

I thought about where that might be, and Claire offered another hint: "You'll need to *key* on my words."

Then it came to me: the key in the snow globe meant she was back at her father's house. "Claire—"

She heard the alarm in my voice and stepped on my protest: "It's safe. I wouldn't be talking to you if it wasn't."

I thought about it. Maybe the house wasn't such a bad choice after all. It was unlikely our enemies would expect us to return there, but that didn't mean they wouldn't think to revisit Garret Harrington's home. It was too dangerous for her to stay.

"You have to get out of there. Now."

"All right," said Claire. "Where should we meet?"

"Get in the car and I'll call you from the road."

I talked to her three times in the next hour. We had come too far to get sloppy now, and I needed to make sure Claire wasn't being followed. After scouting out the city of Columbia I called and gave her directions to a convenience store where I could safely monitor her from a distance and make sure she was alone.

With Claire still at least half an hour away from our meeting spot, I decided to use the time to make a long overdue phone call. When I heard my old friend's voice, all the intervening years fell away. For a moment I wasn't sure where to begin; all that water under the bridge seemed to have formed an ocean.

"I need a favor," I said.

We hadn't talked in more than fifteen years, but Bo didn't say, "Who is this?" He just said, "What can I do?"

"You've been following the news lately?"

"Closely," he said.

"I don't know the latest. Yesterday I had some trouble at a bank in Charleston. Did you hear anything about that?"

"No. But I'm aware of your other recent activities."

"Don't believe everything you hear."

"I don't."

I decided to be less cryptic, and give Bo a rundown of what had happened at the bank. He listened without comment while I told him about the gun, and how others had gone to such great lengths to retrieve it.

"You'll never guess who headed up my welcome committee," I said. "Sam Roper."

"The Baby Bomber?" he asked.

"He's a little touchy about that nickname."

"Poor baby."

"I imagine the local police have been reviewing the security tape, but without sound it might not look like anything more than a bunch of people standing around talking. I have a feeling the police will become a lot more interested in that footage if you tell them that it stars Claire and me and a cosmetically transformed Roper. I'm willing to bet that the gun I returned will suddenly become a top priority."

"And that's what you want?"

"I want it looked at every which way it can be. I think that gun was used in a murder approximately sixteen years ago. Tell me those police shows I've seen are right, and it can still be positively identified as the murder weapon all these years later."

"Sure," Bo said. "Assuming the evidence was collected correctly, there are plenty of things that can match up the gun as the homicide weapon. Evidence techs can study the striations taken off the barrel. Groove impressions can also be linked, and bullet landmarks can be identified by their patterns. Sometimes the lab techs will even compare and link cartridge cases by looking at microscopic details in the marks of the firing pin on the primer. Weapons have their own fingerprints, and ballistics can match them."

"Good. That's what I wanted to hear."

"What you don't want to hear is how many people die from gunshot wounds in this country every year. What you're asking isn't a needle in the haystack kind of search, but it's still a significant undertaking. Back in the eighties at least thirty-five thousand people died from handgun wounds in any given year. That means the problem might not be so much in identifying the gun, as in narrowing down the number of comparisons to get a hit. You got anything to limit the search?"

"The murder probably happened in the D.C. area, and my guess is the victim was someone respectable, maybe even high profile."

"Should I be surprised if I find some association with Garret Harrington in all of this?"

"I wouldn't be."

"Is that what this is all about?"

"It's what part of it is about."

"I'm just a cop," Bo said. "I'm not a fed with a task force, and this is way out of my jurisdiction, but I'll pull whatever strings are available and do everything I can."

"I know that."

"You happen to know the make and model of the gun?"

I told him the specifics, and he said, "That type of gun typically leaves one telltale mark."

"Oh?"

"Yeah, a big hole in the victim."

"No wonder you keep getting promoted. Sherlock Holmes has nothing on you."

Reverting back to our old ways hadn't taken long, but the kid stuff was only temporary. Bo cleared his throat, and then said, "There's something else I wish you would ask me to do, Will."

"What's that?"

"Make arrangements so you can turn yourself in."

"Soon," I promised.

"Remember your advice to me, Will. You always told me to pick my battles."

"This is a good battle."

"Is it your battle? Or is it Claire Harrington's?"

"It's both of ours now. And maybe a lot more people besides."

"You never could resist helping the underdog, could you?"

I thought about saying, *You should know,* but instead I didn't answer.

Bo said, "Be careful, Will."

"I'll call you tomorrow."

From an upper-story office building, I watched Claire park. There was no obvious tail and she looked to be alone. Still, I kept her under observation for five minutes before deciding it was safe to join her.

Claire saw me before I reached the car, and she didn't wait for my approach, throwing the door open and running to me. Our hugs were as unreserved as the kisses that followed. This is what returning home from a war to a loved one feels like, I thought. I didn't want to let her go, but she stepped back from my arms and looked at me critically.

"You look like hell," Claire said.

"You don't."

"What happened to your tooth?"

"It's a long story."

"Then I'll drive and you talk."

We got in the car, and did as she said. I made my story brief, leaving out a lot of details, and felt like a film editor trying to do enough splicing and dicing to make a G-rated version of *A Clockwork Orange*. It wasn't only that I was trying to shield Claire from the violence. My mouth was still an open wound, and everything hurt the exposed nerve— everything, that is, except the sight of her. Though I said nothing about it, Claire noticed my discomfort. She dug into her purse and pulled out a bottle of pills.

"Steer the wheel," she told me, and while I did, she opened the bottle and took out three pills.

"Take these," she said, extending them my way.

"What are they?"

"Tylenol with a little codeine," she said. "They were in my father's medicine cabinet."

I rolled one of the pills in my finger, but didn't bring it to my mouth. "I need to keep a clear head," I said.

"How are you going to think clearly when you haven't slept and you're in pain?"

I was still hesitating when she took a container of bottled water from the cup-holder and slapped it into my hand. "Take them," she said.

I popped one of the pills into my mouth, swigged the water, and repeated the process until all the pills were all gone. As a reward, Claire reached out and took my hand into hers. I preferred that as pain medicine.

"Where are we driving?" I asked.

"D.C. area," she said. "Alexandria."

"What's there?"

"My fiancé is out of town on business," she said. "I know the security code to his building. We can use his apartment."

I released my hold on her hand. Whenever I heard about her fiancé, my perfect little fantasies blew up, exploding not in my head but my chest.

"It's not safe," I said. "The feds will be watching for you there."

Claire shook her head. "Our engagement isn't public knowledge. In fact, we've kept it to ourselves."

"Why?"

"It's complicated."

"If you were my fiancé," I said, "I would want to tell the whole world."

"Don't trust a man on medication," she said, trying to make a joke out of it, but it looked as if her eyes were suddenly misty.

"Are you sure no one knows?" I asked.

"I'm sure."

I was reminded of another situation where no one should have known our whereabouts and intentions. Watching her very closely, I asked: "Yesterday morning we were ambushed at the bank. How could they have known we were going to be there?"

She shook her head without any hesitation, and didn't offer any physical giveaways to indicate she might be telling a lie. "I have no idea."

"Sam Roper, also known as the Baby Bomber, indicated you sold us out."

Claire met my gaze. "That was the first time I ever talked to that man in my life."

"What did he say to you?"

She turned away, choosing to concentrate on her driving. Her expression was no longer as self-righteous or certain. "He said he wanted to talk to me."

The conviction was gone from her voice. I wondered if he had said something else.

"Roper and his team have been after us since the Blue Crab Inn. Judging from our run-ins, I don't think there are that many of them, probably no more than seven or eight. Most don't look or act like professionals. My guess is that they are part of the pro-life underground that's been hiding

Roper and his helpers for the last few years. He might not even have told them why he's hunting us."

My pain was dissipating, and I was feeling more relaxed, but I couldn't lose this tug of anxiety. "What I still can't figure out is how Roper had the inside track this whole time. He knew to go after us at my office, and then the bank."

"They probably found some banking record that showed my father had a safety deposit box. That's how they knew we would show up there."

It was possible, I thought, but it still didn't feel right.

"Why would Roper be involved in this?" Claire asked. "I thought he was only interested in targeting abortion clinics."

"He's broadened his interest to politics. Roper must have finally realized he couldn't target every health clinic and hospital. By getting his candidate elected, he hopes to have abortions outlawed. Killing us is supposed to be for the greater good."

"Did he tell you who he was working for?"

I shook my head. "But there are only two candidates I know running on anti-abortion planks."

"Norman," said Claire. "And all this time I thought it had to be one of the Democratic candidates."

"Why Norman and not Stanton?"

"Because Norman tried to have Stanton killed, remember? It also explains the bomb that was detonated at Stanton headquarters as a diversion before the assassination attempt."

I watched her hands tighten on the steering wheel, saw her knuckles turning white and her lips purse. "By setting me up," Claire said, "Norman thought he was getting rid of two threats. He knew I was looking into my father's past, and he was afraid of Mark Stanton's momentum. When Norman was no longer a shoo-in for the nomination, he wanted Stanton dead, and he wanted me to look like the shooter."

I considered what she was saying, and couldn't find fault

with it. Then again, I doubt whether I could have found fault with much of anything. I was suddenly feeling very good.

"Last night I didn't go to Summerville just for shelter, Will. I was looking for clues."

She sounded as if she was confessing, and wanted my blessing. I was in a mood to bless just about anyone for anything.

"So that's what you were doing," I said, my tone one of approbation. "Did you find any?"

"I might have. I stayed up reading until very late. Do you remember telling me about the invoice to Holly's Secretarial in Ladson?"

"I do indeed," I said.

"Yesterday afternoon I went to Ladson and met with Holly. It was just as we thought. Holly's been doing Father's typing for years, and she was able to print out a copy of *Political Passions* for me. I read the whole book last night."

"You read the whole book!" I enthused.

"The whole book minus one section," Claire said.

"One section," I echoed.

Claire must have thought I had caught on to the significance of her statement, and not that I had arrived at the point of being so loopy that I was repeating things like a bird. "Holly tells me that Father had been working on that section for some time. He told her he wanted to get it just right. Roper must have gotten those pages."

I tried to follow what she was saying, tried to put some brakes on the medication she had given me. The braking wasn't easy. I felt out of balance, felt as if I was spinning out of control.

Claire started speaking very quickly. "There are five sections to his book. The first is 'Dueling and Death'; the second is 'Politics Makes for Strange Bedfellows'; the third is 'God and Mammon'; and the fourth section is 'Pride and Fall.' The missing section is the book's ending. I think the ending was meant to tie all the preceding sections together. From what I can infer, everything built up to the conclusion. I think Father set up the book to show background and historical precedents to better explain his own conduct in the final section."

I knew that everything she was saying was very important, but at the moment trying to hold on to thoughts was like trying to hold water in my hands. Everything was slipping through. Insights and connections materialized for an instant, and then vanished.

"Those pills," I said. "Powerful."

"Yes. They were Father's pain medication for the cancer."

"You said Tylenol and codeine?"

"They might have been a bit more potent than that."

I think I said, "Elephant tranquilizers," but maybe I just thought those words.

It wasn't a time to sleep, but the alarm systems going off in my head were short-circuited. I opened my mouth, and tried to shape into form a few of the many things I wanted to say, but it was Morpheus who had the final word.

CHAPTER TWENTY-ONE

Hands shook me, and a voice said, "Wake up, Sleeping Beauty."

I tried to keep sleeping, but neither the hands nor the voice went away. "Come on, Will. You need to get up. I can't carry you."

I opened one eye. Claire was leaning over me. She was worth opening a second eye for, and I did.

"We need to get inside and out of eyeshot," Claire said.

It was night, and we were in an unfamiliar neighborhood that seemed to consist mostly of high-rise apartment buildings. Claire motioned impatiently, and I got out of the car. On the street there was some car traffic, and a few pedestrians were about.

"Let's look like a couple," she said. "No one will notice us if we walk arm in arm, act like we're connected at the hip, and stare longingly in each other's eyes."

"We could give off that impression better if were making out," I suggested, "and while we're in character we might also consider some heavy petting."

"You always wake up like this?"

"Are you aware of how most men wake up?"

She offered me her arm, and I took it. Claire seemed well-acquainted with the route, as she was able to nestle her head into my chest and navigate without looking up. At the stoop of the building she paused long enough to tap in a security code, and the door buzzed open.

We didn't encounter anyone in either the lobby or the elevator, but we stayed in our roles as lovers. I assumed there were security cameras that were prompting Claire to continue our pretense, but I was hoping there was a part of her that wanted to hold on to me as much as I did her.

At the tenth floor we exited the elevator. Again, there was no hesitation on Claire's part, and it was clear she was no stranger to the building. When she came to a stop and raised a key to the lock, I grabbed her hand.

"There are lights on inside."

"I know," Claire said. "I turned them on while bringing up some things and letting you sleep."

"Where did you get the key to get in?"

"We keep a spare inside the mail slot that opens with just a little jiggling."

The one-bedroom apartment was sparsely furnished. There was a small television in the living room and a single easy chair. The dining room consisted of a card table and two folding chairs. There were no pictures, no paintings, no knickknacks, nothing to make the apartment appear homey or lived-in.

Claire was watching my expression as I looked around. "He's between places," she said. "This is only temporary."

I remembered saying those same words to Claire about my own apartment, and wondered if her explanation was as full of bullshit as my own.

"I already looked for food," Claire said. "There's nothing in the fridge except for a jar of olives, and the only thing in the cupboard is a can of mixed nuts."

"Did I ever tell you how much I love a dinner of olives and mixed nuts?"

"You'll have to fight me for them."

We took our meal, such as it was, at the card table.

Claire's real find of the night was a bottle of merlot. We did our drinking out of some chipped ceramic coffee mugs. After a few handfuls of nuts and a few spoonfuls of olives, I rubbed my stomach in exaggerated satisfaction and said, "You're some cook, honey."

"When I get a chance, smart-ass," Claire said, "I'll make you a six-course dinner that will knock your socks off."

"I'll gratefully take a raincheck," I said, "socks and all. Truth be told, the nuts and olives were as much as my mouth was up to tackling anyway."

The chewing had reminded me how much my mouth hurt. My jaw felt as if someone had beaten it with a hammer. As I lightly massaged it, I realized that Claire was watching me.

"Whatever you do," I said, "don't offer me an after-dinner toothpick."

She thought that was funny, and that made us both a little silly. It was a relief to be able to laugh.

"I didn't want to tell you this," said Claire, "but your face and cheeks are all swollen. It looks like you're storing nuts for the winter."

"That's what happens," I said. "You gnaw on trees and you begin to resemble a squirrel."

We drank some more wine and began to unwind even more. I told her how I had enlisted Lou Bohannon to help us, and that I was sure he would match up the gun with its victim.

"How is it that a cop is helping us instead of trying to arrest us?" Claire asked.

"For two years Bo was my roommate at West Point," I said. And then I added something that I had never told anyone else: "I fell on my sword for him."

I picked up the coffee cup and took a healthy swig of wine. Claire was looking at me expectantly but I pretended not to see.

"I'd like to hear that story," she said.

I shook my head. "Fifteen years ago the honor committee also wanted to hear that story. I declined comment then, and I'm not going to start talking now."

"Truth or dare," Claire said.

"That's a game that involves two people."

She considered that before saying, "Yes, it is."

"Are you telling me that you're in?"

"You Travis men love to draw lines in the sand with your swords, don't you?"

"We're not afraid of showing where we stand."

My challenge prompted us to lock eyeballs for three or four very long seconds, and then Claire finally crossed the line. "Truth," she said.

I took a deep breath and filled my lungs. I had escalated matters, and now had to confront the consequences. That felt almost as scary as someone shooting at me. I considered what to say, and had no idea where to begin.

"By this time you'd think everything would be straight in my mind," I said. "I've certainly had enough time to come up with an explanation that makes sense but that hasn't seemed to help. You remember I told you I was an army brat?"

Claire nodded.

"Twenty-five years ago my family was living in off-post housing in Fayetteville. I was ten years old at the time, and my brother Craig was seven. He never reached his eighth birthday because he died on my watch. It was a tragedy no one in my family ever really recovered from."

Claire could see that continuing with my story wasn't going to be easy for me and she offered an out. "You don't have to go on."

"Truth," I said, "remember?"

The problem with truth, though, is that it is something that can be divided in so many ways, with the seeming contradiction that one person's truth can be someone else's lie.

"I remember leaving our house that morning and hearing my mother say to me, 'Watch your brother.' It was something she was always telling me. Despite my objections, Craig insisted upon tagging along after me, which meant he was supposed to be in my care. On that day I met up with two of my friends, and we decided to go collect some tadpoles at a local pond. Once we got to the water we ditched my brother, and then went about our tadpole gathering. We heard him calling for us a few times, and thought it was funny. I expected that Craig would eventually find us, as he always did, but when about half an hour went by without him turning up, I finally went looking for him. I found him facedown in the water.

"Things were never the same after that. Everyone in my family went a little crazy. I was so guilty I stopped thinking straight. I don't know how I got the idea, but I decided that if I really atoned for what I had done, Craig would come back to us alive. Because of my failure to look after him, it seemed to me the only way to make amends was to take notice of everything. That idea became an obsessive ritual that ruled me for years. I spent more time in class remembering where everyone was seated, and taking notice of how many tiles were on the wall, and how everything was positioned in the room, than listening to the teacher. I became obsessed with trying to notice everything, and started studying memory programs and using mnemonic aids. By the time I was fifteen I memorized the first four books of the New Testament word for word. I was sure God would notice how much I was doing to atone for my huge sin of omission and return Craig back to us, and then everything would be normal again.

"While I was keeping myself occupied with my mind games, my mother and father were finding their own ways to beat themselves up. My father took to binge drinking, and my mother retreated so far inside herself that the real her never came out again. She died four years after the accident in what was diagnosed as an aneurysm to her brain, but I still think it was Craig's drowning that killed her.

"That's what preceded my going to West Point. When I realized that no amount of memorizing was going to bring Craig to life, and when Mom died, I decided that the military was going to be my family for life. There was nothing that would keep me out of West Point. I had this hunger to go there, this absolute need, and even before being accepted I dedicated myself to the commandments of duty, honor, and country. I bought into those concepts without any reservations. I was going to be the best damn officer in the army of my country that I could possibly be. That was my *raison d'être*, my reason for being on the planet."

I stopped talking, and drained the wine left in my cup. Claire reached for the bottle and refilled my glass.

"I didn't get a congressional appointment the first year I applied to West Point, and suffered through a year of junior college. The second year I received my appointment and ended up being roomed with Lou Bohannon. Bo was young. When we started at the Academy I was nineteen going on thirty, and Bo was seventeen going on fifteen. I felt the need to take him under my wing. Looking back, I can see how he became my surrogate little brother.

"The Academy wasn't easy for Bo. He was immature, both physically and emotionally. Bo was one of those guys who always seemed to be a little out of step. He was always getting demerits, and being confined to quarters, and had to do more marching tours than anyone else in our class. Because of his troubles, I let him lean on me. Maybe I even encouraged it.

"Whatever I did, Bo wanted to do. When I had an idea for a dangerous spirit mission, Bo never hesitated a moment before saying he was in. Along with half a dozen other cadets, we pulled off a stunt that's still talked about to this day. Before the big game—and I don't need to tell you that's Army-Navy—a group of us traveled to Annapolis, snuck on the grounds of the Naval Academy, and strung up a huge banner on their quad that read, BEAT NAVY! Our exploit made the local news, and caused a lot of red faces at the Naval Academy. Pulling off that mission was like going behind enemy lines, and Bo was with me every step of the way.

"Bo never had West Point religion like I did. He was there because he was a smart kid who came from a poor family and it was a way for him, maybe the only way, to get a top-notch education for free. Of course, there's a price for that so-called free education. Cadets like to say it's a free quarter-million-dollar education shoved up your ass a nickel at a time. But because Bo didn't come from a military family, he wasn't nearly as prepared for the rigors of that life as I was. He barely escaped his plebe year without being turned back, and things were going even worse for him as a yearling. By year's end, Bo's probationary status was all but used up. His neck was in the noose, and he had been warned that if he flunked any courses he would be dismissed.

"Though I helped tutor him, things didn't look good. The dagger through his heart was a required math course in probability and statistics, a class in the course catalog abbreviated as Prob and Stats, but what we called *probed with bats*. Without a good showing on his final, Bo was going to flunk that course and be bounced from West Point.

"I had the class before Bo did, and took the final. When I returned to our room I found him sobbing, his head in the textbook, his tears staining the pages. Without saying anything to him, I tore some pages out of a notebook and then I reconstructed all the problems on the final. After all my years of mastering memorization techniques, of training to recollect things exactly, it was easy for me to do."

I stopped talking, and shook my head. "I spent all that

time learning how to remember," I said. "Maybe it would have been better if I'd learned how to forget. You know how many times I've replayed her words in my head? 'Watch your brother,' Mother told me. 'Watch your brother.' "

I went back to the wine, and again drained the cup. Claire emptied the last of the bottle in my glass. Without any hurry, with a few sips in between the telling, I eventually resumed the story.

"Bo got a solid B on the final exam, a grade good enough to get him advanced to the second class.

"Bo and I never talked about what I did, though it was clearly an honor code violation. Anyone who attends West Point lives under the ethical obligation of that honor code. The words to the honor code are simple, though its demands are anything but that. The honor code states, 'A cadet will not lie, cheat, steal, or tolerate those who do.' You wouldn't think twelve little words could turn your world upside down, but they did.

"I was a second classman, a Cow, and was just finishing up my first term when I was called before a midnight meeting of the honor committee. Whenever the committee convenes at that hour, you know the charges are serious, and they were. The committee asked me if I had helped another cadet to cheat—specifically, if I had improperly passed on information pertaining to a final examination. I confirmed that I was guilty of that offense. Then they asked me for the name of the cadet I had helped, but I refused to supply it.

"I was escorted over to the Boarders Ward, and by noon of that same day I was expelled from West Point."

"That's terrible," Claire said.

I shook my head. "I was the one who was derelict in his duty. The honor committee did their job. They had no choice but to expel me."

"But what they did was so extreme. I can understand you being disciplined, but not expelled."

I wanted to wallow in her sympathy, but I couldn't. "One time a chairman of the West Point honor committee was asked to describe the most difficult part of his job. Do you have any idea what he said?"

Claire thought about it, and then ventured her guess. "I imagine he said that the most difficult thing to do was expel a fellow cadet."

I shook my head. "He said the most difficult thing was trying to explain the honor code to people who couldn't possibly understand it."

"Maybe there's a reason for most people not being able to understand it. Everyone makes mistakes."

"In the army, your mistakes will kill other people."

"All you were doing was trying to help someone."

"What I did was to be insubordinate to a higher power. Outsiders think that the honor code is some millstone around a cadet's neck, but it's not that way at all. The honor code, and all the responsibilities inherent within it, is a trust that a cadet has to embrace willingly. It's even freeing in a way. You have to abide by its rules."

"There wasn't any appeal for you?"

"No. I wouldn't give up the name, and that made for an unforgivable insubordination. Because I had already attended the Academy for two years, I could have been transferred into the regular army and been forced to serve as a private, but the powers that be just decided to release me from my commitment and cut me loose."

"What happened to Bo?"

"He graduated, received his commission, and ultimately left the army for a career in law enforcement."

"By accepting your help, though, he violated the honor code."

"It was up to Bo to make his own decision about what was right or wrong."

"How do you know he's not trying to have you arrested?"

"Bo's job is to arrest criminals, and he knows I'm not one of those. Our history transcends fifteen years of not talking. When I asked him to help, I could hear the happiness in his voice. Bo wants nothing more than to try and even the score between us."

I started breathing a little more easily. For some reason, my body no longer hurt as much.

"Do you regret what you did?" Claire asked.

"You can't imagine how much I wanted to be an army officer," I said. "When I was escorted off the grounds of the Academy, I wanted to die. All my goals and dreams disappeared."

I stopped talking and shook my head. "Still, even with all the potential consequences hanging over me, I couldn't let Bo down. If I hadn't helped him, he would have been bounced, and I didn't want to stand by and let that happen. I picked my poison."

"I'm beginning to understand now," said Claire, "why my father spoke about West Point with such reverence."

"Once it's in your blood," I said, "there's no eradicating it."

"Duty," she sighed.

"Honor," I said. "And let's not forget country."

"No," Claire said, "let's not."

I raised my cup. "Truth," I said.

Claire touched her mug to mine. Instead of echoing the word, she said, "I'll keep your story in the strictest confidence."

"And I'll respect you in the morning as well."

If Claire was amused, she didn't show it. Her preoccupation showed itself by the nervous running of her finger around the rim of her mug. By being hunched over and making circles with her finger, she avoided any eye contact. Finally she said, "Go ahead and ask."

There was one truth I wanted above all others: "Tell me about your fiancé."

Claire let out a lungful of pent-up air, but my question didn't surprise her. "That's what made all of this so complicated," she said, "but I guess you suspected that."

"I was slow in the uptake. When you're running for your life, the obvious escapes you."

"Mark has been trying to help us," she said, "but he's been in a Catch-22 situation as well."

The first name was finally out in the open. I put the last name to it, something I should have been able to do days before. Claire was engaged to presidential candidate Congressman Mark Stanton.

"To publicly stand by me now would be political suicide," she said. "Mark wanted to do it. He all but insisted. But even when he begged, I refused."

"Why?"

"I did it partly because I didn't want to hurt Mark's chances so late in the campaign. And I didn't want to hurt my chances, either."

"I'm not following you."

"Remember when you said that no one could imagine how much you wanted to be an army officer, and how attending West Point and serving in the army were your reasons for existence?"

I nodded.

"It wasn't hard for me to understand your hunger," she said. "Women aren't supposed to have that kind of driving ambition. If we do, we're taught to put chiffon over it, and somehow try to make it more palatable to men. I have also had a goal since the time I was young. I always dreamed that one day I would be the First Lady."

She studied her fingernails for several seconds, pinched at a cuticle, and then continued. "I suppose I got the bug during my father's time in Congress. We visited the White House on several occasions, and I could never take my eyes off the First Lady. To my young eyes, she looked like a queen."

"I'm surprised you'd settle for the role of spouse when you're smart enough to be the ruler," I said. "Think of Thatcher, Gandhi, Meir, or Bhutto."

"Think of Eleanor Roosevelt, or Jackie Kennedy, or Nancy Reagan. Not only were they an acknowledged power behind the throne, they made their own unique mark on the world."

"Speaking of a unique mark, do you love Mark Stanton?"

"I can't imagine a better partner in life."

"You didn't answer the question."

"I believe I did. I know it sounds calculated, but my experience has been that in matters of importance my brain always rules my heart."

"Why was your relationship kept a secret?"

"You know the story of his wife, don't you?"

Though I read a newspaper every morning, my habit is to start with the sports section, go on to the comics, and then skim the rest. On the scale of what interests me, political stories usually come in dead last. But I did know the story of Jennifer Stanton.

"She was mentally ill, and committed suicide a few years ago."

Claire nodded. "It was a life-changing event for Mark," she said. "He's become a much better father to his two children, as well as becoming more attuned to the suffering of others."

What she was saying sounded as if it had been lifted from one of his political speeches.

"Because of his wife's death, Mark realized he had to put the needs of his children before his own. Sarah is ten now, and Jason is fourteen. When Mark and I started dating almost two years ago, we decided our relationship had to be kept very private."

"The two of you did that for the children?" I said, not hiding my disbelief.

"Not completely. As a widower and father, Mark was in a vulnerable position. He couldn't just start dating. That would look callous and uncaring. For appearances, if nothing else, there needed to be an appropriate grieving period. When Mark decided to run for president, it was still too soon after his wife's death to let anyone know we were dating."

"So it was fine for him to run for president, but not okay to tell the world he was in a relationship."

"There were—considerations."

"Such as?"

"There was polling done that showed Mark's sympathy vote was not inconsiderable."

"Better to run with a dead woman than a living one."

"You're not being fair, Will."

"I already told you that if you were my woman I would want the whole world to know."

"Mark said much the same thing before he announced his candidacy. The polling data was incontrovertible, though. Because he's a widower, the numbers were incredibly positive. People wanted to reach out to him, and they were willing to do it with their votes. If he suddenly had his arm wrapped around a younger woman, that sympathy vote would have vanished."

"So you're saying people should vote for him under false pretenses?"

"No, I'm saying people should vote for him anyway, but there's no reason to toss aside something that's advantageous. That would be like a war hero not using his military record."

"It's not the same thing at all. A war hero has earned his medals. Your man wants people to feel sorry for him because his wife committed suicide."

"That's a cheap shot, Will."

"No, it's his tactics that are cheap."

We both sat there, not looking at one another. Finally Claire said, "I wanted to tell you from the first, but my hands were tied. Like Caesar's wife, I'm supposed to be above suspicion, not someone accused of murder. That's why I was so desperate to clear my name, and that's why I couldn't allow the taint to spread to Mark."

"It would ruin his presidential chances, and your First Lady dreams."

Claire nodded.

"Death before dishonor or the inaugural ball," I said, "or whichever comes first."

"You don't have to be cruel, Will."

"Is this your love nest?" I asked.

"It's where we meet, yes."

"Why not a Boy Scout?" That was the tagline to Stanton campaign commercials, though it was never asked in my facetious manner.

"He was an Eagle Scout."

"Isn't he the candidate that talks endlessly about family values?"

"After the election, we will be married."

"Win or lose?"

"Yes, win or lose."

"But your white dress would look a lot better against the background of the Rose Garden?"

"Why are you so bitter?"

"You know why I'm so bitter. I don't think you love him, Claire, at least not as much as you love the idea of being First Lady."

I waited for her to say something, but she didn't answer.

"What if he doesn't win?" I asked.

"I'll marry him anyway."

"That's right, he's a congressman just like Daddy was, so you'll be able to go to all those receptions and luncheons and balls. You can be that little girl with stars in your eyes once more."

"And I can also have a forum from which to do worthwhile projects. Why is that so terrible?"

"Sometimes we have to give up the dreams of our youth,

Claire. Life takes us on different paths than we want or expect, and that's when you have to remind yourself that it's not the destination, but the journey."

"Any more clichés you care to impart?"

There were three words I was going to impart, but she effectively quashed those out of me. "No, I guess not."

She could see my hurt and anger. "Forgive me, Will. I'm tired."

"Sure."

"When we bring Norman down, I'll try and make all of this up to you. I'm not only talking about paying you for your work. I want everyone to hear how brave you've been."

"Maybe in the future you can get an elementary school named after me," I said. "Hell, that no-tell motel we slept in might even get nominated to the National Register of Historic Places."

"I'm too tired to argue, and I don't want to argue. Would you prefer sleeping in the bedroom or the living room?"

"The bed's all yours. I want to do some reading."

CHAPTER TWENTY-TWO

I had read about half of Garret Harrington's book when I decided to take a break and make some phone calls. Jenny picked up her home phone on the third ring.

"I'm sorry I haven't called you," I said.

There was a slight intake of breath. "Why are you calling so late, Marge?"

Marge was her sister. I assumed Jenny's husband had forbidden her from having contact with me and was in earshot.

"I'm trying to clear my name. I hope in the next day or two to make everything right again."

"An egg has no business dancing with a stone," she said.

Jenny might have been speaking cryptically to allay her husband's suspicions, but it was more likely she was summing up my interest in Claire. "I suppose you're right," I said, "but if you don't scale the mountain you can't view the plain."

"Views are overrated. What good is having your head in clouds? Better to make money selling manure than lose money selling diamonds."

I smiled at the ever practical Jenny's advice. "I called you to see if you could track down a quote for me," I said. "You have your *Bartlett's Familiar Quotations* handy?"

Knowing how much Jenny enjoyed sayings, I had given her a copy for her birthday.

"It's right here," she said.

"I think the line is from Shakespeare, and reads, "Having sworn too hard a keeping oath.""

I heard Jenny turning some pages and mumbling, and then she said, "I found it. That's from *Love's Labour's Lost*."

"Do me a favor," I said, "and read me the line that comes before and after."

"It says, 'Or study where to meet some mistress fine, when mistresses from common sense are hid; or, having sworn too hard a keeping oath, study to break it and not break my troth.' "

The last line interested me most. I thought about the words and how Garret Harrington related to them.

" 'The words of Mercury are harsh after the songs of Apollo,' " said Jenny.

"What?"

"That's how play ends," she said.

While I thought about love and war, Jenny's thoughts were evidently fixated on Claire Harrington. "You still with her?"

"Yes."

"She'll eat you alive. Only fool lives in land of cannibals."

"Thanks for caring, Jenny."

"You watch out. Focus too much on snake and you miss scorpion."

"I'll watch out for both."

"Remember Korean saying: Tap even a stone bridge before crossing it."

"Here's an American saying for you. Sleep tight, don't let the bedbugs bite."

She hung up the phone, and I listened to the dial tone for longer than I should have. Finally I awakened from my thoughts and made a second call.

"Got anything?" I asked.

"Got people interested in your bank deposit," Bo said.

"Good."

"And I found a likely candidate that matches up with the time period and location you specified."

"I'm listening."

"Remember Bradley Walton?"

"Bradley Walton," I repeated, the picture of the man coming to mind. "He had some Cabinet post."

"Secretary of the Interior."

"There was that big scandal surrounding his death."

"He was shot through the heart," he said, "in a spot where gay men were known to cruise for sex."

I remembered the story. "His body was found in some Maryland park."

"That's right. It was in Bladensburg, Maryland."

"Are you sure? Bladensburg?"

I looked at the book I'd been reading. Its pages were spread out over the kitchen table. Bo heard my excitement, but didn't understand it. "What of it?"

"Someone should have made that connection," I said. "In the nineteenth century all the D.C. politicians and notables adjourned to Bladensburg to duel."

"Are you saying Walton was shot during a duel?"

"The last few years of his life, Garret Harrington was working on a book that he titled *Political Passions*," I said. "I've just been reading that book. Duels play a very important part in it."

"I guess the investigation team didn't think to look in the past," Bo said, "because of more recent headlines. Not long before Walton's death, police set up a sting in the park and arrested eight men. The charges ranged from prostitution, to public exposure, to lewd and lascivious acts. When Walton ended up dead, everyone assumed he was at the park trolling for anonymous sex. It was a tidy reason for explaining his being there before sunrise."

I thought about how Walton died. It wasn't as if anyone would have had reason to link a gunshot death to a duel.

"There was a vicious whisper campaign after he died," said Bo. "Everyone was saying that Walton was in the closet, leading a double life. All the speculation tied in with the known facts. Walton was very secretive about his private life, almost obsessively so. After his death, details of that private life kept leaking out. Sources within his staff said he frequently left his office for several hours at a time, and that he never offered any explanations for his absence. Somehow the media was able to obtain some of his credit card expenditures and found that he frequented a number of local hotels and dined in out-of-the-way restaurants. Even his divorce, finalized a year earlier, was grist for the mill. His ex-wife said that Walton was never specific as to why he wanted a divorce, but was adamant that they get one."

I thought about the life and death of Bradley Walton. "Thanks, Bo. I need to check on some things here, and get back to you."

"When should I expect your call?" he asked.

"I'll get back to you in the morning."

"Any idea who the shooter was?"

"You'll need some very heavy tackle to bring this fish in," I said. "We'll talk about it more tomorrow."

When I clicked off I could see Claire standing on the periphery of the dining room.

"That was your cop friend?" she asked.

I nodded. "Does the name Bradley Walton ring any bells?"

"Bradley?" she asked, and then with emphasis said, "Of course."

I wasn't sure if she was answering my question, or making the connection. "Your father knew him?"

"He was the one who was shot with that gun, wasn't he?"

"Bo is looking into that possibility."

Claire put her hand up to her mouth, covering it and looking more vulnerable than I had ever seen her.

"You knew him?"

A nod. "He often dined with our family. My father used to

joke that he and Bradley were part of the 'South Carolina mafia.' They grew up about twenty miles from each other."

I heard fond memories in her voice. "You liked him?"

"Very much. He was always talking to me, always trying to make me laugh. It's hard to separate memories of Bradley before he died, and after he died, and yet I seem to remember there was always an underlying sadness to him."

"Did your father ever talk about his death?"

She shook her head. "My mother and I discussed it several times, though. It was her opportunity to give me a talk about the birds and the bees and human sexuality. I got to hear about Adam and Eve, and Adam and Steve. Mother said it explained why, after Bradley divorced his wife, he never brought a date to dinner, and how she never saw him with a woman out in public. She also thought it explained why he never had children. I remember that whenever he used to visit, Mother always told him that he needed to settle down and have a family. He was only in his late forties when he died."

"He was shot in the heart," I said, "not once but twice."

"What do you mean?"

My own situation and feelings made me certain of Walton's dilemma. "He was in love with a married woman. That would explain the hotel bills, and the out-of-the-way restaurants, and his being so secretive in a town that loves nothing better than gossip. He probably divorced his wife in the hope that the woman he loved would do the same."

"The shooter was her husband?"

"It stands to reason."

"How was my father involved in this then?"

I patted the scattered pages on the table. Claire had read her father's book, so I didn't need to recapitulate its contents. "I think there was a duel."

"A duel?" In her lawyer's voice she asked, "How did you conclude that?"

"The two identical guns are one clue. One of the rules of

dueling is that the weapons are supposed to be the same so that neither side has an advantage."

Claire didn't look convinced, so I pressed on. "You ever see a dueling pistol, or even a picture of one?"

She shook her head.

"Most have long barrels," I said. "The pistols were designed that way for accuracy and to deliver a large shot. Burr killed Hamilton with a fifty-six-caliber bullet, and Jackson did his shooting with a seventy-caliber bullet.

"These days people don't have dueling pistols. The participants would have had to go out and find a modern equivalent. It's likely that the seconds were dispatched to get the guns."

Claire thought about it, offered a tentative nod, and then improved upon that, each bob of her head a little more definitive. "That would explain why Father stored the gun at the bank. And it would also explain his interest in dueling, a subject I never heard him speak of until I read his book."

"That's how I see it."

"And you think Father was Bradley's second?"

I nodded.

Claire looked more troubled by that than the thought of her father's being one of the participants in a duel. "Daddy was very moral. I doubt whether he would have condoned adultery."

"It wasn't some tawdry, short-term affair. I would guess it was a long-established relationship, and that Walton was madly, passionately, and completely in love. I'm sure he wanted to marry the woman, and that her husband had some objections."

"Strong objections."

"Well," I said, "hasn't Bob Norman always proudly proclaimed himself a card-carrying member of the NRA?"

Claire didn't answer, but I saw in her expression that her thoughts were far away.

I decided to forge on: "You know, a few days ago I

wouldn't have been able to understand how Walton could be so stupid, but now I see it clearly. I fell in love, and now I know when that happens you'll do just about anything to be with the woman you love."

She gave a little nod, but I didn't know if it was in agreement, or encouragement, or perhaps just to show that she had heard.

"I need to reread some sections from the book. There might be clues in those pages."

"I'll leave you to it," said Claire, sounding preoccupied.

A few minutes later she surprised me by reappearing. She was holding a pillow and blanket.

"That's not necessary," I said.

"Yes, it is."

She draped the blanket around my shoulders, and then worked the pillow behind my back.

"Thanks for tucking me in."

"I wish there was a more comfortable place for you to read."

"It's fine."

"I can see you're in pain."

"Not too bad," I lied.

Claire left my side and went out to the kitchen. She returned with a mug filled with water and two of the pain pills, and extended them toward me. I shook my head at her offer.

"Take them," she said. "It's evident how much your tooth is bothering you again."

"I want to read with a clear head."

Claire put the water and the pills on the table anyway, and said, "For when the pain gets to be too much."

I almost asked her if they worked on bruised hearts as well, but instead said, "Thanks."

She touched my shoulder in passing, a light caress that lingered for just a moment, though for minutes thereafter it felt as if her hand was still on me. The reminder of her touch made it difficult to read, but I was finally able to immerse myself once again in the pages.

There was no prologue to *Political Passions*, and I wondered if Garret Harrington had planned to write one after he finished the text itself. There was a quotation that preceded the text that was taken from Carl von Clausewitz's *On War:* "Of all the passions none is more powerful than ambition." I wondered if the quotation had inspired Harrington's title.

The book didn't begin with recent history, but opened on a grassy field in Weehawken, New Jersey, on the early morning of July 11, 1804.

> *The two men were almost the same age: the older forty-eight, the other a year younger. In the year 1804, though, people were not so long-lived, and that qualified each as a senior statesman. The men had much more in common than not. Both were admired for their intellect and bravery. As young men they had distinguished themselves in battle, and helped build a nation.*
>
> *In 1775, at the Battle of Quebec, nineteen-year-old Aaron Burr risked his life while attempting to carry the body of General Richard Montgomery from the battlefield. His bravery earned him a promotion to the rank of lieutenant colonel.*
>
> *At about the same time, Alexander Hamilton was commissioned a captain in the Continental Army. On December 26, 1776, Hamilton's artillery company aided General Washington's successful attack on Trenton, New Jersey.*
>
> *During the Revolutionary War, both Hamilton and Burr served on George Washington's staff.*

As I continued to read, I could see the influence of West Point on Harrington's writing. He expanded on Burr and Hamilton's involvement in the Revolutionary War, painting

a picture of two very brave and able men. At the war's conclusion, Hamilton and Burr turned their energies onto new
fronts. Ironically, peacetime seemed to bring them even
more challenging battles than the war had.

*Without the efforts of Hamilton, it is possible that
the Constitution would never have been ratified, and
the government not established. Hamilton was the
main author of the Federalist Papers, writing two-thirds
of its eighty-five essays. In person, Hamilton proved to
be as articulate with the spoken word. He went to New
York with the "hopeless" mission of convincing firmly
entrenched Anti-Federalist delegates to support ratification of the Constitution. For a full month, Hamilton presented his case, ultimately convincing the opposition
to vote with him. After ratification, the monumental
task of building a government began.*

*As Treasury Secretary, Hamilton was given the fi-
nancial reins of a bankrupt nation. All the work that
had gone into establishing the United States of America was poised to fall by the wayside if Hamilton
couldn't find economic solutions that would allow the
new government to operate. By dint of his vision and
hard work, the nation found its economic footing.*

I skimmed over some pages that offered background to
the various trials and tribulations of the two men. Harrington wanted to fully flesh Burr and Hamilton before putting
them in each other's crosshairs. As I read, the pain from my
tooth became a constant distraction, and finally drove me
to take one of the pills.

*Hamilton and Burr did more than rub shoulders
with the Founding Fathers. They were major political
figures of their time, and each desired to lead their re-
spective parties. Burr was a Republican, and Hamil-*

ton a Federalist, but their rivalry was not confined only to the political arena. Over the years, each of the men drew the ire of the other, and their enmity became personal as well as professional.

In 1800 Aaron Burr almost became the third president of the United States. After being chosen as Thomas Jefferson's vice-presidential running mate, the two men ended up receiving the same number of electoral votes. Congress was given charge of breaking the tie. Hamilton considered Jefferson the lesser of two evils, and lobbied against Burr. Congress ended up selecting Jefferson as president, and Burr became vice president, a post he had little stomach for. Ambition had always ruled Burr, and he wanted the reins of power himself. When denied the highest office in the land, Burr sought other kingdoms. For a time he plotted to establish his rule in a new country he hoped to carve out of land from the 1803 Louisiana Purchase. He even considered trying to overthrow the government of Mexico and establishing himself as emperor. Power was Burr's political passion.

Harrington took the readers on a roundabout course to the dueling field, offering up history lessons along the way. It hadn't taken long for America to import the practice of dueling from the continent, with the first recorded American duel occurring in the Massachusetts colony in 1621. On that occasion, swords were the choice of weapon, and no one died. Guns soon supplanted swords, and dueling pistols became popular. In the eighteenth and nineteenth centuries most gentlemen owned their own set of large-caliber, smoothbore, flintlock dueling pistols.

In the South, dueling was particularly popular and Harrington took note of his own roots, saying that "nowhere was it more accepted than in my home state of South Carolina." It was also Walton's home state, I remembered.

"Palmetto State politicians," Harrington wrote, "were wont to shoot off not only from mouth and hip, but from dueling pistols as well." Because of the frequency of duels, cast-iron replicas of men were produced and used for shooting practice. In South Carolina when someone said, "I'm going to the iron man," it meant they were going to do target practice in preparation for a duel.

Shooting at the iron man was one thing, but encounters with flesh and blood were something else entirely.

Alexander Hamilton knew only too well the consequences of political arguments. Philip Hamilton, his nineteen-year-old son, initiated a duel in defense of his father's honor. Young Hamilton offered the challenge after confronting twenty-seven-year-old attorney George Eacker, taking umbrage at some of the man's allegations about his father.

Because the state of New York banned dueling, Philip Hamilton and Eacker chose to meet in a spot just across from the Hudson River on the New Jersey shore. On November 22, 1801, they faced one another with raised pistols. Their "field of honor" on the outskirts of the town of Weehawken would be the same place the senior Hamilton would meet Aaron Burr less than three years later.

Eacker and Hamilton each exchanged a shot. Philip's missed; Eacker's did not. After suffering for a full day, Philip died. The event so traumatized Philip's sister Angelica that she suffered an emotional breakdown from which she never recovered.

Most modern thinkers would wonder how Hamilton, having already lost his son to violence, and by extension his daughter as well, would let himself be put in a position to face the same fate. In early nineteenth-century America, though, many gentlemen felt that honor could best be satisfied by dueling. There were

notable critics of the practice, including George Wash-
ington and Benjamin Franklin, but in the heat of politi-
cal passions, cooler heads often did not prevail. Many
of those challenged to duels felt compelled to proceed.
To back down meant losing face. There were areas in
the country where those who refused to engage in a
duel were "posted"—a practice of posting flyers in
public spots, or publishing announcements in news-
papers, denouncing the cowardice of the individual
unwilling to fight.

I rose from the chair and stretched. My tooth was still
bothering me and made concentration difficult. I decided
I needed some assistance to get through the book, and
went in search of caffeine. In the kitchen I found some instant coffee. While the water heated I noticed a light shining out in the hallway. I turned the corner and followed the
light to its source. Claire was still up and had left the door
to the room open. Her covers were tossed aside, and she
was lying on the bed, wearing a man's button-down shirt.
Maybe she was afraid of the dark. I could understand that
now more than ever.

I suppose she heard my footsteps, and wondered what I
was doing lingering out in the hallway, because she turned
over and looked up at me. I hurried on down the hallway,
cursing my stupidity under my breath, certain that Claire
thought I was a voyeur. In the bathroom I ran some water
over my red face.

The light in her room was still on when I retraced my
steps, but this time I made a point of not looking into the
room. The water was boiling out in the kitchen and I made
my coffee.

Back at the table I sipped from my mug, and tried to for-
sake thoughts of Claire for the simmering disputes between
Hamilton and Burr and their dance with death.

Burr was the challenger. It was clear that Hamilton did not want to fight, but neither would he apologize for the affront that Burr alleged. Both men were keen on reversing recent political setbacks, and neither was willing to back down. Their seconds met and sought an amicable solution, but none could be found. Neither Burr nor Hamilton was short of pride. When the seconds determined they could not reconcile the parties, it fell to them to set the terms for the duel.

It is possible that Hamilton had a premonition of what would happen. The day before the duel he set his affairs in order, writing up his will. His own son had died from just such an engagement, and he was acquainted with others who had met their deaths dueling, among them Button Gwinnet, one of the signers of the Declaration of Independence. Hamilton was well aware that honor offered no shield from bullets.

Aaron Burr's second was W.P. Van Ness. In preparation for the duel, Van Ness and Burr cleared away some underbrush and set up the dueling field. Those two men, as had been agreed, were the first to arrive at the grounds.

Shortly before seven A.M., Hamilton landed onshore after crossing the Hudson on a barge. He was accompanied by his second, Nathaniel Pendleton, as well as a physician, Dr. David Hosack.

It was up to the seconds to make final arrangements. They measured the distance of ten full paces, and then drew lots to determine who would have the choice of position. It was Nathaniel Pendleton, Hamilton's second who won the luck of the draw. Lots were also cast as to which second would conduct the duel. Again, Hamilton's second won.

It would be the last time Hamilton was lucky.

The more I read, the more I was sure that offering up the particulars of this duel was important to Harrington because the past had context with his present. Harrington personalized the encounter, putting faces and feelings to friends and family of the two men. I took notes and tried to pin down some thoughts that were swirling around my mind, but without success. The shooting pain from my tooth didn't make thinking any easier, and I decided to take the second pain pill before getting back to Harrington's account of the duel. Though Hamilton had died two centuries before, Harrington was able to make his death a tragedy. He took eyewitness testimony from Dr. Hosack and Nathaniel Pendleton, and put the readers at the scene of his death.

> The last words of Socrates were, "I owe a cock to Asclepius; do not forget to pay it."
>
> Those who can face death with equanimity and thoughtfulness are rare and remarkable individuals. Few of us would die trying to make good on the debt of a chicken.
>
> In death, Socrates was able to think of others besides himself. Just before his end, he said, "I think that I had better bathe before I drink the poison, and not give the women the trouble of washing my dead body." Few have ever met death with such composure and selflessness.
>
> Hamilton knew he was dying after being shot. He told Dr. Hosack, "This is a mortal wound, Doctor," and then fell into a death-like faint. Later, Hamilton awakened on the barge that was rushing to return him to Manhattan. As he came to his senses, he noticed that his hand was atop his pistol.
>
> "Take care of that pistol," he said. "It is undischarged, and still cocked; it may go off and do harm." Then he tilted his head toward his second and said,

"Pendleton knows that I did not intend to fire at him."

His voice breaking, Nathaniel Pendleton said, "Yes, I have already made Dr. Hosack acquainted with your determination as to that."

If his dying testimony is to be believed, Alexander Hamilton had no intention of aiming his fire at Aaron Burr. To save face, and for what he believed was the sake of his honor, he was willing to die. In the end he was thinking of others instead of himself when he warned his friends about the danger of the loaded pistol. Like Socrates, even in death Hamilton offered lessons in life.

Hamilton crossed over on the Hudson River; his return journey was over the Styx.

Harrington expanded his dueling section beyond Hamilton and Burr. I felt that though the ending to his book was missing, I still had all the answers to the mystery if only I could read between the lines. By that time the pills had kicked in, and I was feeling slightly euphoric.

I read about Abraham Lincoln being challenged to a duel because of lambasting an Illinois state official, and how by Lincoln's naming broadswords as his weapon of choice, his much smaller challenger suddenly had a change of heart and the duel was averted. Not all of our presidents avoided duels. When Andrew Jackson was sworn into office as the seventh president, he carried with him a bullet wound from a duel. The bullet had struck so close to Jackson's heart that surgeons couldn't remove it. Jackson was lucky when compared to his opponent. His shot killed Charles Dickinson.

Political passions seemed to rule Jackson, another native of South Carolina. Jackson's fight with Dickinson resulted from his earlier challenge to the governor of Tennessee. When the governor refused to face Jackson in a duel, Old Hickory posted the man as a coward in a local paper. At the behest of the governor, Dickinson insulted Jackson's wife Rachel, forcing their encounter. Both men squared off, using seventy-caliber balls shot out of pistols with nine-inch barrels.

Rachel Jackson didn't have the stomach for politics that her husband did. Jackson's opponents attacked him through his wife. Because Jackson married his wife before her divorce was finalized, when he ran for president his wife was labeled as an "adulterer" and "bigamist." Even after her husband became the president-elect, Rachel was snubbed by the wives of other politicians. Because of all the attacks, her health failed during the campaign, and she became deeply depressed. She was quoted as saying, "I had rather be a doorkeeper in the house of God than live in that palace in Washington."

Mrs. Jackson got her wish. She died mere weeks before her husband was sworn in as president.

I took my pen and wrote down her words about the palace in Washington in large, bold letters. I wanted Claire to see them.

Tomorrow, I thought, I will acquaint her with Mrs. Jackson's words. Tomorrow, I will make my own case.

I looked up from the table and saw the light in the hallway. Claire still hadn't closed her door or turned off the light. I wondered if she was awake, and was tempted to find out.

The pills were providing me with a bravado that would vanish when their potency expired. There was a part of me that knew this, but I tried not to hear those whispers. I returned to the book and waded through the pages of yet more political duels. I reread the passages that discussed Bladensburg, Maryland, as being the favored shooting ground for eighteenth-century politicians. There was a reason for its popularity; dueling was banned in Washington, but not in Maryland. The town was just a short carriage ride away.

I felt as if I was on the verge of divining all sorts of answers, and had multiple thoughts running through my head all at once, but the pain medicine kept blurring the borders between them and made it hard to focus. I started flipping over pages, skimming through sex scandals, lies, blackmail, and graft. There was no shortage of political scandals. The last chapter available to me dealt with the Cuban missile crisis. At first I didn't even understand why it was included in the book, and then I saw Garret Harrington's continuity.

Another famous duel, I thought, but this time it wasn't two men pointing guns. Kennedy and Khrushchev each had their hands on a nuclear trigger. Harrington demonstrated how political passions could drive people, and nations, to the brink. And sometimes beyond that brink.

"You need to get some sleep."

I looked up from the pages to see Claire standing at the entrance to the hallway. "So do you."

She crossed the room and closed the space between us until she was standing over the table. "I've been thinking about this dueling business," Claire said. "Father always told me you had to do the right thing, no matter how much it hurt. I can't believe he didn't come forward and confess what happened."

"If he had, he would have been guilty of murder," I said, "or at the least being an accomplice to murder, but I don't think that's why he remained silent. The secret bound all of them. It explains your father's telling you that he was a victim of 'having sworn too hard-a-keeping oath.' You know what the next line is?"

Claire shook her head.

" 'Study to break it, and not break my troth.' Your father was bound by his word, and from experience I can tell you that West Point guilt goes a long way."

"Come on," Claire said, touching my elbow. "It's time you went to bed."

In the morning I would look at Garret Harrington's book again. With a clear mind I might see things that I missed. Rising, I took a step and then swayed and almost fell. My balance was off, a combination of the meds and my tiredness.

"Whoa." Claire reached out and steadied me with her arms, and I hugged her for support, and for more than that.

We started moving together on the floor, almost as if we were dancing, and then we were pressing into one another, clinging so close it felt as if glue had been applied to each of us from head to toe.

"This never happened," Claire whispered.

"What?"

"This," she said, and kissed me.

For both of us, it was like touching an ungrounded wire. Our lips trembled and our bodies shook.

I struggled to find words, and just before kissing her back, whispered, "What about this?"

Our second kiss was longer, and if possible, even more passionate than the first. When Claire finally found the breath to answer, she gasped: "Never happened."

"And this?"

I can't tell you how long our third kiss lasted. It was as if I fell into a place I didn't know existed, and Claire was there to share it with me.

Between the table and the bedroom we never separated, never came up for air, just passed hot bursts of breath back and forth between us.

We fell on the bed. Just when there seemed to be no more obstacles between us, we encountered the long row of buttons on Claire's borrowed shirt. She tried to undo one while I worked on another, but her fingers were no more dexterous than mine.

I didn't like the idea of her wearing his shirt anyway. I grabbed the shirt with both my hands and ripped it open. Buttons popped off, flying in all directions.

She had told me her brain ruled her heart. I was glad her

synapses had been short-circuited, and hoped it wasn't only temporary.

My face was upon her, and then my body. We shared the same urgency. I entered her, and pushed deep inside her, and with each thrust offered up my frantic message: this did happen, this did happen, this did happen.

CHAPTER TWENTY-THREE

I awakened to a voice telling me, "Take these."

The room was dark, but there was just enough light to see Claire extending her hands toward me, a glass of water in one hand, and some pills in the other.

"You keep pushing pills on me," I said, still not quite awake.

"You keep groaning," she said, "and the pain is making you toss and turn."

I had no recollection of thrashing around, and at the moment the pain in my mouth was bearable. It didn't even hurt very much to smile, which I did. Claire returned my smile, but hers came across as strained. I wondered if she had slept.

She pressed her offerings into my hands, and gave me a pat of encouragement. "Thanks," I said, and then downed the pills. I took them not for me but for her. Maybe I would stop thrashing and Claire would be able to get back to sleep.

"I hope you feel better," she said.

"Waking up next to you, I feel just fine. How are you doing?"

She answered by running a hand over my chest. I reached for her hand, but she withdrew it from my reach.

"You already deprived me of enough sleep for one night," Claire said, but then added in a soft but teasing tone, "Mind you, I'm not complaining."

"Good."

Claire returned her hand to my chest, and I reached for it, and together we intertwined our fingers. Earlier I had fallen asleep holding her in my arms. This time I drifted off while holding hands with her. The more I tried to hold her, though, the more she escaped me. I couldn't even hold on to her in my dreams.

The pills started speaking to me, and I didn't like their message. For the first time in my life I was in love, and yet that only seemed to increase my troubled feelings. It felt as if my equilibrium was lost, and I was falling. Even when I drifted to sleep, my unsettled mood followed me, and I found no escape in my dreams.

The officer had his back turned to me. When he turned around, I saw who it was. I saluted, and Garret Harrington returned my salute. He looked just like the picture I had seen in his study, a photo taken late in his life. I looked down and found that I was wearing a uniform as well.

I'm impersonating an officer, I thought. I wanted to strip off my clothing. Public nakedness would be better. My shame was absolute. I tried to fight through my paralysis and pull off my uniform.

"It's all right," said Harrington. "Once a soldier, always a soldier."

His words were a balm. My breathing became easier.

"Remember, though, for a soldier, duty comes before love."

"Yes, sir."

"It is difficult, of course. 'The words of Mercury are harsh after the songs of Apollo.'"

The illusion started to pass. I knew that I had heard those words before. Jenny had said them. And with that memory, Harrington disappeared.

I awoke from the dream bathed in perspiration. In all my life I had never dreamed like that. It had to be the meds. I took several deep breaths.

"Only a dream," I whispered, "only a dream."

The curtains were shut and the door was closed. "Claire," I shouted. "Claire."

The room stayed closed, and there was no sound of approaching feet. I reached over to the other side of the bed and touched where Claire had been sleeping. The vacated spot was cold. How long had she been gone? I had wanted to awaken with her next to me, and then somehow surprise her with roses. It was a crazy notion, but she was bringing out feelings I didn't even know I had.

I threw the bedcovers off and opened the door. The curtains were drawn in the living room, but sunlight came through the cracks. What time was it? I stepped over to the kitchen, and the digital clock on the stove told me it was half past two.

It took me a moment of denial before accepting the time as fact. I had never slept in so late and wondered how it could have happened. Then I remembered how Claire had given me the pills in what I thought was the middle of the night, though I had no real gauge as to the time. It was possible that Claire gave them to me just before dawn. That would explain how I had slept most of the day away.

The song of Apollo sang, "Claire knew how exhausted I was, and how much I needed my rest," but in the background Mercury was doing his muttering.

I thought about how Garret Harrington had come to me in his captain's uniform. His visit was not as a congressman or father, but as a soldier. I had been haunted by a gray ghost from the long, gray line. Who was going to visit next, Jacob Marley?

Harrington the ghost, Harrington the enigma. In death he had left so many secrets. At the top of that list was his 911 call. Why would he report a fictitious break-in to the police? That had always troubled me. I took a seat in the living room's lone chair and began to think about it. Insights come at odd times. I believe they are often spurred on by mood or circumstance. Garret Harrington had been put into an impossible situation and had tried to find a way out. The more I considered the man, the more certain I was that I was on the right track. I wished I could say that my conclusions made me happier, but they didn't.

I went in search of the cell phone I had taken from Roper. Bo would be wondering why I hadn't called by now. There weren't many places to look in the small apartment, and when I exhausted them I knew that Claire had taken the phone with her, but I couldn't understand why. She already had the phone I bought at the mall. There was one other item missing as well: Roper's gun. Why would Claire need that?

Suddenly I felt very uneasy. I had to get out of the apartment and call Bo, but before I could act, I heard a key turning in the lock. My first impulse was to find a place to hide, but there was no time. Then Claire walked through the door, and my heart continued to race, but not from fright.

She was wearing a baseball cap, and her new blond hair was coming out the back in a ponytail. Her fashion sense had been compromised by the need for a disguise, and she was outfitted in some of the clothes I had bought her, but she still looked wonderful to me. Claire started when she noticed I was standing there.

"I wasn't sure if you would be up yet," she said.

"I woke up a little while ago."

"That's good," she said, but I don't think she sounded quite sure.

We stood there awkwardly, neither making a move toward the other, and then Claire offered me a tentative smile, and shook the bags she was carrying. "Are you hungry? I bought enough fast food for an army."

"I wondered where you were."

"Out getting food," she said, but didn't meet my eyes. She busied herself by setting up the table, producing a smorgasbord that included hamburgers, chicken sandwiches, salads, and coffee, orange juice, and soda.

"Now I remember how famished I am."

"Fries with that?" she asked, producing some French fries.

"You have a future in fast foods."

"Thanks for your confidence."

We sat down at the table, and I started eating. Claire seemed content to nibble while I shoveled the food in my mouth. "You're not eating much," I observed.

"I ate earlier."

She took her hat off, and without the brim covering her face I could see how deep her dark circles were.

"Did my tossing and turning keep you up?"

"My thoughts kept me up."

"Was I in those thoughts?"

Her silent contemplation was a torture to me. Finally she said, "Last night was wonderful, Will, but in the light of day I can't let personal feelings cloud the bigger picture."

"That sounds rehearsed," I said. "That sounds like a political speech."

Claire didn't answer.

"When you walked into the apartment," I said, "I was looking for my phone. I wanted to call Bo and see if there were any matches to your father's gun, but before doing that I was going to call a florist and order three dozen red roses for you."

The thought of my imaginary roses seemed to move Claire. She bit on her lip, and then said, "I borrowed the phone, but thank you for the thought. It means a lot to me."

"Why did you take the phone when you already had one?"

"The power was low on mine."

"And why did you take my gun?"

"For my protection."

Her answers made sense, but there was still a question I needed to ask: "Did you call your boyfriend?"

She didn't answer.

I put a half-finished hamburger down on the table. "You might love the idea of living in a big house on Pennsylvania Avenue, Claire, but you don't love him."

"When this situation is resolved," she said, "both of us will be better able to put matters in perspective."

"That sounds very reasoned, very dispassionate. That's not the real you, Claire."

She wouldn't look at me. "My head rules my actions, re-member?"

"Last night it didn't."

"Let's hold off on this conversation, Will. I can't deal with it at the moment. It's too distracting."

"What is that supposed to mean?"

Instead of answering, Claire walked over to the closed curtains and opened them. She didn't turn back to me, but looked off into the distance.

"We're still short a few answers here, Claire. I keep think-ing about your father calling the police. Why did he do that?"

She spoke while facing the glass: "Because two men were trying to break into his house."

"There was no physical evidence to indicate that."

"He wouldn't have called if he hadn't seen something."

"I think he did see something," I said, "but not that night. I have come to know your father, Claire. We were brought up on the same values. He believed in duty, honor, and country, as do I. It's the strength we share, and I think it's our Achilles' heel as well."

"How can those values be an Achilles' heel?"

"Because you try and do the right thing in situations that don't allow for it."

"Will—"

I interrupted her. "You remember that story I told you about my helping Bo with that final exam?"

She still wouldn't turn to look at me, but answered by nodding.

"I didn't tell you the full story. When I was summoned before the honor committee at midnight, I wasn't exactly surprised. That's because I was the one who wrote them the anonymous note saying that I had helped another cadet to cheat on his final examination."

That got Claire's attention. She turned around and stared at me with disbelief. "Why did you do that? You said the army was your family. You said you wanted to be a soldier more than anything else."

"That's what I thought, but that was before I violated the honor code."

"You had a moment of compassion."

"I tried to tell myself that. I worked for months trying to convince myself that what I did had no consequence in the larger picture, and yet the more I thought about it, the more I knew it did. The honor code exists to weed out people who shouldn't be officers. Apparently I was one of those people. In a command position you need to make tough choices. Since I broke the rules to help Bo, what is to say I wouldn't do the same in battle? In war, the safe way is not always the right way. There are objectives. You need to be able to meet the enemy and defeat him by whatever means possible, even if that means that those serving under you have to die. You have to be willing to suffer the decisions of command and do the right thing no matter what."

"But you said Bo was like a younger brother to you."

"Maybe I would have looked upon all of my charges as younger brothers, Claire."

She considered the awful truth I had finally faced up to and said, "I'm sorry."

"I think I can finally say it's behind me now. I think your

father had the same struggle, though long after he left West Point. He was involved in something that played on his conscience. His first sacrifice was to leave Congress, but he didn't see that as payment enough. He was in a corner, though, unable to confess because of all the wider ramifications. There was not only his vow of silence, but his concerns about you and your mother, as well as his allegiance to the Republican administration in the White House. The administration was already facing the fallout from Walton's death, but if the full scandal emerged, that would have been a catastrophe for the president. Your father was bound by his loyalties on all sides, and yet he still needed to explain what happened, if only to vindicate the memory of Bradley Walton.

"Years later he still hadn't resolved his dilemma. He worked on the book, which I think he wrote as a long explanation for what occurred, but that wasn't catharsis enough for him. I suspect that writing about the duel made him have to face up to what happened. My guess is that it raised some issues in his mind, and made him realize that perhaps the duel was not as straightforward as he first thought."

Halfway through my explanation, Claire turned her back on me again, but that didn't stop her from listening very closely. Her right ear was tilted in my direction, picking up every word. She had offered no objections, and raised no questions. I would have preferred her to act startled by what I was saying, but she wasn't.

I asked her, "Why is it that very little of what I'm saying seems to be a revelation to you?"

She didn't answer directly. "Last night I watched you sleeping. I think being close to you freed my mind, and I started putting some things together. Maybe with you next to me I realized that was how a relationship should be. You made me feel so warm and so good, but being an engaged woman, I couldn't help but feel guilty as well."

Claire stopped talking. She looked off into the distance and seemed to be taken by the view as if she had never seen it before. "The curtains were always closed in here," she said. "That's one of the rules. Mark is a firm believer in rules."

"I used to believe in rules," I said, "but if rules are keeping you from me, then I want to break them."

She shook the back of her head at me. "When all those revelations of the Gary Condit and Chandra Levy affair came out, I felt so sorry for her even before her body turned up. I suppose there was a part of me that recognized me in her. Mark had a private answering service just like Congressman Condit. I could never reach him directly. I had to page him, and he called back using a prepaid phone card, or a cell phone that wasn't in his own name. Whenever I visited this apartment, I was always supposed to get off the elevator on a different floor, and then take the stairs. I had a cover story ready in the event that I ever ran into anyone I knew, and he even had me memorize the names of two people living in this building so I could always say that I was seeing them. Like Chandra, I was sworn to absolute secrecy, but unlike her, I didn't talk to anyone. I guess I was thinking about my payoff. If Mark succeeded I stood to have my dreams realized."

"You know?" I asked.

"Now I do."

"When are you going to look at me, Claire?"

"I can see you in the reflection of the glass."

"That's not good enough."

"Through the looking glass," she said.

I heard a slight creak and turned to it. Roper was holding a gun on me. Claire must have heard the sound as well, or maybe she caught sight of him in the reflection. She turned around and saw Roper and his gun. I wanted to yell to Claire how sorry I was. I was supposed to be the observant one, never missing anything. I had the reputation of being human Velcro, everything sticking to me, the sponge sucking it all in. But I had missed so many things and now it was too late. I was supposed to be looking out for Claire. I had taken on the responsibility of protecting Claire and failed her. It felt like losing Craig all over again.

Roper said to me, "Don't make a peep, not a sound. If you do anything more than breathe or blink, you're dead."

There was nothing on the table but food, and a food fight wasn't going to cut it.

Roper kept his gun and his eyes on me. His face showed the aftermath of the beating I had given him. It was puffy and the flesh was discolored, but that didn't stop him from smiling. "You can close the curtains now," he said. "I was getting damn tired of waiting for the signal."

For a long moment I thought he had shot me, and then I wished he had. I turned my head to Claire and this time she met my eyes. At least she had the decency to flush. Roper thought our exchange of glances was funny.

"She played you like a fish," he said.

Claire closed the drapes, and put the room back into darkness.

CHAPTER TWENTY-FOUR

The Candidate's trip back to Washington, D.C., had been on the docket for more than a week. Ostensibly he was returning for a key vote on the budget. When plans for his return were made, the Magi had all been in agreement that it would look good for him to show the country he was willing to put his job ahead of the campaign itself. That very notion was bullshit, of course. The hope of all concerned was that he would get more press acting like Mr. Smith Goes to Washington than being just another candidate out stumping for votes.

Things had changed, though. Mark Stanton was now returning to the Hill for a reason other than casting a vote.

The Magi were now seated and waiting expectantly on the campaign's charter jet to hear what he had to say. Stanton had warned them that he needed their help with an important matter and that it would be a working flight for the inner circle. As the jet's wheels retracted and the noise of the engines abated, Stanton announced, "We need to schedule a four forty-five press conference for this afternoon."

The three heads nodded. This sounded like nothing more than a rounding up of the usual suspects for another serving of fodder for the mill.

"At that time," said Stanton, "I'll be announcing my engagement to Claire Harrington."

He saw their eyes widen and their jaws drop. There were noises of incomprehension and disbelief.

The Pit Bull was the first to be able to speak: "What the hell do you mean? Is this a joke?"

"No joke."

"You make that announcement," said his campaign manager, "and we can kiss the sympathy vote good-bye. Some of our strongest numbers come from older women. They sympathize with your being a widower. You also have strong support from single parents who empathize with your trying to raise two kids alone."

Stanton knew those things all too well, but he simply shrugged his shoulders and acted as if he was indifferent to those concerns. There was nothing else he could do. "Let's hope that those constituencies," he said, "will revel in my newfound happiness."

"Why take that chance?" asked the S.O.B. "Why not wait to make the announcement until after the primaries, or better yet, after the November election?"

Because, Stanton wanted to tell him, Claire had made his going public a nonnegotiable point. Try as he might, he had failed to convince her that announcing their engagement might undermine *their* dream and ruin *their* chances of occupying the big house on Pennsylvania Avenue together. Claire said that it was the deal-breaker, and without that public promise she would be singing like a proverbial canary. He suspected she feared for her life, even with her piece of incriminating evidence. Smart girl. She had given Stanton no choice but to capitulate. Their marriage vows might as well include the line, "To love, cherish, and blackmail."

"To wait would look disingenuous," said Stanton. "Claire needs my public support right now."

"Did you say Claire Harrington?" asked the Poet.

She looked horrified. There was some dawning name recognition among the other two Magi.

"Claire did not try and assassinate me," said Stanton. "That's another reason why this press conference is so important. I have to do my part to clear her name. I have already made statements to Justice and the Secret Service to that effect, and now I have to go on the public record."

He looked to the Poet. "We'll draft a statement. It will offer some background into my relationship with Claire, and explain how she was a witness to the assassination attempt on me, and how at the behest of the late Lawrence Deering, Claire reluctantly agreed to go undercover on the Greeley campaign to try and identify the same assassin who was threatening bodily harm against Congressman Greeley. I'll describe how, after I was shot, Claire tried to talk me into dropping out of the race. When I refused, she decided that the best way to assist me, as well as keep me alive, was to work with those trying to apprehend my assailant."

His troops still looked shell-shocked. "Why make this public?" asked his campaign manager. "Why not let the feds make the announcement that the Harrington woman isn't an assassin?"

Because I don't have a goddamn choice, Stanton wanted to say. But he had to play it by the script that he and Claire had hashed out. She had paged him in the middle of the night, and their negotiations had continued on and off for eight hours. He had forsaken sleep and hurried through a morning appearance so he could broker a deal with her. Not all the details were worked out yet, but they had a good game plan. They agreed on keeping their story very simple and then filling in all the fine points after they had a chance to confer in person.

Deering's maverick status would make their explanations easier. The ATF special agent had never played by the usual rules anyway. The man had only failed Stanton once. Claire

Harrington had lived and he had died, but in death Deering was still serving a purpose. Dead men tell no lies, or, even more incriminating, truths.

Even before becoming Stanton's disciple, Deering had been involved in another conspiracy, one that had occupied him until his death. He was passionately pro-life, though he kept that knowledge secret from almost everyone. Deering surreptitiously used his position at ATF to aid his cause. For years he had helped Roper remain a fugitive, his insider information allowing the Baby Bomber to escape the arms of the law continuously.

Stanton finally answered his campaign manager's question. "Because Claire has been hung out to dry for too long," he said. "She wanted to keep her involvement a secret only because of her love for me. I couldn't let her do that, of course. I love her as much as she loves me."

"Mutual sacrifice," announced the Poet. "We can make it sound like O. Henry's 'Gift of the Magi.' "

Theirs would certainly not be the first White House marriage of convenience, thought Stanton. Yesterday he had wanted Claire dead. Today he was going to announce that she was his fiancée.

"Love and doing the right thing," said the Poet, embellishing a little more. "We should be stressing that notion."

The other Magi nodded their heads.

"No matter what the circumstances," said his chief of staff, "people always want a good love story."

"That's what this is," said the Pit Bull.

Or even if it wasn't, the campaign manager seemed to be saying, that's what they needed to make it.

"Play it up like Edward the Seventh and Wallis Simpson," said the Poet. "Women all over the world swooned when Edward abdicated his throne for the woman he loved. We can make this look like the election is secondary to the romance."

"I like that," said the chief of staff. "The thought of a White

House wedding ought to go over big with the voters. Has there ever even been one before?"

"It only happened once," said the campaign manager. "When we first announced, there was a bit of a stir about an unmarried candidate running for the office. Grover Cleveland got married after he became president. What was his wife's name? Fanny Farmer?"

"Frances Folsom," said the Poet. "She proved to be an extremely popular First Lady. There were some reservations about their union at first, as Frances was twenty-one while Cleveland was fifty, but the country became enamored with their young First Lady, especially when the White House became a nursery. She bore two of her five children while her husband was president."

"How old is your fiancée?" asked the S.O.B.

"She's thirty-two," said Stanton.

"Eighteen years age difference," said the campaign manager.

"That's a hell of a lot better than Cleveland and his gal. That was close to cradle robbing."

"It will make you look that much more vigorous," said the chief of staff. "That will help offset some of the negatives of the engagement."

"Clinton survived Gennifer Flowers's prime-time adultery talk in the middle of the primaries," said the Pit Bull. "This smells like a bouquet of roses compared to that."

"We can play it up like that movie *The American President*," said the Poet. "Make it a big stage romance with lots of drama. Who wouldn't want to see a White House wedding?"

It took half an hour for the Candidate and the Poet to agree upon a first draft. While they began the process of fine-tuning his address, the other two Magi kept their speed-dialers burning. "It's love," Stanton heard them saying more than once. They also frequently repeated the line, "He doesn't care about the consequences; he just wants to do right by all concerned."

Appearances, thought Stanton, were so much more important than reality. He shifted his left arm. It was still in a sling. It was a reminder to the electorate that not even a bullet could deter him.

The "assassination attempt" worked better than Stanton could have hoped. It had been a ploy of desperation, of course. Before he was shot, his numbers had been dropping in the polls, but afterward they skyrocketed. Campaigning with a sling on his left arm, Stanton had looked like the wounded hero. Deering was a crack shot, of course. The two men had even choreographed the way he would raise his arms. Deering had put the bullet right where he said he would, in the fleshy part of his underarm. Left arm, of course. Stanton needed his right to shake hands. Ironically, his strong showings in New Hampshire and Iowa had resulted in Garret and Claire Harrington's death sentences. Once he was a viable candidate, he could no longer take the chance of his past surfacing.

Stanton had met Deering many years before when the young ATF agent had surreptitiously given him damaging information about the vehemently pro-choice congressional incumbent he was running against. Over the years the two men had cultivated a close friendship, each offering the other information that had proved useful. In their own ways, the men had furthered each other's career. For years, Deering had been advocating Stanton's running for the presidency, urging him to do it "for the cause." Deering even volunteered the help of his small, secret following, a handful of devoted fanatics who would do whatever he asked without questions. They were the same group that had been harboring Roper, moving him from one safe house to another. When Stanton told Deering that a "past indiscretion" threatened to destroy his campaign, it was

Deering who came up with the plan to kill Garret Harrington. Even then, only Roper was privy to details. The rest had just done as they were told.

The Poet interrupted his musing. "Okay," she said. "Let's try it this way, but you'll need to make it look spontaneous. In the third paragraph I want you to say, 'Win or lose, Claire and I intend to get married next February.' Then you need to look a little chagrined and act as if you're correcting yourself by saying, "Actually, I shouldn't phrase it that way. It's a win-win situation for me, because come next February I will have the pleasure of marrying the woman I love.'"

"I like that," Stanton said.

Claire had lived long enough to figure things out. Clever, clever Claire. She was the ultimate steel magnolia, beautiful to the eye but with a core of cast iron. Now that he thought about it, Claire reminded Stanton of Deborah Everett, the wife of then-Congressman Jake Everett. Deborah's beauty, and Stanton's manipulations, had caused the two men to duel to the death. Bradley Walton had been a fool. Love had blinded him. He thought that Deborah loved him the same way he loved her. Even after the duel, though, Deborah never divorced her husband. She liked his money, and the perquisites that came with being his wife. Walton was rich, but not in Everett's league, and he had no future beyond being a glorified civil servant. Love wasn't enough for a woman like Deborah Everett. She gloried in Walton's adoration, and loved the idea of being in love, but she put herself first. She knew her husband shot and killed her lover, but that didn't stop her from continuing on as the congressman's wife, and then as the senator's. Deborah and her husband never made it to the Oval Office, but to this day she had no equal on the Washington, D.C., social scene. Claire was a woman much like that. She could dabble in love, but what she really wanted was power and position.

Naturally, Senator Everett had been the first to support Stanton in his quest for the presidency. Everett and his flowing and wavy white mane were synonymous with the Washington power scene. The vain fool loved it when his locks were described as "leonine." Over the years, Stanton had been repaid many times for his silence, and for having served as Everett's second. The senator had no idea that it was Stanton's behind-the-scenes maneuvering that had pushed both men onto that so-called field of honor.

Like Deborah Everett had with Bradley Walton, Claire was willing to sacrifice to get what she wanted. In this case Claire would be giving up her soldier-boy pawn. Claire had reluctantly agreed to make the West Point dropout the villain so the two of them could come out smelling like roses. She had tried to plead for his life, but in the end realized the threat he presented to both of them. Roper's latest page told him the package was secure. He would be taking care of him in a matter of minutes.

"And right here," said the Poet, pointing to the page, "I think you should use the line, 'Claire Harrington is a patriot. Her name has been dragged through the mud and all because she is guilty of only two things: loving her country, and loving me, more than she does herself.'"

"That works for me," Stanton said.

The Magi would do better than make lemonade out of lemons. Hell, they would be making heroes out of both him and Claire. If he delivered this talk right, this could be his Checkers Speech.

What Stanton liked most about his union with Claire was that going into it, she understood his ambitions and political passions. Underneath her patrician good looks, behind her Jackie Kennedy aura, were the same base desires that ruled him. Stanton could only admire her raw ambition because it was something they shared. He hadn't known if she would be able to forgive his using her to gain information, and then having her beloved father killed, but Claire had proved pragmatic about the whole situation. She had even said something about being glad that her father hadn't been forced to suffer from his terminal illness. They were alike that way as well, able to forgive much as long as it brought them to the object of their desires.

When it came right down to it, he thought, Claire really was the perfect choice for his First Lady.

CHAPTER TWENTY-FIVE

Roper tossed Claire a roll of duct tape while keeping his gun leveled on me. The small, silenced pistol was a duplicate of the last one I had taken from him.

"Tie him up to the chair," he said. "Make sure there's no wiggle room in his wrists or ankles."

He looked at me, and didn't try to mask the exultant gleam in his eyes. "I'm not worried about him chewing his way out this time," he said. "The first thing I'm going to do is knock out his teeth."

"No, you aren't," Claire said. "There's to be no torture. Mark and I agreed on that."

My stomach felt as if it was being pulled up through my mouth. I couldn't swallow, couldn't speak. Claire approached me with her eyes averted.

"Please sit," Claire said, her voice not much more than a whisper.

There was a part of my brain that was still operational. I considered using her as a shield in the same way I had used Deering, but I couldn't bring myself to move. It had taken me thirty-five years to fall in love, to concede my heart to someone other than myself. I couldn't just suddenly reclaim that heart as my own, nor could I instantly transform that love into hate.

"Sit!" barked Roper with an emphatic shake of his gun.

I collapsed into the chair. Claire knelt at my feet and began running the duct tape around my ankles and the chair legs.

After finishing up the gift-wrapping of my legs, Claire turned to Roper and said, "I'll need something to cut the duct tape with. Do you have a knife?"

Roper shook his head.

"There's a steak knife in the kitchen," she said.

"Then get it," said Roper. "I'll just stay right where I am and hope he gives me a reason to shoot."

Her defense of me hurt more than silence: "That would not serve our interests," she said.

Claire went out to the kitchen and I heard her rummaging through a drawer. There was a part of me still holding out hope. I wanted to believe that when she turned the corner she would plunge the knife into Roper's chest, but that proved to be wishful thinking. Claire used the knife on the duct tape, and then started taping my arms from elbows to wrists onto the armrests. She was so thorough, parts of me began resembling a mummy. I tested my bonds. There was no slack.

I struggled to say the word, but it finally came out, and I hated myself for how weak I sounded asking it: "Why?"

She didn't answer at first, seemingly absorbed in the task of tying me up, but finally she said, "I guess it's like that story of the scorpion and the frog. Do you know it?"

"No."

Claire let out a sigh that seemed to say it was too late for explanations, but she offered one up anyway. In a voice not much louder than a whisper she said, "This frog was contentedly sitting in the shallows of a quiet river when it was approached by a scorpion. 'I need to get to the other bank,' the scorpion said. 'Will you give me a ride atop your back?'

"The frog thought about the request, and expressed his doubts. 'What's to stop you from stinging me once we set out?' he asked.

" 'Why, if I was to do that,' the scorpion said, 'we would both drown in the river.'

"The frog thought about that, and could find no fault with the scorpion's logic. He told the scorpion to get atop his back, and then the two of them set out for the other bank. They were halfway across when the frog felt the terrible paralyzing sting of the scorpion.

" 'You fool!' the frog said. 'Now we will both die.' And as he started to sink forever underneath the water, the frog asked, "Why did you do that?'

"And the scorpion said, 'Because it is my nature.'

"And then both the frog and the scorpion sank into the water and died."

Claire finished her story at the same time she finished tying me up. With the knife she sliced a last strip from the roll of duct tape. I didn't ask her to stick the knife into me. That would have been redundant. Too late, I remembered Jenny's warning. While focusing on the snake, I have missed the scorpion.

"You knew what I wanted more than anything," she said. "I never hid that from you."

"Then I'll credit you with being more honest than the scorpion," I said, "and more poisonous as well."

Roper thought that was funny and laughed. Claire didn't. One single tear dropped from her left eye. It rolled halfway down her cheek and then came to a rest as if stopped by some invisible barrier.

One tear from one eye, I thought. My life had just been summed up. That was how much of her heart she had given me.

"We're a regular Abelard and Heloise, aren't we?" I said. "One of the great love stories of our time."

I wouldn't have guessed Roper had a sense of humor. I was wrong. This, at least, he was finding hilarious.

"I didn't have time to tell you that I dreamed about your father," I said. "I guess my subconscious mind was clueing me in to what my conscious mind already knew, or should have known.

"Your father knew about your secret romance, Claire. You were his only child, and the most important thing in his life, and he suspected you were being used. He needed to have those suspicions confirmed. It wasn't by chance that you overheard that phone conversation where he spoke about the injustice that had been done, and how its perpetrator didn't deserve to be president. Your father heard you enter the house and then orchestrated that conversation. That's why the phone records in your father's file cabinet weren't touched. There was no record of his having made a call, because he never did. There was never anyone on the other line, but he knew you would go back and report what you overheard to the man you were unwittingly spying for."

"That's a lot of guesswork," Claire said.

"What isn't guesswork is how your father set himself up as a target. He probably thought Stanton would approach him with some kind of bribe or offer. Then again, based on what your father uncovered about the duel, maybe he came to believe that Stanton was capable of murder."

"I've already made up my mind, Will," said Claire. Her voice sounded raw.

"If you marry Stanton, you're as guilty as he is. No, you're even guiltier because you know better."

"I don't have time to discuss this."

"Make time, then. You don't want to be like your father and die with regrets. Maybe he was lucky to have died when he did, though. Your marrying Stanton would have broken his heart more than anything else. Think about his

911 call to the police. The man he described as breaking into his house was Mark Stanton. He even alluded to that sling he was wearing. I also should have put a name to his getaway man. The telltale clue there was his description of those wavy, white locks. There's one prominent politician that fits that description. At one time Mark Stanton was Jake Everett's top aide, wasn't he? In his call your father offered up everyone there at the duel: Stanton, Everett, and himself. Oh, and let's not forget the body of Bradley Walton."

"Stop it, Will," Claire said. "There's no point."

"There is a point. Your father was trying to scare Stanton into quitting the campaign, and just as importantly, break off his relationship with you. Garret Harrington tried to play fair, and in the best West Point tradition he tried not to break his vow. I know your father would never have willingly put you in danger, but he had no idea how Machiavellian Stanton could be."

"Shut him up," Roper said.

Claire looked at the piece of duct tape she was holding, and then brought it toward my face.

"Don't—"

She didn't give me a chance to say more, wrapping the tape around my mouth. I tried moving my jaw and freeing my lips, but she cut off two other strips and taped them over my mouth. I screamed in rage, but the sounds were weak even to my own ears.

"I need to get ready for the press conference," Claire told Roper. She tossed the knife on the kitchen table, well out of my reach even if my hands hadn't been bound. Then she left the dining room without giving me a backward glance or a final tear. I heard her walk down the hallway to the bathroom. I wasn't numb anymore. Hate coursed through me. I strained at my bonds, and set the chair to shaking.

Roper and his gun came closer to me. "Uh, uh, uh," he said. "None of that."

He leaned his head, not close enough for me to try a head butt, but near enough to dominate my field of view. "Tell you what, though," he said. "A little later we'll watch that press conference together and hear them announce their engagement. That will be a lot of fun, won't it?"

Softly, so only I could hear, he started humming "Hail to the Chief."

CHAPTER TWENTY-SIX

The Secret Service wasn't happy with the press conference being scheduled outside at the National Mall, but then they had been adamantly opposed to the California whistle-stop tour as well. They didn't like the Candidate being out in the open, or pressing flesh. Given their druthers, they would have preferred him campaigning from inside a bank vault. Stanton wished he could tell them that the threat of assassination was long past.

Two of the three Magi were riding in the limo with him. His campaign manager had gone ahead to make sure everything was set up correctly, and that the media and his supporters were in position, awaiting his arrival.

"Does he know I want the Washington Monument in the background?" Stanton asked. "I don't want the view of the Capitol."

The National Mall is anchored on one end by the Capitol and on the other by the Lincoln Memorial. In the middle, towering five hundred and fifty-five feet high, is the monument. He wanted the obelisk on his right shoulder, knighting him, anointing him. That was the backdrop he wanted, not the Capitol. Too many people perceived that as being the playground for a den of thieves.

"He knows," said the chief of staff. "He's been working

with the National Parks people. They've been very accom-
modating, he said. I guess they must be worried that you'll
cut their budget if they don't play ball with us."

The Poet was scanning the text of Stanton's talk, looking
for any last-minute changes. "Talks at the National Mall
sometimes make people remember Martin Luther King's 'I
Have a Dream' speech on the steps of the Lincoln Memorial. Maybe we should make a passing reference to King and
his speech."

"Your call," Stanton said.

"No," she said, shaking her head with sudden vehe-
mence. "We don't want to mix messages. It's fine as is. It's
perfect."

The Poet was always second-guessing herself. Like any
good speechwriter, she tried to find words that resonated
with the voting public. Her prose was often poetic, and her
words uplifting. Stanton studied her prepared text. It was
certainly longer than the two hundred and seventy-two
words that made up the Gettysburg Address, but it wasn't
overly long. Like all good speechwriters, the Poet had
crafted it for sound bites. The evening news timed out after
commercials at twenty-two minutes, the world news in a
very limited nutshell. If things worked out, they would get
two minutes of the news allotment. The way they had it figured, twenty seconds of those two minutes would consist
of Claire stepping up on the dais beside him, his putting an
arm around her, and their smiling at one another. The spin
would be love in the time of politics.

Stanton pretended he was concentrating on his speech,
though he already had it memorized. He was an actor who
knew his lines. It was strange, but what was really occupying his mind was Garret Harrington's book. Ironically, Harrington had included a section on political suicide. The
chapter had started off quoting from Vincent Foster's suicide note, which said that Washington, D.C., was a place

where "ruining people is considered sport." Saint Garret thought this an apt observation, and discussed both hunters and hunted. One of the great political "sportsmen" of all time was Senator Joe McCarthy. "Tailgunner Joe" had managed to shoot down more people in politics than he had in war. When McCarthy publicly outed Wyoming Senator Lester Hunt's gay son, Hunt drove to his office and shot himself in the head with a .22-caliber rifle. By all accounts, the senator was a good man, but he had no stomach for down-and-dirty politics. He even left a note to his son telling him he was not to blame.

Harrington wrote about numerous other Capitol suicides, including Congressman William Mills, and Jeremy Boorda, Chief of Naval Operations. It was ironic that he himself was now another footnote in that less than illustrious history.

After the duel, Harrington no longer had a stomach for politics. In a way, the duel had killed him as surely as it had Bradley Walton. Stanton had much fonder memories of that duel. After all, he was the one who had engineered it.

At the time, he was chief of staff for Congressman Jake Everett. When Stanton heard rumors of Deborah Everett's affair with Bradley Walton, he decided to have them investigated. Without telling Everett, he hired a private investigator. The pictures the detective took were worth a thousand words, and the ten thousand dollars Stanton paid out of pocket. He knew a good investment when he saw it. The detective also provided some steamy tape recordings picked up from a parabolic microphone. Deborah's unique vocalizations would certainly sound familiar to anyone who had heard them before.

Deborah was Jake Everett's trophy wife—his second, of course—and a former Miss Alabama. She was twenty years her husband's junior. Everett was proud of his wife's looks. She reflected well on him. Though Everett loved himself

more than anyone, there was still a warm place in his heart
for his young wife. As a former college quarterback, Everett
was used to having pretty and adoring women at his side,
though judging by his activities, he was more of a man's
man. Everett hunted, fished, played cards, and drank. He
always considered himself top dog, and hated losing at
anything.

Bradley Walton was the opposite of Jake. He was much
more cerebral, and more private. Walton had few close
friends, and the Washington social scene didn't interest
him. Though he was young to be given a Cabinet post, after
he got his appointment, *Newsweek* described him as a
"young, old man." Hundred-hour workweeks were the
norm for Walton until he fell madly in love with Deborah.

Stanton knew he needed Everett's patronage if he was to
make a successful run for Congress himself. That had always been the plan, but just getting a pat on the back and
Everett's endorsement wouldn't be enough. Money was
needed, lots of it, and he would need Everett to call in old
favors on his behalf. Stanton had to be assured of having
that kind of nontransferable political coin. Everett's I.O.U.s
had to be deep in his back pocket. In Washington, there is
no better currency than political coin.

Everett had bragged about his ancestors "going to the
iron man," and how his great-great-great grandfather Jere-
miah had been in "a dozen duels." As Everett scored it,
Great-great-great-Grandpa had killed three men, sustaining
four wounds in the process. According to Everett, Jere-
miah's last duel was conducted when he was sixty-two. It
was an obvious point of pride for the congressman, but
that didn't mean he was ready to follow the family tradition
without a lot of help. Stanton had played Everett. One of
his political enemies had once described him as a "rooster
who thinks the sun rises just for him to crow." Everett was
vain, hated to lose, and had a legendary temper. Stanton
knew how much Everett enjoyed the admiration of others,

and how he would detest the very thought of his being a public cuckold, especially to some pencil pusher.

Walton was another matter. There was only one way to get to him, and that would be by manipulating his love of Deborah.

Stanton told Everett in what he labeled as "strictest confidence" that a reliable source revealed that Deborah was involved with Walton. When Everett confronted his wife, she at first only admitted to having had a "flirtation" with the other man. Everett would have let the matter drop had Stanton not passed on a few of the pictures showing Deborah with Walton *in flagrante delicto*. It was only the beginning of his feeding the fire. Eventually, Stanton was entrusted to act as Everett's conduit. He warned Walton off from any further contact with Deborah Everett. It was amazing how with just the barest spice of hate, and overtones of threats and ill-will, he was able to escalate the men's antipathy to one another.

When Deborah Everett promised her husband that she was done with Walton, Stanton passed pictures and recordings that made it appear as if Deborah were still having assignations with her lover. Everett was so incensed at what he saw and heard that he blackened his wife's eye. Naturally, Stanton made sure Walton heard about Everett's striking her.

Walton called Everett out for a fight, impugning the man as a coward for hitting his wife. With Stanton's help, the fight escalated into much more. Pride and love intermixed, and neither man was willing to back down. It was Stanton who tweaked the intentions and words of the adversaries, and raised the stakes from a fight to a duel. He quickly went from being an intermediary to being a second. It was a duty he performed very assiduously, reading the *Code Duello: The Rules of Dueling*, and its updated American version of dueling etiquette, *Code of Honor*. Stanton wanted to make sure the duel was conducted in a proper fashion.

There were a few stumbling blocks, though, as it had been more than a century since the last official duel on American soil.

Garret Harrington's selection as the other second was problematic, as Saint Garret did his best to avert the duel. Luckily, by the time he became involved, Stanton had already pushed the men beyond the point of turning back. No one seemed aware of his manipulations, though. Indeed, from first to last, Stanton did his best to appear vigorously opposed to the whole enterprise, and always acted as if he were a very reluctant second.

Looking back, his first mistake was in buying and handling both of the guns. That was the evidence that tied him to the duel. Garret Harrington had refused to fulfill that duty as second. In some ways it was just as well, though. Harrington probably would have chosen peashooters. Stanton selected guns that, in the right hands, were accurate from a long distance, and deadly.

He also picked the dueling grounds. Stanton thought his choice was clever. The park was a known gay cruising spot. There would be a ready explanation for the body being there. The only problem was, he hadn't known his history, hadn't been aware that Bladensburg was famous in the past for being a dueling ground. Luckily, that ricochet bullet missed him.

There was a potential third mistake as well. Stanton needed the patronage of Everett. That meant he had to fix the duel, and ensure that his boss was victorious. The day before the duel, Stanton passed on a "secret confidence" to Walton that Everett's intention was to raise his gun and shoot well over his head. He had to do it that way, Stanton said, because Rule 13 of the *Code Duello* prohibited duelers from shooting their rounds into the air. As the rule stated, "The challenger ought not to have challenged without receiving offense; and the challenged ought, if he gave offense, to have made an apology before he came on the ground." Stanton pointed out that only by firing their pistols with the apparent objective of shooting at an opponent could honor be served. He also told Walton that Everett was willing to let Deborah make her own choice as to who she wanted to live with for the rest of her life. That would be the true test, he implied, of which was the better man.

Stanton remembered Walton's relief. The man had been positively giddy. Not only was a potential death sentence waived, but there was the possibility that Deborah might finally be his.

It was no wonder, then, that on the dueling field Walton was slow to raise his gun. Stanton still remembered the look of surprise on his face when he was struck. For a second or two he stood there, looking in disbelief at the crimson flow spreading across his chest. Then he dropped to the ground, but he didn't die immediately, though, and that was a shame. Several sentences passed between Walton and Harrington. They were words that Harrington apparently couldn't forget, words that haunted him, and words that eventually spurred his curiosity. It wasn't quite a deathbed confession, but it was enough to get Harrington to thinking years later.

Stanton had read Harrington's description of the duel dozens of times. He knew that last chapter of Harrington's book almost verbatim. It had spurred his own memories, taken him back to that day. What a wonderful stroll down memory lane.

We arrived before dawn broke. There were no cars in the parking lot, and we proceeded on the trail to a grassy expanse hidden behind a wall of trees. The grass was very damp, and the breeze was brisk. I remember thinking that even the most hardened centurion wouldn't have pronounced it a good day to die.

Bradley had met me at four-thirty that morning and we drove over to the park together in my car. It struck me as odd that I was more nervous than he was. In my year in Vietnam I had seen how men prepared for battle. Bradley was going up against an armed enemy, but he didn't seem to have the edge that men take into combat.

"Let's walk away now and be done with this thing," I told Bradley. "I'll buy you breakfast."

"He beat Deborah," Bradley said.

"Deborah is a grown woman. She can make her own decisions. She didn't elect you as her protector."

"I appreciate your concern."

He wasn't listening to anything I had to say. In exasperation I asked, "Where are your instructions?"

Two days before, Bradley had promised to put all of his affairs in order and give me a sheet of instructions on what to do in the event of his death.

"I'm sorry," he said. "I forgot to take care of that detail."

Overlooking that "detail" seemed almost inexplicable, and I was puzzled by his behavior. No one enters combat without making provisions for death. He saw my expression of disbelief.

"Don't worry, my friend," Bradley told me.

Stanton admired Harrington's description of what occurred. If anything, Harrington had beaten himself up in the pages of his book more than anyone else. Time and again he offered up his opinion of how he could have stopped the duel, and how he should have stopped it. Saint Garret had no idea of the extent to which everything had been manipulated.

I felt like one of those handlers working the corner in a fight. But this wasn't a fight, but a duel.

*Because of my part in this sordid affair, I was ex-
pected to contribute to the arrangements. Bradley and
Everett waited while Mark Stanton and I conferred.
The two men were separated by no more than a
dozen feet, but I don't think they spoke. I kept hoping
sanity would overtake the proceedings, that Bradley
would raise his voice in the darkness and say, "I'm
sorry." That didn't happen.*

*Stanton was Jake Everett's second, and had taken
his duties as second very seriously. He had memorized both the* Code Duello: Rules of Dueling *and the
more updated American dueling primer,* Code of
Honor. *The way he organized everything made it
seem as if Stanton had been conducting duels for
most of his young life.*

*"It is up to us to determine where each man will
stand," Stanton told me. "That selection will be made by
a coin toss. The winner of the toss will choose position.
Whoever loses the toss will call out the signal to fire."*

*I knew that what we were abetting was very
wrong. "Why don't we cast lots for Christ's robe while
we're at it?" I asked.*

*Stanton ignored my comment. He had brought a
silver dollar for the occasion. "Please make your call
while the coin is in the air," he said. "Miss Liberty signi-
fies heads and the bald eagle is tails."*

*I chose the Lady. In the darkness we hunkered over
the coin to try and see which side had come up. It had
been shined for the occasion, and Miss Liberty and
her thirteen stars came out on top. It fell to me to pick
battle positions. The ground was level, but the shadows were heavier in the south, so I picked that position. I remember thinking that I wanted Bradley to be
shrouded in the shadows, but almost immediately regretted my decision.*

To think of a shroud, I thought, was an ill omen.

What Saint Garret hadn't known, thought Stanton, was that even the coin-toss was rigged. He had carefully filed off some of the silver, putting a little more heft into Miss Liberty to increase the odds of her coming up. He had also anticipated Harrington's calling out, "Heads." It was the more common choice.

He wanted to be the second that called out the order to fire, and not allow either man to have a change of heart. Everything had gone as planned, allowing him to expedite the encounter.

It was Stanton who coordinated the communication between the two rivals, and it was he who selected the mutually agreeable location for the duel to be held.

Stanton had also purchased the weapons, as I had refused to be party to that transaction, but I immediately regretted my decision upon seeing the guns. I have handled my share of weapons, and typically have no knee-jerk reaction to them, but I had a bad feeling about these heavy guns with their long barrels. Though not designed specifically for dueling, they seemed quite fitted to that purpose.

There was no telling the two guns apart. Each contained a single bullet. With heavy heart, I made my choice and selected Bradley's gun.

"We don't even have a goddam doctor here," I said, voicing yet another complaint to Stanton. I was looking for any excuse to stall the duel.

"That was the choice of the principals."

"Stupidity on top of insanity."

"It is a bad situation," Stanton agreed, "but we both know how they have refused to be reconciled."

Stanton and I marched off thirty paces instead of the usual ten to twenty paces. We both expressed the hope that the extra distance would result in both men missing their shot.

In his book, Harrington had been generous in his appraisal of the situation. Stanton remembered his having originally lobbied for the traditional dueling distance of ten to twenty paces, but how Harrington had balked at that. The West Point graduate knew enough about guns to think that spacing too close.

He said, "Weapons have improved since the time those dueling manuals were written. To fire from a distance of ten or twenty paces would likely result in a death sentence."

Stanton wanted to say, "That's the point of a duel," but had thought it best to agree with the other second. Saint Garret would have balked at anything less than thirty paces. Matters had to be resolved, and quickly, before cooler heads could prevail. Right up until the morning of the duel, any delay might have proved costly. Besides, Stanton knew what a good shot Everett was. Harrington was too preoccupied to notice how Stanton hurried the duel along. They needed to act before the world awakened. Stanton was afraid of interruptions, of an encounter with someone out walking his dog, or a birdwatcher invading the brush, or the police doing a drive-by.

He was determined that the duel should be carried out at first light.

> *Stanton and I stepped off the paces, our accounting three feet per step. We marked the spots where Walton and Everett would stand, but to me the distance separating the shooters still seemed much too close. As the guns were handed to the men, I remember thinking how ironic it was that the birds were singing loudly in the surrounding woods.*
>
> *Our being at that place seemed surreal, especially knowing that in a few moments one or both of the men could be dead.*

We directed Bradley and Everett—"the principals," as Stanton referred to them—to their positions. "Once you are posted," Stanton told them, "you are not to quit your positions without being instructed by your second. You will stand firm until given leave to fire."

By that time I could no longer be silent while Stanton quoted from his rules. While the principals went to their spots, I broke dueling etiquette. "For God's sake," I called out, "call this thing off now. Come to your senses."

Neither Walton nor Everett responded. Stanton said, "They have chosen this recourse," he said. "As seconds, it is not our place to interfere at this time."

"I want no part of this," I said.

"Are you abdicating your responsibility of standing as your man's second?" Stanton asked.

He made it sound like a betrayal, and I felt as if I could not just walk away. If I had, though, maybe everyone would have walked. At the least, I should have stepped into the two men's line of fire. In the back of my mind I was always convinced it would never come to this, but now the men were standing there with their loaded pistols. I tried to think of a convincing argument to delay the duel, but Stanton must have interpreted my silence for consent.

"At my word!" he yelled.

Now it was only left for Stanton to give the word to fire, and then the terrible moment came when he did just that.

"Fire!" he yelled.

The ring of the chief of staff's cell phone interrupted Stanton's memories. He fought back his annoyance. After all, it was time to focus on giving his speech.

The call was brief, and mostly consisted of the S.O.B. saying "good." He hung up, and then announced, "Everything's all set."

Stanton decided there was just enough time for recalling the conclusion of the duel as told by Saint Garret.

Everett raised his gun and his experience with firearms immediately showed. His right hand appeared unsteady until he assumed the two-handed shooter's position and sighted on Bradley.

"Shoot!" I wanted to scream to Bradley. I wondered if he had heard Stanton's yell to fire, as he seemed to be moving so slowly. His gun wasn't even completely raised to his shoulder when Everett fired.

At first I thought Everett missed. Bradley just stood there, but then he dropped his gun and staggered. I ran to his side and helped him to the ground. His shirt was already bright red.

Mercifully, he seemed to be in a state of shock. He was shaking his head as if puzzled. As I ineffectually tried to treat his wounds, Bradley said, "It wasn't supposed to be this way."

Then he coughed up some blood and said, "No shots," and after a long pause, added, "His second."

Bradley then seemed to awaken and realize he was dying. As my tears fell on him, he said, "Don't grieve, old friend. Never blame yourself for this."

His words made me cry all the harder, of course.

Then he said, "Tell Deborah I love her."

He said nothing more, though he continued to breathe for another minute or so.

Everett joined us, and the horror of what he had done overwhelmed him. He dropped to his knees, and the gun fell out of his hands into my lap. He cried unintelligible words of sorrow, and seemed to be

*begging Bradley's forgiveness, but it was clear that
Bradley could no longer respond.*

*Stanton reminded everyone of our vows of silence.
He dragged Everett to his feet, and urged all of us to
leave the grounds at once.*

"He's beyond our help," Stanton said.

*To stay would have condemned all of us, so I did
as Stanton bid.*

*Out in the parking lot, Stanton once again re-
minded all the conspirators of our duty to silence. "Remember our promise," he said.*

And then all of us fled the scene of the crime.

That should have been the end of the story, thought Stanton. As a man of his word, Harrington couldn't talk about
what happened. Stanton knew that Harrington probably
would have welcomed jail time for his own involvement as
a way of expiating his sins, but he was denied that relief because of his promise, the same promise all the conspirators
had made.

If only he could have collected the murder weapon,
Stanton thought, but that fool Everett had dropped the gun
into Harrington's lap. Before Stanton could do anything,
Harrington tucked the gun away. It didn't look like a conscious decision. It was just one of those things, but it always bothered him, knowing that Harrington had the gun.
Stanton collected the other trophy, but Walton's gun wasn't
the weapon that mattered. Over the years, Stanton kept
telling himself that Harrington had certainly disposed of
the gun. As his book revealed, though, Harrington neither
got rid of the gun, nor was he able to forget what transpired on that day. Walton's dying words, and his behavior,
played on Harrington's mind. Sixteen years after the duel
was concluded, Harrington was shot with his erstwhile
friend's gun.

Stanton looked up from the pages of the speech he was

pretending to be studying. It was rare for him to be intro-spective. He usually never dwelled on the past, always pre-ferring to look to the future.

In the distance he saw the obelisk of the Washington Monument.

Enough of the past, he decided. The future was now.

CHAPTER TWENTY-SEVEN

I felt like hell and seeing Claire emerge from the bedroom looking drop-dead gorgeous didn't make me feel any better. She was no longer a blonde, but had gone back to her raven locks. Her hair looked professionally styled even though she had done it herself. Claire wore a yellow ribbon that went from the top of her head down along the nape of her neck. Everything fit, as if Claire had worked on this particular wardrobe and look for weeks. Maybe she had, unbeknownst to me. The whole package combined for just the right appearance. With her regal bearing, designer dress, and peaches-and-cream good looks, Claire could have passed muster for her own coronation. All she was missing was a tiara. Somehow, Claire had escaped having any visible marks from our days on the run. The bags I'd seen under her eyes were now hidden by artfully applied makeup, and her haunted look had the appearance of model chic. Just one look at this woman, and the assassin story would be buried forever. I didn't have any doubt that Claire was about to make the same kind of national splash that Jackie Kennedy had. Even Roper seemed affected by how she looked, and was suddenly acting more diffident.

The duct tape muted any and all of my commentary. I wanted to tell Claire that she had sold her soul to the devil, and inflict the same kind of hurt on her as she had on me, but the tape altered the roar of my rage into little more than a whistle. Still, I managed to get her attention with the sounds. I hoped my eyes said it all, but instead of shrinking away, Claire approached me. If I could bowl her over, I thought, give her a bruise or a black eye, she wouldn't look as good for the cameras. Roper must have read my mind. He came at me from behind and pressed down hard on my shoulders, thwarting my plan to spring up.

"It's never advisable to get too near a trapped animal," Roper said.

Claire heeded his advice, and left a few feet of distance between us. "I came to say good-bye," she said.

I tried springing at her, but my chain was jerked short. After several up-and-down attempts, starts turned into stops, my chair must have looked as if it needed an exorcism. When it was clear Roper wasn't going to allow me the opportunity of hopping to my feet, I finally gave up.

Claire twisted her fingers nervously around the yellow ribbon, folding and unfolding it in her hand. "I wish things could have ended differently, Will."

I wanted to tell Claire that she almost sounded sincere, and that being a political whore was a good career choice for her, but I was denied that voice.

She reached her hand back, running her hand along the ribbon. "I'm sure if you asked her why," Claire said, then shook her head and stopped talking for a long moment before regaining control and adding, "I am sorry."

Claire looked at Roper. "No torture," she said. "That would bring about inquiries. Mark will be expecting your page at twenty minutes until five. Don't act until you get his return page after the press conference."

"I know the plan," he said.

By euphemism, my death sentence had just been announced.

"Make sure you follow it, then. We need you to adhere to a strict timeline."

Around the time of my death, Claire and Stanton would have finished their very public forum. I would be the last fall guy, and there would be nothing to connect them to my death.

"When you're done," Claire said, "the apartment has to be cleaned and recleaned. Nothing can appear amiss."

"You're not telling me anything I don't already know."

"It never hurts to go over the details."

Claire walked over to the window and looked down to the street. "Springtime," she said, "in the merry month of May."

She was right. It was now May, I remembered.

Roper didn't say anything. "Still feels like winter, though," she said. "Guess I'm nervous." She took a deep breath and said, "Legs in my stomach and feet in my heart." Then she seemed to spot what she was looking for. "There's my limo rolling down the strip."

She pivoted around like a soldier doing an about-face, and said, "It's time."

Claire didn't say anything as she passed by but did give me a last, lingering look of concern. Her false pity incensed me. I had worked some of the duct tape loose from the corners of my mouth and I screamed at her through the tape. I wanted her to be haunted by my hate, but the sounds didn't slow her. The door closed behind her and she was gone.

Roper loomed over me. "Shut up," he said.

I said, "Fuck you," but through the tape it sounded like a cow with laryngitis. Roper must have translated the words, though. He punched me in the chest hard enough to almost knock my chair over. I made some wheezing sounds, and then did some rapid inhaling and exhaling through my nose. Roper watched with interest, and then lifted his shirt up to get at a pocket knife in his pants, affording me a momentary view of his explosive hair shirt. I guess he didn't go anywhere without wearing his suicide bomb. With his knife he cut another strip of duct tape, and then applied it under my chin and worked the adhesive upward. He further sealed my mouth, and in the process purposely covered up one of my nostrils. I had to fight back my panic while regulating my breathing through half of my nose.

He cut off another piece of tape, and took his time studying it. Roper didn't say anything. He didn't have to. Both of us knew what would happen if he covered up the rest of my nose with the tape. Just the thought of it made me breathe faster. The air rushing in and out of my nostril made the sound of a bellows working overtime. Finally, Roper taped the piece of tape onto my chin and let it dangle from there.

"We'll both be good little soldiers," he said. "I'll follow orders, and you'll die."

He nodded at the idea. "In the end, with her testimony, you'll look like a traitor. They'll make it appear as if you kidnapped her, and were part of a crazed cabal that was plotting assassination and mayhem. I'll make your death look like a suicide.

"Another political suicide," he said.

Roper went over to the table, and poked through the food. He picked up a few French fries and started munching them. "Do you want anything to eat?" he asked. "Maybe another branch to chew on? You thought you had won with that stunt, didn't you? You were so proud. Like Nimrod, you didn't know that pride goeth before a fall."

He took a few more fries and chewed them with his mouth open. "You failed as a soldier," Roper said. "You were kicked out of West Point, but the Academy hasn't said why that was. Were you a cheat? Did they catch you doing drugs? Whatever it was, it will make the rest of the tar stick that much easier to you."

Roper seemed to be considering my shortcomings. "Maybe you were a coward," he concluded. "The army doesn't like a soldier with a yellow streak down his back. I don't allow those types in my own army."

He tapped his bomb undergarment. "You have to be willing to die for your cause. That's what makes you invincible."

Something was bothering me other than being tied up and gagged. There were these echoes I couldn't quite make out in my head. It was like hearing a language familiar to me, but being short the translation. I could feel this pressure in my chest as well. Something was roiling my insides, something other than the imminent prospect of my death. Try as I might, I couldn't figure out what was causing my agitation.

"My role as protector of the unborn has left me little time for other things in life," said Roper. "God called me, and I answered His call. I never succumbed to the temptation of Eve. 'In Adam's fall, we sinned all.' You were weak. The Whore of Babylon comes in many forms."

I decided I couldn't afford to fixate on whatever was setting off my mind's radar. What I needed to do was concentrate on some way of getting out. Escape, or die trying. Rocky Versace, the most recent West Point graduate to receive the Congressional Medal of Honor, never forgot that it was the duty of prisoners to attempt escape. Or die trying. For almost two years Versace was a prisoner of the North Vietnamese. During his captivity he was tortured, beaten, and starved, but that never stopped him from trying to escape. His captors tried to break him by locking him in leg irons, beating him daily, and leaving his wounds untreated. He was periodically paraded through the streets where villagers pummeled him with refuse, taunts, and fists. Rocky screamed back at them in French and Vietnamese and English. He showed his captors that same defiance, demanding better treatment for prisoners. Rocky's indomitable will made him a legend among other prisoners. The last thing his fellow captives ever heard out of Rocky's mouth was his singing. As he was being taken away for the last time, Rocky was singing "God Bless America" at the top of his lungs. He was executed by the Vietnamese.

Rocky Versace died a hero. I hadn't lived the life I wanted to live. Perhaps in death I could make up for my life's shortcomings. Roper was right about one thing. You had to be willing to die for your cause.

I assessed the situation. I was tied up and under guard. My breath was being regulated through one nostril. Straining against my folding chair did no good. My flesh could not break out of the duct-tape bonds nor bend the metal chair. In my mind I tried to choreograph my moves. I would have to hop. Could I somehow overcome Roper? He was wiry, strong, and committed. He wouldn't just roll over.

I considered his living bomb. I had seen wires attached to his fragmentation jacket, but hadn't seen the detonator itself. Roper probably had it in one of his pants pockets, ready for easy detonation.

It isn't the explosion of a bomb that takes most lives, but the resulting fragmentation. As one of my West Point instructors lectured, "It's not the sound, but the fury." Some artillery shells are designed to deliver a payload of several thousand flechettes, needles of metal. The shrapnel spreads out over a wide area, delivering injury and death. The metal casing in many types of artillery shells is designed to split apart in an explosion, raining death. One of the preferred ingredients in a suicide bomb is steel ball bearings. The explosion launches up to several hundred of those balls in a single instant. The result is much like a machine gun going off, with the ball bearings spraying around like bullets. I expected that Roper had armed himself in just such a way.

It wouldn't be a tidy death if my body was found with that of the Baby Bomber. Stanton was adept at covering up his tracks, but if enough potential questions and improprieties reared themselves, his campaign would surely falter. Authorities would have to investigate where and how we died. That would be another smoking gun. I was hoping Stanton's prints would be on that first smoking gun that killed Bradley Walton. Even if they weren't, Bo would insist upon a full investigation. It was up to me to make sure they couldn't manufacture my death in a manner that suited their plans.

I studied Roper. He was right-handed, and there was a bulge in his right pocket. It stood to reason that the detonator was there. For years the man's bombs had wreaked havoc. His weapons of destruction were a part of him, and he wore his fragmentation jacket easily, but even so I doubted whether the weapon was on a hair trigger. He wouldn't want to brush up against something and set off his bomb. There had to be more than a toggle switch. There was probably a casing, something that needed to be raised or broken. I wondered if I could disable him long enough to set off the mechanism.

I tried to think only about my duty, and the task itself. In war, heroes rarely have time to consider the ramifications of their actions. When they jump on a hand grenade to save their comrades, when they throw themselves in front of a machine gun to spare their company, they only have time to react, and then to die.

I was trying to consider the best way to die.

For a minute I surreptitiously wiggled my fingers. Though my wrists were tied, I would still need to be able to move my fingers and set off the detonator. It was possible that Roper had booby-trapped the device to prevent it being removed from him. Maybe I would only need to pull a wire or two to serve my purposes.

I needed to draw Roper to me. He had turned the television on, but he seemed to be alternating his eyes between the screen and me. I slowed my breathing, and with force of will lowered my pulse and heartbeat. My chest stopped moving in and out and my eyes closed.

If Roper noticed, he didn't immediately react. Perhaps a minute passed by before he said anything. "Hey," he yelled. "Wake up."

I didn't respond. A few moments later an object struck my cheek. He must have thrown something at me from across the room. Luckily, I was able not to react.

I detected the barest sounds of movement, and then from close by, Roper screamed one word: "Snake!" Again, I managed to stay still.

Instead of coming at me directly as I hoped, Roper chose a flanking approach. Tied up as I was, I had hoped to strike him with a head butt, but he denied me the opportunity.

Suddenly I couldn't breathe. He had come at me from the side, his finger plugging my nostril and taking away my only source of air. I didn't react, just stayed slumped with my head down. The seconds went by. I tried not to dwell on the growing pressure in my lungs. Maybe a minute passed. Orange stars started dancing around my closed eyes.

I could outwait him. He would break before I did. Eventually he would reach over and take my pulse, and that's when I would throw all my weight at him.

I couldn't breathe, move, or twitch. I had to beat the desperation of my own body to beat him. Mentally I tried to will him nearer.

My lungs were screaming. I started hallucinating, imagining I was hearing Claire whispering endearments in my ear.

I blinked first, jerking my head to the side and sucking in all the air a single nostril could inhale. Then I was on my feet. A smiling Roper danced away from me. He had expected the ploy.

I hopped toward him, and he easily moved out of the way. I jumped again, and he sidestepped me once more. Tied as I was to the chair, my balance was precarious and my maneuverability limited. Roper was just waiting for me to fall over. It was clear he wasn't going to allow me to get near him or his detonator.

The third jump positioned me where I wanted to be. I faked coming at him again, and Roper moved back. That gave me a clear shot to where I needed to go.

The apartment was small, which had entered into my tactics. By feinting I had moved the enemy back. I bunny-hopped forward once, twice. I felt like I was in a three-legged race with a dead person. Roper saw my destination, and was already coming after me. "No!" he shouted.

My third hop got me into launching pad position. From behind, Roper made a flying dive. I was just far enough ahead that he missed me.

On my fourth hop I sprang off as hard as I could, and angled my shoulder into the glass. My eyes closed. I didn't want to watch the impact, or what followed on my drop to the ground ten stories below.

The glass somehow held. I bounced off it, and dropped hard on the living room floor. Roper was on me in an instant. He dragged me away from the window. Tied as I was to the chair, I could do nothing. My back was to the ground, and my legs were tilted and in the air. I was positioned like a baby on a changing table. Roper added his version of swaddling clothes. By the time he finished, I could barely move.

"No rabbit in your hat this time," said Roper. "No magical escape like your tree chewing, or sleight of hand like your gun trick at the bank when you switched guns and made everyone think you deposited the one that mattered. The show's over."

Roper kicked me hard.

"Your death will serve a greater purpose. It will be the glue that binds. You are the sacrificial lamb for both of them. That is what this is all about, you know."

The duct tape gag prevented me from asking questions,

and Roper didn't seem inclined to say anything else. Having failed in my mission of becoming a human flare, I contemplated my failure. I couldn't even die right. Other thoughts kept surfacing through my self-pity, though. What had Roper meant by saying that I had switched guns? That didn't make sense. There was also this vision of Claire that kept coming to my mind's eye, and the harder I tried to push her image aside, the more she dominated my thoughts. I remembered how pretty she looked. As she betrayed me, she never looked more beautiful. I kept seeing her touching that yellow ribbon at the nape of her neck.

Yellow ribbon. Why did that seem significant? Then I remembered her special cadence that she had seemed to recite just for me.

Claire had repeated some of those words when she stood at the window. I reviewed what she had said. She had mentioned it was springtime in the merry month of May, words from the jody. It had been code.

At the time, I assumed Claire slipped up when she said, "If you ask her," but in actuality she was just quoting from cadence. That explained why the words had sounded so familiar. Claire had lifted some lines from the jody call of "C-130," one of her father's favorite airborne refrains.

Through her yellow ribbon, and refrains, Claire had clued me in that she was on an unspoken mission. That had to be it. The pressure in my chest lessened. She hadn't betrayed me after all. But why had she handed me over to Roper? That didn't make sense. Or did it? Roper thought I had duped him by switching guns. He believed that the second magnum had been deposited in the bank—the gun used to kill Garret Harrington, not the gun that killed Bradley Walton. Claire must have used that disinformation to make it look as if she had that weapon. It would have been a negotiating tool with Stanton.

Roper was pacing around the living room, intently eyeing his cell phone. After half a minute of pacing, he punched in a number and apparently left a page. Claire had made a point of telling him he was supposed to page Stanton at twenty minutes until five. Her instructions hadn't been meant for Roper, though. He made it very clear he was completely versed with the plan. Claire had wanted me to know. What was she doing?

I recalled how she had told Roper not to torture me, and to make sure he followed the arrangements to the letter. It would have helped had I known the plan. Roper had said my agreed-upon death had made their union possible. Claire would have needed to make it look as if she was going along with Stanton's plan in order to draw him out.

Roper was watching the television. The network had already announced they would be switching over to live coverage of Mark Stanton's press conference. The news of his surprising engagement to Claire Harrington was being discussed. Spin doctors were already at work.

Duty, honor, country. Claire was her father's daughter. Garret Harrington had always been willing to give his life for his country. The apple hadn't fallen far from the tree.

It was all about to go down. I didn't want to watch the woman I loved die on TV.

I started rocking from side to side. You do what you can. I shouted, whistled, made whatever noises I could. For Claire, I somehow made myself heard through the duct tape.

Roper turned from the TV to me. "What's wrong with you?"

I didn't let up. He came and stood over me and I made him take a measure of my eyes. Making sure it hurt, Roper ripped off a piece of duct tape from the side of my mouth.

"She's got your gun," I said, "the one with the silencer on it. Page him before it's too late."

Roper didn't move, didn't look convinced.

"She's on a mission," I said. "She thought this was the only way to get at him. He painted her as an assassin. Now that's about to be a self-fulfilling prophecy."

Roper reached for his phone and started tapping out a numeric page, but his page never went through. Glass windows all around the room broke, and in synchronized attack, the front door burst open. From seemingly every direction the strike came—screams, shouts, and shots intended to paralyze and neutralize.

The combination didn't work. In his mind Roper must have rehearsed this moment a thousand times. He would go out with a bang. He would take his enemies with him and be a martyr for his cause. Bullets ripped into him, but he didn't fall, didn't even appear to notice the blood streaming out of various parts of his body. Roper reached into the pocket of his pants.

I rolled into him as hard as I could, hitting him just under his knees. It threw him off balance for just an instant, but that was long enough. Bo was on him then, holding his arms, and then there was a pile-up on Roper as if he was a loose ball in a football game.

I was shoved aside and found myself on the ground, staring at the television. Somehow it had survived the bullets and flying glass and onslaught of law enforcement. Stanton's press conference was just beginning.

"Bo! Bo!" I screamed.

Bo was still holding tight to Roper's arms, while others were throwing cuffs on him. The bomb technicians were already looking at Roper's fragmentation jacket and shouting instructions for everyone to clear the room.

Two members of the assault team reached under my armpits and started to lift me up. "No! Leave me!"

I struggled with my body, trying to escape their grip while at the same time keeping an eye on the television. Stanton was already talking. Over all the noise I couldn't hear what he was saying.

My would-be saviors weren't easily dissuaded. I twisted and turned, and again shouted, "Bo! Bo!"

"I've got him, guys," Bo said.

The two men dropped me, glad to be rid of their ungrateful burden. Bo took a knee next to me. He was smiling as widely as the time we'd pulled the banner prank at the Naval Academy. In the years since I had last seen him, he'd lost a lot of his hair, but none of his smile. "So what's so important?" he asked.

"Claire!" I said.

As if the camera was listening for my cue, Claire's face appeared on the television. "She's going to shoot him," I said.

Seeing Stanton die on national television didn't concern me; it was how the Secret Service would respond to the attack.

"You think so?"

My panicked voice hadn't gotten through to Bo. He wasn't doing much of anything but smiling.

"Call somebody!"

"You're right," said Bo. "It's time."

He pulled out a flip-phone and then dialed a number and said something, but the bomb techs were making too much noise for me to hear what he was saying. I watched Bo nod at whatever was related back to him, and then he closed his phone and regarded me with his annoying smile.

"What?"

My one-word shout to him was part question, part frustration, and part venting.

"Let's get that tape off you so you can watch the show," Bo said.

"What the hell is going on?"

"Mark Stanton is committing political suicide, and he doesn't even know it yet. The show is about to get real good."

My Adam's apple felt watermelon-sized. "Claire?" I asked.

"She's the director of all this. Her starring moment is about to occur."

"Then untie me," I said, "turn up the volume, and make us some popcorn."

"Yes, sir."

Fifteen years had passed since a particular sound had come out of my mouth. I made up for lost time, and shouted the Army yell of approval: "Hoo-ah!"

CHAPTER TWENTY-EIGHT

Away from all the cameras, and lights, and people, Claire and I were finally alone.

"Why didn't you just tell me?" I asked.

The question was important to me, but nibbling her ear while asking it was even more important.

"Stanton wouldn't have gone along with the plan if Roper wasn't convinced I had betrayed you for real," Claire said. "That's what I needed him to communicate back to Stanton."

She nibbled my ear in return. That made her explanation sound much more reasonable.

"You didn't think I could act the part of a man betrayed?"

"You're no politician, dear. I've decided that's one of the things I like about you."

"Why didn't you just bring in the authorities?"

"I don't have to tell you how Stanton worked out everything to make the two of us look guilty. On the face of it, our story would have sounded wild and been very hard to prove. The best way for me to gain credibility was to have Mark validate me. I needed him to commit himself to that story on national television and vouch for my character. I let him dig his own grave."

"You used me like a pawn."

"More like a king," she said. "In chess, you have to protect your king at all costs. You were under surveillance from Bo and his team. Stanton wouldn't commit himself until he heard from Roper that all was well with the situation. I couldn't think of any other way to do it. Remember, I was negotiating on the fly."

"But when was it that you knew? When did you put it all together?"

"Not until last night," she said. "I should have figured it out earlier, of course. I talked with Mark a few times while we were on the run. That's how he knew we were at your office, and that we would be going to the bank. While you were making your call at that hotel in Charleston, I briefly talked with Mark and told him what was going on. I felt better because I so wanted to believe he was helping us, just like I wanted to believe he was in love with me. I could kick myself now for being so stupid, but at the time it was almost as if I were under a spell. Luckily there was an antidote for the spell."

"What was that?" I asked.

She looked a little embarrassed. Claire spoke by way of analogy. "Don't you know your children's stories?" she asked. "We're talking the likes of Snow White, Beauty and the Beast, the Little Mermaid, and Cinderella. The more I resisted how I felt about you, the more I was blinded."

I finally got where she was going and barely refrained from thumping my chest. "But once you succumbed to my charms," I said, "your blinders magically fell off."

"You're no Hans Christian Andersen," she said, "but you get the general idea. You made me realize I didn't love Mark Stanton, and that's when everything became clear. It was a hard pill to swallow, but I saw how Mark had manipulated our relationship from the first. At the same time, he worked things out so I couldn't breathe a word to anyone about our relationship. Mark sought me out because he was worried that my father might sabotage his political ambitions, and so he used me to get information. Last night I wanted to wake you up and talk the situation over, but I decided the only way to expose Mark was to make him think he had won.

"He didn't know we had arrived in Alexandria and were staying in the apartment. I called him and pretended to be in a quandary. I said I had the gun Everett had used in the duel, and told him I knew what he had done. 'I should call the authorities,' I said to him, but then let him tell me what a bad idea that was. I had to make him think I was as ambitious as he was. Someone else might not have believed me, but Mark was so blinded by his political ambitions it wasn't that hard a sell. Still, he was suspicions. I had to offer you up, and I knew that meant he would bring in Roper. You had told me about his fragmentation jacket. That made everything chancier, but he insisted on doing it his way to seal the deal. I didn't want to put you in danger, but he wasn't about to commit himself to our public engagement until my hands were also bloodied. The way it was set up made it all a matter of timing. He had to see me, and also know that Roper had you as his prisoner. After we agreed on the details of that arrangement, I called Bo."

"I'm surprised Bo agreed to your plan."

"I'm afraid I didn't give him any choice. He worked out your rescue with the feds. I'm sure he'll be telling you how they were scrambling to make the operation work. If the prize hadn't been the Baby Bomber, I doubt whether the federal agencies would have been as cooperative as they were."

"Before you went public at the press conference about Stanton, you waited to hear from Bo, didn't you?"

"That's right."

"If he had told you I was dead, would you have defended my honor?"

"Men and their honor," said Claire, shaking her head.

"Women look for solutions other than John Wayne heroics. Given a choice of weapons in a duel, I choose wits."

She avoided my question like a good politician. The apple hadn't fallen far from the tree.

"What about that frog and scorpion story?"

"What about it?" she said. "I was trying to clue you in to the fact that I knew who the scorpion was, and that I was now aware of Stanton's true nature. You should have known that I am my father's daughter, and would put service to country above all things."

"Did you carry a gun to the press conference?"

Claire shrugged.

"Come on, Claire, you've got me hanging like a Florida chad."

"If you had been hurt," she said, steel in her voice, "I did have an alternate plan in mind."

"You not only fooled Stanton and Roper," I said, "you fooled me. I almost killed myself trying to foil what I thought was your nefarious plot."

I expected immediate sympathy, more kisses, and a heartfelt apology, but Claire didn't believe in rewarding stupidity.

"Aren't you the person who calls yourself the human Velcro? I expected more out of your vaunted retentive abilities. What did you want me to do, shout the jody out? Do cadence with a baton and majorette outfit? Or would you have preferred me waving the yellow ribbon in front of your face while doing the cancan? I thought the clues were obvious, dear."

"Cadence with a baton and majorette outfit," I mused, "or doing the cancan adorned with a yellow ribbon? You offer such tough choices."

"Shush."

"I can explain why I was slow picking up on your clues," I said. "How could you possibly expect me to think clearly with a broken and bleeding heart?"

I said the statement in a light tone, but she heard the underlying truth. My second sympathy ploy worked much better. Claire moved her lips down to where my heart was, and started kissing my chest.

"Did my kisses work?" she asked. "Has there been a rapid infusion of blood to your heart?"

"I'll go as far as saying there has been a rapid infusion of blood."

"You are incorrigible."

"Get used to it."

We kissed for a long time.

When Claire finally came up for air, she asked, "Are you really a Democrat?"

"Why?"

"Answer me."

"Yes, I really am."

"That could be problematic."

"In what way?"

"The Republican National Committee is looking to make lemonade out of lemons. Believe it or not, they just contacted me. The movers and shakers liked the way I comported myself at the press conference, and wondered if I might be interested in being a candidate for higher office. They want to put the Stanton fiasco behind them, and think my running for Congress would bring a breath of fresh air to the party."

I groaned. "Just when I thought we were clear of politics."

"Will you change your party affiliation for me?"

"No, but if you marry me I'll probably vote for you."

"West Point is a terribly conservative institution. How could you have come out of it a Democrat?"

"I never graduated, remember?"

"You're a hard man to pin down, Will Travis, but I'm determined to get your vote one way or another. By the way, did you just propose to me?"

"Yes."

I kissed her, and then got down on one knee to make it official.

"Yes," she said, and with her arms and lips drew me back to her.

When our lips finally separated, she whispered, "But how will I explain you to the Republican National Committee?"

"Tell them politics makes for strange bedfellows."

ALAN RUSSELL

MULTIPLE WOUNDS

Holly Troy is a beautiful and talented sculptor whose only sanctuary is her art. She also lives with dissociative identity disorder, her personality split into many different and completely separate selves—including a frightened five-year-old girl. But now Holly's gallery owner has been found murdered, surrounded by Holly's sculptures. Holly doesn't know if she was a witness to the crime, or if she committed it. She doesn't know where she was that night. She doesn't even know *who* she was.

Dorchester Publishing Co., Inc.
P.O. Box 6640   ___5579-1
Wayne, PA 19087-8640 $6.99 US/$8.99 CAN

Please add $2.50 for shipping and handling for the first book and $.75 for each additional book. NY and PA residents, add appropriate sales tax. No cash, stamps, or CODs. Canadian orders require $2.00 for shipping and handling and must be paid in U.S. dollars. Prices and availability subject to change. **Payment must accompany all orders.**

Name: _____

Address: _____

City: _____ State: _____ Zip: _____

E-mail: _____

I have enclosed $_____ in payment for the checked book(s).

CHECK OUT OUR WEBSITE! **www.dorchesterpub.com**
_____ *Please send me a free catalog.*

SMILING WOLF

PHILIP CARLO

Anne Fitzgerald is young, beautiful and intelligent—but she may also be dead. She disappeared after interviewing a mysterious man named Santos Dracol, and it's up to detective Frank De Nardo to find her. But the more De Nardo investigates, the deeper he descends into a shocking world of dark clubs and darker perversions, hidden in the shadowy underbelly of New York City. It's a world of power, sex...and blood. It's certainly bizarre, and De Nardo is convinced it's deadly. But will he be able to prove it? Will he be able to stop Dracol and his followers before another body is found?

A HARD TICKET HOME

DAVID HOUSEWRIGHT

McKenzie is an ex-St. Paul cop with time on his hands. That's why he's doing a favor for an old friend with a sick daughter: Nine-year-old Stacy has been diagnosed with leukemia, and the only one with the matching bone marrow that could save her life is her big sister, Jamie. But Jamie ran away from home years ago—and disappeared.

McKenzie starts with Jamie's seedy last known associates. But the trail doesn't lead where Mac expects. It takes him to some very respected businessmen. And every time he starts asking questions, people start dying…in very unpleasant ways.

- -